THE PURE SHORE CLUB

JASON R. LADY

Black Rose Writing | Texas

This is a work of fiction. Names, characters, businesses, places, events, and incidents are either the products of the author's imagination or used in a fictitious manner. Any resemblance to actual persons, living or dead, or actual events is purely coincidental.

ISBN: 978-1-68513-562-1
PUBLISHED BY BLACK ROSE WRITING
www.blackrosewriting.com

Printed in the United States of America
Suggested Retail Price (SRP) $27.95

The Pure Shore Club is printed in Minion Pro

*As a planet-friendly publisher, Black Rose Writing does its best to eliminate unnecessary waste to reduce paper usage and energy costs, while never compromising the reading experience. As a result, the final word count vs. page count may not meet common expectations.

PRAISE FOR
THE PURE SHORE CLUB

"Dive into the captivating world crafted by Jason Lady in *The Pure Shore Club* where wit, action and a bit of supernatural intertwine in an exhilarating adventure! This book is a must-read for young readers, offering an exciting journey that will keep them hooked from start to finish!"
–Tammi Belko, author of *Perchance to Dream*

"Suspenseful and mysterious with humor woven throughout!"
–Christine Laforet, author of the *Being Bree Series*

For my Aunt, Ruth Wright.

ACKNOWLEDGEMENTS

Wow, I can't quite believe I've published a fourth book! I always say, my name is printed on the cover, but it takes many people to make the book happen. This time was no exception. Thanks to my loving and brilliant wife Julie who encouraged me through the thirteen years it took to get my first book published and every book since. You are my chief editor, plot detangler, and morale officer and I couldn't do it without you. Thanks to the past iteration of my amazing critique group who read this manuscript years ago: Bonnie, Chris, and Tammi. I apologize if I left anyone out. The advice you offered on plot and character made a huge difference. Thanks to my awesome group of beta readers: Lincoln, Maddox, Rory, Russell, Sam, and Truett. Your insights are indispensable, and you make sure the book is on the right track. Special thanks to Rory for a wonderful and creative idea for the book cover. Thanks so much to the talented and collaborative team at Black Rose Writing: Reagan, Christopher, David, Justin, and Minna. I am grateful my wacky and weird imaginings found a publishing home with you. Thanks once again for believing in me and promoting my work. Thanks once again to my editor Jess Lawrence for her incredible editing skills (I'm really bad at plural possessive, aren't I, Jess?). Thanks to all the readers, fellow authors, book festival organizers, bookstore staff, library staff, and book bloggers who've been champions of my work. And as always, thanks to all my wonderful family and friends, near and far. I don't have space to thank you all individually, but my world is a better place with all of you in it.

THE PURE SHORE CLUB

CHAPTER ONE
A MYSTERIOUS INVITATION

Abby reminded herself that she didn't have to go. She could turn, walk back to her room, shut the door, and everything would be fine. But she knew full well it wouldn't all be fine. Not really. The voice of her mother sounded in her head, words spoken before both parents had left her at boarding school a week ago: *Joining a club is a great way to meet people and make new friends.* Abby knew she needed all the help she could get in the making friends department. So, she kept walking.

She didn't have to go far. The Pinski English and Humanities Building was very close to the girls' dorm. It loomed before her, a three-story brick structure covered in ivy that doubled as a hall of learning and professors' offices.

Abby paused in the foyer and pulled the invitation out of her back pocket. She remembered the room number just fine, but she felt she had to check it again. Just in case she had it wrong. She didn't want to go to the wrong room and look silly. The words on the invitation, printed in metallic purple ink on cream-colored paper, sparkled in the overhead lights.

Dear Ms. Alvarson,

It is our sincere pleasure to invite you to join our club. You have our congratulations. Be proud! It is quite an honor to be invited to this prestigious and exclusive student organization. Our first meeting is in the office of Mr. Blake Santillian, Room 301, Pinski English and Humanities Building at 4:30PM this coming Friday. We hope to see you there! Again, congratulations to you.

Sincerely,

The Club Executive Committee.

Definitely unusual, Abby reflected. For one thing, it was the only student club that sent her a personal invitation. Secondly, the invitation didn't specify what club she was invited to. That had to be a mistake, she reasoned, though that seemed unlikely. Who sends out an invitation without saying what it's for? Abby hoped it wasn't some bizarre prep school sport like lacrosse or squash; she didn't really care for sports. She slipped the invitation back into the golden envelope it arrived in and headed to the staircase.

Abby headed up the stairs quickly, not wanting to be late. She emerged onto the third floor, only to be hit with what felt like a speeding cannonball. Before she could register what had happened, she was eye-to-eye with the gray and white tiled floor.

"Owww," she groaned. It slowly registered in her brain that she'd been knocked over. Was this just some cruel prank the older kids did to new kids? Did everyone foolish enough to show up for this meeting get an anvil thrown at them, while kids laughed and pointed and took pictures to plaster all over social media?

But there were no mean taunts, there was no cackling laughter.

"Oh no! I am so sorry!"

Abby sat up partway, flinching in anticipation of another strike, and saw another girl a few feet away, already getting to her feet.

"I totally wasn't looking where I was going," the girl explained, walking over and extending a helping hand. Abby tentatively accepted the aid and found herself briskly hauled to her feet like a crane pulling up a load of cargo. Whoever this girl was, she was pretty strong.

"I think I'm late for a meeting," the girl went on, her voice crisp. She wore a Jefford Academy soccer uniform—burgundy and gold jersey with matching shorts and an unzipped warmup jacket—and had a large gym bag hoisted over one shoulder. She whipped out a piece of paper and examined it with serious, dark eyes.

Abby brushed her strawberry-blonde hair out of her face. She wondered how disheveled she must look now, after getting a round trip to the floor. She probably looked like a mess and no one would talk to her at this mysterious meeting.

"Oh, hey, I guess this is yours," the soccer girl said, scooping up Abby's fallen backpack, a J. Crew brand that her parents had bought her right before they'd left, insisting that she needed a new backpack for her new school, even though Abby liked her old backpack just fine. She figured they were doing what they could to make their daughter feel better about a lousy situation.

Soccer Girl went back to examining her invitation. "It says here I need to go to room 301," she reported.

"Oh, uh, really?" Abby said. "I think I do, too. Did you, um, get a weird invitation that doesn't say what club you're being invited to?"

The soccer player smacked her invitation with the back of her other hand. "That's the one. So, you got one of these mysterious invitations too, huh? I'm Maxine Drury, by the way." She extended her hand again, this time in greeting.

Abby took it, unsure if she was supposed to squeeze hard or not. She was never sure how to shake other girls' hands. "Abby Alvarson," she said. She found Maxine's grip to be just as formidable as her helping hand up.

"Nice to meet you, Abby. Now that we've had an introduction that doesn't involve slamming into each other like bumper cars, how about we find this room together?"

•   •   •

They walked together, scanning the room numbers printed on metal faceplates bolted next to each door. This floor was mostly teacher offices, their occupants either already home for the day or at other meetings. The lights in each room were off, and all was quiet.

"Do you have any idea what this is all about?" Maxine asked as they walked.

"Er, none at all," Abby admitted. "I was kind of hoping they'd tell us."

"I don't even know why I'm bothering," Maxine said, a bit of huff in her voice. "As I'm sure you've noticed, I'm on the soccer team—I'm not on my way to a costume party or anything—and I run cross-country, too. I don't have a whole lot of free time. But this seems just weird enough to check out, you know?"

Abby nodded, not sure what to say. Maxine made her feel small, with her obvious athleticism, brisk and confident walk, and the natural manner with which she led the way down the hallway. Maxine had a long dark ponytail that swung from side to side as she strode along.

"What about you?" Maxine asked, glancing over at her new acquaintance. "Why are you coming to this meeting?"

"Well…" Abby began as she struggled to keep up. She paused to think. What should she say? That half of her just wanted to hole up in her room and read, write in her journal, eat snacks and drink hot chocolate, while the other half wanted to make friends? It sounded so lame in her own head; she could only imagine how it would sound to someone like Maxine Drury.

They rounded a corner, and Abby was rescued from having to come up with any kind of response. Down the hallway was a boy, crouched next to an office doorway. He wore a brown fedora, the rim bent and the entire hat askew as he had his head pressed against the door itself.

"Is he doing what I think he's doing?" Maxine whispered.

Abby could only manage a small shrug. She wasn't sure Maxine was really looking for an answer. The soccer player was already striding down to the boy. He evidently didn't notice she was approaching. She came right up next to him, leaned in close and cleared her throat abruptly. "Ahem."

One moment the boy had been in a pose of silence and concentration, the next he was suddenly an energetic explosion of arms and legs, backpedaling wildly away from Maxine. "Holy cow!" he exclaimed once he regained his composure. "What's the big idea, sneaking up on a guy like that? You almost sent me jumping clear over to the next state!"

"What's the big idea yourself," Maxine snapped, her hands on her hips. "What're you doing, skulking around and listening at doors? Are you some kind of spy or something?"

The boy straightened up, puffing out his chest and cocking his fedora back with one hand. "Maybe I am. What's it to you, soccer-girl? Don't you have a rubber sphere filled with air to hit with your forehead or something?"

"I'm supposed to be here," Maxine snapped, pulling out her invitation and holding it in front of the boy's eyes.

By now Abby had caught up with Maxine, and she could see that the door was to room 301.

The boy wore a battered leather attaché case over one shoulder, and he reached into it to pull out a familiar-looking gold envelope. "Yeah? Well, you're not the only one. Seems we've been invited to the same meeting, huh?"

Maxine folded her arms across her chest. "Seems that way."

The boy noticed Abby for the first time. "Another attendee, eh? You as charming and polite as your jock friend here?"

"I-I'm Abby," she said, not sure what else to say. Up close, this guy was pretty unusual looking. Not only was he wearing a fedora, which was pretty strange for a teenage boy, but he wore khakis held up by red suspenders, with a long-sleeved shirt under it with the sleeves pushed up.

"Brett Cho," he introduced himself, tilting his hat towards Abby, a gesture she had never seen anyone perform outside of an old black-and-white movie. "Pleased to meet you, Abby." He fixed an inquisitive eye on the other girl. "And you are…?"

"Maxine," she replied coolly. "Now, Brett, were you going to actually enter the meeting, or just listen in on it? I've always found the former to be much more efficient."

"For your information, Maxine," he replied just as coolly, "the door is locked. And it sounds like a heated discussion's going on in there. I figured I'd listen in, find out what I'm getting myself into, you know?"

Just then, a voice, loud enough to be plainly heard in the hallway, came through the closed door to room 301. "Absolutely not! I forbid it!"

Brett immediately plastered his cheek to the door's wooden surface, clinging there like a fedora-wearing fly. Maxine was there a split second after him, also listening intently to what was going on.

"Um, guys," Abby whispered, "I don't know if…if we should really be listening in on—"

"The Pure Shore Club will be reactivated over my dead body!" came the voice again. Hearing that, Abby found her interest piqued too. She hurried over and squeezed in next to Maxine.

"Blake, you must listen to reason," a much quieter, much calmer voice said.

"Do I really?" the first voice replied, still raised but not shouting anymore. "You and Michael have no solid evidence to present, do you?"

"That must be Mr. Blake Santillian," Maxine whispered, holding up her invitation. "His name is on this invite. This is his office."

"Gee, you think?" Brett whispered back, rolling his eyes. "And here I thought all you jock types were dumb."

"Oh, shut up," Maxine hissed, slugging him in the arm.

"Hey, watch it," he hissed back, cradling a now-sore arm. "No need to get violent, now."

"Nevertheless, you must believe us," came a third voice in reply to Mr. Santillian's skepticism. "If the Smiling Shadow has truly returned—"

"Michael, that is utter nonsense," Mr. Santillian replied dismissively.

"Can you truly take that chance, Blake?" came the other voice, which sounded older than Michael. "You remember as well as I do what happened last time. If our old enemy has truly returned, you know what it will be after. The entire world could be in danger."

The three teenagers shot each other startled glances. The entire world?

What on Earth were the people inside that office talking about?

"You two always come in here with the same old unconvincing arguments," Mr. Santillian replied, much quieter than before but sounding terse. "You're just paranoid, or hoping to ride on former glories and past triumphs; I'm not sure which, maybe it's a combination of both. I don't really care. It's sad, but there's little I can do to help you. I'm not certain why I even agreed to meet with you. Misplaced loyalty to old comrades, I guess."

"So there is nothing we can do to convince you?" Michael said.

"Absolutely nothing," Mr. Santillian agreed.

"That's a pity," the third voice said, "because the three students we invited to the first meeting are right outside your door."

Rapid, heavy footsteps sounded from the other side of the door. All three teenagers scrambled to get away from the door and look as nonchalant and innocent as possible. The door flew open and there stood a tall, broad-shouldered man who looked upon them with blazing eyes.

"In here," he commanded the students through gritted teeth, his eyes blazing. "Now."

All three filed into the office, silently deciding this was not a teacher they wanted to argue with. The office was small and claustrophobic, especially with so many people in it. The teacher stood behind his desk, his hands balled into fists and resting on his hips. The only other occupant of the room that Abby noticed was a young, serious-looking man off to one side. He was in a wheelchair and looked upon them with a grave expression.

"How did you three learn about the Pure Shore Club?" Mr. Santillian demanded.

"We received invitations," Maxine said, a touch of resentment in her voice.

"Let me see," Mr. Santillian said, holding out his hand. As she passed over her invitation, Abby noticed Mr. Santillian was unusually dressed. He wore a white, button-down dress shirt open at the collar, tucked into blue jeans with cowboy boots. The cuffs of his shirt glinted in the room's light. With his hand outstretched, Abby could see he wore gold cufflinks, shaped like old-style flintlock pistols. The only person she'd ever seen wearing cufflinks was her father, when he dressed up for important events. He certainly hadn't worn any as unique as Mr. Santillian's. She wondered where he'd gotten them.

The teacher held the invitations close to his face, reading them intently, like they contained the secrets of the universe. When finished, he slowly turned to the man in the wheelchair.

"It's a safe assumption that you and Reeve sent this out," Mr. Santillian announced.

Abby wondered who this 'Reeve' was. Though there had been a third voice, hadn't there? She glanced around the room with her green eyes as much as she dared. Only Mr. Santillian, the man in the wheelchair, Brett, and Maxine were there. No one else was in sight.

The man in the wheelchair sighed and seemed to deflate slightly. "Yes, Mr. Santillian, we sent them. We thought if some actual candidates were brought before you, you might see to reason."

"See to reason?" Mr. Santillian thundered. "There's nothing to see, Michael!" He turned to address the students. "Listen to me, you three." Abby felt herself stand a little straighter, like she was a soldier being called to attention by her sergeant. "Forget you ever saw these invitations. Forget you ever heard of the Pure Shore Club. It is a defunct organization as of five years ago, and it's going to stay that way. It will not return, nor will it ever return, in any shape or form, is that understood?"

Maxine's eyes narrowed. "What's the big deal? What's a Pure Shore Club, anyway?"

"I don't think we should argue with him, Max…" Brett muttered out of the corner of his mouth.

Mr. Santillian turned bright red and leaned on his desk, palms down, his eyes like two blazing coals. Abby found herself flinching, waiting for an inevitable verbal onslaught. But it never came.

"Trust me, young lady," he said quietly, looking at the surface of his desk, "some things are best forgotten." He crumpled up Maxine's invitation and tossed it into an urn that seemed to double as a trash can. It went right in without the teacher even looking. "Good day to all of you," he said, locking gazes with each of them in turn. His tone was cordial, but his eyes gave off a cold glare.

Brett and Abby hurried to the door. Maxine followed, not happy about it, and making sure her displeasure registered full volume through her expression and body language. She stole a final glance back at the other man, Michael. He looked positively mournful.

•   •   •

The students hurried to the nearest exit, and by unspoken agreement didn't speak to one another until they were outside.

"Okay," Maxine said, the first one to speak, "what exactly just happened in there?"

Brett adjusted the strap of his attaché case. "I feel like I just got in trouble, even though I didn't do anything wrong."

Abby chewed her lower lip and looked at the grass. She hated it when people got mad at her, especially when she couldn't figure out why. She felt guilty, even though logically she agreed with Brett, they hadn't done anything wrong.

"The nerve of that man," Maxine said, tossing her dark ponytail, "speaking so harshly to us. All we did was show up at his door!"

"Mr. Santillian is a bit sensitive on this subject," came a new voice. They turned to see Michael rolling towards them. He came to a stop and looked at them, stroking his chin. "I feel I owe the three of you an apology. This was an ill-advised scheme we thought up…I should have warned you all in advance what you were getting into."

"What exactly were we getting into?" Brett asked.

"And who are you, anyway?" Maxine asked. "You look a little old to be a student, but a little young to be a teacher."

Michael adopted a wry smile. "Michael Alvarez is my name. I used to go to school here, five years ago. I'm in graduate school now."

"Wow, I was in third grade then," Brett said.

Michael chuckled. "Way to make me feel ancient, pal. But anyway, not only am I an alumnus of the Jefford Academy, I'm also a former Pure Shore Club member."

Brett stepped partially in front of Maxine, who glared at the back of his neck. "Wait, what about my question? What's the Pure Shore Club?"

The man in the wheelchair smiled. "You're very curious. Good, that's good. I think it's best that I direct you to the answers you seek. If you want to learn more about the club, I suggest you look to the past."

Then he neatly pivoted his wheelchair and began to roll away from them, down the sidewalk.

"Hold on just a minute!" Maxine called out. "That's it? That's all you're going to tell us? I left soccer practice early for this, I'll have you know!"

Michael did not reply, he just kept rolling onward.

Maxine snorted, then turned to the other two students. "Do either of you understand any of this?"

Abby managed a lame little shrug, and Brett shook his head. Maxine whirled to call out to Michael Alvarez once more—

—only to find that he was nowhere in sight.

"Where'd he go?" she asked, feeling quite confused. They glanced around. The immediate area was all open grass and sidewalks connecting the Pinski Building with other nearby buildings. No one could have gotten inside of any of the other buildings in the few seconds they'd been preoccupied.

"Oh…kay…" Brett said, his eyes wide. He pushed his fedora onto the back of his head. "That's definitely kind of weird."

Abby nodded slowly, feeling a shiver go down her back. "I'd say this is all…kind of weird."

"We could go demand answers from Mr. Santillian," Brett suggested.

"I don't know if that would, er, be such a good idea," Abby said. "He seemed pretty upset."

"She's right," Maxine declared. "The man is utterly obtuse. No, we need to look into this on our own. Maxine Drury is not a girl who has her time wasted with impunity. I demand answers, and we will get them."

"How?" Abby asked.

"Investigating, naturally," Brett said. "Hot dog! I think I smell a story here."

"I don't know about the two of you," Maxine told her two companions, "but I'm starving. Why don't we all discuss this further over dinner?"

CHAPTER TWO
THE INVESTIGATIONS BEGIN

They made their way to the Jefford Dining Hall, which was already packed with kids. Maxine led the way, striding confidently, her soccer bag bouncing as she went. Brett followed, his eyes intent on his smartphone, furiously typing something into it. Abby was impressed he could do that and walk straight at the same time. Anytime she tried typing on her phone and walking at the same time, she inevitably veered off to one side or ran into something. She noticed Brett's unusual style of dress earned their little group some curious glances, but Brett himself appeared to be oblivious.

She wondered what he was typing. Every time she pulled together the bravery required to ask, the butterflies in her stomach would fly up her throat and block the words from coming out. She kept following Brett and Maxine, feeling like a balloon tied to a swift-moving bicycle, bobbing along in the air. Abby consoled herself with the fact that, for once since she got to this school, she wasn't going to eat by herself. That got old really fast.

As soon as they got their food and sat down, they began talking about their bizarre shared experience, keeping their voices somewhat low so their fellow students at the surrounding tables wouldn't be able to listen in.

"Okay, so what do we know so far?" Maxine said between giant bites of food. She had an amazing amount of food on her tray and was chowing down like there was no tomorrow. Evidently doing soccer and cross-country at the same time worked up quite an appetite.

Brett cleared his throat and consulted his phone. "Fact: All three of us received invitations to the first meeting of the Pure Shore Club. Question: Why us? What makes us so special that they invited us?"

"Well…we could see what the three of us have in common," Abby suggested softly.

"I like the way you think, chief," Brett said. "Okay, what grade is everyone in? I'm in eighth grade. Not one of the youngest kids here but definitely not one of the oldest." Which was true. The Jefford Academy started at 7th grade and went all the way up to 12th.

"Me too," Maxine said, and took a giant swig of milk.

Abby confirmed she was also in 8th grade. It also turned out they were all new at the Jefford Academy, starting just that semester.

"A trio of middle schoolers who are all new here. Okay, that's some things we have in common," Brett remarked. He entered notes on his phone. "All right, how about other stuff? Hobbies? Hometowns?"

That turned out to be a bust; the three of them couldn't have been more different. Maxine was from the Seattle area, Brett was from Boston, and Abby was from Charleston.

"I like soccer. And running. And soccer. I like playing a little tennis, too," Maxine said. "And horseback riding. Volleyball can be fun—"

"Super-jock, check," Brett cut her off. "What about you, Blondie?"

Abby realized he meant her. "Oh. I like…reading. Reading stories. And listening to music. I, um, play the saxophone." Abby's cheeks burned. She hated talking about herself to strangers.

"No kidding?" Brett asked. "Jazz musician, huh? Nice. You'll have to play for us sometime. You going out for jazz band here at the school?"

That topic made Abby squirm, so she decided to deflect the question. "What about you, Brett? What do you like to do?"

"Journalism," he answered immediately.

"So that's why you said you smelled a story."

"Good memory." He complimented her with a nod. "Yeah, you two ladies are looking at the next great American news reporter. I'm already on the staff of the school paper. With luck, and a little of that old-fashioned elbow grease, I'll blow the lid off this Pure Shore Club zaniness and make my journalistic rep right out of the gate."

Maxine eyed his phone, lying next to his food tray. "So that's why you've been busily typing away on your phone."

"I beg your pardon, miss," Brett said, sounding truly offended. "This is no mere phone. This is the reporter's lifeblood. In it I not only take all my notes and upload them to the cloud, but I'm writing my autobiography with it, too."

Maxine raised a dark eyebrow, a forkful of food hovering just before her mouth. "Did you say…autobiography?"

"You bet, champ. It's going to be in high demand someday, so I might as well start it now. Hey, maybe if the two of you are lucky, you'll be in it."

"Thrilling, truly," Maxine said, her tone making it clear she found the prospect to be anything but. "I hear the school paper takes any registered student with a pulse who knows how to write."

"Oh yeah?" he countered. "I hear the soccer team…um…well, I'll be Editor-in-Chief of the paper someday. Count on it. I can see it now…" He adopted a dreamy expression, gazing up at the ceiling, a slight smile on his face. "Editor-in-Chief Brett Leonard Cho. It has a ring to it, doesn't it?"

Abby admired Brett's seemingly single-minded devotion to his chosen profession, especially since he was as young as she was. She wished she were as certain about what she wanted to do when she got out of school. Actually, she wished she were as certain about anything in her life.

Maxine just rolled her eyes at Brett's monologue.

"And by the way, it's Fred," he told Maxine.

She had returned to her meal and glanced up at him sharply. "Excuse me?"

He held up his smartphone. "You referred to my little buddy here as 'that phone'. It has a name: Fred."

She raised her eyebrow again. "Are all people from Boston as weird as you?"

"Well, we do things like toss tea into harbors and stuff like that, you know." He laughed at his own joke and swallowed a big spoonful of chili. "How about this? Maybe it has to do with our families. My parents are—"

"Reporters or newspaper editors," Maxine cut in.

Brett smirked at her. "Actually, no, they work on the distribution end of things...they have their own business headquartered in Boston. But I grew up around newspapers and magazines...that's what got me interested in journalism." He seemed very proud of himself, having proven Maxine's expectations wrong.

Maxine looked like she couldn't care less. She turned to Abby. "And you?"

Abby gulped. "Um, my parents are both doctors."

Brett grunted. "Oh yeah? What kind of doctors?"

"Er, they're overseas doctors," Abby explained. "They had a practice of their own back in our hometown, but they gave it up to go help people overseas. You know, in countries that don't have good medical care."

Brett tipped his hat to her. "Your parents sound like good people, Blondie. That's pretty darn cool."

Abby looked down at her food. "I…thank you."

The student reporter swiveled his head to eye Maxine. "And you, champ? I suppose your parents are Olympic athletes or something?"

Maxine's face melted slightly. Abby had only known her for a short time, but it was an odd expression to see on the other girl's face. The mask of confidence and haughtiness faded for a moment. "Well, they're nowhere near as noble as your parents, Abby. My parents own Vermillion Products."

Brett's eyes bugged out. "You're kidding! *The* Vermillion Products? As in, the cosmetics people?"

Maxine didn't meet their eyes and looked away, like something mildly interesting was taking place across the room.

"Holy cow, that's a giant company!" Brett exclaimed. "We're talking mongo huge, here! Venti-size huge! Offices-in-every-country huge!"

Maxine sighed. "Yeah," was the only reply she gave him.

Brett didn't seem to pick up on her obvious discomfort with this topic and kept enthusing. "Hot dog, this is like sitting with royalty or something! Your family must be swimming in greenbacks, huh?"

Maxine gave an almost imperceptible nod. "Yes, my parents are very wealthy." She then leaned forward and pointed at Brett with her fork. "But it's their money, not mine. Just because they're rich doesn't mean I am, so I don't want you treating me all weird now, understand?"

Brett raised his hands defensively. "Hey, hey, champ, cool your jets. Don't worry, okay? I was just gabbing over here." He felt strange, like he was apologizing for something, though he wasn't sure what for.

Maxine threw her fork onto her tray and sat back, folding her arms across her chest. She seemed to have lost her voracious appetite. "Let's move on, shall we? We've established that the three of us have absolutely nothing in common, except we're all in the same grade and attend the same private boarding school and we're all new here. So that's one mystery. What else?"

"Fact: The Pure Shore Club was once a student organization here at the Jefford Academy. Fact: It disbanded…what did they say? Four years ago?"

"Five," Abby put in.

"Five years ago," Brett continued. "Fact: Mr. Blake Santillian, teacher, and Michael Alvarez, alumnus, were both involved in it somehow. Mr. Santillian may have been the faculty sponsor of the club. Michael Alvarez for some reason wants to bring it back. Mr. Santillian is opposed to it, so opposed he seemed like he was on the verge of exploding."

"Him and someone else," Abby spoke up.

"Huh?" Maxine uttered.

"She's right," Brett said. "There was someone else in the room. Or, at least, there was a voice we heard besides Mr. Santillian and Michael Alvarez."

Maxine frowned. "Come to think of it, you're right. There was no one else in there, was there?"

Abby shook her head. "It sure didn't seem like it."

"Maybe the third person was on speakerphone?" Maxine suggested.

Brett looked dubious. "Sounded too clear to be a speakerphone to me."

"Me too," Abby agreed.

"Who do you suppose he was?" Brett asked, not really expecting an answer.

"Reeve," Abby answered.

Maxine and Brett stared at her, expecting more. Abby was startled when she realized they were both looking at her so intently. "By process of elimination," she explained. "Mr. Santillian said that Michael Alvarez and Reeve sent the invitations out. And when we were listening at the door, Mr. Santillian told Michael Alvarez that he and Reeve had no evidence to convince him with."

Brett looked impressed. "Gee whiz, Blondie. Do you have a photographic memory or something?"

Abby's cheeks burned again and she gazed at her hands, which rested on the tabletop. "Something like that," she admitted.

Maxine grunted. She wiped her mouth with her napkin and leaned back in her chair. "Looks like we have a lot of unknowns to figure out, guys."

Brett looked thoughtful. "And chief among the unknowns is one we haven't mentioned yet: Just what is a Pure Shore Club, anyway?"

"I've...been thinking about that," Abby said, looking at her now-empty plate. "I wonder if it was an environmental club. You know, maybe they cleaned up beaches and stuff like that?"

"The nearest beaches are pretty far away," Brett said. "But it's not a bad idea."

"Instead of sitting here speculating," Maxine said, "why don't we do what Michael Alvarez suggested? Look to the past for the answers."

Brett regarded her. "What's on your mind, champ?"

"You're the reporter here," Maxine said. "Where should we go to find out information about old clubs here at school?"

"Yearbooks!" he exclaimed, snapping his fingers. "Those always feature all the school clubs. Let's see if the school has those online." He tapped on his phone for a few moments, then shook his head. "No mention of yearbooks on the school website, or the library's website."

Abby spoke up, "Maybe they, um, have hard copies at the library?"

"Is it even open right now?" Brett asked, consulting his watch.

"Until nine pm every night," Abby reported. "Except for Sunday, when it closes at six pm."

The others looked at her, incredulous. "How do you know that?" Maxine asked.

"Um, I read the student handbook," Abby admitted, feeling totally lame telling that to her new acquaintances. "I figured since I'd be going to school here, I should familiarize myself with everything."

"Let's go, then," Maxine announced, springing out of her chair. "There's a mystery to solve and the night's not getting any younger."

Brett and Abby followed Maxine with their trays, but they had to wait for Brett when he went back for his attaché case, which he had absent-mindedly left behind at the table.

"Almost forgot Gordon," he told them with a grin, brandishing his bag.

"'Gordon'?" Maxine repeated, glancing at Abby and chuckling. "Do you have a name for that silly hat you wear, too?"

"Of course," Brett said. "Its name is—"

"Don't tell me," Maxine interrupted, walking away to bus her tray, "I don't want to know."

•   •   •

"So, this is the library," Maxine remarked, looking around the main floor. "I have to admit I didn't know where it was until today."

"Well, I'm sure they have books on your reading level here," Brett said. "You know, the ones that star Curious George and Winnie-the-Pooh."

She snorted. "I'll have you know that I'm an honors student, thank you very much. Now, where do you suppose they keep the yearbooks?"

Brett glanced around. "Non-fiction would be a good place to start, I guess."

Abby solved their dilemma the easy way, by asking the aide at the information desk. They quickly located a section of shelves filled entirely with Jefford Academy yearbooks stretching back 80 years.

Brett found the yearbook from five years ago, pulled it off the shelf and flipped to the index. "Pure Shore Club…Pure Shore Club…here it is!" He flipped to the appropriate page while Abby and Maxine crowded around to look. It turned out the Pure Shore Club only took up a quarter of a page, a tiny group photo with a list of names, and a small caption that read, 'The mission of the Pure Shore Club is to make the world a better place through community service.'

"Huh," Brett said. "A little vague, but okay, I guess."

"Sure enough, there's Mr. Santillian," Maxine pointed out.

He didn't look that much different than the man they'd seen earlier that day. He even wore the same basic outfit; a white, button-down dress shirt tucked into jeans. But there was one difference between the man in the photo and the man they'd met. In the photo, Mr. Santillian was smiling, and not just with his mouth. His posture looked relaxed, and the picture seemed to capture a glad twinkle in his eyes.

"Looks pretty happy, doesn't he?" Maxine remarked. "Makes you wonder what happened to make him such a grouch!"

"Maybe we just caught him at a bad time?" Abby suggested.

"Hey, look, it's Michael Alvarez," Brett said. Other than Mr. Santillian, there were five people in the picture, arranged in two rows of three. Michael Alvarez, a pleasant smile on his face, was seated in his wheelchair. The other kids were Mindy, Ethan, Stacy, and Steven. They looked like perfectly normal kids. Brett carefully lined up his phone and took a picture of the yearbook entry. "For the article I'm writing," he explained.

"Well, now we know what they looked like," Maxine said, sighing and leaning up against the bookshelf. "But we still don't know anything about the club itself."

Brett pulled out more yearbooks. "Let's dig a little deeper, shall we?"

It turned out the Pure Shore Club went pretty far back. Far enough back, in fact, that they ran out of yearbooks to look through, only going back as far as 1936. They also looked at the five most recent yearbooks and confirmed there hadn't been a Pure Shore Club at the Jefford Academy in all that time. But in every yearbook they looked through that did have the Pure Shore Club in it, the exact same short caption detailing the club was printed. No more, no less. Brett meticulously took a picture of every single year's entry.

"This is all very strange," Maxine remarked. "But I shouldn't have expected anything different; this entire escapade hasn't exactly been a picture of normalcy."

They sat around a round study table, yearbooks strewn all over its surface, a scattering of times past. Maxine sat on the table, holding the strap to her soccer bag, which rested on the floor. Brett stood, one foot on a chair, leaning on his knee with his chin resting in his hand, his felt fedora pushed back on his head. Abby wondered why they wouldn't sit down, like she was. Maybe they were too cool to just sit down? She wondered if she should do something else besides sit in a chair. She just had no idea what. Pace back and forth? Stand on her head? Stand on the table?

"We need to try a different approach, ladies," Brett proclaimed. "We need to delve into school history, and I think I know how we can do it."

Maxine looked at him sideways. "Oh really? Do you have a time machine handy so we can go back and look for ourselves? Come to think of it, that would explain that hat you wear."

Brett either didn't hear her or ignored her. "I learned this week that the old editions of the Skyrocket are online, and the older stuff has been scanned and put in a searchable archive. Unfortunately, it doesn't read well on one of these." He held up his phone. "It shows up all scrambled-looking and stuff. It's something I'm helping them fix. But in the meantime, I bet we can use one of the desktop computers here to take a look. Might as well, it's that or we all go back to our rooms and separately search them on our own computers."

"The school paper?" Abby asked, intrigued. "That's a good idea." She wanted to kick herself for not thinking of that, but she supposed this was why Brett was interested in being a reporter.

Maxine hopped off the table and slung her soccer bag over her shoulder. "Cue Maxine, exit stage left. I'll leave you two to do this research, okay? I went to practice hours ago and by now I probably stink like an overworked racehorse. I'll go clean myself up and come back."

"Sure about that, Max?" Brett asked. "This is where it gets good. Real research, digging up dirt, finding hidden skeletons. Well, hopefully not literally, but you know what I mean."

"I'm sure," Maxine said. "But as fascinating as that sounds, I must clean myself up. I'll be back in a few. Stay out of trouble, kids."

She strode away, her long ponytail swinging from side to side.

Brett and Abby hurried to the library's computer lab.

With just about every student owning a laptop computer of their own, the computer lab was underutilized most of time. And on a Friday night, there was no one else there. Abby suggested they both search for "Pure Shore Club" in the Skyrocket archives on separate computers, and then Brett could sift through the odd-numbered search results and Abby could sift through the even numbers.

"That's very efficient," Brett remarked, clearly impressed. "You might have a future in the investigative journalism biz, Blondie."

For a time, the only sounds were typing on keyboards, the low hum of hard drives.

"Hey, Blondie," Brett spoke up after a few minutes of searching.

"Yes?" Abby replied, growing excited, wondering if Brett had found something.

"What do you want to do?" he asked.

Abby was sitting at the computer opposite his. She leaned over to see him past their two monitors. "Um, what?"

"For a career," he elaborated, without looking over. "A job, you know. When you get out of school. Professional saxophonist, maybe? Or be a doctor, like your folks?"

Abby was taken aback. She was very good at fading into the woodwork, occupying corners in bustling, conversation-filled rooms. Not too many people asked her direct questions like this. Especially not in the short time since she'd moved to the Jefford Academy.

"I…I really don't know," she admitted, sounding foolish to her own ears. Brett was the same age as her, yet he already knew what he wanted. He probably thought she was a loser or something.

He kept on clicking his mouse. "Nothing wrong with that," he told her. "You've got lots of time to figure it out. I was just curious, that's all. There's a lot someone with a great memory like yours could do, I bet."

Abby supposed he was right. She didn't know what to say next, so she went back to her search results.

The next hit she opened took her aback.

"Oh my!" she said, at a higher volume than she'd intended.

Brett was around the table so quickly Abby barely saw him move.

"What is it?" he asked, plopping down in the chair next to her and staring at her monitor. Abby let the text of the article speak for itself. It was from May, five years ago. The same year the Pure Shore Club had broken up. Brett took in the words rapidly, his eyes tracking back and forth like ricocheting ping-pong balls.

Maxine returned just then, wearing jeans and a hooded Jefford Academy sweatshirt. "Hey, guys," she greeted them. "Any luck?" Abby and Brett looked up at her. Their eyes were wide, which took Maxine aback. "Uh-oh. What'd you guys find?"

Brett waved her over, and she came around to the other side of the computer. She read the article Abby had pulled up.

They had kept the yearbook from five years ago with them. It was on the desk next to Abby, and Maxine picked it up, flipping to the group photo of the last Pure Shore Club. She looked at the picture, zeroing in on two of the kids: Stacy McNiece and Steven Endicott. Stacy was a tall, athletic-looking girl with thick, curly hair down to her shoulders. In the picture she was showing off a tremendous smile. She looked friendly, as friendly as a person could look in a picture.

And she was dead. According to the article on the computer screen before them, Stacy McNiece died in an accident five years ago while on a school trip with the Pure Shore Club.

CHAPTER THREE
JOURNEY INTO THE PAST

Brett and Abby busily searched the web.

"Well, that explains everything," Maxine said, leaning up against the wall. "Kid dies on club outing, club closes up shop. Seems pretty straightforward to me."

"But…" Abby spoke up, "what about all the other stuff?"

Maxine knew full well what Abby meant. There was a lot still unexplained, such as the weird talk about the Smiling Shadow and the unidentified third voice emanating from Mr. Santillian's office. Not to mention the vanishing Michael Alvarez. Abby saw the corner of Maxine's mouth twitch, as if she was trying to find something to say but couldn't. Abby had the impression that didn't happen to Maxine very often.

"That wasn't all," Brett pointed out. "The article also talked about another kid from the club who went missing in the same accident."

"Did they ever find him?" Maxine asked.

"Still listed as a missing person," Brett reported. "I guess he'd be this guy…" He produced the yearbook again, pointing out an extremely normal-looking kid with short-cropped hair and average features. The kind of kid who could blend into any crowd. "Steven Endicott was his name."

"Could possibly still be his name," Abby noted.

Maxine snorted. "I doubt it. They were caught in a landslide, doing one of those stupid team-building wilderness things. If he hasn't turned up by now, the poor kid's body is probably under some rocks somewhere. Frankly, I'm amazed Mr. Santillian kept his job here at Jefford after something like that."

"It said he was cleared of any suspicion of wrongdoing," Brett pointed out. "Obviously it's still haunting the guy to this day. Because of course it would, right? Hmm…"

"Something more?" Maxine asked, walking over to look over Brett's shoulder, Abby trailing behind.

"I decided to find out more about this Michael Alvarez guy," Brett told her. "Since he seems like the one who wants to get the club back together, you know? Turns out he's quite the Picasso. See?"

Brett had open an article about Michael Alvarez, from an old edition of the Skyrocket. Michael was a painter, or at least he was when he went to Jefford. The article had several examples of his artwork photographed. One item in particular caught Abby's eye.

"Oh, wow," she said. "Do you guys see the mural he painted?"

The computer screen showed a tiny version of the giant mural they'd all walked past before. It was on a wall at the center of campus. The mural depicted the Jefford Academy as it had appeared in the early 20th century.

"Spectacular," Brett mused. "I didn't know a student had painted that."

"No, no," Abby said. She pointed at the caption below the picture, the caption that listed the title of the piece.

The name of the mural was 'The Past'.

"No way," Brett whispered.

Maxine looked back and forth between them. "What's the big deal?"

"Remember what Michael Alvarez told us before he disappeared?" Abby asked. "He said to look to 'the past' for the answers we seek. Do you think maybe he was leaving us…a clue?"

"There's only one way to find out," Maxine said. "Let's go look at this mural close up, shall we?"

●　　　●　　　●

As they approached the exit doors, they found it had started raining. Maxine proclaimed that a little water never hurt anyone, and strode out into the rain, pulling up her hood and jamming her hands into her sweatshirt's pockets. Abby didn't want to be left behind, and hurriedly pulled her umbrella out of her backpack. It was difficult because it was under all of her books and folders.

She noticed Brett was looking up at the sky with a sour expression. "Gee whiz, and me with no umbrella!" he complained. He pulled his hat down on his head, bringing it almost down to his eyebrows, and prepared to follow Maxine. Abby called out to him to wait and produced another umbrella for him to use.

He took it with a nod of gratitude, but quickly looked curious. "Do you always carry two umbrellas around with you?"

Abby felt her cheeks burn once more, and not for the first time in her thirteen years wished her emotions didn't show up so readily on her face. "Um, I, I like to have backups. You know, in case one breaks, or someone borrows it and doesn't give it back…"

Brett shrugged. "Hey, your paranoia is my gain, Blondie."

Maxine poked her head back into the library. "Are you two coming, or what?" she demanded.

"Is it bad out there?" Abby asked, noticing the tiny waterfalls of water dripping off of the other girl.

Maxine grinned. "Not at all. In fact, I wish it'd done this during soccer practice. It's really not soccer unless it's wet and muddy, you know?"

Brett muttered under his breath a comment regarding 'insane soccer players'. And then they were off.

•   •   •

The mural was near the middle of the campus, not very far from where they were. As they walked along one of the many sidewalks that networked throughout the campus, Abby was struck by how empty the place seemed. Usually it was bustling with students, teachers, and other school personnel going to and fro, playing games, sitting on the grass, reading on the benches. The rain had obviously sent everyone except them running for cover. With the sun setting, no human life anywhere in sight, and visibility down considerably due to the rain, the campus seemed almost eerie, abandoned. Like a school for ghosts.

The gloom could not blot out the sight of their destination, a landmark visible from most points on campus: The Jefford Rocket.

It loomed in the murk, resting in launch position upon a hexagon-shaped stone platform. Its base was adorned with four brass fins, and the remainder of the rocket's hull was bright red, a cheerful beacon on a rainy day. Its tip seemed to defy the weather, resolutely jutting towards the heavens.

Each side of the platform had something different on it, and they had to walk around to the side that had Michael Alvarez's mural painted on it.

Maxine looked up at the Jefford Rocket as they circled its base, getting a face full of water for her troubles but not minding very much. "Do either of you know the story behind this thing?" she asked over her shoulder. "Did some famous astronaut go to school here or something?"

Brett had no clue, but Abby spoke up, "The founder of the school was Aloysius Jefford III, a pioneer in rocket science. This was built in 1964 to honor him. I…I read that in the student handbook."

"I figured," Maxine called back. The words could have sounded mean—Abby knew she was kind of a dork for reading and memorizing the entire student handbook—but Maxine had sounded kind. Abby was grateful for that.

"Rocket science?" Brett repeated. "But if he started the school, he had to have been alive in the 1700s, right? You mean to tell me they had rockets way back in those olden days?"

"Sure," Abby told him. "'The rocket's red glare', and all that. They used them in the Revolutionary War and stuff."

Brett nodded. "That makes sense! Boy, having you around is better than using the internet."

It was too dim outside for Brett to notice Abby's cheeks flaring as red as the rocket monument.

"Ah, we have arrived at 'The Past'," Maxine declared as they rounded the appropriate corner, her quick strides splashing in puddles of water. True to its name, the mural depicted a scene from history, in this case, the campus as it had been in the early 20th century.

"Wowzer," Brett said, pointing to various spots on the painting. "The school was pretty much just the circle then, huh?"

Jefford Circle was a circular road that sat in the middle of the modern-day campus like a pupil on an eye. All other roads radiated outward from it like spokes on a wheel, and the older campus buildings were placed along the circle's perimeter.

"The field house isn't there," Maxine noted. "Neither is the soccer stadium or the tennis courts."

"Or the dining hall," Brett chimed in. "And it looks like the library got redesigned at some point. Hey, there's that little chapel!" He pointed to St. Elmo Chapel, the tiny church building that sat next to the enormous Administration Building, dwarfed like a child next to its parent.

"That was actually the very first building," Abby said. "The rest of the school kind of grew up around it when Mr. Jefford bought the land. Wow…this Michael Alvarez guy is really talented!"

Maxine and Brett had to agree. The painting was enormous, taking up the entire facet of wall, probably a good semester or two's worth of work. It depicted the old-style brick buildings of the campus, with people in period clothing dotting the landscape, all doing different tasks. A girl sat on a bench reading a book. Boys played an improvised baseball game in the middle of a grassy field. People rode in horse-drawn carriages or on old-style bicycles with huge front wheels.

"The details are amazing," Brett said, leaning in so close the rim of his hat bent against the stone surface. "You can see individual blades of grass…cracks in the sidewalks."

Maxine was tempted to point out that Brett could jump right into the painting and, with his anachronistic wardrobe, not look out of place at all. Instead, she refrained, concentrating on looking for clues. Abby and Brett followed her lead, walking around slowly in front of the mural, scanning the wide picture for something out of the ordinary, something that Michael Alvarez meant for them to see. Something that would point the way to figuring out the puzzle that was the Pure Shore Club. Brett took pictures as he went, trying to capture the entirety of the large painting in a series of photographs.

They looked at it from further back, they looked at it from close up. They tilted their heads until they were looking down at the ground. Maxine found herself grateful that the rain had driven all potential bystanders away; the three of them probably looked like they were engaged in some bizarre form of performance art.

Then Brett spoke up, "Hey, this kid here looks like he's looking at a piece of paper."

The girls crowded around him, umbrellas ramming into each other like bumper cars. Of course, the kid in question was in reality a painting, but a very well-done painting. He was wearing knickers and a coonskin cap, and was holding a piece of paper in front of him, as if he was showing it to the viewers of 'The Past'. And perhaps he was.

"He's got something on that paper there," Brett said, "but it's too small to see. Luckily, Cheryl can help us with that."

"Who's Cheryl?" Maxine asked. "Wait, don't tell me—"

"Max, meet Cheryl," Brett said, pulling from his attaché case a magnifying glass.

"Oh, my gosh," Maxine moaned, burying her face in her hands. "Why me?"

Abby smiled and watched as Brett used Cheryl to examine the painting. Not only did this guy dress like someone in an old black-and-white detective movie and use antiquated expressions like 'hot dog!', he carried a magnifying glass around too. How many other boys his age did stuff like that? No boy Abby had ever met, that's for sure.

"Huh, looks like a map," he reported.

"A map of what?" Maxine demanded, squinting her dark eyes in a vain attempt to see what Brett was seeing.

"Here, Blondie," he said, passing the magnifying glass over to Abby. "You've got the photographic memory, tell us what you think."

Abby took the magnifying glass, taking a moment to admire the instrument. It was heavier than she expected, and the handle was made of cherry wood. The handle also bore an inscription carved in gold letters: 'All good reporters need one—Best wishes—G.' She wondered who 'G' was.

She squinted at the painting. "It's a map of the campus," she reported.

"From the olden days?" Maxine asked. That didn't seem like it would be very helpful.

"No, present day. It has all the new buildings on it."

Brett gazed at the stormy skies. "Weird. You think this Michael wants us to find something, maybe?"

"I'd say so. There's an 'X' marked on the map."

"Let me see," Maxine demanded, taking the magnifying glass and a turn peering at the mural. "You're right...it's in the northwest corner of the campus, almost off the map."

"What else is around it?" Brett asked, looking off in that direction.

"Just...woods," Abby told them. "Just empty woods."

Maxine took the magnifying glass away from her face and turned to look at them. "Maybe it's not so empty after all."

CHAPTER FOUR
A SHADOWY VISITOR

At first, it had been a strange sensation for Steven, to walk straight at solid walls and pass right through them. The first few times he'd been understandably reluctant, despite the reassurances of his shadowy companion. It's a natural survival instinct not to run into objects. He'd done this often enough by now to get over his instinct to flinch.

It had been much longer since he'd been back to the Jefford Academy. It was quite unreal to be walking these halls of learning once again. Memories flooded back as he and the Smiling Shadow stalked the halls of the Pinski English and Humanities Building. He'd been such a young fool when he'd first come here, Steven reflected. Now he was older, wiser, and had much better taste in companions.

"Are you certain Reeve will not detect our presence?" he asked as they walked down the darkened corridor to Mr. Santillian's office. The building was closed for the weekend. The lights were dimmed or off completely, its doors locked. The latter was no obstacle to a being with the Smiling Shadow's capabilities. As for the former, well, Steven and his dark friend were quite at home in shadows. They had a lot of experience at it, by this point.

"Steven, Steven," came the smooth voice of the Shadow. "You have my assurances that I am not the same as I was the last time we were here. I've learned how to slip around Reeve's methods of detection." Its voice was like ice water turned to soundwaves. Even after all the time he'd spent with it, the Smiling Shadow still managed to cascade cold down Steven's back.

They found Mr. Santillian's office in short order, right where Steven remembered it being. His former teacher was nothing if not a creature of habit. The door was locked, of course, but the Smiling Shadow's power enabled them to pass straight through, like a pair of phantoms. The office interior, cloaked in feeble light from the rainy day outside, wasn't much different either. Mr. Santillian still retained his fondness for antiques, and they cluttered the room. So much was familiar, it was like coming home. Only for Steven, it was not a good feeling of homecoming. His was the homecoming of a wayward son who despised his place of origin, and longed to wipe it out and forget about it.

The old mahogany desk with the lion's face carved into the front surface. The tarnished, dented helmet of a knight still occupied a space on the bookshelf. A miniature Easter Island statue occupied a space on the desktop. Quill pens filled a wooden cup carved with elaborate etchings in a forgotten language.

Next to Steven, the dark form of the Smiling Shadow undulated, its edges shimmering and flowing and rippling, the only constant the pale white smile that always hovered at its center. "Oh, tiny spy, where are thee? What secrets will you share with me?" The seemingly inane rhyme was actually a passcode. On cue, the Spy-Crystal their agent had planted here months ago floated out from its hiding place behind Mr. Santillian's portrait of William Shakespeare and drifted across the small office to hover before its two masters. It was indeed tiny, no bigger than a pebble, and it glinted in the feeble light coming from the office window.

Immediately it began emanating light, projecting into the empty space a holographic representation of its recordings. It was a recording of everything that had taken place in Mr. Santillian's office from the time the small device had been planted. After much review—and Steven found his already limited supply of patience about to trickle away—they came across a meeting between Reeve, Michael Alvarez, and Mr. Santillian.

"Alvarez," Steven muttered, spitting the name like a curse, his fists clenching of their own accord. He wished the real Michael Alvarez was there in the room with them, and not a three-dimensional representation of the man. Steven would like nothing better than to have his hands around Alvarez's throat.

"Calm thyself, my friend," the Smiling Shadow all but whispered. "Your time shall come, never fear."

Funny, Steven thought, such a sentiment coming from an entity who practically embodied fear to its enemies. He said nothing and watched as his three enemies talked on the recording. He smiled when Mr. Santillian scoffed at the notion that the Smiling Shadow had returned. If he only knew…

Intrigue gripped both Steven and his shadowy friend when three teenagers, middle schoolers or freshmen by the look of them, were caught listening at the door and called on the carpet by Mr. Santillian. The man had lost none of his fiery nature, Steven noted. For all the good it would do him in the days to come.

"My, that pony-tailed one has spirit, eh?" the Shadow said with a ghostly chuckle.

Steven just grunted. The recording ended, and only then did he allow himself a grin of assurance. "Ha! Alvarez has tried and failed to marshal a new generation against us. Mr. Santillian, guilt-ridden and pig-headed as the man is, turned him down cold and sent those youths packing. Good for us, huh?"

"Very good for us," the Shadow said, continuing to look straight ahead as the holographic recording faded and the Spy-Crystal floated back to its concealed station. "Alvarez suspects we are back, but his efforts are in vain, especially without the teacher's support. The Pure Shore Club shall enjoy no resurgence. And those who remain…those who once were members of that accursed assemblage…"

"They will fall," Steven agreed. "One by one, until none are left. And then victory shall be ours. And they shall pay for what they did to me."

"Yes, the hour of reckoning is near," the Shadow said. "Let us return to turning out the lights, Steven. We shall track them one by one, steal what is precious to them, and before Mr. Santillian or Reeve knows it, the icy grip of the hunter shall be upon them."

Steven curled a hand into a fist in front of his face. "And victory shall be ours." Then, without another word, they left the way they came, slipping out as silent as a night breeze. Steven did not so much as look back at the familiar spaces of the Jefford Academy campus, where a younger version of himself once trod. The sinister pair faded back into the rainy evening, seeming to become one with the night itself.

CHAPTER FIVE
A WALK INTO DARK WOODS

"Are you sure this is a good idea?" Abby asked Maxine. She was sitting on Maxine's bed, watching the other girl stuff a backpack full of supplies. It turned out Maxine lived right around the corner from Abby, just five rooms away. The two girls had never crossed paths before, due to Abby's reclusive ways and Maxine's busy sports schedule.

"Which part?" Maxine asked. "Leaving to check out the 'X' on the map, or doing it after dark?"

Abby swallowed hard. "I…both, I guess. We're really not supposed to leave the campus, are we?"

Maxine threw a flashlight into the open backpack. Abby was amazed at the array of equipment the soccer player had stuffed into her tiny room. "You tell me, Abby. You've read the student handbook, after all."

Maxine noticed Abby's cheeks light up an embarrassed shade of scarlet, and mentally kicked herself for being sarcastic with the other girl. Abby had the word 'sensitive' written all over her. With Maxine, if she's making fun of you, then you know she likes you. If not, it's time to be worried. Maxine had to remind herself not to treat Abby the same way she treated most other people.

Abby worked up the courage to reply. "Well…well, no, we can't leave the campus, unless we're on a school trip, or with an adult."

"Well, the way I look at it, the woods around the campus are part of the campus. I mean, the science classes go on nature walks out there. The cross-country team runs on the trails…I know that for a fact. Where's the harm in a little excursion into the forest?" She smiled broadly at Abby. "After all, it's being done for a student organization."

Abby looked conflicted. "I guess…"

"So no problem," Maxine told her. "Come on, we have to meet Brett."

The boy's dorm was on the other side of campus, and Brett had to trek over there to get his own stuff. The girls had agreed to meet him where the woods met the open lawns of the school grounds.

Slinging their backpacks over their shoulders, the girls set out, wearing hiking shoes and rain slickers. Abby hadn't arrived at school prepared to do anything rough outdoors and had to borrow hiking boots from Maxine. Luckily, the other girl had a spare pair, and a shoe size fairly close to Abby's.

Maxine walked briskly out the lobby doors of the dorm, forcing Abby to half-jog to keep up. They pulled their hoods up, even though the earlier downpour had lessened to a steady drizzle.

"What do you think of this Brett guy, anyway?" Maxine asked as they headed off into the darkness.

"Um, why do you ask?" Abby replied.

"Do I really need to spell it out?" Maxine asked. "He's not exactly…normal, is he?"

Abby felt her cheeks burn slightly. "Well, define 'normal'." She sounded more defensive than she intended. The truth was, she was worried Maxine would not like Brett. She was so athletic, and wealthy, despite her admonitions back in the dining hall, and doubtless one of the 'in crowd'. Not the kind of person who gladly hung out with an oddball like Brett Cho. Maxine and Brett were the only people in her life even approaching the roles of friends, and Abby was secretly terrified that after this Pure Shore Club business was over with, they would all go their separate ways, and then she would be alone. Again.

To her relief, Maxine chuckled pleasantly. "Good point. Normal is a relative term…believe me, I know."

They walked together in silence for a few moments, their breath visible in the cool night air. Abby shivered despite the sweatshirt she wore under her rain slicker. "Um, Maxine? There is another reason we shouldn't be doing this."

"The fact that it's after dark?" Maxine guessed immediately.

"Yeah."

"That, Abby, is why we brought flashlights. Come on, I think I see Indiana Jones Junior."

Sure enough, Brett was waiting up ahead. How he had beat them, Abby couldn't fathom, unless he just did it the old-fashioned way and hustled. She suppressed a giggle as they drew closer. Brett really did look like a young version of Indiana Jones. Despite the rain, he still wore his fedora, and now wore a heavy, worn-out brown jacket with scuffed boots, and instead of a backpack he wore his attaché case slung across his torso.

"Ladies," he greeted them, tilting his hat towards them. Abby found she kind of liked that gesture. No other guy her age ever displayed manners like that. He had definitely hustled over here, Abby figured. He was grinning broadly and rocking back and forth on his heels, obviously eager to get going.

Maxine looked him up and down. "Your choice of outdoor gear leaves a bit to be desired, Brett."

"I'm a reporter, not a hunting guide," he retorted. "Look at that backpack. It's gigantic! You planning on camping out there for a month or what?"

Maxine raised an eyebrow, and her mouth opened to fire back, but Abby intervened. "Well, we're here at the woods, in the northwest corner of the campus. The problem is, where exactly do we go? We could set out in any direction and get lost in these woods." She hoped she didn't sound like a scared baby, but as she looked upon the towering trees and the cold, impenetrable darkness they contained, she wanted nothing more than to be back in her warm comfy bed.

"You're worried, huh, Blondie?" Brett asked, reaching out to clap her on the shoulder. "Not to worry, we'll watch each other's backs. Plus, this really is the best time to do this. If we wait until daytime someone might see us and get all nosy."

Maxine frowned, stroking her angular chin. "No, she's right. I'd hate to end up in Timbuktu just because we didn't go the precise direction."

Brett eyed her backpack. "Got a compass in there, then? That might help."

Maxine produced the compass, a heavy-duty military surplus model. "And no, it doesn't have a name. Sorry if that disappoints you."

"Very funny," Brett said, rolling his eyes. "Okay, I took a picture of that little part of 'The Past' that showed the map with my phone." He produced his phone and began pressing buttons. "Between your compass and my phone's GPS, we should be able to—"

"Um, that might not be necessary," Maxine interrupted, her voice suddenly very quiet. She was staring at her compass with a mixture of fear and awe, as if it had grown a face and begun telling her which way to walk.

Her companions rushed to her side and saw that the compass's needle was not pointing north. From the mural, as well as the maps of the campus they'd looked at, they knew which way was north. The way the compass was pointing was not north. It was pointed the direction they needed to go. It was pointed northwest.

"I don't suppose that could be broken, or anything like that, could it?" Brett asked.

Maxine shook her head slowly, still looking shocked. "No, we're being guided. Guided by something."

"Or someone," Abby added.

•   •   •

Every instinct Abby had told her to go back to her dorm and lock the door. Yet, an unquenchable curiosity inside her propelled her to go on, buoyed by Maxine's determination and Brett's own insatiable curiosity. They launched themselves into the woods, the trees surrounding them on every side like colossal, silent sentries, underbrush snagging them and causing them to stumble every now and again. The air was crisp and somewhat misty. The forest seemed filled with the anticipation of the three middle schoolers.

They all had flashlights and used them to avoid tripping and falling on their faces.

"It's too much to hope," Maxine said, "that there would be a nice, easy trail to get out to this…this whatever it is."

She was in the lead, striding purposefully despite the leafy obstacles in their way. Brett was right behind her, shining his flashlight around, seeming to drink in every detail. Abby struggled to keep up, an intense desire not to be left marooned in the wild giving extra speed to her steps.

"Oh, come on, Max," Brett chided her, "where's your sense of adventure?"

"I guess trying out for the soccer team was harder," she admitted through gritted teeth.

Brett did not reply. He pulled out his phone and began typing, tucking his flashlight under one arm to keep it shining ahead.

"You brought that with you?" Maxine asked, looking over her shoulder at him. "Norman, or whatever its name is?"

"Fred, Fred," Brett corrected her. "And I realized a long time ago that I must write whenever I feel inspired. In this case, I'm continuing my autobiography."

"Right now?" Abby asked from behind him.

"Yep," he replied. "We embarked upon our quest, a trio brimming with youthful energy and curiosity, determined to solve the mystery that lurked in the far reaches of the darkened forest…" He continued to read back what he'd just written, causing Abby to smile and Maxine to roll her eyes. He was cut short when he tripped over a root and fell flat on his face.

His nostrils filled with the scents of damp turf and vegetation, he rolled over only to be blinded by the girls' flashlights.

"Is this going to end up in your autobiography, Ace?" Maxine said, mirth gilding her tone.

"Perhaps…there are times inspiration must wait," Brett reflected, rising to his feet, ignoring the offered helping hands of his companions. He shoved Fred back inside his jacket. "What're we standing around for? Let's move, people!"

•   •   •

Mr. Blake Santillian sat in his study at home, trying mightily to concentrate on getting together a lesson plan for his American Fiction course. Normally, the study was the best place for him to focus. His campus office had the disadvantage of easy access, opening him up to all manner of walk-in visitors and phone calls. Both had the same atmosphere—antiques from his extensive collection filled both spaces, though what his office at the school contained was merely the tip of the iceberg. His entire home was stuffed with old things.

With a snarl of frustration, he threw down his quill pen, used his long arms to push himself away from his 19th century roll top desk and rose to his feet. No matter how hard he tried, he couldn't get those three students out of his mind, the ones that Michael Alvarez and Reeve had so foolishly brought into all of this.

It's one thing for those two idiots to risk their own lives, he thought, it's quite another to bring innocent children into their schemes. He hoped he'd shut the door on a renewed Pure Shore Club as firmly as possible, but he knew Michael Alvarez. He knew Reeve. The two of them could be as tenacious as wolves pursuing prey if need be.

Abruptly, he stalked out of the room, walking in his usual long strides. Even at home, he wore his standard outfit—jeans, a white dress shirt, cowboy boots, his special cuff links. Mr. Santillian was a practical man and had found that he wasted much less time shopping for clothes and putting together outfits if he simply did like soldiers, police officers, and Charlie Brown, and wore the same outfit every day.

Though to the outsider Mr. Santillian's home might look like a bomb had gone off in an antique store, he knew exactly where each and every item was. Particularly this item. Heading to a massive wooden hutch in his living room, he reached up to its highest shelf and plucked down a silver brooch in the shape of a cutlass.

It had belonged to Stacy McNiece. He turned it over in his hand, letting the light glint off the surface. The other members of the Pure Shore Club had insisted he have it after Stacy died, to remember her by. Truly a mixed blessing. Some things were better off forgotten.

Except for times like these, he thought, gripping the pin tightly. It was good to remember why the Pure Shore Club had ended, and why it needed to stay that way. Try as he might, he couldn't just write off those three 8th graders as Alvarez and Reeve's responsibility. After what had happened to Stacy, he couldn't bear another young life cut short on his conscience. It would not happen again.

He knew he couldn't get involved personally, but he knew someone who could help. Mr. Santillian shoved the brooch into his pocket and walked to his telephone. Flipping through his leather-bound address book, he found the number of Jolene Colt. She didn't live far away, and she would be eager to help him out in his time of need. Jolene had always been quite reliable.

Mr. Santillian reached for the receiver of his phone—an ivory model with a rotary dial—and was quite startled when the phone rang.

Shaking off the oddity of the coincidence, he answered. "Santillian," he said gruffly. He was not a man who had much patience with telemarketers and survey-takers.

"Mr. Santillian, this is Headmaster Charlton," came the reply.

The headmaster? Mr. Santillian thought, his body stiffening. When did the Jefford Academy headmaster ever call him, let alone any other teacher personally? Usually, his secretary made all of his appointments for him. And it was Friday night, on top of that.

"Yes?" the teacher replied, his mind alive with possible explanations for the unexpected call from the school's highest executive. Could it be…?

"Sorry to bother you at this hour, Blake," Charlton said, not sounding sorry at all, "but a matter has come to my attention that I will need to see you about. It has to do with that…student organization you used to sponsor."

The way the headmaster said it left Mr. Santillian with no doubt as to what the call pertained to.

"What's wrong?" Mr. Santillian asked, hearing the anxiousness in his own voice. Had those three 8th graders gotten into some kind of trouble? Images from the past flashed unbidden through his mind. Mourners in somber attire, weeping in the presence of a closed casket. A headstone. A horrible explosion of bright light…

"It concerns the…past members of the club," Charlton went on. "The authorities have brought it to my attention that they are all falling prey to some kind of…malady."

Past members. Therefore, not those three new kids. A measure of relief entered him, but tension still gripped his limbs. "Do you mean a disease? What kind of disease?"

"Unknown at this time," Charlton reported, sounding haggard. The man was probably terrified at the prospect of potential lawsuits, should the sickness—whatever it is—be traced to the Jefford Academy. "I have representatives from the government coming here, and I would like you to come in and hear more details."

"I'm on my way," the teacher replied, and signed off. He stood in his quiet house for a long moment. A disease…affecting the Pure Shore Club alumni? He had some ideas of what might be going on, but he needed to learn more. But first he had to make sure the potential new recruits Alvarez and Reeve had summoned to his office earlier that day were safe.

He reached for the phone again and dialed Jolene's number.

CHAPTER SIX
THINGS ARE NOT WHAT THEY APPEAR

Brett, Maxine, and Abby continued to follow the compass, and eventually they arrived at the edge of a clearing. In the center was an old barn made of gray wood. The paint was cracked and peeling, and there were gaps here and there where time and the elements had created holes.

"Do we keep going?" Brett asked.

Maxine showed him the compass. It had returned to pointing north, like it normally should. "I guess we've arrived," she replied.

"This is too weird," Brett remarked. "The GPS doesn't show this on the map at all. It just shows forest on this spot, but we can plainly see there's a clearing and a barn here."

Maxine grunted. "No weirder than anything else we've encountered so far."

They slowly approached the barn, trying to stay alert. Abby still wasn't entirely convinced this wasn't just an elaborate prank that upperclassmen pulled on younger kids. Her gaze darted around the clearing, trying to look everywhere at once. They circled the building, discovering a gravel road on the other side that came from a gap in the forest and ended next to the barn. The road looked like it hadn't been used in a while, and it also wasn't showing up on the GPS.

"Very scenic," Maxine remarked, eyeing the ruin of a barn. "I guess if we need some firewood, we're covered. Otherwise, I have to admit this is quite disappointing."

"Don't be so quick to judge, champ," Brett told her. "We haven't looked inside yet." He reached the wide double doors to the barn first, and carefully inched one open, peeking inside. The girls were startled when he shut it abruptly.

"What is it?" Abby asked.

Brett didn't answer. He looked at the front of the barn, then walked to the side a few steps and looked down the length of the old structure. He cracked the door open again. "Holy moley," he said, his voice hushed.

Maxine impatiently strode forward and pulled the other door open. Abby looked over Maxine's shoulder.

'Holey moley' was an understatement. The interior of the barn looked nothing like the exterior. Inside was a long corridor with rounded walls and ceiling. The walls were not made of wood but instead some kind of bright and shiny yellow plastic. At the end of the corridor was another door that looked like an elevator door, but with no controls next to it. All three teens could tell that the hallway was longer than the barn itself.

"What the heck is going on here?" Maxine asked, her dark eyes looking up at the outside structure of the barn and then back to the modern-looking hallway before them.

"This keeps getting weirder and weirder, doesn't it?" Abby said to no one in particular.

"That's just the way I like it," Brett said. He gestured for them to follow, and he entered the barn.

"Brett, wait!" Abby cried. "We don't know what's in there."

He whirled and fixed her with a wry smile. "I know. Isn't that great?"

"But...we don't know much about this Michael Alvarez guy," Abby pointed out. "What if he's a crazy lunatic, luring us here to kill us or something?"

"Oh, Abby, you're being paranoid," Maxine said. "Where's your sense of adventure?" Before Abby could protest again, Maxine grabbed her by the upper arm and pulled her into the barn.

•   •   •

The three students didn't enter the isolated barn unnoticed. From the edge of the clearing, just beyond the tree line, two pairs of eyes watched. They saw three kids—middle schoolers by the look of them—enter the clearing, walk right up to the barn and, after a few moments of discussion neither watcher could hear, enter it. The doors shut behind them.

"How did they do that?" the first watcher asked, his eyes still fixed on the spot where the kids had just been standing. "We've never been able to get into that place." It was true. It looked like any other old, junky building that was forgotten about and left to rot out in the wilderness, but it had become apparent over the years that the old barn was not what it seemed to be.

The second watcher frowned behind her sunglasses. "No one enters that place without the permission of our enemies," she mused. Both her and her companion knew the implications of that. In their long week after being reactivated and ordered to keep watch over this site, they'd seen very few people come this way, mostly hikers and other nature lovers. Those people had always poked around the barn but continued with their individual treks. This was the first time they'd seen someone actually go inside. Despite the decrepit appearance of the building, the walls and door resisted any method they attempted to break in.

"Do we report this to the Smiling Shadow?"

"No! You know his Dark Majesty is occupied right now. No, we will notify Daniken. He will know what to do."

She was senior to him, and he quickly moved to obey her orders. She continued to gaze upon the old building, maintaining her cover inside the tree line. It had been a cold, wet evening thus far, but the elements were no concern for such as they. Only their ultimate goal mattered. And to achieve that goal, the Pure Shore Club had to fall.

•   •   •

It was obvious that the corridor had not tasted fresh air in a long time.

"Mustier than my grandparents' basement in here," Maxine mused. They shined their flashlights around, examining the walls, trying to find any clues that would help them figure out why they had to come to this place. Every surface was spotless, as if someone had been cleaning the place on a regular basis.

"Guys, I'm not feeling very good about this…" Abby said. She was backing up towards the door.

Brett and Maxine turned to look at her. She looked like she was about to run away at any moment.

"Come on, let's just look around for a while," Maxine said. "We've come this far, right? Besides, I personally want to know what's going on. They wanted us in this club, and I think we need to find out why."

"Don't worry, Abby," Brett told her, trying to give her a reassuring smile. "There's no one else here."

That was when the lights came on. All three of them jumped. Strange, soft light emanated from the ceiling. It was weird because there were no obvious light fixtures.

"What did you do?" Maxine demanded of Brett, accidentally shining her flashlight directly into his face.

"Aagh!" he cried, flinching and covering his eyes. "Turn that thing off, will you?"

"He didn't do anything!" Abby cried. "Someone is here! And whoever they are, they know we're here!"

Brett began to look a little pale. "W-what if she's right?" he asked Maxine.

"Calm down, both of you," Maxine said, turning off her flashlight and tucking it in one of her jacket pockets. "Haven't you ever heard of automatic lights? Motion sensors, stuff like that?"

Then the doors to the outside, which they had left cracked open, swiftly clicked shut. Brett immediately ran over and shook them. "Someone just locked us in!" he cried. He spun around and pointed at Maxine. "Still think it's motion sensors, champ?"

"Hey, up until a second ago you were eager to explore this place too," Maxine protested, though Abby noticed the other girl was beginning to look worried. "Now come on, between the three of us we should be able to break that door d—"

She was cut off when the floor started moving. It was like being on a moving sidewalk at an airport. It started up so suddenly that all three of them toppled over. The floor was moving them away from the exterior doors, sweeping them like three dust bunnies towards the elevator doors at the end of the hallway. And those doors were now slowly sliding open.

Brett and Abby were screaming and yelling. Maxine kept a cooler head and managed to get to her feet and try to run back to the outside doors. She could run very, very fast, and was actually making some headway, despite the rapidly-moving floor beneath her. It was like running on a souped up, very long treadmill.

She might have gotten away if not for her companions. Brett and Abby were panicking, and they grabbed Maxine's legs as she reached them.

"Don't leave us alone here, Maxine!" Abby cried.

"We don't want to die!" Brett said at the same time.

"Let go of me, you idiots!" Maxine screamed. "You're going to make me—"

She toppled over, falling on Brett and Abby. The trio quickly became a tangled mass of flailing arms and legs. The moving floor swept them towards the open elevator doors, doors that loomed closer and closer, like a greedy mouth ready to devour all three of them. With a final cry, they were pulled through the door and into the dark abyss beyond.

CHAPTER SEVEN
THE HIDDEN CLUBHOUSE

Mr. Santillian arrived at Headmaster Charlton's offices, a huge suite of rooms at the peak of the towering administration building. Since it was outside of school hours, the building was quiet and virtually devoid of people. Upon Mr. Santillian's arrival, Charlton's personal assistant quickly ushered him into the voluminous office of the headmaster.

The teacher found the head of the Jefford Academy seated behind his desk, his fingers steepled in front of his face, seemingly staring at nothing.

"Headmaster," Mr. Santillian greeted his boss with a curt nod.

"Ah, Mr. Santillian," Charlton replied. "Do come in, please." He waved the teacher over. Mr. Santillian crossed the expanse of plush carpet to the headmaster's desk, seating himself in one of the high-backed armchairs that faced it.

Charlton looked troubled. He was a balding, distinguished-looking man with salt-and-pepper hair and neatly trimmed beard. Mr. Santillian had always seen the man in a suit and tie, but now, perhaps owing to the lateness of the hour, Charlton wore a burnt orange polo shirt and khaki pants. Even seated, Mr. Santillian was taller than him; Charlton was famous on campus for his short stature. Teachers and other school staff called him 'Headmaster Elf' and 'The Gnome in Charge' behind his back.

"Typically, Mr. Santillian, when I get a call regarding problems with alumni," Charlton said, "it has to do with donations to the school, or the alumni association not liking the school's new logo, things like that. I have never heard of this school, or any other, having a group of its alumni just…keel over."

Mr. Santillian frowned. Whatever was going on, it could harm his former students. "Who has been affected so far, Headmaster?"

The headmaster sighed and rose to his feet. Walking to the wall behind his desk, he moved aside a large portrait of Aloysius Jefford III, revealing a hidden safe. With his body blocking Mr. Santillian's view, Charlton put in the combination and swung open the safe's heavy door. He rummaged inside, then shut the door, replaced the painting, and turned back to Mr. Santillian with a file folder in hand.

"That must be a very valuable file folder," the teacher remarked. He wondered what else a school headmaster kept in an office safe.

Charlton glared at him. "It is, Blake, it is. It's the list of every former student who has been in this…this Pure Shore Club." He slapped the folder onto his desktop with a melodramatic flourish and sank back into his chair.

Mr. Santillian had actually been the one who gave Charlton the list, back when Charlton had first signed on as the Jefford Academy headmaster. Every new headmaster was told of the Pure Shore Club, usually by the faculty sponsor. However, the teacher had informed Charlton that although the club had been in existence at Jefford for decades, it would be active no longer, due to the incident five years ago that had claimed the life of Stacy McNiece.

Charlton opened the folder and placed the list where Mr. Santillian could see it. "Here is the list of all former members," he informed the tall man. "And here," he said, removing another list of names from the folder and placing it side-by-side with the other list, "is the list faxed to me by the government just this evening of everyone affected by the mysterious malady. I cross-referenced the lists myself, and as you can see, they are all Pure Shore Club members. And there's something else."

Charlton saw Mr. Santillian's dark eyes come alive with concern as he scanned the two lists. The headmaster had never known what to make of the English teacher. The man was an eccentric, certainly, with his odd and extremely consistent way of dressing, and his strange pistol-shaped cuff links. He wasn't involved in any school clubs or committees, and rarely attended school functions or sporting events.

The man was very much a loner. And on top of that, he once led the Pure Shore Club, which, after all these years knowing about it, Charlton was still not sure what to make of it. It was all so…bizarre. Yet Mr. Santillian was a good teacher, well-liked by his students, and didn't create any problems. Charlton had never expected to really cross paths with the man. Or so I hoped, Charlton thought with an internal sigh.

And Mr. Santillian obviously cared about others, Charlton could see that concern alive on the man's face as he examined the entries on the papers in front of him.

"It's affecting the older alumni first," Mr. Santillian said, without looking up.

"That was the conclusion I came to as well, yes," Charlton told him. "And seemingly working its way to the younger ones. If left unchecked, even your former students may be affected, Blake."

"I realize that, thank you," the English teacher replied curtly, looking up with a smoldering gaze that made the headmaster reflexively sink a little deeper into his chair. Despite Charlton being Santillian's boss, the teacher made him more than a little nervous.

"Blake," the headmaster said, "the government is sending some people here who are arriving any moment. I assume they will be health officials of some sort. I need to ask you—is there anything your Pure Shore Club did in its activities that accounts for such a thing occurring?"

Mr. Santillian mulled the question over, even though he'd thought about it extensively while driving to the administration building. After a few moments, he said, "I do have a theory."

"Anything I want to know about?"

The teacher shook his head. "I don't think so."

"I almost feel relieved. I trust you will investigate your…theory…as soon as possible? We're keeping this quiet for now, but I don't know if we can count on it not leaking out somehow. Can you imagine the panic that would break out if this were to go public?"

Mr. Santillian knew what concerned the headmaster. Panicking parents yanking their kids out of the school. The alumni organization going crazy. The school donors subsequently withdrawing their funds. Disaster for the entire school. Mr. Santillian wondered if he should be angry with the headmaster for being concerned with such matters when innocent alumni were falling victim to some strange malady, but he figured the headmaster was just doing his job, taking responsibility for the future of the school.

"As soon as we meet with your…visitors," Mr.Santillian promised him.

Charlton looked somewhat relieved. Then his intercom beeped and he adopted a stricken expression once more.

"Headmaster," came Carla's voice over the speakerphone, "your visitors from the FBI are waiting."

Charlton and Mr. Santillian glanced at each other. Obviously Headmaster Charlton hadn't expected his visitors to be FBI agents. If he had looked pained before, he looked positively mortified now, his complexion adopting a hue that matched his beard.

"Send them in, please," he replied, his voice expressing confidence he did not feel.

•   •   •

Abby wondered for a moment if she was dead. Darkness surrounded her, and she felt a sensation of weightlessness. But she wasn't floating, she realized. She was slowly drifting downward, held in the grip of some unseen force. It was so pleasant, she almost forgot to be scared.

Suddenly, light surrounded her, and her feet touched a solid surface. She was standing on a gleaming silver floor, deposited there as gently as if she herself had stepped off a curb. Maxine and Brett were with her, looking as bewildered as she felt. She thought to look up, and the others followed suit, just in time to see an overhead door silently sliding shut.

"What just happened?" Maxine demanded. "Where are we?"

"Underground," Brett speculated, "though how far, I don't know. We fell too fast for me to even guess." He already had his phone out, busily taking pictures of their surroundings.

Abby recalled the weightless sensation she'd felt as she'd descended. "Did you guys feel like you were being...guided down? Do...do you think it was some kind of special...anti-gravity elevator?" She felt foolish even saying it. Things like that only existed in stories, not in real life. But Maxine and Brett didn't scoff at the idea. They only looked confused.

"Magic elevators…barns that have different dimensions on the inside than the outside…what have we gotten ourselves into?" Maxine asked, looking around. They were in a chamber with walls as silver and shiny as the floor. Everything was as clean as the inside of the barn had been, yet with the same stuffiness in the air. The chamber was large, about the size of a classroom, with a high ceiling, and was also octagonal, with a door on each wall.

"Guys, look," Brett said, pointing to one of the walls. Above a door was a large inscription, carved into the metallic surface of the wall in block letters. It read 'Pure Shore Clubhouse'.

"This place is their clubhouse?" Maxine exclaimed. "Like, they used to hang out here and stuff? Who the heck were these people?"

"Let's find out," Brett said. He took a picture of the clubhouse sign, then headed for one of the doors.

•   •   •

Special Agent Lauren Saint was already getting on Mr. Santillian's nerves, and he had only met her ten minutes ago. For one thing, she was one of those people who thought it was acceptable to wear sunglasses at night, and while indoors. Second of all, she didn't seem ready to accept anything he told her.

"The Pure Shore Club was what kind of organization, again?" she asked, not looking at Mr. Santillian, but instead pacing back and forth in front of Headmaster Charlton's bookshelves, apparently perusing the titles lined up there. She wore a dark gray business suit, and her hair was tied back with a black hair clip shaped like an owl.

Mr. Santillian's fingers dug into the armrests of his chair. "As I already explained to you, the Pure Shore Club was a community service organization. We did activities like help senior citizens, raise money for charity, clean up parks, things like that." It was an old lie, and one Mr. Santillian was accustomed to telling, even after five years of no Pure Shore Club.

"Mmm-hmm," Agent Saint murmured, still not sounding convinced. She suddenly spun away from the bookshelves to face Mr. Santillian. She was a tall woman, and she towered over the seated men. "And just what would a club like that encounter that would lead to its former members falling into deep, unexplainable comas, beyond the expertise of any physician to treat?"

Mr. Santillian and the headmaster exchanged worried glances. The illness—whatever it was—befalling the alumni sounded worse than they'd imagined.

"I have no idea," Mr. Santillian told her, completely stone-faced.

If the FBI agent sensed he might be hiding something, she gave no sign. "Very well," she said, after a long moment, her eyes a mystery behind her sunglasses, "but we will need you to stay in the area in case we have questions. In the meantime, Headmaster," she continued, turning to Charlton, who was seated behind his desk and sitting ramrod-straight, looking as tall as he possibly could. He was obviously a man on edge. "We will need your cooperation to begin searching the Jefford Academy grounds."

The headmaster frowned. "Search? May I ask what for?"

"And why is the FBI involved in something like this?" Mr. Santillian asked, causing Charlton to suppress a groan. He very much wanted to not antagonize this federal agent. So far only her discretion was keeping any of this mess from going public.

Saint folded her arms across her chest. "My team will be searching for unusual chemicals, biological agents, things like that. The FBI is involved, gentlemen, because this phenomenon is affecting Americans all over the country, limiting itself to no one state in the union. I'm sure you see the implications present in this situation affecting national security. It's affecting relatively few people so far, so luckily we've been able to keep a lid on things and keep it out of the news. Again, your full cooperation is asked for and expected." Her tone made it clear she would brook no argument.

Headmaster Charlton swallowed heavily and nodded. "Of course. Please let me know what you need."

"Excellent," she replied curtly. "We will try to be unobtrusive. Good day, gentlemen." With that, she stalked out, leaving the two men in silence for a few moments.

"Blake, please don't antagonize her," Charlton said, slumping back into his large armchair. "This is already a sticky enough situation as it is."

Mr. Santillian slowly rose to his feet. "I have an intense dislike of bureaucrats putting their noses where they don't belong." That wasn't entirely it, he knew. Agent Saint simply rubbed him the wrong way, mostly for reasons unknown even to himself. "Now, if you'll excuse me, Headmaster, I'm going to go test my theory."

"You do that," Charlton grumbled. He reached for the bottle of antacids he kept in one of his desk drawers. He could tell it was going to be a long few days.

Mr. Santillian left the administration building. He didn't like the suspicions he had, not one bit. If his theory was correct—and he didn't see how it couldn't be—then he was going to have to confront one of his oldest friends.

CHAPTER EIGHT
GIFTS ON SILVER PLATTERS

The Pure Shore Clubhouse had a lot of what you would expect a clubhouse to have inside of it. There was a lounge with lots of soft couches, chairs and beanbags, an empty but functional fridge and pantry, a games room with pinball machines, video games, a pool table, and more, all of it turned off and otherwise mothballed. There were even places to sleep; bunk beds with military-neat bedclothes.

After looking behind a few doors, Brett remarked, "You guys get the impression no one has been in here for a while?"

"But it's all so…clean," Maxine said. "Clearly someone has been maintaining this place."

"Yeah," Abby agreed. "It's…it's like it's all waiting, you know? Waiting for someone to come back and use it."

They tried the next door in line, walking at it and allowing it to slide open automatically before them, like the other doors had. It was like entering or exiting a grocery store.

This next room was where things took a turn for the weird. It was a huge chamber the size of an auditorium, with a vaulted ceiling that rose above them. The other rooms in the clubhouse were normal-sized rooms. This space was like walking from inside a closet to the interior of a cathedral. It was hard to believe a room that gigantic was tucked away underground in the forest.

The size of the room wasn't the only thing that took all three students aback. For one thing, the room did not have a floor, only a narrow metal walkway that stretched out over a bottomless abyss like a silver finger. Brett and Maxine craned their necks to look over the edge. The drop was truly vertigo-inducing, with no visible bottom, just shadows below.

"Great guns!" Brett exclaimed. "Will you look at that?"

"Did you just say…'great guns'?" Maxine asked, looking at him askance.

"Yep."

"Okay."

Brett and Maxine ventured out onto the walkway. It had safety railings on both sides, but despite that feature, Abby hung back near the door.

"Come on, Abby," Maxine said, gesturing to the other girl to follow. "It seems pretty safe."

"Uh, I'll stay over here, if that's okay," Abby called to them.

"I think Blondie there might have problems with heights, champ," Brett whispered to Maxine out of the corner of his mouth. "Hey, check that out!"

He pointed to the far end of the walkway, all the way up against the far wall, where the walkway spread out to form a disc. On top of that, resting there like a cherry on top of a cake, was an enormous sparkling purple globe, as big as a house. It gleamed with a dim yet steady light that threw mesmerizing flashes and patterns onto the surrounding silver walls. Brett and Maxine drew near the orb with caution, its light reflecting in their eyes.

"What do you suppose it is?" Maxine asked. It was large, twice as tall as them and about three times as wide.

"And how does all this stay up here?" Brett asked, looking over the railing. "There's nothing down there to support this hootenanny." Maxine took a look for herself and saw Brett was right. Where she expected to see some kind of support structure for the walkway and the purple sphere's platform, there was nothing but open air.

Maxine boldly walked up to the purple sphere. The surface of the mysterious object crackled with unknown energies that gave off the occasional sizzle or sparking noises.

"It's beautiful," she breathed. Brett walked up alongside her, looking between the orb and the soccer player.

"Yeah, it'd make a great Christmas tree decoration," he said. "I know it looks like a giant ball, but try not to kick it, huh?"

She didn't seem to hear him. Continuing to walk towards it, she touched its surface with her outstretched hand. It was surprisingly cool, and she felt a mild charge go through her body.

Brett grabbed her wrist and pulled her hand away. "Don't," he cautioned her. "Who knows what this thing is. It might give you radiation poisoning or something."

She pierced him with her dark eyes and yanked her wrist from his grasp. "I don't need a nanny, Brett. Touch me again and you'll regret it."

"Hey, hey, hey, just trying to help." He held up his hands in mock surrender. He wished he hadn't grabbed her, on second thought. For a moment there, her caustic exterior seemed to have slipped away, exposing genuine wonder. It had been nice to behold. Brett wondered what made Maxine the way she was, to make her place such walls about herself.

He got a few pictures of the weird sphere, then they returned to Abby, who was all but hugging the door. The room yielded no clues beyond the obvious details, which were so odd that they couldn't begin to guess what it was all for. They resolved to try the next room.

It proved to be a bit more mundane, but still interesting. This new room was taken up by a huge oval meeting table, with high-backed leather chairs along its perimeter. The table had a stylized 'PSC' logo etched into its wooden surface. Along the walls were countless framed pictures, all depicting groups of people. Each photo was marked with a school year, beginning with black and white shots from the early 20th century, and moving up to the present day. The people themselves were a sight to behold. They all wore colorful, unusual costumes, often accessorized with capes, gloves, masks, hoods, helmets, belts, and boots.

"The Pure Shore Club through the years?" Abby asked, her green eyes wide as she took in the bizarre plethora of costumed groupings.

"They sure didn't dress like that in the yearbook pictures, did they?" Brett asked, tilting his fedora back and closely examining the pictures.

Maxine snorted. "Can you blame them? Most of them look absolutely silly. What was this Pure Shore Club? A private cosplay club? If so, I, for one, will be very disappointed."

Abby glanced at Maxine, thinking about how she always thought cosplay was kind of neat. She'd dressed up like different characters for Halloween as long as she could remember, and admired the craftsmanship that people put into the costumes she'd seen in pictures online. But evidently Maxine didn't think very highly of cosplay, and Abby chose to be silent.

Each picture had an engraved metal caption below it that told the names of the people in the pictures. But not real names. They seemed to be code names of some kind. Crystal Lynn. Red Cloak. Eagle Ace. Mister Vim. Kid Gilgamesh. Captain Cloud. Mooncat. The Masquerader. Battle Boy. Solar Girl. Ferrous Wheel.

"Check out some of these names!" Brett exclaimed. "These guys from the 1960s...the Moonbeam...Flower Child...Peace Princess...Aquarius." He was taking a picture of each of the photos as he went.

"The Human Zeppelin?" Maxine said, scowling. "What self-respecting person calls themselves that?"

"Thunderhawk! That's a cool name!"

"The Cometeer!"

"Flying Fist!"

"Down here," Abby called to them. She was at the far end of the wall of pictures. "It's that last class, the one Michael Alvarez was a member of."

Sure enough, the picture was nearly a mirror image of the more normal depiction of the group they'd seen earlier that evening in the yearbook. Except the kids in this picture were wearing strange outfits and the caption did not list their regular names. Two they'd never met were named Heights and Captain Creature.

Stacy McNiece had gone by Buccaneer, and wore a pirate outfit, complete with sword strapped to her hip and wide, floppy hat. She stood with her hands on her hips, smiling broadly, the image of a merry pirate. Mr. Santillian wore a similar outfit to what they'd seen him wearing earlier, except for a black mask that covered the area around his eyes, a black vest, and a cowboy-style gun belt. Michael Alvarez was apparently known as Quantumax, and wore what looked like shiny white armor, complete with a white helmet that had a red visor. Interestingly, he appeared to be standing in the picture.

Steven Endicott was known as Even Steven and wore a simple tunic with the double bars of an 'equals' sign on the front.

"Even Steven?" Brett said, snorting. "Can't give the guy many points for originality, huh?"

"Ease up, Brett," Maxine said. "The poor kid is dead, after all."

"Oh, yeah," he replied, his chin lowering a bit.

Maxine leaned back against the conference table and took in the strange pictures. "So they had magic elevators, weird rooms with bottomless pits and big, round, glowing…things. And they liked to play dress-up.”

Brett was busy taking photos of the photos. “Well, if we thought coming out here was going to help things make more sense, we were wrong.”

“It wasn't our idea to come out here,” Maxine reminded him. “Michael Alvarez directed us here, apparently just to confuse us even more. If he'd wanted me confused, he could have spared us the trouble and just had us do our math homework.”

Abby's attention had wandered to the rest of the room. Suddenly she gave out a sharp cry. Maxine and Brett whirled to see her pointing at the large conference table. On it were three silver platters, the kind you find at fancy dinners. They were lined up side-by-side, like trained soldiers.

“Wh-where did those come from?” Abby asked. She began biting the nails of her left hand.

Brett's head was pivoting back and forth. “Did anybody come in? I didn't hear anybody come in.” He rushed to the door and looked outside. “Hey!” he called out. “What's the big idea, huh? Come out, whoever you are!”

Maxine walked around the table to examine the platters. With her background, she was used to food being served this way, and these particular platters were nowhere near as ornate as some she had seen. But it intrigued her, how they had seemingly popped out of nowhere.

“Um, Maxine, you're not thinking of looking under those lids, are you?” Abby asked. She slowly made her way around the table, not taking her eyes off the three platters. It was as if they were dangerous animals and she had to keep her eyes on them at all times, or else they would lash out at her.

"Why not?" Maxine said. "Someone is offering us something. We might as well take a peek. They could be more clues."

Brett had walked over and was peering at one of the platters, his face so close to it he could see his own reflection. "I don't know, champ. Could be bombs under there…or scorpions…or poisonous snakes…"

Maxine rolled her eyes. "You two are way too cautious. Sometimes you've just got to pull up a lid and see what you get." With that, she yanked the lid off the nearest platter. Brett and Abby flinched, half scared, half fascinated by what might lie underneath.

It was a pair of roller blades. White with golden lightning bolts etched on the sides and gleaming golden wheels to match. They were the coolest roller blades any of them had ever seen. Brett whistled.

"See?" Maxine said, jabbing a thumb in the direction of the roller blades. "Nothing to be scared of. Brett, you try one. You know you want to."

"You bet. It sure would be swell to have a pair of roller blades like those!" He pulled off the lid of the platter closest to him. Underneath was revealed…nothing.

"Hey, there's nothing on my plate!" he bellowed. "No fair!"

Abby's sharp green eyes detected something, and she walked over to point it out. "Look closer, Brett. See?" She pointed, and Brett saw what she meant. On the plate was a tiny blue dot.

"That's all I get?" he asked. "What in Sam Hill is that thing? Some kind of lousy sticker or something?"

"Your turn, Abby," Maxine said. Abby reluctantly removed the lid from the last platter, though with some measure of boldness, now that she saw the others had found the contents of the other platters to be seemingly harmless.

"Oh wow, that's pretty!" she exclaimed. Removing the lid of the last platter had revealed a ring. The band was gold, glimmering in the room's light, with a large red stone in the shape of a heart. The red stone was gorgeous, with light sparkling on its surface like the sun on water.

Maxine plopped down in a chair and began removing her muddy hiking boots. "I've just got to try these on," she told her companions.

"Is it too late to pick a different plate?" Brett asked. He'd put the blue dot on his index finger and was holding it up to his eyes, examining it with his magnifying glass.

"Would you rather have selected Abby's gift?" Maxine pointed out as she slipped the new roller blades on.

"Good point, champ," he said. "That ring is very nice, but not my style. So what is this stuff for? Where did it come from?"

"Yeah," Abby agreed, picking up the heart-ring and sliding it onto her right ring finger. "Once again, this is getting weirder and weirder."

Maxine rose to her feet, balancing on her wheeled footwear like a pro. "Hey, why look a gift horse in the mouth, guys? I've got these sweet new roller blades.

Abby's got some new jewelry. Brett has that…that…whatever it is. Maybe the person behind all of this lunacy is Santa Claus!"

Then, abruptly, Maxine pitched backwards, falling into the chair she'd just been occupying. Her eyes were closed and her head lolled to one side, her limbs dangling. It was like she was a marionette and someone had let go of her strings.

"Max!" Brett and Abby cried out at the same time. Then Brett crumpled, too. He had no chair nearby and ended up in a heap on the floor, his arms and legs spread out at eccentric angles.

Abby cried out, then turned and ran for the door. She'd only gone three strides when unconsciousness overtook her, too. The last sight she had was the floor rushing up towards her face.

CHAPTER NINE
WEIRD COSTUMES, WEIRD OBJECTS

Abby woke up slowly, gradually becoming aware of the fact that she was face down. She felt like she had a blanket on her. Was she back in her room, in her own bed? She rolled over, and strangely, the blanket seemed to roll with her. She twisted and rolled around some more, and realized the blanket was somehow attached to her. By this time, she was fully awake, and she noticed her hands had red gloves on. She slowly sat up, looking down at herself. Her outfit was totally different.

She wore a one-piece bodysuit that was mostly white, with a large red heart embroidered on the chest, and red boots to match her gloves. Rising unsteadily to her feet, she realized the blanket was actually a cape, a mostly red cape with white edges and tiny red hearts around the trim. It was clasped to her shoulders by two golden hearts. The sparkly heart-ring was still on her finger.

Her head felt heavier than normal, and she discovered a hat where there hadn't been one. More specifically, a golden crown of some sort. Her face felt funny as well, and she reached up to feel a mask, one that covered her nose and the area around her eyes. She was dressed head to toe in a costume!

Remembering she had people with her, she looked around to see Brett and Maxine also waking up. Like her, they were garbed in strange clothing, too.

Maxine still had the white roller blades on her feet, but now had on a white outfit that looked like a speed skater's uniform. A lightning bolt was embroidered on her chest, and she also had on a roller blading helmet, knee pads, and elbow pads, all colored yellow. Brett wore a cowl that covered his entire head except for his nose, mouth, and eyes. His fedora was nowhere in sight. Like Abby's costume, his came equipped with gloves and boots, and in his case, the whole ensemble was blue, with a large dark blue circle on his chest.

Their reactions were simultaneous.

"Who put these clothes on us?"

"How long were we knocked out?"

"Hey, you look pretty cool!"

"Hey, you look pretty goofy!"

"How come I didn't get a cape?"

"Knee pads and elbow pads and a helmet? Who designed this outfit, my mother?"

"Wait a minute, where's my hat?"

"At least our backpacks are still here…"

"Do you guys see my hat?"

"What the heck is going on here?"

"Oh, no! My room key was in my pants pocket! Now I'll have to pay a lost key fine!"

"Where's my hat?"

Abby and Maxine turned to look at Brett. He was looking around the room, his arms twitching in half-done gestures, rocking back and forth on his feet.

"Brett, it appears that someone took all our stuff," Maxine told him. "Your hat included. Why are you freaking out about it, anyway? You can get another one, right?"

Brett's eyes were wide inside the eye-holes of his cowl. "You don't understand. I can't get another hat like that. That hat belonged to my grandfather. He gave it to me before…before he died." Brett looked at the floor, ashamed to have freaked out in front of his new friends like that.

Maxine and Abby exchanged glances. "Don't worry, Brett," Abby said. "Maybe we can still find it. Our stuff has to be around here somewhere, right?"

"She's right!" Maxine agreed, slamming her right fist into her left palm. "Someone is playing games with us, and I, for one, am sick and tired of it. We're going to find out who is messing around with us, and why, even if we have to tear this whole place apart!"

As if in reply to Maxine's tirade, the door to the conference room abruptly slid open, and a disheveled-looking older man in a gray suit hurried in. He was tall and lanky, with wild salt-and-pepper hair that grew nearly to his shoulders.

"Oh my, oh my," he was saying to himself. "This isn't how it was supposed to happen at all." He stopped just short of the three teenagers, and was looking around the room, his blue eyes darting to and fro, as if trying to pluck the answers to some unspoken question out of the walls.

"Who are you?" Maxine demanded, while Brett and Abby were still reeling at the man's sudden appearance. Whoever he was, he looked like a college professor. He wore a pine green bow tie and his jacket had patches on the sleeves. He was wringing his hands, adding to his state of seeming confusion.

"No, not at all," he said, either not hearing or ignoring Maxine's question. "It's just not proper, I tell you, not proper." He seemed to regard the three visitors for the first time, his gaze falling on each of them in turn. "Ah, don't you three look splendid! Good to see I haven't lost my touch after all these years."

"What are you talking about, mister?" Brett asked. "Are you the one who gave us these crazy outfits?"

"Yeah, and what is this Pure Shore Club business?" Maxine demanded, rolling a few inches towards the man.

"No time, no time," he said, dismissing their questions with waving hands. "Follow me! There is not much time." He turned and walked out the door.

The three students looked at each other, their facial expressions mirroring each other's surprise and befuddlement. The older man ducked his head back into the room. "Please! Time is short. Come, come!"

"We might as well," Abby said with a shrug.

"Might be the only way to get some answers," Brett pointed out.

Maxine scowled, clearly not pleased with this course of action, but rolled out of the room, her companions jogging to keep up. Despite his age, the old man was already far ahead of them, on the other side of the clubhouse's central area, going through one of the many doors. They followed him, and found themselves in the vast, odd chamber with the giant sphere in the center.

The old man was striding out onto the walkway. Maxine figured they were supposed to follow him and rolled onwards. Brett went to walk after her, pausing when he realized that Abby was once again sticking next to the door. He held out his hand to her.

"Come on, Blondie," he said, injecting as much confidence into his tone as possible. "You can do this. Trick is not to look down, huh?"

Abby nodded slowly, and took his offered hand, biting her lower lip all the while. He led her out onto the walkway, her red cape flaring behind her in a dramatic motion that was totally opposed to the fear she felt. Abby had always hated heights and had to pretend she was somewhere else to make the short trip to the glowing sphere.

Maxine reached the old man first. He was a tall, narrow silhouette against the mysterious sphere's light. She was astonished to see him plunge his arm right into the sphere, as if it had no solid surface at all, but was instead just some kind of hologram. His arm went in all the way to his armpit, and he seemed to be rummaging around inside the giant orb.

"Let's see…Where did I last put this dratted thing?" he muttered to himself.

"What are you doing?" Maxine demanded. "What thing? What are you looking for?"

The man suddenly found what he was looking for, withdrew his arm from the ball of light, and spun to hold up another, smaller sphere, this one magenta in color, no bigger than a soccer ball.

"Take this, Maxine," he ordered her, and shoved the colorful ball into her hands.

She stared at it, then him. "What do you think you're doing? What is this thing? And how do you know my name?" Maxine was nearing the end of her rope. If she didn't get some answers soon, the results were not going to be pretty.

"It is the Empowerer," he told her, as if that explained everything. "Protect it with all your cunning and might. I hate to put you young people into this position, but as I said before, time is short. He's on his way, and I will not be able to look after the Empowerer myself. Protect it. Keep it from the sinister hands of the Smiling Shadow."

Maxine looked between the magenta sphere in her hands and the mysterious old man. "What…? The Empowerer? What kind of dumb name is that?"

"The Smiling Shadow?" Brett asked from over Maxine's shoulder. "What is that? Is it a person? What does he have to do with the Pure Shore Club?"

The old man didn't answer any of their questions. "I must go greet my visitor. He is nearly here. Make all efforts to conceal yourselves."

"What? Why?" Maxine sputtered, clutching the Empowerer tightly. Frustrated as she was at the gray-suited man's lack of answers, she also sensed genuine urgency in his words.

"Everything depends on it, child," he told her. "The world. Everyone in it. Everything, actually. Now I must go."

He didn't wait for them to move aside. To their collective astonishment, he jumped over their heads with no visible effort, and soared in a massive arc that deposited him back near the entrance.

They gaped at the incredible feat they'd just witnessed. The man turned to regard them. "Oh, how rude of me…I never introduced myself. I'm Reeve. In a normal time, I introduce the students to the club, show them around the clubhouse, explain everything. But you three are cursed to live in a time that is anything but normal. Like most beings in this universe, you must muddle along the best you can. My best wishes to you. I'm sorry, so sorry." Then he slipped out the door, leaving three stunned students in his wake.

CHAPTER TEN
PERIL OVER THE ABYSS

Maxine stood still, holding the magenta sphere—the Empowerer, as Reeve had called it—in both hands. Her fingers clenched the sphere tightly, like it was a large fruit she was trying to break into.

"Of all the—!" she exclaimed. "Who does that man think he is, anyway?"

"He's Reeve," Abby said. "We finally know who Reeve is."

Brett was running a hand over the top of his cowled head, as if expecting his fedora to suddenly reappear. "Holy Toledo, did you see that jump he made? Not bad for an old guy. He should try out for the NBA!"

"I don't care if he's the world polo champion," Maxine growled. "I'm going to get some answers out of him, just you watch!" With that, she rolled past Brett and Abby, tossing the Empowerer in Brett's direction. It was so sudden that the sphere nearly flew over the railing and into the abyss below, but Brett managed to catch it in time.

"Hey, watch it, champ!" he cried. "The old man said to take good care of this thing…whatever it is."

"Then he can sue me!" she shouted over her shoulder. She was almost at the door. Abby and Brett glanced at each other and ran after the soccer player.

"Maxine, wait!" Abby called after her. "I think someone or something really, really bad is coming here! I think Reeve means for us to hide until it leaves!"

"I don't care if the Prime Minister of Timbuktu is coming in here," Maxine shot back. "Whatever the old geezer is worried about, it's nothing compared to Maxine Drury!"

Yet despite her bluster, she stopped short of the door. Brett and Abby caught up, nearly running into her. Maxine had an ear pressed to the door, obviously listening to something on the other side. The others joined her without comment, curious to find out what had stopped her in her tracks.

Two voices could be heard on the other side. One voice was the cultured, controlled tones of Reeve. The other was deep and booming.

"Sounds like the visitor is pretty upset," Brett remarked.

Maxine's face scrunched slightly as she concentrated. "It sounds familiar…who could it be?"

"I know who it is," Abby told her companions. They looked over at her to find her green eyes wide inside the holes of her mask. Her unfailing memory had quickly placed who the voice belonged to. "It's Mr. Santillian."

"Mr. Santillian?" Maxine hissed. "What's he doing here?"

"He was the faculty sponsor of the Pure Shore Club," Brett pointed out.

"Is he the reason this Reeve guy is all flustered?" Abby asked. "Why would that be?"

"I think we're going to find out, guys," Brett announced. "Sounds like they're coming this way."

Brett was right. The raised voices of Reeve and Mr. Santillian were growing louder and louder as they approached the strange room.

"Hide!" Maxine cried in a raised whisper. They left the door as if it were suddenly red-hot, but stopped short as they regarded the interior of the room they were in. Vaulted ceiling. Bottomless pit. Narrow walkway. Weird yet beautiful glowing globe in the center. Not the best room to be in if you didn't want to be seen. But Maxine had an idea.

"Come on!" she beckoned to the others, and she rolled out across the narrow walkway, her white outfit making her stand out like a ghost. Brett and Abby followed her, Brett dragging the reluctant Abby along with him. The globe had a small circle of metal around its bottom edge, enabling them to inch around and hide behind it.

They made it just in time. Just as they concealed themselves, Mr. Santillian and Reeve burst into the room. Maxine and Brett each peeked around different sides of the globe, leaving Abby between them, pressed up against the huge sphere with her eyes resolutely shut.

She was trying to imagine herself anywhere else but where she was. While the hiding place was effective, it didn't have a safety railing.

Mr. Santillian was backing Reeve into the room.

"Reeve, this has gone on long enough," he proclaimed in his booming voice. "People are getting hurt out there. You need to be shut down for your own good."

Reeve's back was to them, but they could tell he had his hands in his pockets, apparently not fazed by the teacher's accusations. "Blake, if you ever had any major flaw, it was jumping to conclusions," Reeve proclaimed. "Can you at least accept the possibility our old enemy could be causing this phenomenon you are describing?"

Mr. Santillian grunted, so loud the students could hear it from their hiding place. "The Smiling Shadow? Even now, you're going to bring up the Smiling Shadow? You and Michael have driven me crazy with your paranoid theories…"

"It's more than just paranoia, Blake," Reeve replied. "If you would just give Michael more time to investigate—"

"There is no more time," Mr. Santillian interrupted him. "You haven't been the same since our final battle with the Shadow. You're malfunctioning, and it's making people sick. It's time for that to end."

Maxine and Brett could tell Mr. Santillian had produced something from his pocket, something small that glinted in the room's light.

"So it has come to this," Reeve said, placing his arms behind his back. "I gave you that to use in case I was compromised by a third party…every teacher of the Pure Shore Club has had one. Funny, despite all my abilities, I never predicted it being used like this."

Mr. Santillian seemed to be having problems looking Reeve in the eyes. "It…it gives me no pleasure to do this, old friend. You have opened my eyes up to wonders I never imagined. I owe you a great deal." The teacher was having a difficult time talking. His words sounded as if they were being squeezed from his throat.

"You must do what you feel is right, Blake," Reeve said sharply. "Get on with it, then."

"Goodbye, old friend," Mr. Santillian said, sounding like he was in physical pain. He did something with the small object in his hand, and Reeve's form became shimmery at the edges. Maxine suppressed a gasp when Reeve dissolved into several glittering sparkles. The sparkles quickly vanished, like the falling remnants of fireworks.

With Reeve out of the way, there was a greater chance Mr. Santillian would spot them huddled behind the mysterious sphere, but he didn't so much as glance their way. He remained where he was, staring at the spot Reeve had just occupied. It was strange to see on the face of a teacher, let alone Mr. Santillian, but he almost looked sad.

Then he did something else with the object in his hand, and the lights went out. Abby whimpered involuntarily, but Mr. Santillian didn't hear. The giant ball they were hiding behind continued to glow, like a giant round night light in the dark. The teacher then turned and quickly stalked out, his long coat billowing behind him.

As soon as the door shut, Brett began talking. "What the heck was that all about? He turned Reeve off? Like he's a toaster oven or something?"

"Who knows?" Maxine said with a shrug. "Come on, we need to get out of here. I have a bad feeling about this."

She began to inch her way around the globe, back to the walkway, when something terrible happened. She slipped. Walking on a ledge with wheels on her feet in the dark wasn't the easiest thing to do, even with her natural grace. With a cry of alarm, she tumbled off the edge, but snapped out a gloved hand just in time, catching the rim of the ledge.

"Max!" Brett cried.

"Oh, no!" Abby chimed in, seeing her worst imaginings taking place right before her eyes, and happening to her new friend to boot.

Brett squeezed around Abby and went to Maxine's aid. She was now hanging on with both hands, straining to pull herself back up.

"Hang on, Max," Brett told her, and he stooped to offer her a helping hand. He forgot he had the magenta sphere known as the Empowerer tucked under his arm, and as he leaned forward to help Maxine, he lost his hold on the sphere and it fell.

Maxine reacted with whip-like speed, reaching a hand out to catch the falling sphere neatly in one palm, while continuing to hold herself onto the ledge with her other hand. Brett had tried to catch the sphere himself, but all he accomplished was throwing himself off-balance. He ended up tumbling off the ledge too!

The abyss loomed beneath him, and he frantically clawed the air for a handhold, any handhold. Time seemed to slow down. He wondered if he would hit the bottom or just fall forever. He wondered if he would see his parents again. He wondered why he had to die while wearing blue tights.

But he found a handhold; his hand encircled Maxine's right ankle.

"Aaaaah!" she cried, almost pulled off the ledge from the sudden weight. Maxine was now dangling by one hand with a thirteen-year-old boy hanging onto her ankle. It felt like her entire leg might pop out at the hip. She gritted her teeth, holding on with all the considerable determination she could bring to bear.

Below her, Brett was hanging on with both hands, going, "Oh man, oh gosh, oh man, oh gosh…" over and over.

Then she remembered Abby was still on the ledge. She opened her scrunched eyes, and saw the other girl still rooted to the same spot, her arms hugging the giant glowing sphere like it was her anchor in a typhoon-struck sea.

"Abby!" she cried out. The other girl looked on fearfully but didn't move. Maxine knew the bottomless pit was freaking her out, but they needed her help if they were going to survive. "Abby, get over here and help us! I know you're scared, but you can do it!"

This seemed to snap Abby out of her state of panic, and she shuffled over, her cape fluttering around her, making her look like the world's most tentative bird ever, balancing on a telephone wire and not liking the experience one bit.

Brett was suddenly galvanized, and shouted upward, "Give her the sphere!"

Maxine thrust the magenta orb up towards Abby, who closed her eyes, crouched, and reached out blindly with one gloved hand. Maxine shoved the orb into the other girl's outstretched palm, and Abby immediately pulled back, squatting on the ledge, clutching the sphere close to her chest. Maxine was finally able to use both hands to hang on, and the relief that coursed up and down her body was palpable. However, the tremendous strain of holding herself and Brett up almost immediately began to take its toll. She was strong, but not this strong. In a vague, distant corner of her mind, she marveled that she was able to do this at all. She was already finding her limits and exceeding them.

If we survive, Maxine swore to herself, someone is going to pay for this.

Abby felt ashamed of herself. Two people—two friends—were in grave danger right in front of her eyes, and she was so chicken she could barely lift a finger to help them. The magenta sphere was warm, and she clutched it even closer, closing her eyes and leaning back on the larger sphere behind her. Maybe her parents were right to leave her behind, to stick her in this school.

She'd been so sad when she didn't get to join them on their overseas mission of mercy. But now she realized they'd known what they were doing. She couldn't have handled the pressure, the danger. She was better off reading her books in her dorm room, safe and cozy, out of harm's way. No life or death situations. No hardship. Nice, comfortable security.

Her friends cried out, Maxine in pain, and Brett in alarm. The noise shocked Abby to her senses. She couldn't just sit by and let them die. She had to help, no matter how terrified of heights she was.

Abby carefully placed the magenta sphere down on the ledge, and squatted near Maxine, holding out both hands.

"C-come on, Max," she called out. "Take m-my hand!"

Maxine was prepared to do so, but Brett cried out from below, startling them both. "Don't!" he yelled. "We'll pull her down, too!"

Maxine grimaced, knowing Brett was right. No way was Abby strong enough to pull both of them up. Only a weightlifter could do that, or maybe Superman. If Maxine gave Abby her hand, the combined weight of herself and Brett would surely pull the other girl over the edge.

"W-what are we going to do?" Abby asked, still squatting. Maybe she could go find a rope. She could tie it to something, and her two new friends could hopefully pull themselves up. "I'll be right back!" she told them and took off.

She raced around the globe, ignoring the dizzying drop all around her, and ran along the walkway to the door. She expected it to slide open as she approached it, like all the doors in the clubhouse seemed to do, but it didn't move an inch. She looked for a button, or a latch, or a knob, something that would enable her to open it manually. She even waved her hands in front of it, like it was an automatic soap dispenser. The door remained stubbornly shut.

"Oh no!" she said, gripping the edges of her cape in frustration. Even the cape wasn't long enough to tie to something and lower to her imperiled friends. She clenched her teeth, frustrated at their hopeless situation. If she could only fly...

As if on command, a small object appeared near her, floating in mid-air. It was a small rectangle that quickly grew. Abby realized it was a playing card, and it expanded until it was the size of a small carpet. It hovered in mid-air. Squinting, Abby focused on the thing. It was a giant queen of hearts, which she supposed was fitting, considering her costume. Had she thought the thing into existence? And if so, could she control it?

She thought with all her might, willing the thing to move. And it did, moving a few inches in the air. The card responded to her thoughts, moving up, down, back and forth. Her eyes widened.

"Hold on, guys!" she shouted, and she sprinted back to the glowing globe, the card flying ahead of her like a herald.

"What the—?" Brett cried upon seeing the thing flying down to them. Abby peered over the edge and used her mind to hover the card below Brett's feet. He saw her intent and let go of Maxine's leg. For a split second, Abby's stomach dropped into her knees when she realized she'd never tested the mysterious card to see if it could hold up a human being. But she didn't have to worry. Brett dropped a few inches, landing on the card, and it seemed to handle his weight easily.

Abby quickly willed it to lift him up to the ledge, and he hopped off. Brett watched in amazement as Abby directed the flying card back down, this time placing it under Maxine's dangling feet. With profound relief, the soccer player released her tenuous yet mighty hold on the ledge, and allowed her body to fall on the card, where she immediately crumpled into a ball.

Abby flew the card upwards and onto the more secure area of the walkway. Maxine tumbled off the card and lay still on the floor. They raced to her side, only pausing to scoop up the magenta ball. The card seemed to sense it was no longer needed and shrank back to normal playing card size, then winked out of sight as abruptly as it had appeared.

"Max!" Abby called out, kneeling at the dark-haired girl's side.

"She's not dead, is she?" Brett asked, kneeling on Maxine's other side and checking the pulse on her neck and wrists.

"No, not dead, Ace," she murmured. She rolled over and regarded them with her mahogany eyes. "Just feeling very tired, very sore…and very, very stretched out. I think I've grown at least two inches."

"She's alive!" Brett cried happily, clapping Abby gently on the shoulder. "Way to go, Blondie! You too, champ! You must eat your Wheaties, huh?" He clapped Maxine on the shoulder.

"Ow! Watch it, you moron!" she snapped, punching him lightly in the chest. "I'm a little sore from you hanging off my ankle. Do you have bricks in your pockets?" Brett could tell Maxine was just kidding, and he and Abby laughed, partially hysterical from their recent ordeal.

"So, are you two going to help me stand up or what?" Maxine demanded. They obliged, pulling her to her feet. She wavered, then stood up straight. Her arms felt like she'd just held up the entire world. She felt like she could sleep for a week, but she knew she couldn't rest just yet.

"Seriously, how'd you hold both of us like that?" Brett asked. "Your soccer training must include some pretty intense weightlifting, huh?"

In truth, Maxine couldn't quite believe she'd been able to do that either. But she remained silent as she rubbed her sore arms.

"Where did that big flying playing card come from?" Brett asked Abby. "That thing was pretty swell!"

Abby shrugged. "I don't know. It kind of…appeared. And it seemed like I could control it with my mind."

"As 'swell' as that thing was," Maxine said, leaning on the railing and rubbing her sore arms, "we aren't out of the woods yet. I'm guessing we're locked in?"

Abby nodded, her crown glinting in the dim light of the glowing globe. "It's like Mr. Santillian somehow turned everything off. The lights are out and the door doesn't work."

"Reeve is gone," Brett added. "Yeah, Mr. Santillian seems pretty serious about making sure the Pure Shore Club doesn't come back." He held out the magenta ball, the mysterious object Reeve called the 'Empowerer'. "Whatever this thing is, it had better be worth the trouble it—"

The ball suddenly flared with purplish light, so abruptly that Brett almost dropped it. The light was out as soon as it started, and their heads turned in unison when they heard the door open, seemingly of its own accord.

"Well," Brett said, "Mama Cho's little boy has never been accused of looking a gift horse in the mouth. Shall we, ladies?"

The ball enabled them to get back into the meeting room, where they retrieved their backpacks and other gear. Abby expected Brett to want to hunt through the dark clubhouse for his lost hat—she really didn't want to stay there any longer; the clubhouse was spooky with all the lights out—but Brett put the sphere in his side bag and surprisingly didn't mention his grandfather's hat.

They walked out into the central chamber. Before any of them could think about what to do next, the ball flared again, and the magic elevator that had brought them down originally swept them back up to the surface.

The three students stumbled out of the clubhouse. Darkness still shrouded the clearing around the barn, the surrounding trees looming like sinister giants, partially obscured by a blanket of fog. The rain had stopped, leaving the earth wet and muddy, the air moist.

"Great, now we have to hike all the way back to campus," Brett said.

Abby looked between them. "This trip only seemed like it raised more questions."

"We can continue to look for answers later," Maxine told her. "Right now, all I want is a hot shower and my bed." She started off towards the tree line, Brett and Abby at her heels, but she stopped short, causing them to run into her back.

"Hey, what's the big idea?" Brett asked.

Maxine grabbed his arm so tightly it made him wince, pointing off towards the tree line with her other hand.

They were not alone.

Several shapes, silhouettes of people, lurked in the mist. There was the crunching of grass and the squishy sound of trodden mud as the visitors strode towards them. There were between fifteen to twenty of them, and their features became more distinct the closer they came, emerging fully from the fog. They were all tall, wearing somber clothes of black and grey. Their eyes were obscured by sunglasses, despite the utter lack of sunshine. They had untamed manes of hair, sticking out in all directions from their heads, reminding Abby of multitudes of horns.

The students stepped backward in unison.

"Good evening, children," called the one in the middle, an especially tall and lanky man. His voice was horrible, like silverware scraping glass. "I trust you had an enjoyable visit to your little clubhouse?"

"W-who are you?" Maxine demanded, trying to inject as much bravado into her voice as possible.

"We are Outriders," the man rasped. "Forerunners of the Smiling Shadow. Those who serve him and prepare the way for his return."

CHAPTER ELEVEN
THE MENACE OF THE OUTRIDERS

Now that they were closer, Abby could see the faint lines of smiling faces drawn on each of the Outriders' shirts, looking like the half-materialized faces of ghosts.

"The Smiling Shadow again," Brett whispered, sounding terrified yet intrigued.

"Don't take any pictures, Ace," Maxine hissed at him. "Now is not the time."

"Wouldn't dream of it," Brett whispered back, looking around at the sinister assemblage before them. The men and women in gray and black—the Outriders—had stopped walking towards them, and now stood around them in a semi-circle. With the barn at their back, and the Outriders on every other side, the students were trapped.

"What do you want?" Brett snapped, wincing when his voice cracked in the middle of the sentence.

The lead Outrider grinned, revealing a mouthful of brown, jagged teeth. It was a nasty smile, like the grin of a hungry wolf. "Oh, nothing much. You see, children, we've been trying to get into that clubhouse of yours there for a long time now. Our master wants its secrets and riches." He spread his hands before him. "But here's the thing…it just won't let us in. Not very hospitable. It's a shame, eh, fellows?" The other Outriders emitted a chorus of giggles, cackles, and guffaws that sounded like bottles being thrown down a flight of stairs.

"So you want us to show you how to get in, is that it?" Brett asked, his voice holding up a little better this time, but not much.

The Outriders stopped laughing abruptly, their grins replaced by expressions like grim, night-stalking corpses. "That's precisely what we want, boy," the leader rasped. "And you will let us in. If you choose not to, believe me, the consequences will be…shall we say…unpleasant." Then the Outriders began striding towards the students once more.

Maxine and Brett crowded close together, feeling each other shaking, neither having any idea what to do now. Behind them, they could feel Abby's presence. She was moving, and they wondered what on earth she could be doing.

Suddenly, Abby stepped around them. She extended a hand towards the Outriders, brandishing a golden wand that they'd never seen before. It had a glowing red heart on the end, and she pointed it at the somber group like she meant business.

"Stay back!" she ordered. "Turn around and walk away, or else!"

Maxine and Brett stared. They had never heard Abby sound so confident. With her golden crown and flowing cape, she struck an impressive figure. The Outriders stopped in their tracks, given pause by Abby's sudden show of courage.

But only for a moment. The leader chuckled. "If you knew how to use that thing, girl, you would have done it by now."

Abby knew he was right. The wand had appeared out of nowhere, like the flying card, but she had no idea what to do with it. She gulped and lowered the wand to her side, staring at the group of Outriders with wide eyes.

"Nice try, girl," the leader remarked. "Too bad it will do you and your friends no good at all." Suddenly, every Outrider had a weapon in his or her hands. They were dark weapons, almost as if they were made of solid shadows. Swords, hatchets, chains, clubs, pistols, short rifles.

"Leave us alone!" Maxine cried out. "You have no idea who you're messing with…My parents are powerful people…"

"And I don't see them anywhere around here, do you?" he snapped in reply. "Face it, kids, this is the end of the line. No one can save you now."

As if in reply, the clearing suddenly filled with dazzling light and the roar of a powerful engine. A red automobile zoomed into the clearing, driving straight at the Outriders. The students watched in astonishment as several of the Outriders leapt out of the way, soaring into the air in impossible arcs, landing among the trees or along the edges of the clearing. Others were not so lucky, and were struck by the car, flying several feet across the muddy turf.

The car stopped right in front of the three students, and its passenger side gull wing door flipped up. The car was a thing of beauty, all aerodynamic lines with a fin on each rear side, red hubcaps, and a giant spoiler that swept backwards behind the vehicle.

"Don't just stand there!" commanded a voice from inside the car. "Get in!"

Maxine, Brett, and Abby looked at each other. The driver seemed to be there to save them, but could they be sure? Nothing was what it seemed.

Their decision was made easier when they saw the Outriders who had been struck by the car slowly getting to their feet, and those who had evaded being hit collecting themselves and starting to close in.

"Come on!" the driver admonished again, and this time they didn't hesitate. Maxine led the way, diving into the car's shadowy interior. The passenger seat was pulled forward, enabling all three of them to pile into the back seat. As soon as Brett, who gallantly jumped in last, was inside, the door slammed shut and the driver announced, "We're out of here! Hold on!"

The passengers were startled when the interior of the car began to change before their eyes. The upholstery and metal flowed like water. They found themselves shunted forward, then flipped around. In a matter of nanoseconds, the front of the car had become the rear, and vice versa. The driver had turned the car around without turning it around in the conventional sense.

Without a pause, the driver gunned the engine. It roared like an enraged puma, and they were thrust into the back of their seats as the vehicle leapt into action, racing away from the barn and leaving the Outriders behind.

"W-who are you?" Brett asked the driver.

"The Crimson Cruiser," the driver replied. All they could see of their rescuer was a red-clad arm on the wheel, a hand inside a thick red glove, and the edges of a helmeted head. "Mr. Santillian asked that I keep an eye on you. And with good reason, I see. Now hang on."

Trees whipped by on both sides and then they were out on a country road. The Crimson Cruiser negotiated a turn with ease that would have sent most vehicles skidding off the road and raced away. The Cruiser's passengers could see the dashboard, all green lights and displays laid out in front of the driver. Brett mouthed 'Holy Toledo' when he saw how fast they were going. The digital speedometer read that they were traveling at a hundred miles per hour and climbing.

"How do you know Mr. Santillian?" Maxine asked. "Were you in the Pure Shore Club, too?"

"Sure was, sister," the Cruiser replied. "Years ago. But we need to talk later, I have to concentrate now." The Cruiser's voice was muffled by the helmet, but sounded grim and determined.

"Why?" Brett asked. "You gotta have left those clowns in your dust by now. Can't you lay off the pedal a tiny bit?"

"I haven't left them behind," the Cruiser told him, still staring resolutely ahead, hands gripping the wheel with the intensity of a racecar driver.

Brett, Maxine, and Abby strained their necks to look back and see what the driver was talking about, and they were shocked to see several Outriders in hot pursuit, riding black motorcycles.

"Whoa!" Brett exclaimed. "They didn't have those cycles back in the forest!"

"The Outriders have an annoying ability to conjure up the equipment they need," the Cruiser replied. "And the bozos haven't become any less tenacious or ornery over the years, I see. This could get nasty."

The Cruiser whipped the car around a tight turn, yet the Outriders doggedly remained behind them, expertly maneuvering their black motorcycles.

"These guys are like the world's scariest motorcycle gang!" Brett remarked, straining his neck to look behind. Something smacked into the rear window and caused him and the girls to flinch.

"What was that?" Maxine asked, her voice a mix of fear and resentment.

"I think they've given up on trying to catch us and have started shooting," the driver replied. "My Chameleon Car can take a few hits, but I'd rather not test its limits if I can help it. Hold on, kids!"

The passengers were thrown forward as the Cruiser applied the brakes. Only their seat belts kept them from flying out the front window. The car was suddenly at a dead stop, and the Outriders were barely able to take evasive reaction as they swept towards it. Half of their number wiped out, rider and cycle flying in different directions as they attempted to save themselves. A few avoided the obstacle and came to a stop as well.

The students stared out the windows with wide eyes as the mounted Outriders took careful aim with their dark pistols.

"Well, I got a few of the nasty varmints," Cruiser said, and the scarlet-clad driver gunned the engine once more. Abby gaped as the car went from a standstill to eighty miles per hour in the time it took her to blink. She looked back, and amazingly enough, the Outriders were once again in hot pursuit. Who were these people?

"Well, I'll be," the Cruiser said, assessing the situation in the rearview mirror. "The Smiling Shadow must be feeding these boys a little extra juice these days. Well, don't worry, I've got a few more tricks up my sleeve."

All the passengers could do was glance at each other worriedly and remain scrunched back into their seats. Abby imagined it was what it felt like to be on a spacecraft rocketing to outer space. Then Brett saw what loomed ahead on the road and pointed.

"Hey, sharp turn coming up!" he yelled, and the girls looked on in horror. A yellow sign proclaiming a hard right turn was fast approaching, and all that lay beyond it was guard rail and night sky.

The Cruiser grunted. "Didn't want to do this before…it can attract too much attention. But those fellas back there are giving me no choice." The driver didn't slow down at all, but instead sped up!

"What do you think you're doing?" Maxine demanded.

Brett went pale. "We're going to dieeeeee!"

Abby just gaped in astonishment.

All three of them screamed as the car plowed through the guardrail and flew out into empty space. There was a sickening moment of terror as gravity seemed to take hold and the car dipped towards the ground. But then the interior began to change. It expanded, turning slightly roomier, with a rounded roof. The windows shrank to oval-shaped portholes, and the car's roaring engine sounded different.

Abby looked out the window and, to her amazement, saw a wing. An airplane wing. The car had turned into a plane!

Behind them, most of the Outriders were unable to stop in time, and they plunged off the edge, falling into the abyss.

CHAPTER TWELVE
MEET THE CRIMSON CRUISER

The car-turned-airplane soared through the night sky. After making sure there was no sign of pursuit, the Cruiser activated the auto pilot and swiveled the pilot's chair to face them.

"Everyone okay? No bruises or broken bones?"

"This car of yours is pretty slick," Brett remarked, looking around at the red airplane interior. "But why didn't you just come pick us up in an airplane to begin with?"

"You need room to land an airplane," the Cruiser explained. "Room that a narrow gravel road in the forest doesn't provide. Plus speed and a long enough road to take off from."

Cruiser's helmet looked like a racecar driver's helmet, and they could see their reflections in the faceplate. They'd all forgotten about the outlandish outfits they were wearing.

"I take it from those clothes you all have on that you've met Reeve," the Crimson Cruiser said.

"Briefly," Maxine said. "He seemed very confused."

"Yeah, I imagine so," the Cruiser said, sounding weary. Red-gloved hands reached up and pulled off the helmet. All three of them were startled to see the Crimson Cruiser was a young woman, probably in her late twenties, with short blonde hair and blue eyes.

"Well, I know who you all are," she said, looking at each of them. "Brett, Abby, Maxine. Mr. Santillian told me about you guys." Her voice had a slight southern accent, more obvious now that her helmet was removed. "It's only polite that I tell you who I am. You know I'm the Crimson Cruiser, but I normally go by Jolene. Jolene Colt."

Maxine folded her arms across her chest. "So, Mr. Santillian sent you to babysit us. Lucky you."

"Max!" Brett exclaimed. "This lady here saved our collective bacon. You could stand to show a little gratitude."

"Sorry, sorry," Maxine said. "There's just been a lot to take in today."

"I bet you guys are a little overwhelmed," Jolene said. "I don't blame you. No eighth grader would be prepared to do what you all have done today. In fact, it seems to me you three did pretty well. So let me guess, Michael Alvarez gave you guys clues, you followed them to the clubhouse, and Reeve was there waiting for you."

"All true except that last part," Abby said. "Reeve showed up after we woke up with these crazy outfits on." She gathered up the folds of her cape and then dropped them for emphasis. "Then Mr. Santillian showed up, too. He did something to Reeve…made him disappear."

Jolene frowned. "He did what?"

"Made him disappear," Maxine said. "One moment, you had this nervous professor looking guy, the next moment, no nervous professor looking guy. Like turning off a light switch. But before that, Reeve gave us—"

"These nutty clothes," Brett said quickly, cutting Maxine off. She glanced at him, her face smoldering, and he gave her a quick wink that he hoped Jolene wouldn't notice. "Now it's our turn to ask a question. How did you know where to find us? It seems like you didn't know Mr. Santillian had just been at the clubhouse."

Jolene's eyes were far away, and she snapped back to reality. "Oh…yeah, I didn't know he was there. As for how I found you, well, I have my ways, and we'll just leave it at that, okay?" She shot them a sweet smile, yet her steady blue gaze made it clear there was no room for argument.

"And you also didn't know Mr. Santillian was planning on doing anything to Reeve," Brett said. Jolene nodded. "So then," Brett went on, "what's going on here? What's Reeve, that he can be made to disappear like that? Where did you get this crazy car…plane…vehicle? What's a Smiling Shadow? Why do those Outriders want to get into the clubhouse so badly? What is the Pure Shore Club?"

Jolene's eyes widened under the barrage of questions. Her mouth twitched. "You're pretty curious, aren't you? Ever think of becoming a reporter?"

"Most of the time," Brett said with a grin. "So…answers, Ms. Colt?"

She looked out the nearest porthole, toying with a strand of her blond hair. "I wish I could tell you all what you want to know. Mr. Santillian asked me not to tell you guys anything about the club. He's clear he doesn't want you to know anything about it."

"Oh, whatever!" Maxine exclaimed, rising to her feet, standing steady on her golden roller blades. "Look at us! We've been stuffed into these insane outfits. We've witnessed one man make another man vanish. We hiked through a wet, dark forest to a hidden underground clubhouse. We've been threatened by a horde of refugees from a heavy metal fan club. And you won't tell us anything, just because Mr. Santillian says so?"

"Yeah!" Brett chimed in, leaning forward. "Do you have to do what he says? What do you owe him, anyway?"

Jolene's mouth tightened into a determined line. "He was my teacher, when I went to school at Jefford. He was also my boss for a few years, while I was his teaching assistant. But most importantly, he saved my life once."

Abby's green eyes grew wide. "Really?"

"Really. So, you see, kids, as much as I'd like to answer all your questions, I can't. Now, I should get you all back to the campus."

"That's it?" Brett asked. "You're just going to say 'no comment'? Stonewall us? You'll save us from the Outriders but not tell us what's going on?"

They glanced at the clock on the airplane's main console.

"10:45!" Brett exclaimed. "Wow, I lost track of how late it is."

"We have to get back soon," Abby said. "Our curfew—"

"Is 11:00," Jolene said, turning back to the controls. "I know, I used to be a student at Jefford too, remember?"

"If we're late," Abby said, "it gets put on our record. They call parents, too!"

"Not to worry," Cruiser replied as she guided them towards the ground, "I'll have you all back in a jiffy."

"I sure hope so," Abby said, gazing out the window.

"Getting back by curfew is the least of my worries," Maxine said. "After all we went through tonight, and we don't know anything more than when we went in."

"It stinks, champ," Brett agreed. "It really does." They all exchanged glances, then looked at Brett's satchel, which sat next to him, bulging with the spherical shape of the mysterious orb called the Empowerer.

•   •   •

It was 10:55 when the Chameleon Car sped through the Jefford Academy's side gate. To get the students back to campus before curfew hours, the Crimson Cruiser had to fly around until she found a long enough stretch of road to land on, and then broke some speed records to get them home in time. She stopped at Jefford Circle, equidistant between the boy's and girl's dorms.

"Everybody out! Hope you had a nice drive…and flight!" she told them as they climbed out.

"Yeah, it was great," Maxine said, "if I wanted to experience what it's like to be in the Indy 500."

Abby looked around them. There was no one in sight, but that could change in an instant. "Um, what do we do about these clothes we're wearing? Tell people we were at a costume party?"

Jolene bit her lower lip, then leaned back in her seat heavily and sighed. "Concentrate really hard on the clothes you were wearing before. Imagine them back on you. That should do the trick."

They obeyed, and their garish outfits vanished, replaced by the same clothes they'd been wearing before.

"Hot dog!" Brett cried, reaching up and pulling down the brim on his fedora. "Grandpa Cho's hat came back! Woo-hoo!"

Jolene looked at him quizzically, then decided she didn't want to ask. She reached out to shut the gull-wing door, but Maxine stopped it with one hand. "Hands off the car, girl," Jolene told her.

"Wait a minute. What about those Outriders? Aren't they going to be after us?"

Jolene shook her head, tossing her blunt-cut blond hair. "The Outriders stay away from the Jefford

Academy as a rule. They're worried about upsetting Reeve."

"But Reeve is—" Abby began, but Jolene cut her off.

"I know, I know, but they don't know that now, do they? Plus, I'll be around just in case. Sweet dreams, kids. Don't worry about anything, okay? It's all being taken care of."

Abby thought Jolene sounded sincere, but she saw worry in the young woman's blue eyes.

Then she yanked the door from Maxine's grasp, and the car immediately shifted into high gear, racing around the circle to head back the way it came. Jolene somehow had silenced the roaring engine, so it merely emitted a hummingbird-like hum.

"Wow," Brett said, watching the car speed out of sight. "That is one swell hot rod she's got there. I wonder what else it can do?"

"Who cares?" Maxine grumbled. "I'm dirty, sore, frustrated, and tired. I need to go lie down."

Brett snapped his fingers. "Darn it! I forgot to take pictures or some video during that chase! That would've been real swell in my article…" He stopped, noticing that Maxine still had on the golden roller blades.

Brett pointed at Maxine's feet. "Hey, champ, looks like you get to keep those crazy roller blades." Maxine looked down. She'd become so accustomed to wearing them that she hadn't realized they hadn't disappeared along with the rest of her outfit. The golden wheels glinted in the moonlight. Maxine immediately went into her backpack and found her mud-plastered hiking boots stuffed in there.

"Weird," she remarked. "Definitely, absolutely weird."

Abby held out her hand, showing them she still wore the special ring she'd found at the clubhouse. "Looks like I get to keep my new jewelry, too."

Suddenly, Brett began to spin around in circles, looking around frantically. The girls watched him, both puzzled and amused by his antics. He began clawing through his pockets, then his backpack. He took off his hat and looked inside of it.

Maxine couldn't remain silent. "Um, Brett? You okay there, Ace? Did your clothes reappear, but Luke, or whatever your phone's name is, isn't in your pocket anymore?"

"His name is Fred, I'll have you know," Brett said, still turning his pockets inside out, "and no, that's not the problem here, champ. I have Fred, Fred's A-okay. No, it's that little blue dot. That was my souvenir from the Pure Shore Clubhouse, and I've lost it!"

Abby felt bad for Brett. It would have been neat to see what the little blue dot could do. If anything. Then she spotted something floating in the air near him. It was so dark, at first she thought it was a mosquito or some other bug, but it was way too still for that.

"Brett, I think I've found it," she told him.

"Where?" he asked, halting his search abruptly and looking at her with wide eyes. The ground was covered with the objects from his pockets: magnifying glass, small notebook, pens and pencils, gum, a tiny flat stone, and more.

"There!" Abby said, pointing to the spot next to his head.

He whirled and immediately spotted it. He reached out, plucked it from the air and held it in his palm. It was the size of a blue quarter, and unlike Abby's sparkling ring or Maxine's roller blades, didn't glitter in the moonlight. It just lay there, small, blue, and flat.

"Whew!" he breathed. "So this thing can pull a hummingbird and float around. Nice to know. Good eye, Blondie, good eye."

"If we're all quite finished taking inventory," Maxine spoke up, "we need to get indoors, in case you two have forgotten."

Brett held up his satchel, bulging with the mysterious, spherical Empowerer. "What about this thing? Reeve made it sound like it was pretty valuable."

"Hold onto it for now," Maxine told him. "We can think of a place to stash it in the morning. Right now, your room is as good as any."

"Why my room?" he asked.

Maxine raised a dark eyebrow. "You didn't want to just turn it over to that Crimson Cruiser lady and be done with it, so I think you should look after it."

Brett slipped the satchel back over his shoulder and sighed. "Hey, I just didn't know if we could trust her or not. We're taking it on her word she even is who she says she is, after all."

"And here I thought I was the cynical one in this group," Maxine remarked. "Really, Brett. I don't know what that thing is, but I bet it's nothing but trouble. If we'd given it to her, it would have been her problem. Now can we get some rest? I have a game tomorrow, and I'd like to not fall asleep while I'm driving a ball downfield."

"I guess it would be a good idea to sleep on it," Abby said, putting her own backpack over one shoulder. "Want to meet for breakfast and compare notes?"

The others agreed, and Brett and the girls went their separate ways. Maxine and Abby walked together in silence, each lost in their own fatigue-hazed thoughts. They reached the dorm along with a gaggle of other girls who were sneaking in under the wire. The nightguard on duty, an older female student, locked the door behind them and they all went to their rooms, trying to be as quiet as possible. At the Jefford Academy, coming home after curfew was a huge offense, but almost as huge was violating the noise rules.

They reached Abby's room first and she pulled out her swipe card.

"Um, good night, Maxine," she said quietly. She felt utterly bewildered, like her mind had been wrung out like a wet towel and stuffed like a turkey. She wondered if she'd be able to fall asleep.

"Hey, Abby," Maxine said, pausing in her walk down the hallway. She was a near-silhouette in the dim after-hours lighting. Her hands were stuffed into her pockets and her face was masked in shadows. "I wanted to let you know…well, you did really good tonight. You saved my life with that crazy flying playing card of yours. You also saved Brett's life, but he probably hasn't had time to consider that yet."

Abby felt her face flush and was glad it was hard to see in the hallway. "I couldn't just let you guys die," she said with a shrug. "It's what anybody—"

"You also stood up to those Outriders," Maxine pointed out. "That was seriously impressive. I haven't known you that long, but you seem like you have more courage than you know."

Abby didn't know what to say. Then their floor monitor, a curly-haired senior named Clarice, poked her head out into the hallway. "Hey, you two, quit yakking out there, huh?" she hissed.

"Good night, Max," Abby said, hurriedly unlocking her door. She didn't want her floor monitor to write her up. It could go on her permanent school record, after all.

"Night, Abby," Maxine replied, and headed to her own room. She ached all over and, like Abby, felt like her mind had taken in much more than it could handle. And the thing was, she knew this Pure Shore Club business wasn't over yet.

CHAPTER THIRTEEN
A SINISTER COUNCIL

"Daniken approaches," the Smiling Shadow told Even Steven, "and he is most displeased."

"How unfortunate," Steven replied without looking.

Steven was sitting in a high-backed armchair, staring into their hideout's fireplace. The fireplace was a huge maw of flame, throwing undulating light all over the room, yet doing nothing to warm the place up. Any area the Smiling Shadow occupied seemed to become chillier by several degrees.

The Smiling Shadow filled one dark corner of the room, a vast chamber with a gray, stone-tiled floor and a vaulted ceiling. The Shadow was in touch remotely with its many Outriders, using them as mobile sets of eyes, ears, and hands. From their hideout, the Smiling Shadow could direct his forces, and receive information from them as well. No matter what news it received from its Outriders, its broad white smile never changed expression. Its own black mass blended in with the natural shadows that surrounded it.

The hideout was one of the many homes owned by Steven Endicott's family, this particular one a remote stone mansion nestled in a mountain range that Steven was certain his family didn't bother using. It was a perfect place to hide out while their plan was underway. Steven liked the place. He hadn't visited it much growing up, but he'd always been intrigued by its resemblance to a castle. In his childhood visits, he'd usually run around and pretend to be a knight, a wizard, or even a king. Especially a king. Even then, he'd enjoyed the idea of ruling his own kingdom. Perhaps that was when his ambitions to rule and conquer had been born, he reflected. When he'd realized his rightful place in the order of things.

Steven's contemplation before the fire was interrupted by heavy footsteps in the hallway. The door to the sitting room flung open suddenly, and the Outrider known as Daniken strode in. Given that the Smiling Shadow knew what his Outriders knew and could see what they see, Daniken coming all this way and reporting in person seemed a bit unnecessary to Steven, but he supposed the Shadow liked to remind his minions who was in charge.

Daniken was one of the Outrider Commanders, and was proud of his position, walking with his long-haired head held high and striding boldly everywhere he went, his long limbs containing barely-concealed destructive power. Yet when this fierce, powerful man came into the presence of the Smiling Shadow, he knelt on the Oriental rug with his head bowed.

The Smiling Shadow took several moments before acknowledging his servant. "Arise, Commander Daniken," it finally whispered, its voice little more than a hiss.

Daniken rose, as did Steven, circling around the armchair with his hands behind his back. Daniken didn't appear to acknowledge Steven's presence, which didn't surprise the former Pure Shore Club member in the least. The Outriders resented Steven's close bond with the master, and the fact he was once one of their most hated enemies. Daniken's eyes, as ever, were concealed by sunglasses, despite the darkness outside.

"Report," the Smiling Shadow ordered.

"My liege," he said, standing at attention like a soldier, "our spies monitoring the Pure Shore Clubhouse spied three youngsters entering the structure earlier this evening."

"Youngsters?" Steven snapped, taking a quick step forward. "How old were they?"

The Outrider made a point of ignoring the question, not even looking in Steven's direction.

"Answer the question, Daniken," the Smiling Shadow said.

Daniken's lip twitched. "They looked to be middle school or freshman age. They came from the direction of the Jefford Academy. I gathered my squad, and we confronted them when they exited the clubhouse. They are young, inexperienced, and stupid. We should have had them."

"Should have?" the Smiling Shadow said, its whispery voice containing a core of malice. "Should have? What mighty force did these inexperienced children summon that enabled them to escape the clutches of my Outriders, Daniken?"

The Outrider Commander visibly swallowed. "It was the Crimson Cruiser, my liege. She arrived out of nowhere and spirited them away. We gave pursuit, but she flew away before we could stop her."

"The Crimson Cruiser!" Steven exclaimed. One of his hands gripped the back of the armchair tightly. "After all this time? Could Mr. Santillian suspect us?"

"He suspects nothing, Steven," the Shadow chastised him, its eerie smile not turning in his direction. "Likely he has the Cruiser on hand to prevent the children from doing what they have already done. Going to the clubhouse. Meeting the accursed Reeve. Tell me, Daniken…had the children…changed in any way, while they were in the clubhouse?"

Daniken's hands clenched and unclenched. "Yes…yes, they had on costumes when they emerged. One of the two girls in the group brandished a wand of some kind at us but appeared to not know how to use it."

"Costumes?" Steven cried. "They wore costumes?"

The Smiling Shadow drifted from the corner to hover near Steven. Its unchanging smile made Steven wonder, not for the first time, if everything amused the strange being. If the entire universe was one big joke. A comedy show put on for its amusement.

"Calm yourself, Steven," it said. "What are three more Pure Shore Club members to dispatch? We have taken care of so many of them already." The smile grew wider. "Yes, taken care of them…taken away the gifts Reeve so lovingly doled out…and left them broken, in body and spirit." He sounded positively giddy, and that would have chilled Steven's heart, but Steven himself drew satisfaction from the steady annihilation of that club he hated so much.

"As for you, Daniken," the Smiling Shadow said, "I trust you and your squad put up a good fight? Made the Crimson Cruiser pay, at least somewhat, for daring to interfere in your business?"

Daniken gritted his teeth. "In truth, my liege, I lost several of my squad. They drove off a cliff while giving chase."

Steven let out a nasty bark of a laugh. "I question your competence, Outrider. The Crimson Cruiser is a glorified chauffer, after all."

The Outrider slowly turned to regard Steven, acknowledging him as an adult might regard a whining child. "I don't remember asking for your input, boy," the Outrider said, his voice even more low and raspy. His eyes were a mystery behind his ever-present sunglasses.

"Really, Daniken," Steven said, chuckling and folding his arms, "if you can't defeat a woman driving a car, it's probably for the best you never had to fight those children. They likely would have given you and your shaggy friends a sound thrashing."

Daniken was a skilled fighter and gave no sign whatsoever that he was going to strike. He simply did. With speed enhanced by the power granted him by his dark lord, and the shadowy blade that snapped into being in his grasp, he struck at Steven with a blow that would have beheaded an ordinary man.

But Even Steven was no ordinary man. As quick as Daniken struck, a silver sword appeared in mid-air, deflecting the Outrider's blow. The two blades clanged together, echoing off the stone walls of the vast house. The silver blade continued to hover in mid-air between Steven and Daniken, awaiting a new strike. Daniken, frustrated from his night of defeat and embarrassment, was more than happy to oblige.

He struck, and struck, and struck again, a dark dervish of deadly power. But everywhere he tried to hit Steven, a defense sprang into being to thwart him. The silver blade deflected his own shadowy blade. His dark throwing stars were met in mid-air by a silver shield that replaced the hovering blade.

With a howl of frustration, he finally summoned twin obsidian pistols and unloaded a barrage of jet-black cartridges Steven's way. This, too, was thwarted, by a silver breastplate that appeared on Steven's torso. The shots bounced harmlessly off of it, flying against the walls and ceiling, only to be swallowed up by the shadows there.

Through all of it, Even Steven stood with his hands on his hips, malicious amusement dancing in his eyes, and a mocking smile on his face.

Daniken finally gave up. Dropping his hands, the dark pistols vanished, and he stood there, panting from his exertions.

"Feel better?" Steven asked. "Foolish Outrider. You should know that there is a reason I'm called 'Even Steven'. Any force you direct against me, I have the best defense immediately available to cancel you out. I am, therefore, effectively invincible."

The Smiling Shadow, silent through the one-sided fight, spoke up. "Daniken, surely you know that Steven's power is the reason I was able to return from certain death to lead you. So apologize. Now."

The half-hidden malice in the whispered words chilled Daniken's blood, despite his anger. The dark clad man grimaced, then inclined his head towards Steven. "Forgive me, Even Steven," he said, managing to sound sincere.

Steven didn't reply but gave a small nod in return.

"And he is right," the Shadow went on. "If we are to win this second campaign against the Pure Shore Club, we cannot waste precious resources, is that understood?"

Daniken gave the living shadow a much more heartfelt bow. "Yes, my liege."

"Very good," the Smiling Shadow said. "Now, enough squabbling among ourselves, gentlemen. We have a war to win. Even now, my Outriders, scattered across the land, are massing together. Our operative is in place at the Jefford Academy, ready to give us the word. I have traveled through this wretched world, as only I can, striking down the Pure Shore Club one member at a time. Victory is within sight, growing ever closer with each passing moment."

Steven leaned on the mantle, contemplating the fire that still blazed within the fireplace, despite the heat-absorbing presence of his shadowy ally. "Do you really think this will work? Will Mr. Santillian himself really play into our hands as you predict?"

The Shadow chuckled, a noise that made both Steven and Daniken shudder. "You doubt my plan, Steven? Your former teacher is nothing if not predictable. Yes, he will play his part, like a good little pawn. The clubhouse will be wide open to us. As soon as we get the word, we will sweep into that accursed place. We will destroy the thrice-hated Reeve. And at long last...I will seize...it."

"The Empowerer," Steven said, his voice barely a whisper. He knew full well the consequences of the Smiling Shadow gaining possession of that object.

"Yes...yesssss. The Empowerer," the Smiling Shadow said. It drifted to hover in front of the fire, its proximity raising goosebumps on Steven's flesh. Only an act of will on his part kept his teeth from chattering. The Shadow's mass nearly blocked out the light of the fire, like the moon eclipsing the sun.

"With the Empowerer, I shall be unstoppable," it hissed. "And light shall be but a memory." Suddenly, its dark mass sprung forth, falling upon the fire like a sinister blanket. The flames sputtered and died instantly, as if a switch had been flipped. The Shadow lingered in the fireplace for a moment, then slowly withdrew. Not even embers were left in its wake. Steven gulped.

The Smiling Shadow laughed then, a shrill, horrid noise, like a chorus of merry banshees. Daniken joined in, throwing his long-haired head back. The man known as Even Steven gamely joined in, drawing amusement from the imminent fruition of their plans, the utter destruction of the Pure Shore Club. He felt tremendous glee at the prospect of paying back Mr. Santillian, Michael Alvarez, and the others for what they did to him.

Yet, in the back of his mind, he wondered…once he had his revenge, what would he have then? What place would he have in the dark kingdom of the Smiling Shadow?

CHAPTER FOURTEEN
EXPLORING STRANGE GIFTS

Abby didn't even bother tossing and turning. Once she entered her room, she realized she was way too wound up to fall asleep. Her desk had a bookshelf built into it, and she looked at the row of books there, special ones she'd brought from home. Home. Where was home anymore? The closed-up, mothballed house she'd grown up in, back in Charleston? Where her parents were, a battle-scarred and faraway country she'd never visited? Or here, at the Jefford Academy?

She sighed and sank into her chair. Pulling her cell phone out of her pocket, she looked at it for a long moment. Even with the time difference, she could call her parents. They were probably awake. But what could she tell them? *Hello, Dad. Hello, Mom. You'll be happy, I made some new friends. How did I meet them? Oh, I took your advice and joined a club to get involved in the school community and meet other kids. Well, sort of…it's a little complicated. Okay, make that very complicated.*

With a grunt of resignation, Abby plopped the phone down on her desktop. There was no way she could tell her parents about any of her experiences this past afternoon and evening. They were too bizarre, too harrowing. Too mysterious. How could she explain what was going on? She didn't even understand it all herself.

And she wasn't even certain she'd made new friends. Certainly, she and Maxine Drury and Brett Cho had shared some unique experiences so far. But they'd only known each other for a few hours. Not even a whole day. She wanted friends very badly, but she knew she couldn't expect to be best friends with Maxine and Brett.

She liked them, to be sure. She admired Maxine's strength, her courage to say what was on her mind, the certainty in all the dark-haired girl's words and actions. She also admired Brett's willingness to be who he really was, however oddball and retro it might be. He showed a courage of a different kind, a comfort in his own skin that Abby was certain she could never emulate.

No, both of them were way cooler, way smarter, way more confident than she was. Once this Pure Shore Club business was over with, they would go their separate ways. There simply wasn't enough in common between the three of them to stick together long-term.

But a small part of her continued to hope for the opposite.

"Well, what can I read?" she said out loud. Thinking aloud was something she did when she was lonely and silence surrounded her like an invisible fortress. She scanned her row of books. "Hmm. Should I read *Percy Jackson and the Olympians*? *Inkheart*? *The Scarlet*

Pimpernel? That's my favorite of all time, as we all know. That would be a great choice. *The Adventures of Robin Hood*? Very inspiring, lots of fun. Will Scarlet is way cool." She mimed loading a bow with an arrow and took aim at the spine of the book. Abby stopped when she realized none of the books sounded good at the moment. There was way too much to think about.

She flopped onto her bed and stared at the ceiling. What was the Pure Shore Club? She felt like she and her companions were no closer to finding out the answer to that question than when they'd first arrived at Mr. Santillian's office. Pure Shore Club. Something about it all nagged at her, but what? She couldn't put her finger on it.

"Wait a minute!" she exclaimed, sitting bolt upright. She might be confined to her room until 6AM, but she could still do some investigating. She still wore the sparkly heart-ring, after all. The Crimson Cruiser had told them how to switch back to their normal clothes. She'd never said they couldn't return to the colorful costumes again, did she?

Abby concentrated, and sure enough, the Queen of Hearts outfit appeared on her. She hurried over to look at herself in the mirror and was startled. She looked…grand, somehow. Like she was more than just a middle school girl in a silly outfit. Abby ran her hands around the edges of the crown, the edges of the mask that covered the area around her eyes. She twirled, letting the cape swirl around her. With these clothes on, she really felt like a queen. Or at least a princess of some kind.

She strode up and down the length of her small dorm room. "Watch out, world," she said, dropping as much regal drama into her voice as possible, "Princess Abby is here! What shall be my first royal command? Ah, I have it! Chocolate ice cream for dessert every night! My second? Mandatory reading of *The Scarlet Pimpernel* in every high school. My third? OFF WITH HIS HEAD! Who? What do you mean, who? Don't annoy me with your petty questions, you fool. I am the QUEEN! I answer to NO ONE!" Abby's monologue ended in a stream of giggles.

Then she stood still. She figured she was just being stupid. She was no princess, no queen. At the end of the day, she was just a girl in a gaudy costume. Maxine would've mocked her something fierce if she'd seen all that carrying on.

Abby remembered the flying playing card that had popped out of nowhere when they'd needed it most. She wondered if she could summon it again. It turned out she could. Just like making her costume appear, she thought hard about the flying card, and it was suddenly there, hovering a few inches away from her head.

After examining it from all sides, she determined it looked like an ordinary playing card, except for the fact it could, in Brett's words, 'pull a hummingbird' and float in mid-air. With her mind, she made the card expand. It grew to the size of a small carpet and wouldn't go any larger than that. Apparently it had some limits.

Concentrating carefully, Abby willed the card to lower onto the floor. She didn't quite believe it could hold her weight, even though she'd seen it carry Maxine and Brett earlier that night. But she couldn't resist trying. She sat cross-legged on the card, letting her cape dangle over the edges.

With a thought, the card rose an inch off the ground. Then another. Then another. Abby had her eyes scrunched shut, and slowly opened them when it became apparent that the card would not collapse underneath her. Galvanized, she lifted herself up further, until her crown almost brushed the ceiling.

"Wow!" she exclaimed. "I can fly…or at least float!"

Then she remembered the other equipment she had with her. Reaching to her side, she pulled out the long wand. The heart-shaped gem on the end glittered. She'd brandished the wand earlier in a desperate attempt to scare off the Outriders, though she hadn't a clue what she was doing. But the wand had given those sinister men and women pause. Why did it scare them?

Probably nothing, she thought. For a lark, she pointed her wand down, towards her stuffed duck, Mr. Quack. He was sitting on her nightstand, all downy and plump and green. Maxine and Brett would probably ridicule her for sleeping with a stuffed animal at her age, but she didn't care. She'd owned Mr. Quack since she was a little girl, and she wasn't about to give him up.

On a whim, and because she had the wand in her hand and having something to point with made her feel much more queen-like, she barked, "Off with his head!"

And to her astonishment, Mr. Quack's head fell off. Abby gasped, and was so startled she fell off the floating card.

•   •   •

Maxine awoke the next morning feeling refreshed and full of energy. Sunlight streamed through her window, coating her room in gold. She blinked her dark eyes and stared into the sunshine. Some part of her acknowledged its beauty, but such sights hadn't seemed so great for a while now.

Throwing on running clothes and shoes, she headed outside for a morning run, despite the fact she had a soccer game later that same day. Most people wouldn't go for a run the morning of a game, but Maxine took pride in not being 'most people'.

She stretched in front of her dorm, enjoying the quiet. Not too many other kids got up so early on a Saturday. Maxine enjoyed this time, when the world was still. It was like she had the whole planet to herself, at least for a while. Then she realized roller blading sounded better than a run. She bounded back up the stairs, and after a moment's consideration, picked her new roller blades—the ones given to her at the Pure Shore Clubhouse—over her older pair. If these things were going to be hers, she might as well break them in.

Maxine rolled down Afterburner Drive, her dark ponytail streaming behind her like a contrail. She felt good, considering the exertions of the previous day. Her arms were a little sore, but she figured that was okay. She didn't need them to roller blade or play soccer, anyway.

She left the campus and turned out onto the two-lane road that ran perpendicular to Afterburner Drive. Gazing at the open road ahead, she realized this would be a good time to think about all the craziness she'd just been through. The Pure Shore Club. Reeve. The Crimson Cruiser. The clubhouse. The Outriders. She wasn't sure what to make of it all.

None of it made sense, and as she bladed along, none of it made any more sense. Maxine disliked mysteries, she didn't have the patience for them. She grew frustrated, which made her push herself harder, and go faster. And faster.

She realized she was going very fast indeed. The landscape was rushing by at a rate she usually associated with car rides. But she didn't slow down. Her legs moved faster, her arms pumped, and she leaned forward into the wind, letting speed sweep her away.

The passing landscape became indistinct. The golden wheels of the roller blades made sparks on the asphalt as her feet became a blur. Maxine didn't know how it was happening, how these mysterious roller blades were granting her such speed, but she found she didn't care. Giving herself over to the exhilaration of rocketing across the countryside, she grinned the most genuine grin she'd worn in ages.

She became a laughing, whooping, cackling blur, streaking towards the horizon.

•   •   •

Maxine arrived at breakfast, freshly showered, wearing a Jefford Academy hooded sweatshirt and walking with a spring in her step. She found Abby at the same table they'd used the previous day for dinner. The other girl was chewing on a pencil tip, staring at a piece of paper on the table in front of her.

"Morning, Abby," Maxine greeted her.

Abby looked up sharply, fumbling with her pencil. "Oh, hi, Maxine. I called your room a couple of times, but I guess you were out…"

"Yeah, I went roller blading," Maxine told her. She had her new roller blades with lightning bolts on the sides slung over her shoulder. "I have a lot to tell you."

"Oh, so do I!" Abby exclaimed. "But you go first."

"I should maybe wait until Brett gets here," Maxine suggested. She put her roller blades down and gazed at the breakfast buffet across the room. "Watch those, huh? I'll be right back."

Maxine strode away, leaving Abby staring at the paper on the table, and occasionally glancing at the sparkling, heart-shaped ring on her finger.

Brett and Maxine arrived at the same time. Just like dinner the previous day, Maxine had a tray piled high with food: waffles, bagels, scrambled eggs, a bowl of Froot Loops, a banana, an orange, a grapefruit, a small carton of milk, and three glasses containing different kinds of juice. Brett wore what seemed to be his usual outfit: fedora, khaki pants with suspenders, and an open-necked white shirt with the sleeves rolled up. He had his leather jacket slung over his shoulder, and he hung it on the back of his chair before sitting down.

"Holy cow, champ!" Brett said, his eyes wide. "You leave anything for the other kids to eat?"

"Shut up," Maxine muttered, plopping her tray down and settling gracefully into her chair. "I'm an athlete. I need lots of calories. Especially on a game day."

Brett only had a bowl of some tan grain-looking stuff that looked like birdseed, and a mug of coffee. Abby didn't see too many kids her age drink coffee; she personally found the stuff revolting. If she ever got shanghaied into going to a coffee shop, she usually drank hot chocolate or tea.

"I'll have you know," Brett said, eating a spoonful of his food, "that you're not the only athlete at this table. I happen to have an exercise regimen of my own."

Maxine coughed. "You? What do you do, pen-lifts?"

"Actually, I jump rope," Brett said.

The dark-haired girl had been drinking apple juice and nearly spit it out on the table. Abby had to suppress a smile too. She wondered if Brett was being serious.

Apparently he was. "What's so funny?" he demanded as Maxine chortled merrily, unable to shovel any food in.

"Oh, nothing, nothing," she said. "Jumping rope is a perfectly good form of exercise…if you're a third-grade girl!"

Brett jabbed at the air with his spoon. "My grandfather jumped rope all his life and he lived to be ninety-nine years old. I figure there must be something to it. And I do more than just jump rope. I do push-ups, too. And I have a punching bag, an old-school one on a post, in my room."

Maxine raised an eyebrow, her amusement vanishing after the mention of Brett's grandfather. "You…punch a punching bag? What are you, a boxer or something?"

"The old guy taught me a few things," he said evasively. "But let's stop jawing about my health habits. I've got something amazing to share with you two. You're not going to believe it, you're really not."

Maxine and Abby exchanged glances. They had their own stories they were eager to tell, but Brett kept on talking.

"See this little guy?" he said, looking around to make sure no one was looking, and showing them his blue dot, nestled in the palm of his hand.

"Yeah, it's still tiny and blue," Maxine observed. "We've seen it before. Exciting stuff, Ace."

Brett just smiled and stared at his dot. It began to grow in his hand.

Abby stared with wide green eyes. In short order, it was as big as a dinner plate. Brett placed it on the tabletop. "It can get a lot larger than that, too. I found that out messing around last night. I couldn't sleep until I'd written down everything we'd experienced. My phone had to do an update and I couldn't save the stuff I'd written earlier to my laptop, so I decided to start from scratch. When I got to the part about being given this little guy, I realized I'd better learn all I could about it."

Maxine chomped on her food, looking only half-interested. She smugly contemplated knocking Brett's socks off with what her roller blades could do. "So, it can change size. Anything else?"

"You'd better believe it, champ," he told her. "Watch this!"

He half-rose, took one hand, and plunged it directly into the blue circle. The girls gasped at the same time. Abby dropped her pen. Maxine dropped her fork. Brett's arm disappeared into the blue circle like it was a hole! Both of them immediately looked under the table. The blue circle was also on the underside of the table, and Brett's arm was protruding from it! It was like there was a hole in the table and he'd stuck his hand through it. He waved at them and chuckled.

"Pretty nifty, huh?"

They sat up quickly, eyes bugging out, mouths gaping.

"Oh my gosh!" Abby cried out. "That's amazing!"

Maxine looked around. "Brett, get your hand out of that thing before someone sees you!"

He saw her point and hurriedly withdrew his arm. He shrank the circle to its default dot state and placed it in one of his pants pockets. Brett sat back, smiling crookedly. "Like I said, it can get bigger than that. Big as a person. Big enough to allow me to walk through walls."

"No way," Abby breathed. "How...how did you figure that out?"

Brett's smug expression was replaced by a look of sheepishness. "Well, if you must know, I made it grow all huge, but it was too big to fit in my room easily, so I put it against the wall. I did my exercises, then I cleaned up and got dressed. I was putting on my pants when I, um, tripped."

"Tripped?" Abby asked, as if it was an undefined foreign term.

"Yeah, I fell. Got all caught up in the pants and lost my balance."

Maxine snorted. "Brett, was there some sort of mix-up that got you admitted to this school? Because I'm pretty sure there's a rule that to enter eighth grade you have to dress yourself without toppling over."

"Zip it, champ," he growled. "Anyway, so I trip, see? And I fall towards the wall. Good thing it was the wall where I put the blue circle, otherwise I'd probably have a king-size goose egg on my noodle right about now. You can imagine I was pretty surprised that instead of cracking my head, I fell through the wall, into the room of Davidson, the kid next door."

"Oh no!" Abby exclaimed. "Did...did he see you come through the wall?"

"Naw, he was asleep. I fell right onto his bed. Didn't wake the guy up at all. Me and the other guys on the floor, we call him 'Deadman Davidson', 'cuz the kid sleeps like Rip Van Winkle. I could probably play a trumpet right next to his head and it wouldn't so much as make him roll over. So, I was all disoriented and stuff, but I got my wits together, realized what had happened, and got back into my room in a fast New York Minute."

"Wow," Maxine said. "That little dot might not be as useless as it seemed, huh? Well, listen to my morning. I took these new roller blades out, for a little morning exercise, to get warmed up for the game today and all. It turns out, these babies let me go…really fast."

Brett continued to eat his mysterious food. "Yeah, so what? Most roller blades can do that. There was this kid back in the old neighborhood named Muldoon. We called him 'Molasses Muldoon' on account of him being real slow. Well, when Molasses Muldoon got a pair of roller blades for his birthday, let's just say we didn't call him 'Molasses' much anymore. In fact, we started calling him 'Mach-One Muldoon'."

Maxine shook her head. "You don't understand. I went really, really fast. As fast as a car. Maybe even as fast as an airplane."

"How fast?" Abby asked, looking at the white roller blades, their golden wheels glinting in the morning light.

"I have no idea," Maxine admitted. "Fast enough that I ended up far away from campus before I knew it. I'm not even totally sure where I was…I had to use my GPS to find my way back. But it was fun. A lot of fun."

"It didn't hurt, traveling that fast?" Abby asked. "You know, wind burn?"

Maxine thought for a moment. "That's a good point…no, it didn't. It was just like I was out for a jog.

After I got to a certain speed, that white outfit I was wearing last night appeared on me, with the helmet and the pads and everything. And a visor of some kind slid down over my eyes automatically, I guess to shield them from the wind. It was weird…like the clothes knew on their own to protect me. Oh, and I found out I can retract the wheels into the boots if I want to. I wish I'd known that when we were above that bottomless pit. But yeah, these are incredible!"

Brett leaned over to touch the roller blades. "Sounds like a swell time! Think I could borrow these sometime…?"

Maxine pulled the roller blades out of his reach. "Sorry, that Reeve guy gave these to me."

He folded his arms. "Fine, see if I ever let you use the blue dot."

Before Maxine could retort, Abby spoke up. "You guys have had some amazing things happen to you. Well, you're…you're not the only ones."

"No way!" Brett exclaimed. "That crazy Queen of Hearts getup do something oddball for you, Blondie?"

Abby nodded. She told them about how she'd accidentally disassembled Mr. Quack, taking care not to mention exactly what object she'd disassembled. She'd been upset, since Mr. Quack was a memento from her childhood, a link to her faraway parents. But she began to wonder if the wand could not only split objects apart, but also reform them. So she pointed the wand and hoped for the best. And it worked! Mr. Quack was as good as new.

Then she grew curious. What else could her wand do? A lot, it turned out. She experimented on many things in her room. It turned out she could change an object's appearance, making them look however she wanted. She transformed a paperclip into a potted plant. She changed the color of her evergreen bedspread to pink, to red, to brown, and back to evergreen. She made an aspirin as large as an ottoman, and made her desk chair the size of a dollhouse chair. Long into the night, her room was alight with flashes of pink light as she delighted in her wand's astounding powers.

"That's incredible!" Brett said. He'd stopped eating altogether and was staring at her. "So, you can basically turn anything into anything, then?"

She shook her head, tossing her strawberry blonde curls. "No, not anything. I tried to make a kitten, but it wouldn't let me make any animals, only plants. I also tried to turn one of my pencils into a cell phone, but that didn't work. I couldn't make anything electronic. And it seemed to tire me out the more I did it. But it was fun!"

"I bet," Maxine agreed. "So, we've all been given these funky objects that enable us to do these…magical things. The question now is…why? Why did Reeve give us this stuff? Why did Michael Alvarez point us in that direction? What are we supposed to do now?"

"That's what I'm going to find out," Brett told her. "I still have a story to finish here. I'm going to get to the bottom of this, or my name isn't Brett Cho."

Maxine pointed her fork at him. "You're still thinking you're going to put this in the school paper? Do you realize what they'll think of you if you try? They'll call you a raving lunatic, that's what they'll do. Heck, that's what I would call you if I wasn't in the middle of this craziness with you."

He shook his head and leaned back in his chair. "It doesn't matter, champ. The truth is the truth, no matter how outlandish or unlikely it might seem to some. The kids at this school have a right to know about the supernatural shenanigans going on right under their noses."

"Then get up on this table and show this whole room what your blue dot can do," Maxine told him. "If the truth is so important to you, then show it right now. You have evidence right there with you. Why don't you use it?"

"Not yet," he replied, fixing her with a steely glare. "Not until I find out the 'how' and the 'why'. Especially the 'why'."

Abby had returned to the piece of paper on the table in front of her. On it she had written the words 'Pure Shore'. Before the others had arrived, she had been staring at the words. Something about them had been bugging her ever since the previous day.

"Pure Shore Club," she muttered to herself. Then it clicked. The little safe in the back of her mind that contained the answer opened, and it rushed to the forefront of her consciousness like a flash flood. "Oh my gosh!" she exclaimed.

Maxine and Brett stopped in mid-bicker and looked over at her.

"What is it?" Maxine asked. "Something wrong?"

"The name," Abby said. "Pure Shore. There's a clue right there, right there in the name!"

Brett leaned over to stare at the words on the page. "I don't follow you, Blondie."

"Look," she said, pulling her pen out of her inside jacket pocket and writing furiously on the paper. Then she flipped it over to show Brett and Maxine.

"It's an anagram," she explained. "You can rearrange the letters to spell out another word."

At the top of the page, Abby had written 'Pure Shore'.

Below that, she had written another word: Superhero.

CHAPTER FIFTEEN
THE FATE OF THE PURE SHORE CLUB

Brett looked like he might fall off his chair. He leaned heavily on the table, putting his head in his hands. "No way!" he said, shaking his head. "No way, no way! That's…that's impossible!"

Abby put the paper down and sat back. "I agree with you, it seems crazy. But with everything we've seen, it kind of makes sense. As much as anything like this can make sense."

Maxine was frowning. "Wait a minute. Abby, you're saying that the Pure Shore Club is a club for…for teenage superheroes?"

The other girl shrugged. "I guess I can't say it for certain. But it sure fits, doesn't it? The funky costumes. The secret underground clubhouse."

"Not to mention these crazy…magical objects we've all been given," Brett put in. "I think you might be on to something, Blondie."

Maxine still had her fork in her hand, and furiously tapped the tabletop with it. "Superheroes? You two have to be kidding. You mean…superheroes like Superman…or Batman?"

"Like Spider-Man," Abby said, nodding. "Or Wonder Woman."

"Or the Green Lama," Brett said. "Or the Blonde Phantom."

Maxine looked over at him, eyebrow raised. "What are you talking about, Brett?"

"Old-time comics," he explained. "From my grandpa's attic. The point is, we're just like the guys in those stories. Somehow, we've been gifted with strange abilities. Supernatural skills beyond the reckoning of mortal men."

"But why us?" Maxine demanded, tossing her fork down onto her tray. "Why is any of this happening in the first place?"

Brett glanced at Maxine. "Calm down, champ," he tried to reassure her. "We'll get to the bottom of this. I think the first order of business should be hiding this thing."

He held up his backpack. It had a globular bulge in it, making it very obvious to the girls what was in it: the magenta sphere that Reeve had called the Empowerer.

"That old geezer said to keep this thing safe," Brett reminded them.

"I think he said to 'protect it with all your cunning and might'," Abby recited from memory. "That 'everything depends on it'."

"I'll take your word on that," Brett said. "Regardless of his exact words, that geezer wants us to take care of this hootenanny. How about we do that and then try to figure out the rest of this business?"

"Sounds great," Maxine said, resuming the consumption of her titanic meal. "We just need a hiding place where no one can get to that thing. Somehow, I don't think that stashing it under one of our beds is a good long-term solution. Know of any safes or vaults around here?"

Brett smiled. "As a matter of fact, I do."

•　　•　　•

"I can't believe you broke into the headmaster's office!" Abby said as they walked.

"Calm down, Blondie, you're gonna bust a gasket," Brett told her. The trio were walking across the campus. It was a cool Autumn day, breezy and partly cloudy. The campus was alive with students hanging around outside, some playing games, others studying. The school was gearing up not only for the same soccer game Maxine would be playing in, but also for the first football game of the season.

"I just don't get why you did it," she went on, waving her hands. "You can go into the Administration Building any time you want, Monday through Friday, from eight in the morning until five in the afternoon. Why would you break in there on a Saturday?"

"Stop saying I broke in," Brett said. "You're making me sound like a cat burglar or something. Thanks to my little blue circle buddy, I didn't have to break anything to get in there. I just put my blue circle on one of the outside walls and I was in, simple as that!"

"Her original question still stands, Ace," Maxine spoke up. She had her hands in her pockets, her white roller blades dangling by their laces from her forearm.

"What a couple of killjoys. Haven't you two ever done something just because you could? When I realized I had this new ability, I decided it would be fun to waltz right in there, sit down, and put my feet up on the big man's desk. So that's what I did. That old codger's got one fancy office, let me tell you. Plush carpets and everything. Anyway, it'll make a great anecdote for my memoirs."

Abby waved her hands before her. "Okay, I get why you did it. Well, not really, but okay, I can move past that. But I don't understand why we're going there now. Surely there's some other option? Like a safe deposit box at a local bank?"

"Yeah, that would go over well," Maxine remarked. "'Hi, we're underage minors. Please give us a safe deposit box'."

Abby blushed. "All right, I know that wouldn't work. But you get what I mean...Can't we find somewhere else to put the Empowerer instead of the headmaster's personal safe?"

"Who's going to look for it there?" Brett said. "It's the perfect place to stash it."

"For once, you and I are in agreement," Maxine said. "If we're not going to turn the thing over to Mr. Santillian or the Crimson Cruiser...and I'm still very much in favor of doing so…then getting it out of our hands is the best option."

"Never let it be said you aren't a bright gal, champ," Brett told her. "We'll get this taken care of, then maybe we can start getting to the bottom of things."

As they passed the towering Jefford Rocket, a person on a bicycle zoomed into their path and stopped. Startled, all three of them jumped and hopped backwards a step. It was Jolene, also known as the Crimson Cruiser, atop a cherry red bicycle.

"Mornin', kids!" she greeted them, smiling broadly and sipping water from a bottle. She wore black tights, athletic shoes, a white Jefford Academy t-shirt, with a red bicycle helmet atop her blonde head and a red jacket made of a material that shimmered in the sunlight. "Hope you guys got a good night's rest."

Abby noticed that while Cruiser was smiling genially and slowly sipping water as she leaned on her handlebars, her blue eyes were alert and serious, tracking slowly between all three of their faces.

"Um, yeah," Maxine answered first. "Slept like a log." Brett and Abby muttered their agreement.

"Good, good," Cruiser replied. "Nice to see you three have formed yourselves a little group. It's so hard to make friends your first semester. Great to see you guys haven't had many problems."

They glanced at each other, feeling awkward under Cruiser's scrutiny. The blonde woman sighed and gazed around at the open spaces of the campus, the green lawns drenched with sunlight.

"Boy, it seems like ages since I went to school here," she confessed. "I remember weekends like these…procrastinating on my homework, hanging out with my friends, relaxing…just like you guys are doing, right?"

"Right!" Brett said, and they all nodded vigorously.

"What are you doing here?" Maxine asked. "Visiting your old haunts?"

Cruiser shook her head. "No, I'm keeping an eye on you. I promised I'd look out for you for a while, remember? Just being nearby, you know?"

Brett grimaced, hoping it wasn't obvious. How could they possibly hide the Empowerer if the Crimson Cruiser was watching them? He glanced at Maxine, wondering if she was right. Maybe they should tell Cruiser what had happened. But the same question came back to his mind: Who could they trust? It's not like they really knew any of the people involved. They didn't even know one another that well. How could they possibly confide in Cruiser? Not to mention Mr. Santillian. Brett touched the strap of the backpack he carried. Suddenly its mysterious contents felt not only very heavy, but like they were burning a hole in his back.

"Good morning, everyone," came a booming voice out of nowhere, startling all four of them. Mr. Santillian approached them, wearing a long tan trench coat over a white button-down shirt, blue jeans, and cowboy boots. Abby noted the teacher's clothes and wondered if Mr. Santillian and Brett were related. Both of them wore similar outfits every day, it seemed.

"Good morning, Mr. Santillian," Cruiser greeted him in return, seeming a little flustered at her former teacher's sudden appearance. He had come out of nowhere.

"So, Ms. Alvarson, Mr. Cho, Ms. Drury," Mr. Santillian said, nodding at each student in turn, "enjoying your first week at Jefford so far?"

The teens murmured an affirmative chorus.

"Good, good," he said absently, as if he hadn't heard them. His mind was clearly on other things, his dark eyes darting around in their sockets. Abby was impressed he remembered their names. It wasn't as if he had any of them in class or anything. From her studies of the student handbook, she knew that Mr. Santillian taught upperclassmen.

"What brings you to campus on a weekend, sir?" Cruiser asked. She was clearly as surprised at his sudden arrival as they were.

"Some business to take care of," he said. "I was going to call your cell phone, but since I've run into you, I think a more traditional conversation will serve just as well." He turned to the three students. "If you will excuse us, I need to speak to our friend Jolene here in private."

"Sure thing, Mr. Santillian," she said. "I'll see you kids around, all right?"

She pedaled away, the teacher keeping up with her easily with his long strides. Abby wondered if Cruiser's red bike was her amazing Chameleon Car, transformed into another kind of vehicle.

"Weird," Maxine remarked, watching the bicycle-riding woman and the broad-shouldered man recede into the distance. "Is it just me, or do you guys get the impression Cruiser hasn't told Mr. Santillian anything?"

"Like our powers?" Abby asked. "Or even being attacked by the Outriders?" She felt her body shiver at the thought of the dark-clad men and women with their dark blades. She sincerely hoped she'd never encounter them again.

"Yeah, he didn't want us anywhere near the Pure Shore Club," Brett said, tipping his hat back so he could scratch his head. "If he knew about those shenanigans last night, he would've freaked out."

"Well, let's not look a gift horse in the mouth," Maxine said. "As long as he's talking to Cruiser, she's not following us around. We can go hide the Empowerer if we move quickly enough."

Brett nodded. "Right-o. Let's get to the Administration Building, ladies."

•   •   •

Cruiser couldn't believe what she was hearing.

"You're serious?" she said, still pedaling slowly along, Mr. Santillian loping beside her. "You've really…shut Reeve off?"

Mr. Santillian pursed his lips, squinting. "I'm not proud of it, Jolene, but yes, I did what I had to do. The Pure Shore Club alumni are all getting…sick. Somehow, the powers Reeve gave them are hurting them, expiring in some way."

Cruiser stared straight ahead but didn't really see what was in front of her. Her legs mechanically pumped her bike's pedals. She could have rolled right off a cliff for all the attention she was paying to the world around her. "But how do you know turning Reeve off is going to help?"

"Well, I can't claim to understand all this extraterrestrial science any more than anyone else, but there is a link between Reeve and all the people he's given powers to since the club began. As you know, he was severely damaged in the last battle with the Smiling Shadow."

Cruiser nodded, unwelcome memories coming back. She remembered the hordes of Outriders invading the headquarters. She remembered the final fate of Stacy McNiece, the Buccaneer.

"He's been slowly repairing himself over the past few years," Mr. Santillian went on, "but he'd be the first to admit he's still a bit glitchy. I think the link between him and all the Pure Shore Club members became corrupted over time, despite his efforts."

Cruiser nodded slowly, her mind trying to accept this turn of events. She realized that Mr. Santillian had stopped walking, and she turned her bike to pedal back towards him. He was looking off to the tree line at the northwest corner of the campus. The direction where the Pure Shore Clubhouse was.

She wondered what he was looking at. Had he spotted something? Were there Outriders lurking in the vegetation, and his sharp eyes had seen them?

Mr. Santillian turned to look at her, and she was surprised to find her former teacher's eyes watery.

"I didn't do it gladly or easily, Jolene," he told her. "Reeve was a friend to me. He was a friend to many of us. I'm just doing what's right. Now that he's shut off, everyone will get better." He almost sounded like he was trying to convince himself, not her.

"I'm sure you did the right thing," Cruiser said mechanically, though she was anything but sure.

"But it's not over," he told her. "There's still more work to be done."

She squinted at him. "Sir?"

He looked back towards the forest, seeming to regain his composure. "Reeve could always be turned back on. Then the entire mess would start all over again. Not only that, but the club could be restarted, too. New kids, like those three eighth graders. Brought into the ranks and trained to be heroes. I can't let that happen."

Her mind was already seeing where this was going, but she asked the question anyway: "What are you saying?"

"I'm saying that we need to use drastic measures," he told her, crossing his arms. "I can't just let the clubhouse sit out there, not while Reeve and Michael Alvarez are trying to restart the club. I will not have another Stacy on my conscience, not while I know I can do something about it."

Cruiser's heart sank. "You're…you're going to destroy the clubhouse," she said softly, her blue eyes wide.

Mr. Santillian nodded. "It's the only way to ensure it doesn't happen again. The means to grant more teenagers superpowers must be annihilated. Wiped out. Only then will the risk be over."

"But you need three people to do that, right?" she asked. She barely sensed her bicycle underneath her. Everything seemed unreal, like she might float away.

"I've already called Mindy," he said. "She's flying in today. I wanted to take care of this as soon as possible. I…hope you will help us, be our third."

Cruiser swallowed the lump in her throat. The way the system was designed, it took two Pure Shore Club members and one faculty advisor to activate the clubhouse's self-destruct. Could she really bring herself to help with that? To destroy something that, for her and for many others, had so many cherished memories attached to it?

But she realized she had no choice. She owed Mr. Santillian far too much.

"Yes, sir," she said, her voice cracking. She managed to look him in the eye.

"Great, I really appreciate it, Jolene."

"No problem, Mr. Santillian."

He chuckled. "Jolene, you know you can call me Blake. You're not my student anymore."

"Of course, Mr. Santillian."

He shook his head and sighed. "Well, I'll need you to pick up Mindy from the airport. I have to stay here and run interference. The FBI is snooping around for clues to what's affecting all the alumni. If they only knew, eh?"

He texted Cruiser the details on Mindy's arrival time and flight numbers, and they prepared to part ways.

"Mr. Santillian?" Cruiser asked as he turned to leave. "What about our powers?"

He knew what she was getting at. "Why do they still work? Even though Reeve is shut off?"

"No, sir," she said. She gripped the handlebars of her bicycle, as if a tornado was going to sweep in and whisk it far away. "I know that even though Reeve's personal program is turned off, a lot of his peripherals still keep running, including maintaining our powers. No, I mean after we destroy the whole shebang…then it's really over, isn't it? Our powers will be totally gone."

Mr. Santillian's mouth compressed into a tight line, and he squinted at the sidewalk. "Yes, Cruiser," he said, his voice quiet. "That's right. Yourself, Ethan, Mindy, Michael, all the others, even me…it will all be gone."

"But…" Cruiser went on, her mind racing through the implications, "all the good we do…all the help we give…"

"I think that's a small price to pay to help the alumni get well, and to make sure no new powers are granted to eager young teenagers. Yes, the Empowerer must be destroyed, along with all the rest of it, to make sure there are no new incarnations of the Pure Shore Club."

Cruiser nodded and looked down at her bicycle. "Well, I'd better get moving, I guess." The Jefford Academy was in a pretty isolated area. The airport would be a long drive, so it was best to start as soon as possible. They said their goodbyes and she steered her bicycle to the nearest road. Once she ensured no one was watching, she willed the red bicycle to transform into the same amazing super-car she'd used to rescue the kids the previous evening.

The powerful vehicle formed around her, and she zoomed off campus and towards the airport. Driving the Chameleon Car was quite a rush, one she'd never taken for granted. The car was like an extension of her body.

She realized she'd better enjoy it while she could. Conflicting emotions welled up within her. Anger at Mr. Santillian for unilaterally making these huge decisions and taking away something so wonderful. Yet she saw his point. She thought of those three eighth graders, how they were probably stumbling around with their newfound superpowers, and how young and innocent they were. How easily they could end up like Stacy McNiece. Or Steven Endicott, given the right circumstances. They could become casualties, or monsters. Giving up her own powers was a small price to pay to make certain similar tragedies never happened again.

Yes, destroying the Empowerer was the only way to ensure that no one else received superpowers, ever.

CHAPTER SIXTEEN
WALKING THROUGH WALLS

"I still can't believe we're doing this," Abby whispered as they entered the Administration Building. Travelling through the blue circle was just like walking through any open doorway. She had expected it to at least tingle or something, but it didn't.

"Hey, I said you could wait outside," Brett said, not unkindly. "I'd hate to make you do something you're uncomfortable doing."

"We talked about this, Ace," Maxine said, stepping out of the blue circle. She was last in line, and after she was through Brett willed the circle to shrink back to its normal dot-size and float near him. Maxine had on her new roller blades, just in case fast work was needed. "We're in this together," she went on, rolling into the darkened corridor before them. "We can't think of a better place to put that thing under wraps, so we might as well share the risk along with you."

"Very neighborly of you, champ," Brett told her, walking along next to her. "I think I just might be touched."

"You can say that again," the dark-haired girl muttered. "So where is the big man's office?"

Brett led the way, walking quickly yet cautiously. The building seemed deserted, all the lights shut off and entirely quiet, but they had to be cautious, nonetheless. If they ran into a school staff member working weekend hours, they would have some very awkward explaining to do, not only about why they were there in the first place, but how they got into a locked building.

The three intruders didn't like the possibility of getting into an elevator and being stuck if someone else got on with them. The only other option was to climb eight flights of stairs to the top floor of the building. They opened the door to the nearest stairwell, trying to be as quiet as possible, but every creaky hinge and every footfall sounded like bass drums to their ears. The stairway was lit by dim after-hours lights that did little to alleviate their paranoia. To Abby, it seemed as if they were climbing the inside of a shadowy, sinister tower.

They reached the top and crept towards the headmaster's office. The doors were made of some kind of polished cherry wood, standing in contrast to the more everyday-looking doors on all the other offices. The doors were locked, of course, but that was no obstacle to someone with Brett's abilities. Moments later, they were stepping out of the blue circle, into the offices of the school's headmaster.

"Are you guys sure there are no cameras in here?" Abby asked, looking around worriedly. She had visions of hidden cameras, all relaying information to rows and rows of screens in some security control chamber somewhere. At any moment she expected a SWAT team to pop out of nowhere and arrest them all.

"Abby, this is the Jefford Academy administration building, not the White House," Brett told her. "I haven't spotted a single camera. Come on."

The girls followed Brett past the reception desk, and he used the blue circle again to pass through the outer room into the inner office. Abby reflected on how amazing it was to pass through walls and locked doors like this, like they were nothing. Like the three of them were ghosts. The possibilities of what Brett could do with his newfound ability both fascinated and scared her.

The inner office was where the headmaster conducted most of his day-to-day business, and it was decorated to impress. A plush carpet muffled their footsteps. Floor-to-ceiling bookshelves lined one wall, filled end to end with scholarly-looking leather-bound books.

"Wow," Abby said, upon seeing Headmaster Charlton's massive wooden desk. "I think his desk is bigger than my entire dorm room!"

She looked around the room, wide-eyed, while Maxine grunted in reply. She'd seen plenty of offices like this over the years, her parents' offices included. Dens of Important Business, designed to impress—or perhaps intimidate—any and all visitors who came in. Being in such a room again caused her stomach to tighten in an unpleasant fashion.

Brett walked over to the room's most unusual feature, a safe built into one of the walls.

"Kind of weird," Abby remarked. "I mean, to have a safe but not hide it?"

Maxine rolled over to examine the portrait of Aloysius Jefford III, mounted on hinges so it could swing in and out like a door. "Huh," she grunted. "Just like you said. Almost like he got absent-minded and forgot to shut this. I can't imagine he just lets the safe be out in the open all the time."

"Who knows?" Brett said, shrugging. "Everybody gets distracted sometimes. Now, just give me a second or two…" He placed his blue circle up against the safe door and stuck his head into it. From the girl's perspective, it looked like Brett had his head stuck in the wall, like it had been built around his blue circle.

He shortly came back out, holding a tiny box. "Okay, now for Abby's part of our plan." He gave her the box and she examined it closely. He removed the Empowerer from his backpack. The magenta sphere glowed faintly in the dark room, like a large, bizarre night-light.

Abby looked at her heart-ring, swallowed heavily, then concentrated. In a split second, her regular clothes were gone and she was clad in the garish, caped outfit of the Queen of Hearts. She tried not to look Maxine and Brett in the eyes. Next to them, wearing their street clothes, she felt rather foolish in the fantastic ensemble. She produced her heart-wand and pointed it at the Empowerer.

"Do your stuff, Blondie," Brett encouraged her, holding the Empowerer out to give her a clear line of sight.

There was a flash of pink light that momentarily dazzled all three of them—their eyes were adjusted to the room's darkness—and then Brett examined Abby's handiwork.

It had worked! The Empowerer—whatever it actually was—had been transformed into a duplicate of the tiny box Brett had produced from the safe. He took it from her and held them side-by-side. "Nice work. I wouldn't be able to tell the difference, if not for our little clue."

That had been Maxine's idea. The headmaster's safe apparently was filled with file folders, envelopes, random objects, and a stack of tiny boxes that Brett had discovered contained gemstones. Maxine had sensibly pointed out that if they were going to hide the Empowerer in the pile of boxes, and if the Empowerer was really as all-important as Reeve had made it out to be, they might want to give themselves a way to identify it in its transformed state. To that end, they had agreed that subtle letters on the underside of the box—'BAM', the first letters of each of their first names—would do the trick.

Brett buried his head in the safe again, placing the two boxes inside. There were so many of them, he hoped the headmaster wouldn't notice an extra. Then the girls heard Brett call out, "Hey, wait a minute!" He withdrew his head, sans hat, from the safe. He was holding a manila envelope, staring at it with wide eyes. When he touched the top of his head, he jumped as if startled his hat wasn't there, then thrust his arm through the blue circle. He plucked his hat from the safe and placed it back on his head. "Guys, you won't believe what I have here," he told them, flipping through the envelope's contents.

"Brett," Maxine said, rolling her eyes, "I don't know about you, but I have better things to do than go through Headmaster Charlton's tax records."

"No, this isn't anything like that," he told her, looking up. "This is a list of names."

"What names?" Abby asked, growing curious.

"Names of people in the Pure Shore Club," Brett replied.

Maxine frowned. "How do you know? Let me see."

She and Abby crowded around Brett. Sure enough, the ream of paper had a simple heading of 'Pure Shore Club: Members' and a long list of names and the year each person graduated. For some reason, there was a red check mark next to each name. Brett kept flipping forwards, moving on to later and later years, until the red check marks stopped. Only a few names remained unchecked, all people who had graduated just before the Pure Shore Club had been disbanded. Familiar names, like Jolene, Mindy, Michael Alvarez, and Ethan. Stacy McNiece and Steven Endicott were not checked off, but crossed off, a sight that made Abby's stomach go queasy.

"Why are so many names checked off?" Maxine wondered aloud.

"I have one even better than that for you, champ," Brett said. "Why does the headmaster have this list in his safe in the first place?"

"Yeah," Abby spoke up. "I assumed…I thought this club was a big secret."

Maxine stared at the list of names. "You have to wonder how something like this could be a secret at all. I mean, all those people with superpowers? Unless they did absolutely nothing, how did they stay on the downlow all these years?"

The question hung unanswered in the still air of the headmaster's office. Then they heard voices in the outer room. Someone had entered the reception area. They could hear muffled voices talking animatedly.

"Someone's here!" Brett whispered, staring at the still-shut door to the headmaster's office, looking quite guilty despite his earlier bravado.

"Get the blue circle!" Maxine hissed. "Move it!"

Brett sprung into action, replacing the folder back in the safe where he found it, mentally plucking the blue circle from the safe door and pasting it onto the nearest wall. Maxine leapt through the opening first, followed by Abby. Brett jumped through last, the voices in the outer room growing louder as he went. He leapt a little too high, and the top of the portal brushed his hat, knocking it off. He landed on the other side and found Maxine and Abby staring at him.

"Brett, your hat!" Abby cried, pointing at his head the same instant his own hand flew up to touch his bare scalp. If the headmaster—or whoever was coming in—

found a fedora on the floor in this office, it could not turn out well. Moving faster than Abby had ever seen anyone move, Brett swept through the blue circle once more, and came back through, hat clutched tightly in one hand. Then he willed the circle to come off the wall, just as the inner door to the office opened.

CHAPTER SEVENTEEN
SNEAKING AND SPYING

Headmaster Charlton flicked the lights on and shed his long overcoat, tossing it onto his office's conference table. Mr. Santillian was right behind him, striding along with much less urgency than the diminutive headmaster. He took off his trench coat and draped it over one forearm.

The headmaster noted that Mr. Santillian wore his usual outfit of white dress shirt and jeans, including the strange golden cufflinks shaped like flintlock pistols. Did the man ever wear any other clothes? Headmaster Charlton wondered. *Perhaps we should raise his salary so he can go shopping.*

"That Agent Saint is driving me stark raving mad, Mr. Santillian," Charlton complained, plopping into his high-backed desk chair. "She wants to know about everything that comes into the school, going back twenty years. How does the woman expect us to know where we got our school supplies from back then? For Pete's sake, there weren't even computer records then!"

"It sounds like she's very thorough," Mr. Santillian said, remaining on his feet. "She's still keeping all of this quiet, right?"

Charlton nodded. "And believe me, I'm thankful. Otherwise, I'd probably be searching for a new job. Anyway, I called you here to find out your…progress. Have you, ahem, investigated the solution to our little crisis?"

"I have. The sick alumni should be getting better soon. And by the end of the day today, I'll have taken steps to make sure that this can never happen again."

Charlton looked at him carefully. "Anything I want to know about?"

Mr. Santillian shook his head. "I doubt it."

"Just as well, just as well," the headmaster replied, leaning forward and holding his head in his hands. "All we can hope for now is that the alumni will get better, and this whole thing will get brushed under the rug."

Mr. Santillian found himself growing angry with the small man, and he knew it was irrational. The headmaster was looking out for the interests of himself, to be sure, but he was also looking out for the school as a whole. Still, Mr. Santillian's thoughts drifted to the heritage he was soon to destroy, the capacity to do good wiped away, and he couldn't help but find the headmaster's concerns utterly trivial.

Agent Saint stormed in like a launched missile, not bothering for social niceties such as knocking. The sudden entrance caused the headmaster to jump a few inches off his chair, but Mr. Santillian merely turned to regard the FBI agent, his expression calm.

"Gentlemen," Agent Saint greeted them. "So far my people have turned up nothing of interest." She strode in and stood next to Mr. Santillian, her eyes a mystery behind her ever-present sunglasses.

Mr. Santillian felt the tight knot at the center of his stomach loosen a bit. He had been worried that the FBI would find out about the Pure Shore Club during their investigation. To his knowledge, no person or agency had poked around the edges of anything concerning the club in all its history. Now it seemed that the secretive club had gone undetected by the government agents. He had been afraid of the club being discovered, which would have been extremely ironic, as close as he was to destroying it forever.

•　　•　　•

In the next office, Maxine, Brett and Abby were hearing everything. They had created an impromptu ear hole between the offices with Brett's blue dot. He placed it very low on the wall, near the floor, and shrunk it to a tiny size, so hopefully it wouldn't be noticed.

"The FBI is here?" Maxine whispered. "Why would the FBI be at the Jefford Academy?"

Brett and Abby looked at each other and shrugged. They continued to huddle around the blue dot and listen.

"Mr. Santillian," Agent Saint addressed him, "I wanted to pass along a bit of information you may wish to know about."

Her tone sounded almost grave. Mr. Santillian had been lost in his own thoughts, but he snapped back to reality. "What is it?" he asked, his voice scratchy. He wasn't sure he could take any bad news at that moment.

"One of your very recent students, Ethan Goldman, was found unconscious on a back street in Chicago late last night. He appears to be suffering from the same coma-like symptoms as other members of the Pure Shore Club. They estimate he may have been out in the elements for quite a while…he's been taken to Derrymore Memorial Hospital where they're doing what they can, which admittedly isn't much."

Several thoughts and emotions hit Mr. Santillian at once. This explains why Ethan didn't return my calls or my texts, he thought miserably. He'd contacted Ethan before Mindy because Ethan lived closer to the Jefford Academy and could get there faster. When Ethan hadn't responded, Mr. Santillian had moved on to Mindy.

Mr. Santillian shoved his hands deep into his pockets, his shoulders slouching. He'd taught several of the people who'd grown ill, of course, but his latest Pure Shore Club had been especially near and dear to him. The fact that Ethan had been touched by this sickness alarmed the teacher. Ethan must have been afflicted in the hours right before Reeve had been shut off, and hopefully even now was getting better. But honestly, he didn't know how long that would take.

Another student of mine hurt, he reflected sadly. He could feel the cool metal of Stacy McNiece's brooch in his pocket, a small yet stark reminder of his past failures.

To Mr. Santillian and Headmaster Charlton's shock, Agent Saint actually walked over and placed a hand on the big man's shoulder. "Don't worry, Mr. Santillian. It might take some time, but we will get to the bottom of this. The important thing is that Ethan and the others are all still alive. If any cure can be found, it will."

He glanced at her, unsure how to take this gesture of kindness. Saint had been nothing but abrasive and suspicious since she'd arrived on campus. Maybe she wasn't so bad, he reflected. Maybe she was just doing her job, and now that it was apparent he had nothing to do with the alumni getting sick, her attitude was softening somewhat.

"Thank you," he said finally. Saint nodded and withdrew her hand.

"We will, of course, let you know as soon as we find something," she told them. "I'll be in touch."

•   •   •

The three teenagers exchanged curious looks. Of course, they remembered Ethan from the pictures in the yearbook and at the clubhouse. What was this illness everyone was talking about? And why was the FBI interested?

They heard the FBI agent leave, and Brett glanced over at the door. It led out into the hallway, and had a semi-opaque window built into it. He could see the silhouette of the FBI agent in the hallway. She wasn't walking away. Instead, she stood right there beyond the door. What was she doing? Just hanging around out there? Or did she suspect she'd been spied upon?

The lights were off, so Brett highly doubted the agent could see into the room, and they were hiding behind a desk. He peeked over the desktop and wondered if she was looking in their direction. Did she detect their presence? He found himself holding his breath.

She continued on down the hallway, disappearing from view. Brett allowed himself to breathe again. These might be the perils of being a reporter, but it was pretty nerve-wracking.

The girls had been oblivious, still listening through the blue dot. Brett crowded next to them to hear what was going on. Mr. Santillian was talking.

"I need to leave, Headmaster, I have an appointment later this afternoon I must prepare for."

"I am sorry about your former student, Mr. Santillian," the headmaster replied. "I truly hope the measures you have taken will allow the young man to heal."

"So do I," the teacher replied. "By the way, Headmaster, you might want to think about closing up your safe…What's the point of having it built like that if every random visitor to your office knows it's there?"

"Quite right, Mr. Santillian, quite right," the headmaster said, sounding quite exasperated with himself. "I've been so scatterbrained lately…" They heard a loud click, presumably the headmaster shutting the painting over the safe. Then they heard both men leave the office and go down the hallway. Brett retrieved his blue dot, tucked it into his inside coat pocket, and sat against the wall.

"We hid the Empowerer right in the nick of time," Maxine said.

"What do you mean?" Brett asked.

"Think about it, Ace. That Cruiser lady was promising to keep a close eye on us. We couldn't have done this little stunt without Mr. Santillian showing up and taking her aside. Apparently, Mr. Santillian's next appointment after talking to her was meeting with the headmaster and that FBI agent. She's probably out there looking for us even as we speak."

Brett groaned, slumping back against the wall. "Great. Hopefully she's not going to interrogate us about where we've been."

Maxine grunted. "We don't have to tell her anything. It's not like she's a teacher or our parents or something."

"Did you guys catch what they said?" Abby asked, jabbing her thumb towards the headmaster's office. "They said alumni from the Jefford Academy are getting sick. And somehow it's connected to the Pure Shore Club."

Maxine frowned. "Do you think the stuff Mr. Santillian alluded to about fixing that problem…has something to do with him shutting off Reeve?"

"It can't be a coincidence," Brett mused, rubbing his chin. "I think this whole sick alumni business could use some looking into."

Maxine got to her feet. "Well, you'll have to do it without me, guys. I've got to get to my soccer game. If I'm late, my coach will dream up some diabolical punishment for me."

Brett looked up at her. "You're still going to your soccer game? With all this stuff going on?"

"I don't know if you know something I don't, Ace, but from where I stand, we have no clue what's going on. I, for one, do not intend for this Pure Shore Club nonsense to interfere with my life. If I have a soccer game, I have a soccer game, and not even those Outrider punks are going to keep me from it."

Brett and Abby got up. "It's your lookout, champ. All right, me and Blondie will continue trying to break this story. Which is, I'll have you know, the thing those Outrider clowns aren't gonna keep me from."

"I'd be disappointed if they could, Ace," Maxine said, and she slugged him in the arm for emphasis. She was impressed when he didn't flinch.

"We should get going," Abby piped up, shifting from foot to foot. "Someone might come in here at any moment."

"Uh-uh," Maxine said. "These snazzy new roller blades of mine mean that I don't have to leave with anybody. See ya!" She gave them a little wave, then there was a rush of wind, and Maxine was gone.

Brett looked at the space Maxine had just occupied, then at the now-open door. The wind had blown his hat off and he stooped to pick it up. "I bet she enjoyed that way too much."

CHAPTER EIGHTEEN
THE RETURN OF THE SMILING SHADOW

Mr. Santillian sat in his office, leaning on his desk and looking at his cell phone. He didn't want to make this call. He really didn't. He was angry at Michael Alvarez for attempting to bring more innocent children into the Pure Shore Club, to start the madness all over again. Plus, he had annoyed Mr. Santillian over the years with his absurd theories of the Smiling Shadow's return.

Theories that Michael had been trying to prove, with the help of Reeve…and Ethan. If anyone should know about Ethan's condition right away (and Mr. Santillian assumed Ethan's family had already been notified) it was Michael. Plus, Michael might be worried if Ethan was not returning his calls and such.

The teacher's conscience won out and he decided to make the call. He ended up getting Michael's voicemail. He closed his eyes. He hated to leave bad news in a message, but he didn't think he had a choice. Michael deserved to know this as quickly as possible.

"Mike, this is Mr. Santillian. I know you're probably shocked to get this message from me. I'm afraid I'm calling with bad news that you may or may not know about already. I know you've been, um, working with Ethan Goldman, and I just wanted to let you know that he has…fallen into a coma-like state."

Mr. Santillian briefly considered telling Michael everything. How all former Pure Shore Club members were falling prey to a mystery illness, and how Reeve's damaged state was the most likely cause, and how Ethan would likely be better very soon. He decided against it the next moment. Tipping Michael off about the fact Reeve was deactivated would only cause the young man to storm the clubhouse. That was a complication Mr. Santillian did not need, not when he was planning on destroying it.

"Ethan is in Chicago, at Darrymore Memorial Hospital. He's reportedly in good hands and…he'll be fine, eventually. I just thought you would want to know." He felt like he needed to say more, at least 'goodbye', but in the end he just ended the call.

•   •   •

Even though they were estranged, Michael Alvarez had Blake Santillian saved as a contact in his phone and knew right away it was his old teacher calling. After their last meeting, he wasn't feeling especially charitable toward his old teacher, so he let the call roll to voicemail.

When he listened to the message, he grew quite alarmed. So that's what had happened to Ethan. The two of them had been working together, following up on clues and leads regarding the reemergence of the Smiling Shadow and his Outriders. He hadn't heard from Ethan in a few days but chalked it up to Ethan's busy schedule—he was in graduate school, the same as Michael, and often was out of touch for days. Michael hadn't thought much of it.

The last Michael knew, Ethan had been following up on an Outrider sighting in Chicago. The same city that Ethan was now occupying a hospital bed in. Unless he had been unlucky enough to fall ill while in that city, the enemy had caught wind of him investigating them and stopped him.

Michael decided he would go see Ethan for himself. He lived in Phoenix, a long ways from Chicago, but distance was no obstacle to the man also known as Quantumax. With a thought, Michael summoned his superhero regalia—shining white armor with a stylized 'Q' on the chest and a white helmet that concealed his features.

He could draw upon the universe's quantum energy field for various abilities, and one was the power to levitate. He rose from his wheelchair, hovering in his apartment. He smiled under his helmet, enjoying using his superhuman powers. But his enjoyment was short-lived. His friend was in trouble, and he could delay no longer.

Michael Alvarez concentrated, and one moment he was in his apartment, the next he was in Ethan's hospital room. It was daytime, and the room was filled with sunshine. Michael took a quick look around, and luckily no one was in the room. That was one risk of teleportation, that you may happen upon and shock some unsuspecting bystander. It was a risk he wouldn't normally take, but time was of the essence.

Ethan, my old friend, what has happened to you? He contemplated the prone form on the hospital bed in front of him. Ethan's complexion was close to gray, and he was hooked up to various machines that monitored his vital signs. An IV tube fed into his arm, and he was dressed in hideous pea-green hospital garb.

He grabbed the clipboard that hung from the end of the bed and flipped through it. Michael was an art major and had no more than the average person's knowledge of medicine, but the notes he read were pretty clear. Ethan was in a coma-like state, the reasons behind it unknown. Although he didn't know the details, he had a pretty good idea what had caused it. Ordinary dangers were no threat to Ethan, the man also known as Captain Creature. He could turn into any animal, from a stinging yellowjacket to a charging rhino if he was in trouble. Whatever did this had to be powerful indeed. As powerful as…

"Greetings, Michael Alvarez," came a voice from behind him. A voice Michael knew well. A voice that he heard from time to time in his nightmares. A sound like wind sweeping through a graveyard.

A churning cauldron of dread emerged in his stomach. He knew that voice, he also knew this feeling. The feeling everyone got in the presence of the Smiling Shadow.

He turned around. There it was, the Pure Shore Club's old enemy, lurking in the back of the room, where the sunlight streaming in from outside did not quite reach. The ghostly white smile hovered in the air, surrounded by an undulating mass of living darkness. Four Outriders, a sinister sight in their gray garb, sunglasses and wild hair, flanked their master, but Michael barely noticed them.

For a while now he and Ethan had been certain the Smiling Shadow was back. There had been rumors here and there, bits of information they'd been following up on. The Outriders had also begun to reappear, a sure sign their dreaded liege was still alive. But having a theory and actually seeing that he was back were two very different things.

He had to escape.

"Trying to disappear, Michael?" the Shadow said. "I'm afraid you will find that to be quite impossible at this moment. You see, I have learned much since last we met. Many, many new things. Blocking your signature mode of transportation is but one of them."

Michael realized he was right. He concentrated as hard as he could, but he could not make himself teleport.

Suddenly the blinds closed, startling Michael and cutting off the dazzling sunshine from outside. They'd been closed by another man Michael hadn't noticed before. A man who stood mostly obscured by the shadows.

"Can't have any passive onlookers observing our personal business, can we?" the man said. This voice was also familiar. It didn't elicit fear, as the Shadow's voice did, only surprise.

"You...?" Michael said feebly, squinting into the darkness.

"Hey, Mikey. Long time no see." He stepped closer, out of the shadows. He was dressed quite differently to his companions. His outfit was all primary colors, and he had a giant equals sign on his chest. At first Michael didn't believe it, that it had to be another man wearing the costume. Some kind of trick. But there was no mistaking the face and voice. The Smiling Shadow was not the only person back from seeming death. Somehow, improbably, Even Steven had returned too. How was it possible? It was understandable how the Smiling Shadow had survived what had happened—he was the Smiling Shadow, after all—but Even Steven was merely human.

Seeing Steven again brought back long-buried rage and hurt, giving him a bit of courage to offset the Smiling Shadow's fear-effect. He concentrated and a nimbus of light surrounded him. The Smiling Shadow and his Outriders appeared unfazed by the sudden brightness, but Michael was pleased to note Even Steven at least squinted.

"I prefer the lights to be on," he said. He peered closely at Steven, who was blinking, his eyes adjusting to Michael's luminescence. In the light, there was no mistaking it. "Steven…it really is you, isn't it? What deal did you make with the Smiling Shadow to survive, huh?"

Steven glared at him. "Maybe I'm just extraordinarily resilient, Mikey. By the way, I wouldn't start firing off any of those fancy energy beams of yours. In these close quarters, you might end up hitting your zoned-out buddy over there. Though honestly, if you killed him, you might be doing him a favor."

Michael glanced around the room. The Outriders were in motion, walking to take up positions to his left and right. He couldn't teleport away, and he didn't see an easy way to escape otherwise. He could blast a hole in the wall and fly away, but Ethan could get hurt by shrapnel.

"What did you do to him?" he asked, gesturing towards Ethan.

"He led us on quite the chase, didn't he?" the Smiling Shadow said. He chuckled, a horrid sound like a thousand bats racing up a chimney. On cue, the Outriders also laughed, a chorus of unpleasant rasps. Steven merely smiled a nasty, hateful smile. "But not good enough," the Shadow continued. "In the end, he was no match for us. We caught him, and we took from him what Reeve gave him."

Michael's eyes widened behind his visor. "You don't mean…?"

"Oh, we do, Mikey," Steven said. "We do. We've done the same thing to almost every other member of the Pure Shore Club. And now, old buddy, old pal, it's your turn."

"This is a trap?" Michael asked. "What, do you have Mr. Santillian's phone tapped or something?" His mind was reeling. He couldn't think straight. The Smiling Shadow and Even Steven were still alive. He had to get away. He had to warn the others!

"Something like that," Steven replied. "Truthfully, you are a dreadfully predictable chap, Mikey. We knew as soon as you heard your friend was in trouble you'd come running like a loyal dog."

"Loyalty is a concept you know nothing about, Steven," Michael said, glaring at his former teammate. "You'd think that after all this time you maybe would've reconsidered your ways, but apparently you're just as stupid as you were then. Sad, really."

Steven stepped forward. The light given off by Michael reflected in his eyes. "Me, sad? You're the fool who possesses incredible powers but doesn't use them in a proper fashion…to rule, to dominate, to conquer!"

"That was always your hang-up, wasn't it?" Michael snapped back, trying to keep his eyes on all the enemies at once. "Powers. You thought Mr. Santillian should have made you the leader of the club because—"

"Of my powers!" Steven cried, clenching his fists. "I was the most powerful member of the club! I deserved to be the leader!"

"Same old Steven," Michael said. He would have to act now if he had any chance of getting away. He lashed out with a bright white laser beam from his left hand, hoping to nail the Outriders that stood between him and the door.

But Steven was too quick. He lunged into the path of the beam, and automatically his own power generated a black energy beam that intercepted Michael's blast. Michael increased his power output, hoping to overwhelm Steven's counter-laser, but it held firm.

Before Michael could try anything else, the Smiling Shadow lashed out with his own black energy blast. Michael was caught in the side, knocked out of the spot where he hovered in mid-air, and collapsed onto the floor. The blast hadn't hurt, exactly, his personal force-field had blunted much of it. He'd forgotten the Shadow could make a person feel so cold. His teeth chattered and he shivered uncontrollably. He found he couldn't move. The Shadow must be turning up his fear effect, Michael realized in the back of his mind. Unnatural terror engulfed him, driving out most rational thought and leaving him pinned to the floor like a giant, chilly hand.

Through blurred vision, he looked up to see the Smiling Shadow, Even Steven, and the four Outriders looking down on him. All were smiling. He wished he could punch all of them, though he knew a punch would do no good against enemies such as these.

"Foolish, foolish Michael Alvarez," the Smiling Shadow chided him. "You were defeated from the moment you materialized in this hospital. Now I will do to you what I did to Ethan. Then we will hunt down Mindy…and the Crimson Cruiser…and Mr. Santillian. And then we will storm the clubhouse. And we will, once and for all, seize the Empowerer."

Michael gritted his teeth. The Smiling Shadow didn't have to tell him all this. They were gloating, taunting him. He worked on focusing his rage, his anger, through the haze of chill and fear the Smiling Shadow was laying on him with its evil powers.

"Y-you'll never succeed!" he spat out. "Reeve will stop you!"

The assemblage of foes cackled.

The Smiling Shadow hovered closer. "Reeve cannot stop us. Your overzealous Mr. Santillian will see to that. Won't he, boys?" Steven and the Outriders laughed again.

Michael didn't know what they were talking about. He just knew he had to escape. The Smiling Shadow's dark form rippled, and multiple tendrils of shadow reached out towards Michael Alvarez. But just past the Shadow, he could see Steven's grinning face.

The Shadow had made a mistake, Michael realized. If he and his Outriders had been here alone, they probably would have had him. The Shadow's powers were just too overwhelming. But the Shadow had brought Even Steven, and Michael's dislike for the traitor was so intense that it enabled him to section off a corner of his mind. By sheer force of will alone, using the power of his mind, he strained against the interference projected by the Smiling Shadow.

He refused to let Steven win. Just before the shadowy tendrils reached Michael Alvarez, his entire body suddenly flared with white light, and he was gone. No remnant of him remained in sight, just an empty spot on the floor of the hospital room.

"Where…?" Steven said, his eyes flickering around the room. "Surely he didn't get away!"

The Shadow was already withdrawing his tentacles, his ever-present smile unperturbed by this turn of events. "I think not, Steven. The jamming I had in place to block his annoying teleportation ability was quite thorough. No, I think the poor lad made such a great effort to escape he disintegrated himself."

Steven's eyes narrowed and his jaw twitched. He wanted to be sure his hated enemy was indeed gone forever. "You are certain? How do you know?"

"Remember, Steven," the Shadow said, "I can sense the existence of all of these Pure Shore Club vermin. Each one of them, a vague presence on the edge of my consciousness. I do not sense Quantumax anywhere on this planet. Yes, he is quite dead. Destroyed himself, trying to escape our clutches. He evidently preferred death to what we were going to do to him. How utterly tragic."

Then he laughed his horrible laugh, and his Outriders laughed along with him, good underlings that they were. Steven merely smiled a tight, nasty smile. Michael Alvarez dead. It was almost too good to be true. The man who had vexed him for so many years, gone forever.

Steven Endicott knew he should feel elated, but somehow, he didn't. It was almost as if Michael's death was…anticlimactic. He wondered if this was what revenge was supposed to feel like. If so, was it truly worth it?

The voice of one of the Outriders disrupted Steven's thoughts.

"My liege, if I may be so bold, perhaps we should leave this place soon."

"Quite right, Karlsson, quite right," the dark one agreed. He was using his fear effect in a subtle manner, steering hospital personnel away from Ethan's room, but that wouldn't last forever. "Let us return to our isolated abode, shall we? I have a feeling the final phase of our master plan shall commence soon…very soon…"

He spirited his five human companions away in a cloud of blackness, leaving behind only the senseless form of Ethan, and if anyone had been around to notice, a definite chill lingering in the air.

CHAPTER NINETEEN
ADVENTURE HAS A WAY
OF FINDING YOU

Brett found he was grateful Abby had a photographic memory. She had seen the list of Pure Shore Club members for only a few moments, but that was all she needed to file them away in the steel trap of her brain. Now she and Brett were at the library, entering the names into search engines, looking through news articles from across the country. They were not liking what they found.

"Every last one of them," Brett said grimly, leaning forward and peering at the monitor as if he could wrest answers from its depths with his gaze. "Every name we've put in, they've all caught some kind of mystery bug and are down for the count."

"Not all," Abby said. Brett was an amazingly quick typist, so he was in the driver's seat while she sat next to him. "It seems like Michael Alvarez hasn't, or at least it hasn't made the news. Or Mr. Santillian, or Jolene Colt, for that matter."

"So this bug, whatever it is, hasn't affected everyone," Brett observed. He made notes in his phone. "At least, not yet. And despite what Mr. Santillian said back in the headmaster's office, there are no reports of anybody getting better."

Abby shrugged. "Well, um, maybe it just takes time for them to get better?"

Brett looked thoughtful, tapping the side of his phone against the table. "It makes sense the FBI is here. To them, the whole thing probably looks like a terrorist attack, or a conspiracy, or maybe an alien virus from outer space. But they don't know about the Pure Shore Club."

A sudden, horrible thought occurred to Abby. "Brett…do you think maybe we might get sick and go into comas too? After all, we're members of the Pure Shore Club now."

Brett sat back abruptly, his eyes wide. He pushed his fedora to the back of his head. "I guess I hadn't thought about that, Blondie. Gee whiz, that makes me a little freaked out, let me tell you." He looked at her. "How are you feeling? Okay? Not okay?"

Abby turned a bit pale and bit her lower lip. "Fine until I thought about this. Now my stomach feels all queasy."

Brett scooted his chair away. "Hey, if you need to hurl, I'll get you a trash can…"

She shook her head firmly. "No, I'm fine, I'm fine. Just scared, that's all." Abby held her hand up, regarding the sparkling heart-ring granted to her by the mysterious Reeve. "Wow, some superhero I am. They really screwed up when they let me into this club!"

Brett eyed her closely. He'd never seen her act like this before. "Don't be so hard on yourself, Blondie. This is wacky stuff no normal eighth grader has to deal with."

"No, you don't understand," Abby replied, crossing her arms and looking across the room. "Even my parents don't think I can be brave."

"Your parents? What do you mean?" All Brett knew about Abby's parents was they were doctors in a third-world country.

Abby swallowed hard. "They went on a dangerous mission—an adventure—and they left me behind. They put me in this school while they faced danger to help others."

Brett thought for a long moment. "They told you that?"

"No," she replied, sinking into her chair. "But I can tell."

"Seems to me that maybe they wanted their daughter to be safe."

"Well, being safe is overrated," Abby said. "Anyway, I think they thought I couldn't handle it, so they left me here."

They sat in silence for a few moments. Then Brett chuckled and said, "Well, if it's adventure you want, Blondie, you've got it. All three of us are in the middle of something nutso. Grandpa always said that adventure sometimes has a way of finding you, even when you don't want it to."

Abby smiled. "Your grandpa sounds like he was a wise man."

She noticed him look away sharply, going back to typing on the keyboard and continuing searching the internet. "The wisest," Brett replied, his voice hushed.

"Um, you were close to him, huh?" Abby asked. She wasn't sure if Brett wanted to talk about this or not, but she was curious. After all, she'd watched Brett have a borderline breakdown when he thought he'd lost his grandpa's hat.

"He taught me everything I know about being a reporter," Brett said, eyes still riveted to the computer screen. "Among other things."

"You said your parents worked in the newspaper business too," Abby said.

Brett sighed. "Yeah, but they're not reporters, Blondie. The itch to dig up dirt and discover truth skipped a generation, I guess. No, they run their distribution business and pretty much let me be raised by my grandfather."

Abby realized this explained a great deal about Brett. He really wasn't a weirdo; he was raised by a man from the old school. Well, she reflected, Brett is still kind of a weirdo, but at least he's an understandable weirdo now.

"When did he die?" Abby asked.

She noticed him grimace, just slightly. "Just this past summer. My parents were so used to him looking after me, they didn't know what to do. They're kind of workaholics…I've barely seen them over the years. They took what they felt was the only option available and sent me here. And here we are."

"Here we are," Abby repeated. In the middle of some utterly unexpected craziness. She felt sorry for Brett, the only real parent in his life having passed away and his actual parents having no time for him. She wondered if all the kids at the Jefford Academy had similar stories.

Brett gave up his web browsing and sat back heavily in his seat. Abby noticed he had his blue dot balanced on his knuckles. With subtle movements of his fingers, he was making it flip from one knuckle to the other, to one side of his hand and back again. He also began spinning his chair around. The sight made him look like some bizarre, fedora-topped amusement park ride.

"That thing you're doing there, um, with your knuckles is pretty impressive," she said. "Your grandfather teach you that, too?"

He slowed and came to a stop facing her. "Yeah," he said with a smile, watching the dot flip-flop along his hand. "He knew all sorts of stuff, and he taught me all of it. Reporting, card games, car repairs, old-time music and movies and comic books, boxing…"

"That's right!" Abby exclaimed. "You mentioned earlier that you box. Do you ever, um, get into fights?"

"Only when I have to," Brett said with a gleam in his eyes. "Things got rough sometimes, back in the old neighborhood. Fellow has to be ready to handle himself in case there's a rhubarb."

Abby blinked. "Um, a what?"

"Rhubarb!" Brett repeated. "You know, a fight. A brawl."

The last time Abby had checked, rhubarb was a kind of pie. But she chose not to pursue the issue.

"That's what my grandpa called fights, anyway," he went on. "Guess I kind of picked up some of his lingo over the years. That was his favorite part of baseball games, he always said, the rhubarbs. When the benches on both sides clear off and there's a giant pile of guys wrestling on the pitcher's mound. Yeah, he loved those."

Abby didn't know much about sports, so she took Brett's word for it about the rhubarbs. "Well," she said, changing the subject and hoping it wouldn't offend Brett, "now that we know about all the Pure Shore Club alumni getting sick, what do we do now?"

Brett put the blue dot in his inside jacket pocket and began typing on the keyboard again. "When you need to get to the heart of a news story," he said, "you've got to talk to some key players. I think we could stand to talk to a certain painter guy who got us into this mess in the first place."

Abby remembered Michael Alvarez and the amazing mural he'd painted. "Yeah, where's he been?" she wondered out loud. "I kind of had the impression that he and Reeve were working together. Mr. Santillian turned Reeve off, so where's Michael Alvarez? You'd think he'd be pretty upset."

Brett grunted. "You're assuming Alvarez even knows that happened, Blondie."

"Oh. Good point."

It was a simple matter to find out from the school's alumni records that Michael Alvarez was a graduate student at a Phoenix-area art school. From there, Brett was able to use the internet white pages to look up Michael's phone number.

CHAPTER TWENTY
THE DISAPPEARING OUT OF SYNCH MAN

Michael Alvarez found himself back in his apartment, not quite certain how he had arrived there or how long it had been since he'd left. He looked around. He was still hovering in the air, an indication his Quantumax powers still worked.

He felt a rush of elation as memories of the recent past came rushing back. *Good! The Smiling Shadow and that smug Even Steven haven't beaten me yet!*

He felt a chill then, as he fully recalled the Smiling Shadow's fear effect, the shock of seeing Even Steven alive after all these years, and how close he'd come to losing everything. He'd managed to break through the Smiling Shadow's power and escape, teleporting away. Apparently he'd brought himself to a familiar place, his home. He realized poor Ethan had been left behind, but he also knew Ethan wouldn't want him to waste time going back for him.

Time was of the essence now. Michael didn't know if the Smiling Shadow knew he'd escaped or not. A horde of Outriders could be breaking down his door any moment. The villains themselves had stated they were going after Mindy, Cruiser, and Mr. Santillian next. And apparently they'd somehow tricked Mr. Santillian into lowering the clubhouse's defenses. As much as Michael and his old teacher had their differences these days, he was certain the man would be horrified if he knew he'd played into the Smiling Shadow's hands. Everyone had to be warned. Mr. Santillian could not brush off Michael's fears now.

Before teleporting to Ethan's hospital room, Michael had left his phone on his kitchen counter. He floated over to pick it up and try calling Mindy or Reeve or someone else who might be able to help him. But he received yet another surprise when his hand went right through the phone. He tried again and got the same result. His white-gloved hand passed right through the phone like it wasn't there. With trepidation, Michael realized what had happened. Somehow, his escape, an act of willpower that enabled him to break through the Smiling Shadow's interference, had an unwelcome side effect.

He hadn't materialized all the way. His body was slightly out of synch with the objects around him. Testing his theory, he floated through the apartment, and found himself going through walls, furniture, and anything else in his path. Surely I can overcome this, he thought. I will just concentrate on becoming solid, and everything will be fine.

But the man known as Quantumax found becoming solid was not that simple. No matter how much he concentrated, he could not resume a fully solid form for more than a second or two. With supreme effort, he could will himself to be solid and lightly touch something, but he'd quickly revert to being a living ghost. Somehow, he'd transformed into a phantom that couldn't interact with the real world.

He floated back to his phone to make another attempt to pick it up and was startled when it began to ring. Michael tried with all his mental might, but could not will his form into a solid enough state where he could press answer, let alone pick it up. He'd never felt so helpless in his life. He didn't know the number on the caller ID, but if it was someone from the Pure Shore Club, he had to answer and warn them the Smiling Shadow was back and had Even Steven on his side.

The call went to voicemail. Michael made a supreme effort—he worried he was going to burst a blood vessel in his head—and managed to play the message.

"Hi, this message is for Michael Alvarez," came a youthful-sounding voice. "Mr. Alvarez, this is Brett Cho. Hopefully you remember me…eighth grader, Jefford Academy? You invited Abby Alvarson, Maxine Drury, and I to join the Pure Shore Club. Well, I got to tell you, things have gotten pretty dicey here. Your little clue to get us to the clubhouse worked. Nice mural you painted there, mister, very nice…"

Despite his current predicament, Michael felt glad. The plan he and Reeve had cooked up was working out. The Pure Shore Club had some brand-new members, and apparently just in time.

"Yeah, yeah, I'm getting to that," Brett said to someone else. Evidently, Brett was not alone, wherever he was. Hopefully it was Abby or Maxine he was talking to. The less people that knew about the Pure Shore Club the better, and these three new members may not know the club's rules of secrecy yet.

"Anyway," Brett went on, "we've been through a lot here. We got some crazy costumes and powers from that Reeve character, but no sooner than we meet Reeve than that sunny Mr. Santillian marches in and does something to him. The old guy just vanishes. Freaked us all out to no end, let me tell you."

Michael's eyes went wide under his helmet. His thoughts, already racing, went into overdrive. He didn't! Mr. Santillian didn't actually—

"We get out without him realizing we were there, but then right outside we run into a gaggle of jokers who call themselves Outriders. They were about to put the hurt on us, but then a lady in a red car named Crimson Cruiser rescues us. I imagine you know her."

How did Cruiser get involved? Michael wondered. And what's this about Outriders near the clubhouse? Michael's throat tightened. Had he inadvertently put these kids in greater danger than he'd expected?

"You and Reeve wanted us to join this mysterious club of yours, but you guys didn't exactly give us a manual or anything. You might say we're flying blind, and we don't know who to trust. But you and Reeve got us into this mess and like I said before, Reeve ain't going to be helping nobody anytime soon from the look of things. So, that leaves you, Mr. Alvarez. It seems that Pure Sure Club alumni are getting sick all over the place, the FBI is snooping around the campus about it, and everyone's mentioning this 'Smiling Shadow' thing. We want answers, Mr. Alvarez, and we want them now…yes, I know this message is really long, Abby…let it go, okay?

"So anyway, Mr. Alvarez, you've got three confused and annoyed middle schoolers here. You pushed us into the deep end of the pool. Pony up some answers or…well, I can think of a few things we've learned this weekend that might be inconvenient for you if, shall we say, certain parties found out about them. But I'm a reasonable guy, and I think from my brief hanging out with you that you are probably a reasonable guy, too. No one needs to find out nothing they're not supposed to if you just get in touch with us and give us the lowdown. Capeesh? Hopefully we understand each other now. We look forward to hearing from you. My cell number is…"

Brett rattled off his cell phone number and hung up. If Michael Alvarez had a solid body, he'd have floated backwards and slumped into his overstuffed easy chair. Instead, he drifted backwards, and sank into the chair, until all that was visible was the very top of his head. Any other time, he would have laughed at how ludicrous he looked.

That was what the Smiling Shadow and Even Steven had been gloating about. Somehow, they'd tricked Mr. Santillian into shutting Reeve off. Michael couldn't believe it. Even as strained as the bond between Mr.

Santillian and Reeve was, he couldn't fathom his old teacher doing that unless there was a good reason. Whatever the Smiling Shadow and Even Steven had done, they'd played Mr. Santillian like a harp.

Michael groaned aloud. The plan had been for the kids to find the clubhouse and Reeve would grant them their powers and explain everything. But from the sound of things, Reeve hadn't had the chance to do that. Given all of that, plus the fact they'd had to tangle with Outriders, Michael realized he couldn't blame the kids for being upset. He couldn't imagine what it would have been like to have been given his Quantumax powers with so little information and guidance to go on. He would be mad too.

He drifted up out of the chair. This new information didn't change anything, except add even more urgency to his task. If Reeve was shut off, the clubhouse was wide open to anyone who knew where to look. And the Smiling Shadow and his cronies definitely did. After all, they'd been there before.

And as the villain himself had told him, Michael knew the Smiling Shadow was once again after the Empowerer. This had suddenly become bigger than Mindy, bigger than Ethan, bigger than Cruiser, or Mr. Santillian. Now, the safety of the entire world was at risk.

His last teleport, from Chicago back to his apartment, had left him in a phantom state. His powers might be permanently damaged. Who knows what another teleport might do to him? He realized he might end up in even worse shape. It doesn't matter, he thought, with grim resolve. *There's too much riding on this, too much at stake. If there's a chance I can make it to the others, I must try.*

He focused his mind, drew upon the quantum energy of the universe, and threw himself into uncertainty.

•   •   •

"I can't believe you threatened him!" Abby exclaimed as they walked out of the library.

"'Threatened' is a very strong word, Blondie," Brett replied, walking briskly with his hands in his jacket pockets. "I think what I did was more…leaning on the guy a bit."

"I fail to see the difference, Brett!" Abby said, her own hands gripping the straps of her backpack tightly. "I mean, you're supposed to be a reporter, not some…some…street hoodlum!"

Brett grinned. "People might say there isn't much of a difference between the two. Hey, lighten up, all right? We need some facts, and to get those facts, we need to get things moving a little."

"Well, you could have consulted with me before doing that," she pointed out. "What you do affects me and Maxine, in case you've forgotten."

He stopped walking and looked at her. "Oh? Why do you say that?"

Brett was surprised to see Abby wore a crestfallen expression. "Well, um, we're…I mean, we're a team, right? The three of us, trying to figure this stuff out?"

"I…guess so," Brett replied, not sure where exactly Abby was coming from. "But don't forget, Blondie, I'm after a news story here. Maxine just wants revenge or something for being jerked around. And you…" He trailed off, realizing he had no idea really why Abby was taking on this mystery with him and Maxine.

She was not forthcoming, certain Brett would think it was stupid if she told him. Sure, he would be nice to her and all, but deep down he'd think she was stupid. After all, she wasn't trying to solve this mystery in order to make a name for herself, like Brett, or to settle a score, like Maxine.

She wanted to go on an adventure, to face danger, to prove that she could overcome great hardship and great odds. She wanted to prove to herself she wasn't a helpless girl who needed protection like her parents thought she was. She wanted to prove she had what it takes. So here she was, on the adventure of a lifetime, and scared out of her wits for most of it.

"Anyway," Brett went on, "like I told you guys before, the world, and especially the people at this school, deserve to know what wacky supernatural hokum is going on right under their noses, and Brett Cho's the guy who'll tell them all about it. And if that takes twisting a few arms to get that done, then by golly, I'm going to twist a few arms. I'll do it to that Alvarez character and I'll do it to that Cruiser dame and maybe even Mr. Santillian, too."

Abby's eyes widened. "Mr. Santillian? Surely you wouldn't! If he even knew we were involved with the Pure Shore Club—"

"So what?" Brett interrupted. "Mr. Santillian needs to level with us. You know what's going on. Those Outrider guys could come after us again. And like you said earlier, this illness affecting the alumni could affect us, too."

She bit her lower lip and looked at the ground. "Yeah, I'm trying not to think about that too much, I guess."

"It's okay…I'm freaked out by all this stuff too. I just want to find out what's going on. And I guess…I guess you're right. I should have consulted with you and Max before I put the screws into Alvarez. After all, we're all in the same club, huh?"

She looked up at him, smiling. "Yeah, the Pure Shore Club," she said. "First new members in years."

"Also the most clueless members in years," Brett said, chuckling. "If not the most clueless ever."

She laughed. "Yeah, I guess we are, at that."

They stood in silence for a long moment. The afternoon was growing cold, and the shadows on the ground were growing long. The autumn sun was bright in the sky.

"Well," Brett said, adjusting his hat, "how would you like to catch the end of a soccer game?"

•   •   •

Brett and Abby had obviously never seen Maxine Drury in her element before, and they realized at least partially why she was so arrogant. She was an amazing soccer player. There were few other girls on the field who matched her level of skill. And not only was she fast, and agile, and had incredible endurance, she was also a smart soccer player. She fit into a team very well, scoring her share of goals but also assisting her teammates many times.

"Holy Hannah," Brett said softly. "That girl can play herself some soccer, huh?"

"Definitely," Abby said, her eyes wide as she watched the gameplay. She didn't know much about soccer—or many other sports, for that matter—but even she could tell Maxine was highly skilled.

They sat in the last row of the bleachers, cheering for the Jefford team in general and Maxine specifically. There was a pretty good crowd there, plenty of students and some adults as well. Brett remarked on the fact to Abby.

"Yeah, lots of school spirit," Abby agreed. "It makes you think."

His eyes remained riveted to the game. "Think? About what?"

"The Pure Shore Club," she explained. "They…we…are technically an official Jefford Academy team. Yet who really knows about them and what they do? They probably don't ever get cheers or awards or applause or any kind of recognition."

Brett tipped his hat backward on his head. "I hadn't thought about that angle," he admitted. "But hey, they're the ones who've chosen to operate in secret all these years. If they want crowds cheering for them, they could at least have the decency to tell the rest of the school—not to mention the entire world—what they're all about. Heck, we're technically in the club and we don't even know what the Pure Shore Club really is."

"Beyond being a secret society of superheroes," Abby said, drawing her knees to her chest and hugging them. She rested her chin on her knees. "We saw that list of names…all the pictures on the walls of the conference room. There's got to be dozens of them out there. But it seems like they've never sought the spotlight."

Brett grunted. "People in wild costumes with crazy superpowers…you'd think we'd have heard of them by now. Unless they graduate from the Jefford Academy and then don't do anything. That would be weird, though."

"Maybe," Abby said tentatively, "they're out there, but they somehow go under the radar. They do good deeds without being noticed. I mean, isn't that what true heroes do?"

Brett cheered as Jefford scored another goal, aided by a slick pass from Maxine. Then he told Abby, "I don't follow you, Blondie."

"Take my mom and dad, for instance," Abby said, her eyes staring off to the horizon, as if she could look hard and far enough and see her parents there. "They don't expect to get any reward for what they're doing. They're just doing it. They're doing it because it's the right thing to do. Isn't that the mark of a true hero? Doing the right thing with no thought of any reward?"

Brett thought about it for a moment. "I guess that's true. I don't know about you, though, but I'm not out to be any kind of hero. I just want a story out of this. A big story. The story that will launch my reporting career."

Abby scrutinized him with her emerald eyes. "You don't want to stay in the club?"

He shrugged. "I…I don't know, I…" Brett didn't have to finish his sentence. The game was over, and he stood up to cheer and clap along with the other Jefford Academy supporters. Maxine spent some time on the field slapping backs and giving high-fives to her teammates. They'd won 8–2. The bleachers began clearing out.

"Well, I guess we should go down and talk to her," Brett said finally.

"Yeah, we have a few things to tell her," Abby said.

A voice suddenly came from the bleacher seat behind them. "And I have a few things to tell you."

Brett and Abby whirled. Behind them was a man, a man who could have been there the entire time or maybe he hadn't. They hadn't noticed him when they sat down.

It was Michael Alvarez.

CHAPTER TWENTY-ONE
REGRETS AND REVELATIONS

Michael was dressed in a navy blue fall jacket and jeans. Brett wondered how long he'd been sitting there, and how he had gotten himself up into the bleachers. The last time they'd seen him, the man used a wheelchair.

"Hey!" Brett exclaimed. "How long have you been there?"

Michael smiled, though the expression didn't quite make it into his eyes. He looked tired, Brett noticed. Tired, and maybe a little scared. He kept looking around, as if he was expecting someone to sneak up on them at any moment.

"Actually, I just got here," he said. "Listen, I have to apologize for how things have played out. Your induction into the club is not how it's normally done, believe me. But current events have necessitated an atypical mode of operation."

Brett laughed. "That's one way of putting it, chief. Hey, I left you a voicemail just a little while ago."

"I know," Michael said. "I heard it."

Abby thought about how Michael had vanished the day before, and how he had mysteriously appeared on the bleachers just now. "You have some kind of…transport ability, Mr. Alvarez," she said. "Um, am I right? You can vanish from one spot and pop back in at a different spot?"

Michael smiled again. "Very good, Abby. Yes, I can indeed do that, among other things. Much as the three of you now have amazing abilities, I'm sure."

"Yeah, you could say that," Brett said. "Now look, mister, if you heard my message then you know the three of us are through playing around—"

"No, that's just you, Brett," Abby muttered.

Brett ignored her. "—and we want some answers, pronto. Or we take what we know and make things uncomfortable for you, see?"

Michael's face went deadly serious. "Yes, I do see, Brett. That is partially why I'm here now. You two, and Maxine, are in great danger. Not only that, but you might be our only hope."

"Only hope?" Abby said. "What do you mean by that?"

Then came Maxine's voice from behind them. "Hey, guys, good thing I spotted you up here," she called to them. Abby and Brett turned to see the soccer player climbing up the bleachers, a sports bag slung over one shoulder. "Why are you up here chit-chatting? What's so interesting?"

Brett jabbed a thumb over his shoulder. "Good question, Max. Why don't you ask him?"

He and Abby turned back to Michael Alvarez. Or rather, to the spot where he had been sitting. It was just an empty spot on the bleachers. He had vanished again.

•   •   •

Mr. Santillian sat in his office, gazing around at the various antiques scattered around the room. For a long time now, he reflected, he'd fooled himself into thinking he'd put the Pure Shore Club behind him and devoted himself entirely to teaching. But that was not the case, he now realized. With the end of the club so near, Mr. Santillian saw that he had never totally severed those ties.

He turned one wrist slightly, allowing the flintlock-shaped cuff link to glint in the office's light. Yes, he had still held onto certain things. He had never totally let go of the club, and the result was this decision was much harder than it had to be. Mr. Santillian wondered if, when the moment came, he could go through with it. Totally destroy Reeve, the Empowerer, the clubhouse, all the powers of all the members across the country.

His cell phone rang, providing a welcome interruption from his brooding. He answered swiftly and was greeted by the southern accent of the Crimson Cruiser.

"Hiya, Mr. Santillian," she said. "Mindy arrived right on time. Downright miracle if you ask me. Darn airlines. Anyway, we've just started on our way back to Jefford. Where do you want us to meet you?"

"At the clubhouse," he told her, a slight unreality settling into his words even as he spoke them. "With Reeve out of commission, we will have no problem gaining access."

"And activating the self-destruct," Cruiser replied. Mr. Santillian could hear ruefulness in the young woman's words but chose to ignore it.

"Yes, and activating the self-destruct," he agreed. "Call me when you're about twenty minutes away and I'll meet you there." He hesitated a moment, then added, "Drive safely. And tell Mindy I say hello."

He snapped his phone shut and looked across his desk. The cutlass-shaped brooch lay there, acting as a proverbial northern star for him, guiding him towards his goal.

This will be for you, Stacy, he thought.

CHAPTER TWENTY-TWO
SHADOWS ON THE MOVE

Steven Endicott gazed out of a rear window of his mountain chalet. The sun was still high in the sky, covering the slopes with swaths of light. It was a dazzling sight, and a welcome alternative to the gloomy interior of the house and its grim occupants. Steven appreciated the aid of the Smiling Shadow and its Outriders, but he could only take so much darkness.

He wondered what that said about himself, but rejected that line of thought, choosing instead to replay in his mind once more their slaying of Michael Alvarez. It had been glorious, Steven thought. To see the look of shock on Michael's face when the fool realized Steven was still alive. To see him struck down and destroyed. It had all been just as Steven had imagined it, and he savored each portion of the memory. It had been a long time coming. He smiled to himself.

Then he lost the smile. What he had never thought about, even in his wildest daydreams of vengeance, was the aftermath. How he would feel after claiming his revenge. He wasn't sure what he expected, but he hadn't expected it to feel…quite like this. What elation he'd felt was more or less gone, leaving him feeling oddly empty. The sensation disturbed Steven. Revenge had been his goal for five years now. Surely it had to feel better than this. Perhaps when it was all done, when all of his old comrades rested in their graves…

He realized he was no longer alone. The room had grown noticeably chillier, and he spun to see his dark ally there. The amorphous black blob drifted over to Steven, its ever-present smile an oasis of ghostly white in a sea of shade.

"Steven, the time has come," it said, its voice a giddy hiss. It sounded like a cobra eager to feast on its prey. "I have received the word. The fool Santillian has fallen into our hands, as neatly and predictably as we thought he would."

Steven's mind whirled. He'd hoped it would come to this, but some small part of him had doubted their plan. "You don't mean…?"

"Indeed," the Smiling Shadow replied, floating next to him. "Our intelligence tells us Reeve is deactivated. The clubhouse is ripe for the picking."

"Excellent," Steven said, his fists clenching involuntarily. "When do we make our move?"

"Immediately," the Shadow said.

Steven's eyes narrowed. "What's the rush? If Santillian has truly shut off that accursed Reeve, we can walk into the clubhouse at our leisure."

"Circumstances are such that we cannot take our time, my dear Steven," the Shadow said. The longer

Steven was standing near the malevolent creature, the colder he became. He resisted the urge to rub his arms for warmth, not wanting to look weak to his partner in vengeance.

"What's happened?" Steven asked.

"Santillian is going one step further than we anticipated," the Shadow said. "He plans to activate the clubhouse's self-destruct."

Steven frowned. That was definitely not what he and the Shadow wanted. They wanted the Pure Shore Club destroyed, but they needed the clubhouse intact. More specifically, they needed the Empowerer. "But he needs at least two club members to do that. The only ones left are—"

The Shadow didn't let him finish. "Both are en route even as we speak."

"Both of them?" Steven said. "How convenient for us. Then we can't waste any more time standing here arguing. Have you summoned the Outriders?"

"But of course! They converge upon the clubhouse with all possible haste," the Smiling Shadow said. "Your former teammates shall be no match for us."

"They must be taken alive," Steven reminded him. "If any of them are killed before I get there—"

"Do not worry yourself, my dear boy," the Shadow chided. "I've not forgotten the details of our agreement. Rest assured, you shall have the revenge you dream of."

Soon they departed, the Smiling Shadow spiriting its human compatriot along in its darkness. As they travelled, Steven thought about what was to come. He couldn't believe the day was finally here, and what he and the Smiling Shadow had managed to do in the space of a weekend. The entire Pure Shore Club hung on a string, and they were about to cut that string.

Yet, in the back of his mind, he was aware none of it made him feel as good as he had hoped.

•   •   •

"He did it again!" Brett exclaimed. "Teased us and then took a powder when we weren't looking!"

Maxine raised an eyebrow. "Are you sure Michael Alvarez was actually here? The two of you didn't have a hallucination or something?"

"No, he really was!" Abby said. "He was right there, talking to us!"

Maxine held up her hands. "Relax, I believe you. If it was just Ace there saying he saw Michael, then I'd wonder. But with you backing him up, I believe it. Plus, it's nothing Alvarez hasn't done to us before."

"What about what he said?" Abby said, her eyes wide. "That we're in danger? That we're the only hope?"

"He said those things?" Maxine asked.

"Yeah!" Brett said. "Then the guy pulled a fade! Again!"

Maxine's eyes narrowed. "This is all becoming highly obnoxious to me."

Abby looked around. The soccer field was largely cleared out, with only a few stragglers remaining, mostly people talking in small groups.

"You seem anxious, Abby," Brett observed.

"Like I said, Mr. Alvarez said we were in danger," she replied, looking back at them. "For all we know, those Outrider guys could be creeping up on us even now!"

Maxine stole a glance around. "Well, I wouldn't worry too much about that. Cruiser is supposed to be watching out for us, right?"

"Is she?" Brett asked. "I don't know. If that's true, then why haven't we seen her around since this morning?"

Maxine shrugged. "Maybe she's really good at staying out of sight. My dad has bodyguards who are pretty good at that. Anyway, we don't know what wacky powers she has besides that crazy car of hers. Maybe she can turn invisible or something."

"Well, whatever she's able to do," Brett said, "she's next on my list to get answers from. If Mr. Santillian is going to be a jerk and Mr. Alvarez's going to pop in and out like this, maybe the dame in the red car can tell us what's going on."

Maxine arched an eyebrow. "Oh really? And how, precisely, do you expect to make her do that? In case you've forgotten, she wasn't exactly forthcoming last night when she drove us home."

Abby spoke up. "You missed it, Maxine. Brett took it upon himself to threaten Michael Alvarez."

Maxine's eyes widened. "To his face? Wow, I figured you to be a fairly street-smart guy, but that's pretty bold!"

"No, not to his face," Brett said, suddenly becoming very engaged in typing information into his phone.

"Over the phone then?" Maxine asked.

"Not exactly," Brett murmured.

Maxine raised an eyebrow, eyeing Brett closely. "Don't tell me you texted him."

"He left a threatening voicemail message for Mr. Alvarez," Abby explained.

Maxine smirked, then broke out into all-out laughter. "You did not!"

"He did," Abby said with a small smile. "You should have heard it, it was, like, seven hours long. He even said 'capeesh'."

"It was hardly that long," Brett said, resolutely staring at his phone. "Anyway, cut the chatter, huh? I'm updating my memoirs."

"Oh, great," Maxine said, her laughter having dropped to chuckling. "I'm sure future generations will be impressed and inspired with you threatening a wheelchair-bound man via voicemail. Truly, a journalistic maneuver worthy of the masters of the medium."

Brett shot her a withering glare and went back to typing.

"What'd you threaten him with, anyway?" Maxine asked. "Locking him in the headmaster's safe? Hitting him with your blue dot?"

"For your information," Brett said, slowly raising his head to look at her, "I told him we'd take what we know and blab it all over the place. Make stuff real uncomfortable for him, you know?"

Maxine frowned. "Okay, I'm more impressed now. But did you ever think maybe you should consult with Abby and me before doing something like that?"

"That's what I said," Abby put in.

"Because did you ever think about what would happen if Mr. Alvarez decided to call your bluff?" Maxine went on. "If you think the FBI is interested in a bunch of sick alumni, they'd be really interested in magic wands and blue circles that let you walk through walls and super-speed roller blades. And I, for one, like my super-speed roller blades. I'd be really, really upset if some government agent took them away to study."

Brett spread his hands wide. "Look, I'm sorry, all right? I have bigger priorities than playing with magic wands and racing around the countryside at Mach Six. You two may be taken with all this superhero hoodoo, but I'm only interested in the truth."

"That's right," Maxine said, crossing her arms. "Your lousy story. Well, you're doing a stellar job pursuing that little goal so far."

"Hey, Michael Alvarez came here, didn't he?" Brett pointed out. "Obviously my tactic worked."

"Yeah, too bad he disappeared again," Maxine said, looking off into the distance. "I wonder where he went to, anyway?"

CHAPTER TWENTY-THREE
IT'S ALL FALLING APART

Cruiser drove with both hands on the wheel of her Chameleon Car, knowing this was her last spin in the amazing vehicle. Once Mr. Santillian destroyed the clubhouse, the source of all their powers would be gone, and who knew what would actually happen to the car. Perhaps it would revert to being a normal automobile, she reflected. A regular car, one she couldn't morph with her thoughts. She wouldn't be able to take it flying, or boating, or off-road biking, or any of the other alternate modes of transportation she had at her disposal. It would definitely be missed.

Mindy's voice broke into Cruiser's reverie. "Do you think he's really going to go through with this?"

Cruiser gripped the wheel tightly. "You mean Mr. Santillian?" she said, though she knew full well who and what Mindy was talking about.

"Yeah," Mindy said. "I mean, do you think he's really going to throw the switch? Blow up the clubhouse?"

"From my understanding, it's less of an explosion and more of a disintegration. Draws less attention…less chance of a forest fire, too."

Mindy's scientific expertise was in archaeology, not psychology, but she knew an avoidance tactic when she heard one. "You know what I mean, Jolene. Can he really do it, when it comes down to it? For that matter, can we really help him do this?"

Cruiser shot Mindy an annoyed glance. "You're here, aren't you?"

Mindy shrugged. "I'm here probably for the same reason you are. We're loyal to our old teacher. But I wonder, in this case, if he's right. And what about Michael and Ethan?"

"What about them?" Cruiser stared hard at the road ahead, as if she could melt the asphalt with her stare.

"You know, their theories about the Smiling Shadow and all that. What if they're right? If we blow up…excuse me, disintegrate the clubhouse…and we lose our powers, and the enemy is still out there somewhere, what do we do then? Throw rocks at it?"

Mindy saw a muscle in Cruiser's jaw twitch. She was definitely hitting a nerve. "We don't know if Ethan and Michael are right," she said.

"We also don't know if they're wrong," Mindy shot back.

"Nice to have some support," came Michael Alvarez's voice from the back of the car.

Mindy and Cruiser both screamed, and Cruiser nearly drove off the road. She narrowly avoided taking the car into a ditch and jerked them back onto the road. The only problem was she took them too far out, into the other lane, where a semi truck was barreling down on them.

The two women screamed again, and Cruiser jerked the car back into the right lane just in time. The semi raced past, honking its horn furiously. Cruiser couldn't blame the trucker; he had probably been as freaked out as they were.

She snapped her gaze to the rearview mirror, and Mindy was already craning her head back to look into the back seat. Michael Alvarez was sitting there, wearing normal street clothes and looking very tired.

"Michael?" Mindy cried upon seeing her old friend in the back seat.

"What are you trying to do, mister?" Cruiser said, glaring into the rearview mirror. "Get us all killed?"

He held up his hands. "Sorry, ladies, sorry. I had no idea you were in motion. In fact, I had no idea I was teleporting into a moving vehicle."

"What do you mean you had no—Michael!" Mindy exclaimed as she looked at him more closely. "What's happened to you?"

Cruiser had enough. She pulled off into a gravel patch on the side of the road and whirled to face Michael directly. Her jaw dropped as she realized what had Mindy so concerned. Michael was transparent. They could see the car upholstery right through him, as if he were a ghost.

"My powers are messed up right now," Michael said. "Listen, I don't have time to talk. I could vanish at any moment."

"What…? Why…?" Cruiser stammered, unable to form a coherent sentence due to her thoughts bottlenecking somewhere between her brain and her mouth.

"It's true. It's all true. Everything Ethan and I have been looking into the past few years. The Smiling Shadow is back."

Cruiser's eyes grew wide. "You have proof, Mike?"

A visible shudder rippled through the man's transparent form. "I've seen it."

It was Mindy and Cruiser's turn to shudder. So, it was true. The old enemy was back. And it was likely not too pleased with how their last encounter had ended.

"It's been picking off all the old members of the club," Michael told them, speaking quickly. "I think it's stealing their powers, throwing them into comas."

"Oh my gosh," Cruiser said softly. "It's causing this mystery illness that has the FBI all riled up."

Michael's eyes narrowed. "It got Ethan. He must have gotten too close to finding them out, so he was zapped. They ambushed me when I went to check on him. They're going to go after you guys next. And that's not all."

"Yeah?" Cruiser asked, anxious to hear more.

"There are some new kids in the club," Michael said. "Three students that Reeve and I coaxed into joining. Only it all got messed up. They don't know what's going on, but they have powers, and the Shadow's gonna gun for them eventually, too."

"Yeah, I know all about the new kids," Cruiser said. "I've met them, actually."

"Yeah, Brett Cho left me a voicemail," Michael said. "How did that come about, anyway?"

"Brett Cho?" Cruiser asked. "Why was he calling you?"

"New kids?" Mindy said at almost the same time. "Michael, you brought new kids into the club? What were you and Reeve thinking?"

His face contorted into a grimace. "I know, I know, it sounds stupid. They're part of a plan Reeve and I cooked up, but it's all falling apart. We might be able to salvage things, though. But listen, there's more. The Smiling Shadow is not the only enemy after us. There is also St—" Michael's voice cut off, like a television having its mute turned on. Mindy and Cruiser could see his mouth moving, his hands gesturing and his eyes wide, but they couldn't hear him. His transparent body began fading even more from view.

"Michael!" Cruiser cried. Both women reached out to him, a desperate attempt to pull their old friend fully into reality. Their hands grasped nothing but empty air. Cruiser had never felt so helpless. She could do nothing but watch as Michael faded away totally, his mouth never ceasing its movement.

They stared at the space Michael had just occupied for a long moment, neither knowing what to do or say.

CHAPTER TWENTY-FOUR
APOLOGIES

Despite everything that was going on, Maxine insisted on going back to her dorm and taking a shower. Brett, being a boy, was confined to the lobby while Maxine and Abby went upstairs. Maxine wasn't one to take forever cleaning herself up, and soon she was dressed in a Jefford Academy sweatshirt and jeans, tying her still-damp hair back in a ponytail.

"Good game, I must say," Maxine said as she put on her shoes. "I didn't think I'd be able to play so well after being a human rope last night and roller blading this morning, but sometimes I surprise myself. I'm on a good team, so that helps. The last school I was at, I was surprised they let half of those morons even try out, much less play."

Maxine finished tying her shoes and glanced up at Abby. The other girl was sitting on Maxine's bed, staring off into space. "Hey, there, Abby," Maxine said, "you listening to me?"

Abby's head jerked around, obviously startled out of deep thought. "Oh, sorry, Maxine…it's hard for me to concentrate on school stuff just now, with all this Pure Shore Club stuff going on."

Maxine grunted. "Like you haven't thought at least a dozen times this weekend about when you're going to get your homework done."

"Um, I already did it," Abby said. "While Brett was doing his internet searches at the library."

Of course you did, Maxine thought. She hadn't known Abby very long, but it was likely she was as driven about academics as Maxine herself was about sports.

"But school stuff seems so trivial now," Abby said. "I mean, Michael Alvarez seems to think we're in great danger. Reeve seemed pretty freaked out, too. Everyone's going on about this Smiling Shadow. I don't know, aren't you scared? At least a little bit?"

Maxine shrugged. "I don't scare easily. Besides, I'm not convinced that anybody is telling us the truth. No one seems to want to level with us, and until someone does, I refuse to become even the slightest bit anxious."

"I would feel the same," came a voice from across the room, "if I were in your shoes."

Both girls jumped, startled, and Abby let out a frightened squeak that she immediately regretted doing in Maxine's presence. They spun to see Michael Alvarez sitting in Maxine's desk chair.

"Hey!" Abby cried. "You're not supposed to be in here, this is a girl's dorm!"

Michael's eyes widened and he looked around, realizing where he was.

"Get out!" Maxine shouted, and she picked a heavy textbook off of her dresser and lobbed it at him. Both girls were amazed when the book passed right through him. It crashed into the wall and fell to the floor, its cover wide open.

"You...you can turn intangible?" Abby said, awe overriding her earlier outrage.

Michael had instinctively flinched when Maxine hurled the book at him, and he opened his eyes, looking wary that more heavy objects might get flung his way. "No, not normally. My powers are all messed up right now. But that's not important."

Maxine and Abby both noticed, the closer they looked at Michael, it was apparent that everything was not normal. His body seemed to fade slightly every few moments, like he was a ghost that couldn't make up its mind to live in the physical world or not.

"Give us some answers, mister!" Maxine yelled, pointing a finger at the intruding alumnus. "No more hints, no more stupid games. I've been jerked around all weekend and I will not stand for it anymore!"

Abby gasped, shocked that Maxine would talk that way to an adult. Michael responded by looking sheepish and holding up his hands. "You're right, you're right. I've screwed up majorly here. I should have just told you everything flat out, right outside of Mr. Santillian's office, before things got out of hand. You guys have been through a lot, and it could have been avoided if I'd been less of an idiot. I left it to Reeve to tell you guys everything while I went off hunting for bad guys. It was wrong and it wasn't fair to you three."

Maxine folded her arms and tossed her soggy ponytail. "Well, it's good to hear you admit that."

"Listen, I don't know how much time I have. Like I said, my powers are behaving strangely, and I keep teleporting away involuntarily. I keep coming back to the people I need to talk to, but not in the order I want or when I want. So hear me out. Your answers about the Pure Shore Club, Reeve, the Smiling Shadow, all of it…can be found in the club's time capsule."

"What?" Maxine said, one eyebrow lifted. "You've got to be kidding me!"

"Where is it?" Abby asked, not wanting to waste any time.

Michael's form almost faded out of sight entirely, and with visible effort he faded back in again. "Under the Senior Rock. And watch your backs, please…I can't protect you, not in this state, and the others are otherwise occupied. You're on campus with lots of people around so you should be safe."

Maxine frowned. "What, we're supposed to dig this thing up? In front of all these people you just talked about?"

And right when she was finished with her question, Michael winked out of sight.

She sighed. "I am getting so sick of that."

CHAPTER TWENTY-FIVE
THE TIME CAPSULE

Maxine burst into the lobby, her special roller blades slung over her shoulder. Abby trailed behind, doing her best to keep up. Brett was lounging in a chair, his hands behind his head. When he saw the girls, he leapt to his feet.

"I think I know what our next move should be, gals," he said. "We need to talk to Cruiser, but she may not come out of the woodwork unless we're in danger. I think we should go get in a fight…maybe with those Outrider guys if we can find them…and she'll come running. Or driving, in her case."

"No need," Maxine snapped. "Come on." She grabbed a handful of his leather jacket and pulled him out the door.

They explained their latest encounter with Michael Alvarez to Brett.

"Hold on a second," Brett said, "let's think this through, huh? Don't you guys think that if we start digging there a person or two might just notice and get us in trouble? Plus, I hate to rain on your parade, but none of us have shovels."

"It's true," Abby said. "I didn't bring a shovel with me to school. It wasn't on the list of recommended items to bring."

"It doesn't matter," Maxine said, shaking her head. "What matters is that this is a time capsule buried by the Pure Shore Club. The same people who are secret superheroes, have an underground clubhouse, and cars that turn into planes. I highly doubt that any time capsule they use is going to be normal."

Brett and Abby glanced at each other.

"Soccer queen's got a point," Brett said with a shrug.

They soon arrived at the Senior Rock, a gigantic stone the size of a small minivan. It was blotted and splashed with every color imaginable, and covered with initials, slogans, and symbols, all painted by last year's senior class.

"Whoop-dee-doo," Brett said, nodding at it. "You pay your tuition, you study for four years, and you get the privilege of painting a huge pebble with your graduating class."

"It probably was a pebble at one point," Maxine said, her eyes scanning the ground near the Senior Rock. "There's probably a trillion layers of paint on that sucker."

"Actually, it's only been around since 1932," Abby spoke up. "It was brought here from a nearby quarry, and—"

"I think we need to focus here," Maxine said, interrupting the other girl. "No offense, Abby, but finding this time capsule has got to be our top priority."

Brett frowned. "Too bad that Michael Alvarez couldn't just tell you guys what the scoop is instead of us having to stand around out here like goons."

"Who knows?" Maxine said. "He might reappear at any moment." What she didn't say, and all three of them knew, was that Michael Alvarez's powers were messed up somehow. They guessed that his difficulties weren't due to happenstance; there was something really big going on. Big, and very dangerous. And the three of them were wrapped up in it. To survive, they would need information, the very information that, hopefully, they were about to find.

"Well, I don't know about you two," Brett said, "but maybe shovels would be the way to—"

He never got to complete this sentence. The ground simply opened up, swallowed him, then closed back up. It had opened and shut like a snapping mouth, dropping him into the earth like a penny into a wishing well. The spot where he'd been standing looked undisturbed and perfectly normal.

Abby gasped and stepped backward from the spot Brett had just occupied. Before Maxine could even react, Abby was gone too. Then she felt the ground beneath her feet disappear, and she fell into nothingness.

•   •   •

"Maxine, is that you? Abby, are you there?"

"I'm here."

"Are you guys okay?"

"What happened?"

"I think we've been buried alive!"

"Are you serious? Tell me you're joking, Brett…"

"Don't panic, Abby, he's just being a fool, as usual…"

"Can anyone find a light switch?"

Right then, the lights turned on. They found themselves in a small chamber with smooth walls that sloped inward and a rounded ceiling. Everything was colored a shiny coppery hue. They barely had room to stand up. The top of Brett's hat brushed the ceiling.

"What in Sam Hill is going on here?" Brett asked. "Where are we?"

"I think we're inside the time capsule," Abby said. The air reminded her of the Pure Shore Clubhouse. Musty, stale. The kind of air no human has moved through in a long time.

"I wonder how far underground we are?" Brett asked.

Abby really, really wished he hadn't asked that question. The thought of hanging around beneath the earth, with who knows how much dirt and rock over their heads and no discernible exit made familiar waves of panic erupt from her stomach.

"What are you, a geologist?" Maxine snapped. "Who cares how far underground we are? What I want to know is, what kind of time capsule is this?" Maxine demanded of no one in particular. "There's nothing inside of it!"

Then came a voice. A voice that reminded Abby of classical music and libraries filled with leather-bound books.

"Welcome, Pure Shore Club members," the voice said. They looked around, trying to spot a speaker along the walls. Then light swirled near one of the walls, making all of them take a step back. The light coalesced and began to take on a discernible shape.

When it was finished, there was an image of a man standing there, a man they all recognized, even though they only encountered him briefly the day before. He wore a gray suit with patches on the elbows of his jacket, and a pine green bow tie. His head was framed by a wild mane of salt-and-pepper hair that extended almost to his shoulders. His hands were clasped in front of him, and he regarded the three teenagers with a kind, grandfatherly smile.

It was Reeve.

CHAPTER TWENTY-SIX
THE ORIGIN OF THE PURE SHORE CLUB

Mr. Santillian gazed upon the various pictures of the different Pure Shore Clubs throughout the years. There was so much history, he thought to himself. So many people had walked through the clubhouse halls. He reflected on the task before him and nearly quit. He felt unworthy to end this club. Who was he to destroy this legacy?

Then he reached the end of the line of pictures and his gaze settled on the final Pure Shore Club. Michael, Ethan, Mindy, Steven, and…Stacy. They all looked so young. So full of energy and optimism. How had it all gone so horribly wrong? How did it come to this, he wondered, with two alienated from him, two about to help him destroy the clubhouse and Reeve, and another two dead? It was all so…unjust. He wished he could go back and change the course of events, but that was not among his superpowers.

A chime sounded within the clubhouse, indicating someone on ground level had opened the entrance. Within seconds, the low hum of the anti-gravity elevator could be heard. Mr. Santillian stepped out of the meeting chamber just in time to see Cruiser and Mindy floating downward. The sight of the anti-gravity elevator in action usually amazed him. Now it made him sad, for he would likely never see it working again.

The duo landed and immediately saw him. Mindy looked very much the same, always appearing younger than she really was. Both regarded him with solemn expressions.

"Hello, Mindy," he greeted his former student. "It's been a long time, hasn't it?" He reached out a hand for Mindy to shake. He was surprised when she did not return the gesture.

"Mr. Santillian," Cruiser spoke up. "We need to talk."

•   •   •

"Reeve!" Brett exclaimed. "What happened to you? What are you doing down here?"

The old man continued to smile serenely, his hands clasped in front of him. "I do not understand this input," he said. "Please restate your query."

"What the…?" Brett said, his eyes squinting.

Abby stepped forward. "Um, are you Reeve?"

"I am not Reeve," came the reply. "I am a prerecorded interactive database with a holographic interface designed to mimic Reeve due to the Pure Shore Club members' familiarity and resultant comfort level with him."

"Ah," Brett said, pushing his hat onto the very back of his head. "I guess that explains that little question."

"Enough of all this cryptic nonsense," Maxine said. She stepped forward and jabbed a finger at the image of Reeve. "Are we inside the Pure Shore Club's time capsule?"

"Yes, indeed you are, young lady," Holo-Reeve said. "As I was about to say when you first dropped in, this time capsule was constructed by Reeve and the last group of the Pure Shore Club before the club was disbanded. It was the hope of the members that if the club never was restarted, future generations might know of the organization and what it was truly about."

"So this…time capsule is just below the ground, on campus grounds?" Brett asked. "Where kids and teachers are just walking over it and near it all the time?"

Abby let out a soft whistle. "Wow, that's kind of crazy to think about."

"How'd this thing get down here, then?" Brett asked, touching one of the eggshell-smooth walls. "Does the Pure Shore Club own excavating equipment or what?"

Holo-Reeve actually chuckled. "No, no, my boy. Such crude methods are not needed given the unique abilities of the Pure Shore Club. You see, the time capsule itself was constructed at the clubhouse while Mr. Santillian was away, and then—"

"Stop right there," Maxine snapped, holding up a hand like she was stopping traffic. "I can't speak for all of us, but I could care less how this stupid time capsule was buried here. And I don't want to stand here asking questions. Can't you give us…a menu or something?"

Brett winced inwardly. He understood Maxine's frustration—he was eager for answers himself—but he worried that her tone might make the Holo-Reeve uncooperative. It seemed like an automated system, but who knew what stimuli would make it stop talking to them? And it wasn't like other sources were a dime a dozen. His gambit to flush out the Crimson Cruiser and demand answers from her had been a desperate one, despite his outward confidence.

But the Holo-Reeve seemed unperturbed. "Switching to Graphic User Interface format."

The hologram of Reeve remained where it was, but a two-dimensional display appeared next to him. It looked like a touch-screen, but instead of something you read on a tablet or a phone, it floated in mid-air.

"Jeepers," Brett said, the display reflecting in his eyes. "I wouldn't mind having a TV or a computer like this."

They clustered around the floating screen and read the listed options.

CLUB ORIGIN
CLUB MEMBERS
THE CLUBHOUSE
THE TIME CAPSULE
CASES
CLUB TIMELINE
ARTIFACTS
MORE

"I think our best bet is 'Club Origin'," Brett announced.

"Best idea you've had all day," Maxine replied without glancing at him.

He decided not to give her the dignity of a response and touched the 'Club Origin' section. And all three of them screamed as the smooth, bronze floors and walls vanished, leaving them standing in what seemed to be empty space.

"Yaaaaaaaa!" they howled in unison, clutching each other for support, for a good thirty seconds. Their screaming trailed off when they realized they weren't falling. They could still feel solid ground under their feet. And Holo-Reeve was still there, looking implacable, with his hands behind his back. He seemed unmoved by both the disappearance of the room and the obvious discomfiture of the three teenagers before him.

Stars began to appear in the blackness all around them. Abby gazed at them in wonderment. She knew her constellations pretty well, but she didn't recognize any of these patterns. Maybe this view was from another side of the Earth, she speculated. She didn't want to voice the theory out loud though. Maxine was already impatient as it was.

"What the heck's going on?" Brett demanded, disengaging himself from Abby and Maxine, the former of whom had a near-death grip on his leather jacket. "Where'd the room go, wise guy?"

"You selected the 'Club Origin' option," Holo-Reeve said crisply. "The holographic nature of the time capsule is engaged. You are seeing a representation of a section of what you call outer space."

"Outer space?" Brett exclaimed. "But why?"

Holo-Reeve cocked his head. "Because, young man, this is where the Pure Shore Club started."

CHAPTER TWENTY-SEVEN
THE COMPUTER FROM OUTER SPACE

"Sir, we think there may be a problem," Mindy said. "We…saw Michael."

Mr. Santillian's eyes flashed. Cruiser knew that, as much as Michael drove Mr. Santillian crazy, their former teacher still cared about him. "Is he all right?" Mr. Santillian asked, his eyes darting between their faces.

"His powers seemed to be messed up," Cruiser explained. "He appeared in the car while we were on our way over here."

"Yeah," Mindy said. "He got all transparent after a few minutes and totally vanished. He hasn't reappeared since."

Mr. Santillian nodded, thinking that he saw what his former students were getting at. "I see. His teleportation might be malfunctioning. If we destroy the clubhouse now, he might lose his powers and end up who knows where."

"No, that's not what we mean," Cruiser said. "He said…he said the Smiling Shadow is back."

Mr. Santillian scowled and immediately walked away. He strode into the meeting room, the sliding door still open from when he'd come out to greet them.

"That went well," Mindy said, looking at the space where Mr. Santillian had just been standing.

"We knew this wouldn't be easy," Cruiser said. She shook her head, tossing her blond hair. "Come on."

Mindy followed Cruiser into the meeting chamber. Mr. Santillian was at the far end of the long table, sitting in one of the high-backed chairs. He had it swiveled so his back was to the door.

"Mr. Santillian, please hear us out," Cruiser said.

He abruptly spun his chair to face her. "Why are you wasting precious time with this nonsense, Jolene?" he asked, not quite yelling but not talking in a normal tone of voice, either. "People out there are sick and they're not going to get better until we do our job here. The job I summoned both of you for." His dark eyes swept over both of them. "You know how I feel about Michael and his stupid theories. He's living in the past! The Smiling Shadow is dead and gone! We need to act now, to prevent more hardship and pain—"

"Michael says he saw the Smiling Shadow," Cruiser interrupted.

Mr. Santillian looked like he was going to continue his diatribe, then he settled back into his chair. He considered Cruiser's words for a moment. "Where did he see it?" he asked finally.

Cruiser shrugged. "I guess wherever Ethan is right now."

"Ethan's fallen into a coma too," Mr. Santillian said. "I was going to tell all of you after you arrived."

"Well, I guess the Shadow ambushed Michael when he went to check up on Ethan," Cruiser continued. "This is what Michael told us before he vanished."

"He also told us about the new kids," Mindy said, taking a step forward.

Cruiser winced. She'd forgotten to mention to Mindy that Mr. Santillian didn't know the eighth graders had been brought deeper into the business of the club by Michael.

Mr. Santillian quickly rose and leaned on the table, piercing her with his gaze. "What about the new kids?" he asked. "Are these the new kids I'm thinking of? The ones who Michael recklessly and without my knowledge sent invitations to, bringing them to my office, hoping that somehow, magically, I would see things differently and agree to restart the club? Those new kids?"

Mindy gulped. "Yes…I guess, those ones. I actually haven't met them."

Mr. Santillian's eyes shifted over to the woman in the red jacket. "Cruiser?" he prompted her.

She took a deep breath. "Mr. Santillian, those kids have acquired powers. Costumes, too."

"*What?*"

·   ·   ·

"The Pure Shore Club started in outer space?" Maxine exclaimed.

Brett snorted. "Are you really surprised, champ? Do you really think anything this bizarre could have started on Earth?"

"Precisely, young man," Holo-Reeve said. He looked at the star-speckled darkness all around them. "I did not mean that the club started in the cold vacuum that is most of the universe. To narrow it down just a tad, it actually started here."

The stars suddenly began to streak by. The surrounding view was shifting. It reminded Abby of all the science fiction movies she'd ever seen. It was incredible, like she was standing in space and moving faster than light.

A planet came into view, colored differently than the Earth. It was a world covered with orange clouds, with patches of yellow and green visible here and there.

"Great guns!" Brett said, staring at the planet-image. "That's no planet in our solar system, is it?"

"Indeed not," Holo-Reeve answered, walking over to the world and leaning close to it, peering at it as if he was examining its surface. "It is quite a few light years from the Earth. So many, the number would be incomprehensible and therefore does not bear mentioning."

"So…people live on this world?" Abby asked. "Like, I mean…extra-terrestrials?"

"Aliens?" Brett put in. "Like in War of the Worlds? Or The Day the Earth Stood Still?"

Holo-Reeve chuckled. "Not quite like them, no. They have never left their planet with the intention of causing trouble for others. In fact, they have a humanitarian streak. You see, students, these aliens nearly destroyed their own world in a series of devastating wars. Once they picked up the pieces and realized once and for all the error of their ways, they formed a peaceful society. But that wasn't enough for them."

This was all a bit much for Maxine. It was one thing to accept superpowers, but aliens from other planets? She folded her arms across her chest and remained silent, allowing Holo-Reeve to keep talking and trying to keep an open mind. Her mind, however, threatened to slam the door shut every moment of his story.

"They postulated that if life existed elsewhere in the universe, that life may have the same problems they once faced and might need a little help. They formed what would translate into your language as the Galactic Hand Project. They sent several long-range craft into the depths of space, each one aimed at a world that, through their telescopes, they deemed likely to have intelligent life. One of these craft, as you may have guessed, made it to Earth."

"This craft," Brett cut in, "did it have a crew? What happened to them?"

Holo-Reeve shook his head, tossing his stringy white hair. "No, no, my lad. These craft were entirely unmanned, run by computers. It was the directive of each craft's computer to reach the world they were assigned to, travel to the surface, conceal itself, and proceed to help the inhabitants of its assigned world, all without being noticed."

A sudden thought struck Abby. "Wait. The computer you're talking about…that's Reeve, isn't it?"

Holo-Reeve nodded. "Yes, indeed."

Maxine and Brett stared at her. "How did you guess that?" Brett asked. "I assumed Reeve was a regular guy with powers, like the other Pure Shore Club members."

Abby shrugged. "He could be turned off like a computer. And Mr. Santillian said that he thought Reeve was malfunctioning."

"You're right," Maxine said. "Doesn't sound like a regular person to me. Sounds like a machine. So that's all Reeve is…a machine!"

Holo-Reeve snorted. "A most sophisticated machine, young lady. Far beyond anything your science has been able to produce. For one thing, Reeve is self-aware. He knows he is real, and as you may have noticed, he has a personality. And when it comes to how he conducts his mission here on your planet, he has a great deal of latitude. He is creative, which is more than I can say for any computer you humans have invented."

"Gee," said Brett. "For a glorified tour guide you sure can get defensive."

"Just setting the record straight," he replied. "So anyway, the craft carrying the computer intelligence you know as Reeve left many centuries ago." They watched as several dart-shaped craft broke through the orange world's atmosphere and sped into the darkness of space, all going in different directions. The stars began to streak by them again. Their view was following one craft in particular. "The ship reached Earth in the 1920s."

The stars stopped flying by and the craft seemed to slow down. The Earth came into view, the big blue marble that they had all seen in pictures. Seeing it like this was very different. It was in 3-D and was almost as tall as them. It was like they were cosmic giants, flying across space from world to world. As much as the experience was disconcerting, Abby wished she could do it for fun sometime. She glanced at her companions, wondering if they marveled at this experience as much as she did. Brett's face was the picture of concentration, likely soaking up all details for his news story. Maxine had one eyebrow raised, her arms folded, and a faint smirk on her face. As if she was daring the Holo-Reeve to make her believe in the fantastic history they were hearing about and seeing.

The image of the craft slowed as it neared the Earth and with apparent ease glided into orbit around the planet.

"Reeve arrived and began scanning your world, gathering data with long-range sensors and discreet probe devices," Holo-Reeve explained.

Brett grunted. "Good thing ol' Reeve showed up in the 1920s," he remarked. "It's not like there was a space race on then. No one had any satellites or anything up to see him coming."

Holo-Reeve smiled kindly. "Even if Reeve had arrived in the present day, my young friend, he would still have gone undetected."

"Reeve was built on another planet, doofus," Maxine said, slugging Brett in the arm. "He'd better be able to make himself invisible to our technology, or he's not worth squat."

"I guess that makes sense," Brett muttered, holding his now-sore arm.

"So," Holo-Reeve went on, "Reeve scanned your world, and in a short amount of time he realized he could help the human race by creating what you call superheroes."

"Why superheroes, though?" Abby asked. "I mean, if Reeve is so powerful, why doesn't he, I don't know, end war or cure all diseases or something like that?"

Maxine figured Abby was thinking of her parents. If Reeve could end the terrible conditions overseas that necessitated the services of doctors coming from other countries, her parents wouldn't have to be separated from her. Maxine wondered what that kind of relationship with parents was like. Where the child actually wanted the parents around. *I wouldn't know*, she reflected bitterly.

"Reeve is not that powerful," Holo-Reeve explained. "Also, part of his programming is an imperative that he keep his presence on Earth a secret to all but a select few. His creators were worried that a violent race could get ahold of him, reverse-engineer his functions, and use those technologies for unpleasant purposes.

"He settled on the idea of creating super-powered guardians who would operate in secret, righting wrongs and doing good without being noticed by mainstream society."

"So that confirms why we never heard of real-life superheroes running around," Brett said. "They don't want to be noticed."

"Reeve also realized that if these secret guardians were to have any effectiveness, they would need to go through some kind of training. Upon finding the Jefford Academy, at the time a smaller private school, he decided this would be the place to do it. It had the advantage of being relatively isolated."

Maxine frowned. "Why train his superheroes here at Jefford? I mean, he could have opened his own secret school somewhere else right?"

Reeve nodded. "Certainly. The problem with that approach, Maxine, is that young people such as yourselves have a degree of accountability that is a factor. Your parents have a general idea of where you are and what you are doing. Society as a whole frowns upon children running around willy-nilly with no one to look after them."

"A school that already existed was needed," Brett said. "People could believe the kids were here for normal studies."

"Yes, indeed. Reeve settled his craft into an area of land near the Jefford Academy." The image of the spacecraft descended to the Earth's surface, and they seemed to follow it, going through clouds and leveling off over green forests. The craft hovered over a spot and from its underbelly a red shaft of light lanced down towards the ground, burrowing a giant hole in the earth. The craft then settled into the hole, and more red lights came up from inside the hole. These lights didn't move dirt out of the way but were somehow pulling dirt into the hole. The craft was burying itself in the ground.

"So Reeve hid itself there," Abby said. "What happened to the spaceship?"

"Converted, over time," Holo-Reeve replied. "The craft's on-board nanobots can work very quickly, and Reeve directed them to rebuild the ship, to turn it into a sort of underground lair, hidden from prying eyes on land or air. While he was working on that, he reached out to a likely candidate to be his human contact at the school. You see, Reeve has certain mental and empathic abilities. He can scan the minds of others, read their thoughts, and know their hearts."

Brett grimaced. "Yeesh, that kind of thing gives a guy the heebie-jeebies!"

"Just be glad he's on our side," Maxine muttered.

"Well, as far as we know," Abby added, her tone low and ominous.

Holo-Reeve continued as if he hadn't heard them. "He searched through the faculty of the Jefford Academy and found a man named Hugh Ellwand." The forest disappeared, and in its place was the image of man, dressed in period clothing. He had red hair, a pipe in his mouth, and twinkling green eyes.

"Mr. Ellwand was a literature professor, horseman, and fencing enthusiast. He was a man of high heroic ideals and interest in old legends such as Robin Hood and William Tell. He enjoyed reading about classic Greek heroes like Perseus and Jason, and was an avid reader of books such as *The Three Musketeers* and *The Scarlet Pimpernel*."

Abby was startled to hear her favorite book named in Holo-Reeve's lecture. She looked at the image of Hugh Ellwand and realized she probably would have liked the Pure Shore Club's first teacher very much. She wondered if he was still alive; but realized that was foolish thinking. He looked to be in his late twenties or early thirties in the hologram; he was likely long-deceased by now.

"In other words, he was just what Reeve was looking for. He approached Mr. Ellwand while the latter was out riding in the forest. The two struck up a friendship, and Reeve gradually revealed his true nature. He proposed they recruit young heroes from the student body each year and train them in the use of their abilities. Mr. Ellwand was quite receptive to the idea, and added some ideas of his own, like not assigning powers at random, but instead assigning them based on the personalities of the club member."

"So, we were somehow…drawn to the silver platter with the power meant for us?" Brett asked. "I guess that makes sense. These powers line up with who we are too neatly for it to be otherwise."

The view shifted again, showing the interior of a very familiar room. It was the bottomless room from the Pure Shore Clubhouse. At its center was the giant, faintly glowing purple globe. Just seeing the inside of that room made Abby's stomach feel queasy. She hugged herself and hoped the others wouldn't notice.

"Behold, the power source of the Pure Shore Clubhouse," Holo-Reeve said, gesturing to the image before them. "It is called the AmazeHeart, named so by Hugh Ellwand himself when he first laid eyes upon it. It powered Reeve's faster-than-light craft and houses many important components, such as Reeve's central CPU and the drives that store the Pure Shore Club's files. It also houses this."

The AmazeHeart changed before them. It shifted to a cross-sectional view, as if someone had peeled one side of it off like an orange, revealing its innards. Inside, the sphere was hollow, and floating within it were several geometric shapes, all different colors. One in particular was quite familiar to Maxine, Abby, and Brett.

"The Empowerer," they said in unison.

If Holo-Reeve was surprised they knew the name of the gadget already, he didn't show it. The magenta sphere—an image, they had to remind themselves, not the real thing—floated out of the AmazeHeart and hovered before them.

"The Empowerer, when activated, grants superhuman abilities to those chosen by Reeve and the club's faculty advisor. The mechanism by which it selects what power to give a person is totally random, as intended."

They glanced at each other. So that was what the mysterious object was for. The question lingered why the Smiling Shadow—whatever that was—was so keen on retrieving it, so keen that Reeve had seen fit to shove it into their hands for safekeeping.

"Empowerer…AmazeHeart…." Maxine mused, "they sure laid on the cheese when they named these things, didn't they?"

The image of the Empowerer disappeared, and the view shifted to four teenagers, dressed in similar clothing to Hugh Ellwand. Mr. Ellwand and Reeve were giving each of them a silver platter.

"Well, that looks familiar," Maxine murmured.

The teenagers took the lids off their platters and revealed small objects on each shiny surface.

"I think we know what will happen next," Brett said, watching intently. Sure enough, all four teenagers fell into unconsciousness right where they stood. Reeve kept them from toppling over via pillowy constructs that materialized in the air to catch them.

"Hey!" Brett exclaimed. "We didn't get the soft treatment those characters are getting. All three of us took our chances with the floor."

Maxine rolled her eyes. "So much for things being harder back in the old days."

Then each of the four teenagers was enveloped in a white cocoon of light.

"Whoa," Abby said. "I guess we were knocked out for that part. What's happening to them?"

"When each new member is granted their power, a period of unconsciousness is necessary as the gift given to them calibrates itself to the new member's body and mind. Some members have powers inherent in their own forms, others have powers derived from special items."

"I guess all three of us are that last kind, huh?" Brett mused, rubbing his chin. "When you say it calibrates itself to the user's body and mind, that means it's kind of…synched up to them? Meaning only they have that power or can use that item?"

"Correct, my lad," Holo-Reeve said. "However much they may have wanted to over the years, either for fun or for necessity, Pure Shore Club members cannot swap powers or otherwise loan them out to non-members. Once you are granted your power that is your power and no one else's."

The view shifted once again, and instead of four teenagers in bright cocoons, before them stood the image of the same four teenagers, this time dressed in garish costumes, with Hugh Ellwand at their side.

"Every school year, more kids are added to the club, and generally remain in the club for their entire time at the Jefford Academy. After which they graduate, go out into the world, start a career, live what is on the surface a normal existence, and operate behind the scenes as a secret superhero. But it all starts here, with small groups of select kids at the Jefford Academy."

Brett, Maxine, and Abby were quiet for several moments as they processed the incredible information they'd just been told.

Abby broke the silence. "But how? I mean, how is this all done? I mean, are the aliens who made Reeve, like…wizards or something?"

Holo-Reeve chuckled. "I could explain how it all works, my child, but I highly doubt your scientific education is up to understanding it all. No offense, of course."

"It just seems like magic," Brett offered. "I mean, what if someone from the Middle Ages came forward in time, and were shown a television or a phone?"

"Or heard a voicemail message?" Maxine put in, grinning fiendishly.

"Enough about the voicemail message, okay? Anyway, my grandpa always said that one man's innovative technology is another man's magic."

"Interesting," Abby said, mulling it over. "It seems like sorcery to us, but it's really just…machinery." A terrible thought occurred to her. "Gee, guys…do you think this means that the three of us have…technology inside of us? You know, to make these powers work?" She shivered, and not just because of the cool air inside the time capsule.

Maxine frowned. "That is disturbing. Okay, Answer Man, fess up. Have we all turned into cyborgs or what? What will it do to our long-term health?"

A disturbing link between two unconnected pieces of information hooked up in Abby's mind. "Wow, guys…remember how, when Mr. Santillian confronted Reeve, he said that people were getting sick because of Reeve malfunctioning?"

Maxine didn't totally remember that being said, but she took Abby's word for it. She'd only known the girl for a couple of days now, but her memory seemed to be second to none.

"And Mr. Santillian turned Reeve off because of it," Brett added. "He told Headmaster Charlton that he hopes the sick alumni will get better."

"What about it, then?" Maxine asked. "Are we all going to get sick?"

Holo-Reeve remained unperturbed. "Members of your species get sick an average of—"

"That's not the right question," Brett interrupted him. He turned to Maxine. "This thing can't carry on a conversation the way the real Reeve can." He looked back to Holo-Reeve. "Is it true that Reeve is malfunctioning? And if so, does his malfunctioning have health consequences for the Pure Shore Club members, including us?"

Holo-Reeve frowned. "To answer your first question, my boy, yes, Reeve sustained extensive damage in the Pure Shore Club's final battle with the Smiling Shadow and his minions. He is in the midst of a self-repairing process that is estimated to be done in four more of your years. As for your second question, no. Reeve has no direct link to the Pure Shore Club members. It is the AmazeHeart that is connected to them, not Reeve. No damage that Reeve sustains could affect them, beyond being denied his full capabilities."

Abby was absent-mindedly biting the nails of her left hand as she thought. "So Mr. Santillian is wrong," she said. "Maybe to figure all of this out, we need to know more about this Smiling Shadow. Um, can you show us the menu again, please?"

The Graphical User Interface reappeared. After a few moments surveying the options, Brett turned to Holo-Reeve. "Hey, pal, got any suggestions as to where a guy would get the scoop on the Smiling Shadow?"

"I would suggest the 'Cases' section. It is grouped by case number and case name."

Sure enough, after drilling deeper into the submenus, they found an entry titled, simply, 'The Smiling Shadow'.

CHAPTER TWENTY-EIGHT
WHAT IS THE SMILING SHADOW?

"Those new members actually received costumes and powers?" Mr. Santillian barked, his eyes darting between Cruiser and Mindy. "How long have you known about this? How long has this been going on under my nose?"

Cruiser spread her hands in what she hoped was a placating gesture. Mr. Santillian had always possessed a bad temper. Not that she could blame him for being upset. Michael and Reeve had undercut and bypassed him quite thoroughly.

"Mindy didn't know until I told them on the car ride here," she told her old teacher. "I knew Michael and Reeve were planning to recruit some new members, but they'd told me they were involving you in the plan. I guess since I was still in the area, they wanted me in the loop in case the new club had transportation needs."

Mr. Santillian's eyes narrowed. "So why didn't you say something when I called you and had you keep an eye on those kids?"

Cruiser sighed. "Because I knew you'd be upset. When you told me what had happened, how you'd shown Michael and the new kids the door, I knew you definitely had not approved of Michael and Reeve's plan. So yeah, when I first encountered them, they had costumes and powers and everything. But I didn't tell them anything. I just took them back to campus."

Mr. Santillian snorted. "Well, that's something at least. Of course, I don't know what would have been worse, telling them everything about the club or letting them run wild with superpowers and not know what was going on."

"I know, I know," Cruiser said, reaching up with a red-gloved hand to massage the bridge of her nose. The strain of the past couple of days was getting to her, operating under conflicting loyalties and seeing the onset of a crisis. She was tempted to run out of the clubhouse, get in her car, and ride off to the horizon at Mach 3, leaving this entire mess behind her. But avoiding doing the tough thing had gotten her into this mess, she knew. She wasn't going to solve anything by continuing to stick her head in the sand.

"Look, sir," Mindy put in, stepping forward, "I know you're mad about what Michael and Reeve did, but it's really not what we need to be concerned about now."

Mr. Santillian's eyes flashed. "Putting innocent children in danger is always something that gets me concerned. I know all of you think I'm just some kind of jerk. Mean old Mr. Santillian being a grouchy, crotchety killjoy, not wanting to start up the club again." He pointed a finger at them. The pistol-shaped cuff links on that wrist flashed in the room's light. "You two, of all people, should know why I don't want to induct new members and why I don't want the club to start up again! Maybe Michael, Ethan, and Reeve are right. Perhaps the Smiling Shadow has returned."

"So you're willing to admit that?" Cruiser asked. She was surprised. Mr. Santillian had never admitted that it could be true, that their old enemy might have returned from certain death.

Mr. Santillian swept one hand through the air. "Michael can be delusional and too earnest for his own good, but he's no liar. He never told me he wouldn't recruit new members, for example. If he tells you he's actually seen the Smiling Shadow, then I believe him. Or at least I believe he saw what he thinks he saw."

Cruiser was taken aback. That was far more than she'd ever expected Mr. Santillian to admit. "So…you're worried about those kids. That they're in danger. That the Smiling Shadow is after them."

"Of course I'm worried about them!" Mr. Santillian thundered. "I'm worried about all of you. I don't want the Smiling Shadow to face any of you any more than I want it hunting those students."

"We can take care of ourselves, sir," Mindy said, folding her arms.

"No," Mr. Santillian said. "If it's true, if our old enemy is back, I don't want any of you to deal with it."

"So what, then?" Cruiser demanded. "You'll fight it on your own?"

"If I have to."

She couldn't believe he was being this obtuse. "You won't stand a chance, sir. No disrespect intended."

Mindy piped up. "She's right. If the Smiling Shadow is back, it's going to take a team effort—all of us—to defeat it again. Surely you know that."

He rested a hand on the back of one of the high-backed conference chairs. Memories arose of meetings at this very table. He closed his eyes and he could almost hear the voices of his students. Mindy, Michael, Ethan, Steven, all as teenagers. And Stacy.

He allowed one hand to drift to his pocket, and he gripped the cutlass-shaped brooch. With a pained expression, he pulled it out and opened his palm, allowing the others to plainly see what he held. They all recognized it, of course. It had been the source of the powers of one of their best friends.

Mindy gasped. Cruiser looked at her feet.

"You have to understand," he told them, his voice low and husky, "my conscience cannot handle another student of mine dying."

•   •   •

When they selected the 'Smiling Shadow' option, the menu disappeared and a sinister image appeared before them. Brett and Abby took an involuntary step back, their mouths agape. Only Maxine stood her ground, peering intently at the image, almost daring it to come to life and mess with her.

It was a dark, formless, shadowy mass, hovering inside the time capsule. Its inky blackness was so absolute that it was as if a black hole had erupted right in front of them. The edges of its form undulated constantly, as if it would not maintain even a rough shape for any length of time. All of that obviously gave it the 'Shadow' part of its name. The 'Smiling' part came from, they all observed, a faint white smile slashing across the approximate center of its form. While the rest of its mass was in constant, albeit slow, motion, the smile was fixed in place, like the eye of an evil hurricane.

"Blue blazes," Brett whispered, sizing up the Smiling Shadow's image. "What in Sam Hill is this thing?"

"The Smiling Shadow," Holo-Reeve explained, his hands clasped behind his back, "is another alien construct, from the same world that created Reeve." He began to walk around it, studying the three-dimensional image from all angles. "You see, young sir and young ladies, not everyone on that distant world was enamored with the idea of using time and resources to send help to faraway places and peoples none of them would ever see. These rogue elements in that peaceful society decided to do what they could to sabotage those efforts. Hence, when the craft that contained Reeve was launched into the void of space on an errand of peace, it was tracked and followed by another craft, a craft containing a malign artificial intelligence on an errand of evil."

Holo-Reeve finished his circuit of the hologram and came to a stop on their other side, looking at them expectantly.

"This…thing…is an artificial intelligence?" Maxine asked, walking up to it and looking into the depths of the inky projection. She'd been on a tour of underground caverns once, where there were creatures that evolved with no eyes due to the utter and complete lack of light. The park ranger conducting the tour had turned off the lights for a few moments, just to show the visitors what it was like to be down there with no light whatsoever.

Looking at the Smiling Shadow reminded Maxine of those moments underground, where man-made lights and the sun did not reach. It was a darkness your eyes had no hope adjusting to, a darkness that could render you blind if you spent enough time within it. She suppressed a shiver, hoping the others wouldn't notice.

"It is quite intelligent," Holo-Reeve confirmed.

"So why's it got everybody all freaked out?" Brett asked. "I mean, it's freaky-looking and all, but how much of a threat can a shadow be? Everybody casts a shadow, and as far as I know, you can wipe the floor with them by turning on enough lights."

"Or by turning the lights off," Abby pointed out.

"The Smiling Shadow is not a shadow as you know it," Holo-Reeve said.

Maxine grimaced. "I was afraid of that."

"It may look like a living shadow but it is actually a colony of microscopic machines, machines that work together and have various powers. It can pass through solid objects, and also become solid enough to strike at opponents. It can project dark blasts that can paralyze or kill. It can expand or contract its mass. It can fly at speeds exceeding Mach 5. It can generate irrational fear and dread in the minds of its opponents to help incapacitate them. And it can also create followers."

Brett snapped his fingers. "Those Outrider guys! With their dark knives and motorcycles they could conjure up. They have powers too. This happy silhouette thing gave them those powers, huh? But why? Does he control their minds or something?"

Holo-Reeve shook his head, and the image of the Smiling Shadow faded away, to be replaced by three-dimensional representations of a handful of Outriders. The sinister assemblage looked similar to the ones who'd accosted them outside the clubhouse. Black clothing with gray t-shirts emblazoned with faint white smiles, sunglasses, and wild, spiky or shaggy hair.

Even though they knew they were just holograms, the sight of them still made the stomachs of all three teenagers tighten in unpleasant ways. If Cruiser hadn't arrived, Abby thought, who knew what the Outriders might have done to them? And what if they had to face the Outriders again? She knew more about her heart-wand now, but not that much more...did she?

"The Outriders are all disaffected individuals," their guide went on. "Outcasts from society, criminals, loners, anti-social miscreants and scum. People who are eager to latch onto a leader who promises power and fortune. They are all volunteers, and each go through a painful process where the Smiling Shadow alters them. They gain the ability to conjure weapons and other objects made of solid dark energy. And all of their baseline human abilities are enhanced. Strength, speed, reflexes, endurance, durability, agility, senses, memory are all far above normal human levels."

Maxine folded her arms across her chest. "These guys are pretty much users of freaky steroids. Figures."

"They are also extensions of the Smiling Shadow, in that they can mentally communicate with him, turning them into a formidable network of evil."

"How many of them are there?" Abby asked.

"Their numbers have greatly varied over the years. The group has been as few as ten, and as many as fifty."

Maxine grunted. "No shortage of jerks with too much time on their hands in the world, I guess."

Brett pointed at Holo-Reeve. "Okay, Mac, so we know who the Smiling Shadow and his flunkies are. I can fill in the blanks; he arrived on Earth and went after Reeve."

"Indeed," Holo-Reeve replied. "The Pure Shore Club faced the menace of the Smiling Shadow several times over the years, but was never able to strike a decisive blow. Never was the Smiling Shadow, either. It has always been extraordinarily good at eluding capture and remaining undetected."

The holograms of the Outriders disappeared, and another menu appeared in front of them. The header read 'Smiling Shadow Encounters' and had a list of dates. Obviously they could select any of them and hear about the clash that took place on that date between the Pure Shore Club and their shady nemesis. One date drew their attention: the last date in the list, also marked 'Final Battle'.

"As much as I hate skipping to the end of the story," Abby said, "I think that's the one we want."

Brett and Maxine nodded, and Abby touched that date with her hand.

The menu vanished, and Holo-Reeve resumed speaking. "The Smiling Shadow grew frustrated not being able to strike a decisive blow against his enemies. So he tried a different strategy.

"He decided to bring a Pure Shore Club member over to his side."

CHAPTER TWENTY-NINE
A VISIT FROM LAUREN SAINT

Before any of them could further argue with Mr. Santillian, a shrill chime came over the clubhouse's overhead speakers.

"What's that?" Mindy asked.

"Proximity alarm," Mr. Santillian explained, walking to the conference table and tapping the wooden surface. It might have appeared to be ordinary wood, but in reality it housed several devices, including a three-dimensional hologram system. Parts of the wooden table slid back to reveal control interfaces. Mr. Santillian tapped keys, and a holographic image appeared above the conference table, projected by unseen equipment built into the table's wooden surface.

"Who are they?" Mindy wondered aloud.

"The FBI," Mr. Santillian said. Cruiser noted that Mr. Santillian rarely sounded shocked about anything, but he did now.

"The FBI?" Mindy exclaimed. "How do you know that?"

"They've been snooping around the campus," Mr. Santillian explained, "trying to find a link between the Jefford Academy and the mysterious ailment affecting the alumni."

The hologram showed six people, one of them recognizable as Special Agent Lauren Saint. She appeared to be examining the barn's door, unaware of what the unassuming exterior hid. The other agents were standing in a loose semicircle around her.

"Were you followed?" Mr. Santillian asked Cruiser.

She threw up her hands. "No way, sir. You know me better than that. I can spot a tail with the best of 'em."

"You're right," he conceded. "Stupid question. Well, regardless of how they found us, I need to go up there."

"Why?" Mindy asked. "All we have to do is keep quiet and they'll have to go away eventually, right?"

"You're thinking of this situation as if Reeve is still active," Mr. Santillian said, not bothering to mention that Reeve being inactive was his fault. He didn't need to elaborate any further. Everyone knew that without Reeve running the clubhouse's various safeguards against unauthorized entry, it wouldn't take much for the team of FBI agents to find their way in. Mr. Santillian had counted on the clubhouse's remote location and its obscurity keeping interlopers at bay. Now that fragile protection was gone, people were literally knocking on the door.

He turned and swept out of the room. "I'm going to talk to them," he said over his shoulder. Entering the foyer, he pulled his small remote control out of his pocket and began to thumb the key for the anti-gravity elevator that would sweep him up to the surface. Hearing footsteps, he turned to see his old students had followed him, varying degrees of concern and surprise on their faces.

"What are you going to tell them?" Cruiser asked. "That you like to hang out in old, dilapidated barns in the woods in your free time?"

Mr. Santillian gritted his teeth. "I'm sure I'll think of something once I reach the top." He sounded much more confident than he felt.

"We should come with you," Mindy suggested.

"No," he replied with a firm shake of his head. "You two being with me raises way too many questions. If need be, I will leave with them. You two can remain here until the coast is clear."

"And then what?" Cruiser asked. "Hide here in our hole like a couple of scared possums?"

"We'll reconnect later," he promised them.

Activating the controls, he left Cruiser and Mindy behind. Unlike the security measures, simpler clubhouse features like the lights, the holographic display, and the anti-gravity elevator could be turned on and used very easily. The security measures were more complicated to turn on and set up, and Mr. Santillian was uncertain he could do that without Reeve's help.

Arriving swiftly at the top, he reflected on how long it had been since he'd last used the elevator. He'd forgotten what it was like, the sensation of weightlessness. He'd forgotten about many things, he realized. How enjoyable it had been, in some ways, to be part of the Pure Shore Club. Banishing those nostalgic thoughts, he stalked to the door and opened it a crack, just enough to peer out at his visitors.

If Agent Saint or her cohorts were surprised to see him there, they didn't show it. All wore business suits, apparently dispensing with any pretense of operating undercover, along with their ever-present sunglasses. Clean-cut, fit, and serious-looking, they were every inch what you would expect government agents to look like.

"Yes, what is it?" he asked, realizing simultaneously that he probably sounded ridiculous, and that he hadn't thought of any explanations for his presence in the barn.

"Mr. Santillian," Agent Saint said, "we need you to come with us, please."

He hadn't expected that. "What's going on?"

Saint's expression didn't change, remaining calm. "We need to ask you a few more questions. Shouldn't take long."

Mr. Santillian decided to stall them, to try and find out more. "Questions? About what?" He looked past them and saw two black SUVs, that were doubtlessly the agents' vehicles, parked next to Crimson Cruiser's Chameleon Car.

"New facts have emerged that are realigning our investigation," Saint replied. "Now," she went on, her tone dropping a few degrees in temperature, "you will come with us."

Why so vague? he wondered. He narrowed his eyes. "How did you find me here?"

He expected that question to rile the agent, but instead her mouth twisted into a tight-lipped smile. "We've been tracking your movements," she told him. He noticed that Saint's fellow agents were also smiling. What's the big joke?

Before he could respond, Agent Saint reached out, and with surprising speed gripped the edge of the door and pushed it wide open, causing him to stumble backwards. He recovered quickly, but Saint had already stepped into the hallway, apparently not surprised by its modern appearance as compared with its exterior. With another swift movement, she reached out and took something off his shoulder.

"What...?" he started to ask, anger welling up inside him. He stopped short as Agent Saint showed him, palm up, what she had taken. It was a small, gray disc about the size of a nickel.

"A tracking device," she explained. "Made to turn the color of whatever we plant it on. In your case, the same color as that trench coat you always seem to wear."

He remembered Agent Saint's kind words to him during their last meeting back in the headmaster's office. The comforting touch on his shoulder. All she had been doing was planting the device on him.

"It's not just a tracking device," she went on, her thin smile spreading into a grin that reminded Mr. Santillian of a predatory animal about to take down its prey. Then he thought about her words, and various horrifying implications began to occur to him, sending his thoughts into a tailspin.

"You mean…" he said, fear strangling his voice to a raspy whisper.

"Oh, yes," Agent Saint replied. "It's also a listening device. We've heard everything you've said since we planted that device on you, and everything everyone around you has said as well. Now, what say you get your friends out here, and all of us return to the campus for a nice little chat?"

CHAPTER THIRTY
THE FATE OF STACY MCNIECE

"The Smiling Shadow got one of the Pure Shore Club on his side?" Brett asked. "But how? And who?"

"If you be quiet for more than a few seconds," Maxine said, "I bet he's going to tell us, Ace."

"Most of the club members would never betray their comrades," Holo-Reeve said, "not to mention ally themselves with a horror such as the Smiling Shadow. However, there was one. One who, somehow, was selected by the AmazeHeart to be a member, despite certain…character flaws. Selfishness, jealousy, and greed filled the heart of one young man, and made him a perfect target for the Smiling Shadow's insidious plan."

Abby thought, for what amounted to an automated narrator, this hologram of Reeve had a flair for the dramatic. Then she watched as the holograms of the Pure Club members began to disappear, one by one, until only one remained.

"Steven Endicott?" Abby said. "The boy who everyone thinks is missing?"

Brett walked up to the hologram of Steven, making quick notes on his phone. "So this is the guy who betrayed the club, huh? He doesn't look so tough."

And indeed, he didn't. Of course, they remembered seeing him in the yearbook photo of the Pure Shore Club. The only person shorter than him in the group was the petite Mindy Nakajima. He had a round, doughy face and otherwise bland features. Unlike the impressive costumes of some of his cohorts, his outfit consisted of simple pants and boots, and a tunic with an equals sign emblazoned on the chest.

"What were his powers, anyway?" Maxine asked. "The ability to do math?"

Holo-Reeve drifted over to peer closely at the hologram of Steven. The holograms looked so real they had to remind themselves that neither man before them was real. "Hardly. Steven, who went by the codename Even Steven, may have been the most powerful Pure Shore Club member in all its history."

Brett whistled. "Wow, that's a pretty strong statement."

"Indeed, my boy. You see, Even Steven's power is to counteract any attack made against him. If you try to hit him, burn him, shoot him, drop something on him…you name it, his power comes up with a countermeasure all on its own without him even thinking about it."

"Then it requires no conscious thought," Abby mused. "He can be walking along and if someone drops a piano on him from above he's still okay."

"Correct," Holo-Reeve confirmed. "But despite his impressive power, Steven was discontent. He wanted more power, and to be the club's leader."

"He wanted to take Mr. Santillian's place?" Brett asked.

"No, Mr. Santillian is only the faculty advisor. After each year's club is formed, a student leader, usually a senior, is selected. Even from the time of his freshman year, Steven thought it was his right to be the leader. From his point of view, the person who cannot be defeated should be the leader."

"Power by might alone," Maxine said aloud. Her parents and their corporate tactics, what she knew of them, came to mind.

"He didn't understand that there were other qualities sought after in the club leader…selflessness, tactical thinking, the ability to inspire. When his senior year came around, he felt that even though he was turned down for the position in previous years, his chance had finally arrived. Surely he would not be turned down then. But the position went to Michael Alvarez instead, and Steven was secretly enraged. It was in this state that the Smiling Shadow, perhaps sensing the dark state of the young man's heart, approached him and made him some sort of offer, the details of which are unknown. But the long and short of it is, he let the Smiling Shadow and its Outriders into the clubhouse."

The view around them began to shift, showing them quick snapshots of the Outriders in the clubhouse with the Smiling Shadow and Even Steven. Just like the previous images Holo-Reeve had shown them, it was hard to believe they were inside a small underground enclosure. The illusions all had depth and looked realistic enough to touch. Even Maxine found herself wanting to duck or flinch when what seemed like living bodies came too close.

The Pure Shore Club had evidently arrived at their clubhouse to find their enemies had stormed the place. Images flashed before their eyes of a huge fight. They saw Michael Alvarez in his superhero regalia, the outfit gleaming like it was made of white light, blasting away at Outriders with some kind of energy he projected from his hands. Brett noted that Michael appeared to be capable of flying and floating. Stacy McNiece was also present, fighting the Outriders with a sword, not surprising for someone who dressed like a swashbuckling pirate. The other Pure Shore Club members fought too and appeared to be outnumbered about five to one.

"There was a big rhubarb, obviously," Brett said. "So did they win?"

Maxine looked at him, one dark eyebrow raised. "Did you say…rhubarb?"

"I can explain later," Abby whispered to the other girl.

"It depends on how you look at what happened," their guide told them. "It turned out, the Smiling Shadow was not just out to destroy Reeve and the Pure Shore Club. When the club members arrived, they found that the Smiling Shadow was trying to access the AmazeHeart. More specifically—"

"It wanted the Empowerer," Abby interrupted. "That's why Reeve gave it to us…he even said so! That we had to keep it safe from the Smiling Shadow!"

Brett rubbed his chin. "But why? What's the big grinning inkblot's interest in that doohickey? Does he want to hang it on his Christmas tree or something?"

Holo-Reeve had halted the rapidly shifting barrage of images, stopping on one that showed the Shadow next to the AmazeHeart. Outriders were all around it, and Even Steven was nearby as well. They appeared to be holding the good guys off while the Smiling Shadow's dark form protruded multiple shadow-tentacles. Each one was inserted into the AmazeHeart, obviously trying to crack open the giant orb and gain access to its contents.

"Yes. As you know, the Empowerer is what grants powers and special objects of power to the Pure Shore Club. When Steven told him about it, the Smiling Shadow realized that if he gained access to it, he could figure out how to increase the powers of his followers, but also his own power could be enhanced exponentially as well. No one ever figured out what exactly he intended to do once he gained access to the Empowerer."

"They stopped him from getting it, huh?" Maxine asked.

Holo-Reeve's expression grew grave. "Yes…but at a terrible cost. Watch and learn, my young visitors."

The image showed Reeve moving in to stop the Smiling Shadow, even as the rest of the club fought a mob of Outriders. The image of the professorial old man was gone, and Reeve had manifested as a golden giant. He looked like an Oscar statue come to life, shiny and featureless. He slammed into the Smiling Shadow and the two began to grapple, gleaming titan versus dark mass. As they struggled, it became evident their clash was taking place on deeper levels than what was obvious. Reeve's golden surface began to crack and lose its luster in spots, while the Smiling Shadow's dark form began turning gray. Parts of it broke off and floated aimlessly in the air, not re-connecting to the central body. It was obvious they were hurting one another.

Yet through it all, the Smiling Shadow's ever-present ghost-grin never faltered. Then Reeve appeared to be dealt a grievous blow, staggering backward, his golden form fuzzy around the edges, then winking out of sight completely. All the Pure Shore Club members looked stricken at what had happened and began fighting with a renewed determination. They appeared to be driving the Outriders back. Some of the black-clad warriors were fleeing the area, others were unconscious on the floor, others were bitterly fighting on.

The Smiling Shadow, his primary opponent vanquished, immediately returned to his task of cracking the AmazeHeart. Rather than the many small tendrils it had extruded before, it assaulted the glowing sphere with a single, massive, continuous dark blast. The orb's surface began to crack where the blast struck it. It was obvious that the villain was very close to getting what he wanted.

Then they watched as Stacy McNiece, the Buccaneer, managed to break away from the melee and rushed towards the Shadow. Mr. Santillian, occupied with fighting several Outriders at once, reached out a hand in her direction, obviously calling out to her. Abby was pretty good at reading lips, and she was certain the teacher was calling after his student, "No, Stacy…stay away…" All three of them winced as Mr. Santillian, distracted by Stacy's heroic effort, was struck by an Outrider and sent flying into a wall, where he crumpled to the floor, obviously knocked out.

Stacy reached the Smiling Shadow, who seemed not to notice her. Her sword flashed, held high, ready to strike. She was not the only one in motion; Even Steven was running in to intercept her, to protect his chosen ally. But he was too late. Stacy brought her blade down, severing the Smiling Shadow's connection to the AmazeHeart.

Then everything was obscured by bright light, so bright they had to shield their eyes. The light was gone as quickly as it had appeared, and when they could see again, their surroundings were the rounded copper walls of the time capsule once more. Holo-Reeve stood before them, his hands behind his back.

"What happened?" Maxine asked, blinking to get the afterimage of the sudden flash out of her eyes. "Your fancy equipment go on the fritz or something?"

"Good to know even alien super-technology breaks down, huh?" Brett asked. "Here I was beginning to feel like a caveman with all this high-tech hokum all around me."

Abby realized what had happened. Brett and Maxine were assuming there had been a technical malfunction in the time capsule's hologram projectors, but that was surely not the case.

"There was an explosion, wasn't there?" she asked. "When Stacy McNiece cut the Smiling Shadow."

Holo-Reeve nodded, his eyes steady and unblinking. "Yes, apparently the Smiling Shadow's intrusion into the AmazeHeart was, shall we say, quite volatile. By severing the connection, Stacy triggered a rather large feedback pulse. Mr. Santillian and the other Pure Shore Club members were protected by an energy shield created by Michael Alvarez. But the Smiling Shadow, Even Steven, and Stacy McNiece were all annihilated, due to their proximity to the explosion."

"Annihilated?" Brett asked. "You mean…just…" He struggled to find words.

"Vaporized," Abby said, her voice almost a whisper. She couldn't imagine what it would have been like for the survivors. One minute your friend is there, the next, they simply…are not. The very thought made her feel ill.

"But wait a minute," Maxine put in, "there was a funeral for Stacy and everything. Didn't they bury a body?"

"That's a good point," Brett said, making more notes on his phone. "Obviously Mr. Santillian and the others covered up what really happened. That field trip accident story was just a smokescreen. So, how'd they explain no body?"

Holo-Reeve spread his wizened hands. "Before the explosion, Reeve was severely damaged. After the explosion, he was in even worse shape. It was decided how they would cover up the deaths of Stacy and Steven, and they realized they would have to stage everything so at least one body was recoverable to allay suspicion. Reeve was able to use what little power he had left to construct ersatz remains to resemble Stacy."

Abby shuddered at the thought. "Mr. Santillian really went along with that? That's really…gross. Gross and wrong!"

Maxine folded her arms across her chest. "I'm with Abby. Awfully macabre, isn't it? Is that really the sort of thing superheroes do? If so, I'm not sure I want any part of this club."

Brett rolled his eyes. "Oh, come on, you two. Desperate times call for desperate measures. What would you have done? Blown the lid off the whole shebang for the whole world to see? They had to cover their tracks."

"I'd expect you to be the last person praising their obsessive need for secrecy," Maxine said, stabbing an accusing finger at the fedora-wearing teenager. "Aren't you Mr. Newsflash? Taking notes this whole time, hoping to make your rep by exposing the Pure Shore

Club to the world. Aren't you being a tiny bit hypocritical by agreeing with what they did?"

"I don't agree with it, champ," Brett protested. "It's just that I can see where they were coming from. If I was in their shoes, and all that. But obviously I'm not."

Abby thought about the entire situation. How the parents of Stacy and Steven had been lied to. How the whole school had been lied to, the whole community. It all struck her as very unethical. Not to mention the Outrider who had been transformed for that purpose. As evil as the Outriders seemed to be, they surely had parents and siblings like anyone else. But she realized Brett might be right. If she was in their shoes, faced with those tough choices, would she have argued for a different outcome?

"Believe me," Brett went on, "I'm still planning on telling the whole world about what's going on here. They'll be sorry they inducted Mama Cho's little boy into their club, that's for sure!"

"That's more like it," Maxine said with a nod.

"Although," Brett said, stroking his chin, "surely there was an investigation of some kind. Steven and Stacy's families would've wanted answers."

"There was an investigation," Holo-Reeve confirmed. "But Reeve did his work well, and Mr. Santillian was cleared of any wrongdoing, and maintained his position here at the Jefford Academy. The families were devastated, of course, but they accepted it was a simple, unfortunate accident."

Something occurred to Abby. "Wait a minute…if the Smiling Shadow was blown up, how come everyone thinks it's still around?"

Brett continued to take notes. "Well, I wouldn't say everyone thinks that. Michael Alvarez and Reeve might, but Mr. Santillian sure doesn't. Okay, Answer-Man," he addressed Holo-Reeve, "tell us about that. Why does Alvarez think this bad guy is back? Does he have any evidence or something?"

Holo-Reeve continued to stand there, his hands behind his back. "I am not programmed with the answer to that question," he told them.

"Figures," Maxine muttered.

"If it is back," Abby said, wheels spinning in her mind, "then maybe it's somehow responsible for what's happened to the Pure Shore Club alumni. Maybe it has nothing to do with Reeve at all!"

Maxine leaned against one of the sloping copper walls. "Well, that's a possibility, I guess. The problem is, our friendly guide here listed off the Shadow's superpowers. Putting people into incurable comas wasn't one of them."

Abby looked at each of them. "Maybe it learned a new trick?"

•   •   •

Mr. Santillian couldn't close the door because Agent Saint was standing in the threshold, blocking the way with her body. He also didn't think he stood much of a chance of darting past the phalanx of agents just beyond her. Even if he could, he would be out in the forest, on foot. He couldn't start Cruiser's Chameleon Car, it was linked to her and drivable by her and her alone.

But if he went backwards, the FBI agents might find the anti-gravity elevator and reach the others. The FBI knew they were in the area due to their listening device, but Mr. Santillian still didn't want to contribute to them being arrested by the government. So he took the only option available to him.

He fought. The trench coat-wearing teacher charged at Agent Saint like a football player. She was a tall woman, and doubtless in good shape, but he counted on his large frame being sufficient to bowl her out of the way.

Mr. Santillian collided into her and realized that his life was destined to be full of rude surprises. It was like running into a wall. The wind knocked out of him, Mr. Santillian staggered backward a few steps. Then it was Saint's turn to rush him. Her hands were outstretched, obviously intending to get him in some kind of hold. They began to grapple, his long coat flapping in the air like useless wings. She was much stronger than he expected, but he managed to bash her in the face with his elbow, sending her ever-present sunglasses flying against the wall. Saint's iron grip loosened and he broke free.

He intended to race past her, even though he was unsure how to deal with the other five agents who stood outside. Stealing a glance at Saint to make sure she was still stunned, he began to run—

—and stopped short. For the first time, he could see Special Agent Lauren Saint's eyes. He'd thought her wearing sunglasses at all times was just a silly affectation. He was wrong.

She wasn't stunned, merely staring at him, her mouth scrunched into a nasty smirk. And her eyes were not normal eyes. There was no white part of the eye, no iris. It was like her pupils had stretched out and covered her entire eyeballs. It was a sight he knew well. It meant dark power resided within Agent Saint, and likely the other agents as well.

They were Outriders!

CHAPTER THIRTY-ONE
DARKNESS FALLS

"Okay, history lesson's over," Maxine announced. "I think we know everything we need to know, don't you?"

Brett chewed the tip of his stylus. "Not quite. We still don't know where we fit into all of this."

"What's not to know?" Maxine asked. "Michael Alvarez the Vanishing Wonder and Reeve the Alien Superhero-Creating Computer wanted to revive their little club. Mr. Santillian put the kibosh on it. They still managed to pull us into it, mostly due to our own curiosity. We wanted to find out what was going on, what this stupid club was all about. Now we know. I think we're done, right?"

Maxine's words caused Abby's stomach to clench. Here it was, everything she was afraid of. The mystery was solved, they had reached the end of the road. The adventure was over, and they were now going to split up. Her new friends were going to each go their own way and leave her alone again.

But the adventure wasn't over, was it?

"No," Abby spoke up, her voice meek as a mouse. "It's not over yet."

Maxine squinted at her. "What do you mean?"

The blond girl was staring at the floor, her eyes wide as her mind whirled with possibilities. "What if they weren't just trying to start up the club again? What if it's true, and that Smiling Shadow…thing…isn't dead? What if it's still out there, and we're the ones who have to fight it?"

Brett held up his hands. "Say what? Hold on, Blondie. Even if that's true…you really think they recruited the three of us to fight that living blackout? Come on, we're just a bunch of kids!"

"So were any of the Pure Shore Club members," Abby shot back, startling Brett and herself with her bluntness. "Since when does age matter when it comes to fighting evil? Do you know how many people our age lied about how old they really were and signed up to fight in World War II? Or how in the English Navy, kids even younger than us signed on as officers? Just because we're kids doesn't mean we can't do our part."

Brett looked thoughtful. "I guess you have a point there…Heck, my grandpa was sixteen when he entered the Army, back in the day. But regardless, it's not like Reeve had the chance to give us any training or anything. We barely know how to use these crazy superpowers they stuck us with."

"That's true," Maxine said. "If they'd wanted us to help them, they should have done things right. If we go fight that Smiling Shadow creature—if it's even real, or back from the dead—we're likely to get ourselves killed. I, for one, want to live to graduate high school."

"Lofty goal you got there, champ," Brett said. "Speaking for me, I'd like to write this story up. It's going to be like a booster rocket for my reporting career, let me tell you."

Abby couldn't believe Brett was still sticking to that after everything they'd heard. How could he think about being a reporter when something like the Smiling Shadow might be running around loose?

Brett tucked his phone into his inside coat pocket and took a step towards Abby. "Look, Blondie," he said, his voice placating and kind, "I know you feel like your folks abandoned you here at Jefford and went off on an adventure without you. I know how you feel like this Pure Shore Club business was your adventure. But sometimes things don't work out exactly like we want 'em too."

Maxine looked at Abby, noticing how the other girl's eyes were watering. Abby was biting her lower lip and looking at the floor. Maxine guessed this was all coming from some conversation Brett and Abby had when she hadn't been around. It didn't bother her, she had already guessed this about Abby Alvarson from what she knew of her background.

"But...the sickness," Abby said, her voice even quieter than before. "The thing that's making all the other Pure Shore Club members ill. What if it gets us, too?"

Brett smiled. "I think if that was going to affect the three of us, it would have by now."

Maxine couldn't let that one go by. "What, are you some kind of medical doctor? How could you possibly know that?"

He shrugged, causing his leather jacket to crinkle loudly in the enclosed space of the time capsule. "I don't. But come on, the FBI and Mr. Santillian are on the case. I bet that Crimson Cruiser dame is helping them too. Whatever is going on, they'll fix it, and we can go on our merry way."

Maxine walked to Abby's side and placed a hand on the other girl's shoulder. "Look, Abby. If it makes you feel better, we'll go to Mr. Santillian, or find that Crimson Cruiser lady. They don't have us in the dark anymore. We can talk to them, straighten things out. We can even give them the Empowerer back, let them handle it from here."

"Since when are you Ms. Make-Nice?" Brett asked, pointing a finger at Maxine. "For the past two days you've been ready to lay into all of those people for jerking us around."

"I'm full of surprises," Maxine replied without looking at him. "So, what do you say, Abby? We can go talk to them? Maybe talk them into letting us keep these wonderful new toys?"

Abby continued to stare at the ground. "Sure," she said, her voice as morose as they'd ever heard it. She thought about her dorm room. Her books. Her saxophone. She didn't want to go back to just doing those things. She'd had a glimpse behind the curtain, she thought. She'd seen a layer of reality beyond the day-to-day things everyone normally saw. Superheroes. Secret underground headquarters. Living computers from outer space. She wanted to keep on exploring this new world, as scary and confusing as it all was. But that was about to end.

Brett was looking at the Holo-Reeve, who had stood by the entire time they'd been talking, still as a statue and staring into space.

"Jeeves," Brett addressed him, "back to the surface, pronto. We appreciate the info overload, but we've got business to take care of topside. Mama Cho's little boy has himself a story to file, and—"

The time capsule elevated them to the surface just as suddenly as it had sucked them downwards. The trio popped back out to ground level, the earth crunching shut under each of them in a split second. It was as if the holes had never existed. But they didn't notice that—other things were seizing their attention at that moment.

The campus was very different than when they'd gone into the time capsule. The first thing they noticed was the bitter cold, a winter chill that had no business being in the autumn season. Abby could see her breath, and she hugged herself to be warm. Brett zipped shut his jacket, and Maxine just took the unexpected extreme of temperature stoically.

It was also dark. The sun wasn't visible, not even the vestiges of a sunset. The sky was completely black, with no stars or moon. All around them, the campus was shrouded in darkness.

"Holy cats!" Brett exclaimed, looking around in shock. "How long were we down there?"

"Not this long," Maxine remarked. They pulled out their phones to check the time.

"It's only four thirty," he said, his horrified expression barely visible in the darkness. "What's going on? Is it the end of the world? Because if so, I'm gonna be mighty hacked off!"

Before either of the girls could reply or suggest what to do next, they heard a noise. It had been eerily quiet, but now there was a noise, drifting to their ears over the still, chilled air. It was the sound of laughter. Horrible, cold, evil laughter. Soft, in the distance, but growing louder and louder with each passing moment.

They stood rooted to the spot in awe and fear as a dark shape drifted past the nearby Jefford Rocket. It was only noticeable because it was even darker than the unnatural nighttime all around them. That, and there was a faint, ghostly white smile in the center of its form.

It was travelling rapidly, crossing the campus and soaring past them before any of them had a chance to react. The sinister laughter faded into the distance, and all three of them found the air had grown even colder with its passing.

"W-was that...?" Brett asked, his eyes wide as coasters.

"Sure looked like it," Maxine replied grimly, staring into the empty sky with narrowed eyes. "And unless I'm mistaken, it's heading in the direction of the clubhouse."

Abby hugged herself even tighter, hurting her own arms. She'd been trying with all her might not to let her teeth chatter, but after seeing the Smiling Shadow, she gave up and chattered away. "W-well, Brett…I g-guess y-your grandfather was r-right."

"How's that?" he asked, still staring at the area where the Smiling Shadow had flown by.

"Adventure has a way of finding you."

CHAPTER THIRTY-TWO
ENEMY ATTACK

With the realization the FBI agents—if they were even truly FBI agents—were actually Outriders, Mr. Santillian decided the time for holding back, for concealment of his true nature, was long over.

He swept his hands towards each other, each hand brushing the opposite wrist's pistol-shaped cuff link. There were twin flashes of light as the cuff links transformed into full-size pistols. They looked like old-time flintlock pistols, colored silver with black accents, but their output was decidedly not old-time.

With a pistol in each hand, he mentally selected the appropriate ammunition, and in fluid motions, he aimed and fired at his assailants. Lightning bolts, blue and white and crackling, burst forth from the twin barrels and lanced across the distance between him and the Outriders.

Saint was too quick, diving to one side. The bolts streaked through the space she had just occupied and struck two of her cohorts. Each one jerked and danced where they stood for an instant, then the lightning enveloped them and each man blew up in a burst of red sparks and a smell of brimstone.

Ignoring the loss of her two comrades, Saint rolled and came up in a crouch, her back braced against the corridor wall, and in a split second had her own weapon in her hand. It was a dark pistol, one of the typical weapons of the Outriders. She fired quickly, sending a swarm of dark bolts towards Mr. Santillian.

He willed one of his pistols to project a round, clear force field that appeared just in front of the pistol's barrel. The dark bolts bounced off the force field, spraying into the walls, creating fiery, smoldering micro-craters.

At least my old tricks still work, he thought. He sized up his situation and realized it wasn't promising. He had no cover whatsoever inside the barn, and there were still four of them and only one of him. With his other pistol, he raked the entryway with more lightning, creating a near-deafening crackling and an ever-increasing odor of ozone. He was keeping the other three Outriders at bay, but it was only a matter of time before they rushed him.

Yet he couldn't retreat. He couldn't let these scum into the clubhouse. Not again. So, he decided to do the unexpected, and charge.

Saint seemed genuinely surprised when he rushed past her and charged the door, firing with both guns as we went. His only hope was to keep them pinned down long enough to get into the forest. Then he could plan his next move.

He was surprised when Saint came flying past him, like she'd been shot out of a cannon. She flew through the air and plowed into one of the Outriders in front of him. They went into the dirt like someone had lobbed two sacks of potatoes. He glanced backward—

—to see Mindy and Cruiser running behind him, both wearing their superhero gear. They'd come up the anti-gravity elevator, he realized, having seen what was going on using the clubhouse's external cameras, and they were coming to his rescue. He was simultaneously annoyed with his former students for disobeying him and relieved.

Cruiser reached out to her Chameleon Car with her mind and remote-started it. The engine roared to life, obviously startling the Outriders who remained on their feet. They spun towards the car, just in time to see it barreling towards them. Both men were hit, flying off in different directions.

Saint and the man who she had been thrown at were already back on their feet.

"Surrender, Mr. Santillian!" Saint cried. "Your defeat is inevitable!"

"Next time, Outrider," he growled in return, not really caring if she heard him or not. They were running towards the Chameleon Car, its doors already swinging up to admit them. He fired wildly behind them, trying to occupy Saint and the other remaining Outrider with evading his blasts instead of aiming at their backs.

Cruiser and Mindy dove into the car, and Mr. Santillian was about to follow when something caught his eye. Cruiser had the car angled towards the only road out of the woods, and coming down that road was a veritable sea of Outriders. There were Outriders on black motorcycles and Outriders gliding through the air on dark wings like wicked, human-sized bats. They were a grim sight, all black and gray clothes, rolling and soaring into the clearing like a sinister tide.

Mr. Santillian got over his shock quickly and jumped in.

"Looks like our buddy the FBI agent has reinforcements, sir," Cruiser remarked as Mr. Santillian dropped into the seat next to her.

"Pretty certain she's not a real FBI agent," Mr. Santillian told her. "I've been played for a fool, I'm afraid."

"Getting out this way is going to be pretty difficult," Mindy spoke up from the back seat. "They've even got the skies blocked off, so you can't switch to helicopter mode."

Mr. Santillian's mouth compressed into a tight line as he assessed the situation. "We shouldn't have tried to escape this way," he said. "We should have gone below, destroyed the clubhouse. If we leave, it belongs to them."

"Can't be helped now, sir," Cruiser snapped. "There're too many of these yo-yos. We've got to get out of here!"

He hated to admit it, but she was right. Their best hope at this point was to escape to fight another day. "Go!" he ordered.

The car sped into high gear, racing towards the phalanx of Outriders driving down the road towards them. The Outriders were loyal to the Smiling Shadow but not stupid. They steered their cycles out of the way, but fired at the car as it raced past. Dark bolts scored dents and tiny smoking craters in the Chameleon Car's gleaming scarlet surface, but it zoomed onward. Cruiser drove too fast for anyone to get a direct hit.

It seemed like they were about to get away—the Outriders weren't willing to block them, and the swarm of black-clad warriors was thinning—then Cruiser's sharp eyes spotted something up ahead, blocking the road. Whatever it was, it was dark, and it was large.

"What is that?" Cruiser asked, leaning forward and gripping the wheel tighter. Mr. Santillian peered closely, and Mindy also squinted into the distance. Cruiser briefly switched the windshield to magnification mode, showing a blown-up view of the mysterious obstacle.

It was a dark, amorphous mass, with a huge white smile in the center. The sight chilled all three of them to the bone, bringing to mind unwelcome memories of bitter betrayal and loss.

"Michael was right," Mr. Santillian whispered, his voice so low the noise of the Chameleon Car's engine almost drowned him out. "Reeve, Ethan…they were right. It's not dead. It's really, truly not dead." His hand went to his coat pocket, and he felt the bulge of Stacy McNiece's brooch there. Involuntarily, he swallowed hard.

"What do we do?" Cruiser asked, her blue eyes wide. She was already slowing down. She glanced at Mr. Santillian, but his eyes were riveted on the Smiling Shadow, an expression somewhere between horror and awe on his face. Cruiser grit her teeth, having no idea what to do next. Mindy's powers were short-range, and Cruiser couldn't ask her friend to close the distance with the Smiling Shadow.

She was cycling through options of other vehicles she could transform the car into so they could escape when Mr. Santillian suddenly broke out of the seeming trance he'd been in.

"Roll down my window, Cruiser," he ordered.

She immediately complied, seeing he still had his super-pistols gripped in each hand. Mr. Santillian leaned out the window and did the only thing he could do: blast the Smiling Shadow with everything he had. Twin bolts of blue-white lightning streaked forth from his pistols, lighting the darkness between them and their old enemy.

From the center of the Smiling Shadow, red lightning bolts shot forth as if in response. Mr. Santillian, Cruiser, and Mindy barely had time to register that this had never been one of the Smiling Shadow's powers when the energy blasts met in mid-air and exploded. The shockwave hit the Chameleon Car like it'd run into a wall. The car flipped backwards, and they all yelled and grabbed for handholds as the world tumbled outside the windows all around them.

Then, with a bone-crunching BOOM, the red car landed on its roof. It rattled, wheels still spinning, then was utterly still. The Smiling Shadow drifted towards them, taking its time, cackling softly, serenely confident in its victory. Outriders were coming up from the other direction, sandwiching the car between them.

The car morphed, solid metal flowing and ebbing like water, until it was a dented, cracked motorcycle, lying at Cruiser's side. Mr. Santillian and Mindy were unmoving on the ground, limbs splayed out, both quite unconscious from the impact. By some miracle, Cruiser still had some of her wits about her. Through blurred vision, she surveyed the scene around her. Her fallen, senseless comrades. The villains, closing in from the front and rear. Her only chance, she knew, would be to take off into the forest on her bike, try to evade capture and hopefully track down some Pure Shore Club members who hadn't fallen into comas yet. She hated to leave the others behind, but she knew she was their only hope.

Staggering to her feet, she tried to raise the motorcycle up on two wheels. But the strain was too great, and she fell to her knees, the cycle clattering to the road. As far as she could tell, she wasn't that badly hurt, but something was sapping her will, overriding her desire to fight with an unnatural, paralyzing fear.

"Feeling rooted to the spot, my dear Crimson Cruiser?" the Smiling Shadow said, floating up to a few meters away and coming to a stop. Cruiser had forgotten how horrible the sinister hiss of the thing's voice was. "That would be my doing. I can't have you leaving us, not when our little party has only just begun."

Her eyes narrowed as she fought a wave of nausea that racked her body. "How…?" she whispered. "That red lightning…you've never been able to do that…"

The Smiling Shadow chuckled. "Quite right. I've never been able to do that. And I still cannot. You see, my sweet Cruiser, the Pure Shore Club are not the only ones who can work as a team."

Its form rippled, bubbled in the center, and broke apart. Out walked a man from inside the Smiling Shadow. It was a man Cruiser remembered from the past, a man she knew full well could have created the countermeasure to Mr. Santillian's lightning blasts.

"Steven," she whispered. The horror being projected into her mind by the Smiling Shadow went up several notches. Even Steven strode right up to her, his walk casual, confident. Like a conquering general striding on occupied land. It wasn't just the Smiling Shadow who had survived certain death. But how? The Shadow she could understand, it was an extraterrestrial construct, an unearthly power. Steven was just a human being. He had no business being here, walking around and alive. Her head swam, and she fought the urge to black out.

"Yep," he said. "Back from the dead, ready to pay back some old debts. I've had a long, difficult time as I've recuperated. A long time to lick my wounds, nurse old grudges." He stopped right in front of her and bent down to look into her dazed, unfocused eyes.

"I think I'm going to enjoy this," he said, his round face splitting into a broad grin. He motioned to a nearby Outrider. The black-clad man produced a gun made of solid darkness. He aimed at Cruiser and fired.

Then all was darkness.

CHAPTER THIRTY-THREE
THE FROZEN CAMPUS

"What's wrong with them?" Abby asked, her voice hushed.

"I don't think you need to whisper, Abby," Maxine replied. "I don't think they can hear you."

Abby found she had to agree. As they made their way through the campus, walking in perpetual shadow, their breath making clouds in the air, they encountered fellow students here and there. To a person, they were frozen to the spot, utterly still, each with a thousand-yard stare.

"It's like they're all statues!" Brett remarked, peering closely at a boy named Dean from his History class. Dean's mouth was as wide open as an airplane hangar door, his arms dangling at his sides like slack vines. Brett waved his hand in front of Dean's face. "Hey, Dean-o! Say something, buddy!" Dean displayed no reaction whatsoever.

As they continued through the darkened campus, they kept seeing other students, and the occasional faculty member or school worker. Some stood alone, others clustered in groups. It was as if they were all walking along and some strange phenomenon came by and rooted them all where they were.

Maxine saw girls she knew from the soccer team, others from cross-country. Brett saw Jen Mallory, the editor of the school paper, and Deadman Davidson, his next-door neighbor. Abby didn't know the names of too many people but saw plenty of familiar faces, including a short upperclassman girl who pulled a regular shift at the front desk in the girl's dorm.

"This is really creepy," Maxine said as they continued wandering the campus. Brett and Abby agreed. They had never been anywhere so quiet in their lives. There were no voices, no car engines, not even the sound of wind rustling tree leaves. Everything was utterly still. Still, and very, very cold.

Abby hugged herself tighter, shivering in the unnatural chill. Brett doffed his leather jacket and passed it over to her. She accepted it gratefully, quickly donning it but finding it didn't entirely screen out the unseasonable temperature.

"What did the Smiling Shadow do?" she asked, knowing Maxine and Brett wouldn't know any more than she did. "And where did it go?"

Brett gulped. "I'm not sure I want to find out."

"Well, what we can do is stick with the original plan," Maxine said. "Find the Cruiser, or Mr. Santillian. Tell them where the Empowerer is. They can deal with this mess."

"You're assuming they haven't been frozen, too," Brett pointed out.

Maxine blinked. "Why would they be? We're not."

"Who knows why that is? Maybe it's because when the Shadow did this, we were underground in the time capsule, so we didn't get affected. If we find either one of them, they might be useless for anything except being a department store mannequin."

"Or maybe it doesn't affect Pure Shore Club members," she snapped. "You heard that talking encyclopedia down there. We're different now, somehow…changed. Alien technology working inside of us. Maybe it makes us immune to this…freeze effect."

Brett folded his arms across his chest. "I don't think you can assume that. Besides, if Mr. Santillian and Cruiser were around and not frozen, don't you think we'd have noticed them by now? They'd be just as freaked out as we are. I think Cruiser would be racing to us right now if she could."

Maxine jabbed her index finger into Brett's chest. "Okay, smart guy, then tell us what to do. What great plan do you have, Ace? Leave a threatening message for Michael Alvarez again? Oh, wait, I forgot! He's turned into a ghost and for all we know has faded away for good."

Abby shoved her hands deep into the pockets of Brett's jacket and closed her eyes. Something was nagging her, dancing on the edge of her mind. If only Maxine and Brett would stop arguing for a moment, she could think of it.

"I say we call our parents, get them involved," Brett was saying. "Heck, the FBI is already snooping around here, so people outside of the school are already aware something is up. Maybe the cops can be called in, or the army."

Maxine rolled her eyes. "I am not calling my parents, Brett."

"Fine, then I'll call mine," he shot back. He whipped out his phone from his pants pockets and selected a number from his contacts. No signal. His phone just returned dead air, no matter what number he called to reach his parents. He even tried some of his buddies from the old neighborhood. Nothing. "Okay, fine," he said, snapping the phone shut and stuffing it back into his pocket, "that doesn't work. The Smiling Shadow must be laying down some interference or something."

"Great," Maxine muttered. "Now what?"

Abby spoke up. "Why don't we see how far this goes?"

They looked at her.

"Come again, Blondie?" Brett asked.

"This," Abby said, spreading her arms to indicate the freeze effect. "Why don't we walk and see how far we have to go before it stops? I mean, what if it's not just the campus that's like this? What if it's bigger? What if it's—"

"The whole world?" Maxine asked. "That's a pleasant thought. But a good one. Just leave it to me."

She placed her shoulder bag on the ground and opened it, pulling out her white and gold roller blades. It was so dark the golden wheels couldn't gleam.

"I'm not walking anywhere," she told them.

CHAPTER THIRTY-FOUR
THE TRIUMPH OF EVEN STEVEN

Michael Alvarez found his powers were stabilizing. Somewhat. This time he was able to will himself to appear in the clubhouse, instead of careening between various places he wanted to go. He'd theorized that if he calmed down and waited, whatever effect the Smiling Shadow had on his powers would correct itself, that the amazing nanotechnology that enabled his abilities to work would perform self-maintenance. It seems he'd been right.

Looking down at himself, he saw he wasn't transparent anymore. That was a start, he thought. He pushed his hand toward the nearest wall and it sank into the solid surface. Unfortunately, he was still intangible.

Oh well, he thought. Baby steps, baby steps. Now that he was at the clubhouse, he needed to talk to Mr. Santillian and the others. Cruiser was likely at the clubhouse already, but Michael highly doubted his former teacher was listening to reason.

When he materialized, he found himself in the boy's bunk room, unused bunk beds lining the walls. Reeve had kept the place up well, Michael observed. The clubhouse was kept at a state of near-readiness the past few months, preparing for the time the club would rise again. Only it hadn't quite turned out the way they'd planned.

Hearing voices, he floated to the door and began to descend the staircase. He stopped short when he caught glimpses of people moving in the foyer beyond. Stomping footsteps alerted him that all was not well. Using his intangible state to his advantage, he jumped into a staircase wall, then tilted his head out just enough so only one eye looked out. Hopefully, whoever the visitors were, they wouldn't be too observant.

Michael was shocked to see Outriders. Dozens of Outriders, streaming down the stairs, barking orders, laughing, pushing and shoving each other. Was he too late? Had the enemy struck so quickly?

He made his way down the stairs, staying inside the wall but keeping an eye out—literally—to see what was going on. Reaching the clubhouse's center, he saw wave after wave of Outriders floating down the anti-gravity elevator. It was just as he'd feared. Mr. Santillian had shut down Reeve and played right into the enemy's hands. Now they were running loose in the clubhouse. Alarm welled up in his gut. If the Outriders were here, then where were Mr. Santillian and the others?

His unspoken question was answered when a group of Outriders floated into view, descending from above like a host of dark angels. The Outriders were in pairs, each pair carrying a limp, unconscious, battered form.

Michael's jaw clenched as he saw Mr. Santillian, Cruiser, and Mindy were prisoners. Each of them looked like they'd been in a fight, which didn't surprise him. He just wished he could have been there to help them.

But as he looked at the number of Outriders entering the clubhouse, he knew his presence wouldn't have done much good. He probably would've been captured, too. He watched as all three of his friends were dragged into the AmazeHeart chamber, the door sliding shut behind them.

Michael was startled when the Outriders suddenly stopped what they were doing and lined the walls, snapping to attention like soldiers. Floating down the anti-gravity elevator was the black, ever-shifting form of the Smiling Shadow, Even Steven at his side.

Michael gulped. He wasn't sure if the Smiling Shadow could sense his presence, but he wasn't about to find out. Sticking around wasn't going to do much good anyway. Now there was only one hope, and he had to get out. With the speed of thought, he vanished.

●　　●　　●

Steven felt like a conquering celestial entity floating to earth, ready to claim the world as his own. He couldn't believe it. Here they were, back in the clubhouse! The old defeats didn't matter now. Through trickery and might, they had achieved their goals. The Pure Shore Club was at their mercy, the clubhouse ripe for the picking.

"Good to be back, eh, my friend?" he asked the Smiling Shadow, striding past the assembled, grim-faced Outriders. The Shadow did not reply. Steven turned to regard his sinister companion. The Shadow seemed to be surveying the room, rotating slowly in place.

"What is it?" he asked.

"For a moment…" the Shadow hissed after a long pause, "I thought I sensed…"

The Shadow trailed off. Steven looked around too, curious as to what the Shadow detected that he didn't. He knew the Smiling Shadow's origins, how the dark intelligence was the product of a science that he, Steven, could never understand. The Smiling Shadow had more capabilities than were generally known.

Finally, he stopped rotating and looked at Steven. "I suppose it was nothing," he said. "Come, Even Steven. Let us enjoy this moment."

They entered the AmazeHeart chamber. As usual, the room was bathed in the soft purple light of the extraterrestrial construct. The Outriders activated the room's hidden controls so the bottomless pit was now covered by a gray metallic floor. The minions of the Shadow lined the walls, ready to do their master's bidding. Mr. Santillian, Cruiser, and Mindy were slumped against the wall, all in shackles made of dark energy and still knocked out.

All in all, it was a beautiful sight.

The Smiling Shadow turned to Steven. "And now, my friend…we do what we came here for. We claim what is rightfully ours."

The AmazeHeart's light reflected in Steven's eyes. "Ultimate power," he whispered. His face split into a giant grin.

The Shadow drifted towards the AmazeHeart, laughing all the way.

CHAPTER THIRTY-FIVE
RECONCILIATION WITH THE VANISHING MAN

Abby and Brett didn't have much time to react to Maxine's speedy return. Just a golden streak of light coming around a nearby building, a rush of air, then she was standing there in front of them. Smoke trailed from her roller blades.

Maxine placed her hands on her hips. "It's crazy, guys. This dark and cold, all around us right now…it only goes to the edge of the campus."

"No way," Brett said, raising his eyebrows. "How is that possible?"

She shrugged. "I don't know. It's like someone put a giant, dark, freezer-dome over the entire school."

Abby frowned, looking around as if to see the darkness's edge. "I don't get it…I mean, can you see the darkness from the outside?"

Maxine shook her head. "That's just the thing. Once you get outside, you can't even tell the campus is like this. Everything looks normal, sunshine and everything. I suppose if you had some binoculars, you could zoom in and see the slack-jawed students all over the place. But otherwise, it's like nothing's happened."

"An illusion?" Abby mused. "But what happens if someone enters the campus grounds?"

"I've got an answer for that one," she replied. "I saw a car that had come down Afterburner Drive, just sitting there with the engine on. The driver was turned into a space-case like all these other people we've seen. Car must have rolled to a stop."

"Great guns!" Brett exclaimed. "So if you cross a certain line, you get brain-dead like everyone else. This just gets worse and worse!"

Maxine cocked an eyebrow. "Still going to go file that story now, cowboy?"

"Not yet," he told her, tilting back his fedora. "It's just delayed for a while. Well, I bet if there's light and heat outside this 'dome' you talked about, there's phone reception too. Let's head out and call our parents!"

"Yeah, about that," Maxine said, "are you sure you want to do that? I mean, do you really think your parents are going to believe this? They're going to think you went off to school and promptly lost your mind."

Brett looked glum and kicked a rock on the sidewalk. "You're probably right. I think they're convinced I'm kind of crazy, anyhow."

"I can't imagine why," Maxine stage-whispered to Abby, who tried not to chuckle.

"Let's call your family, Max," Brett said. "They've got power, influence. Even if they think your story is nuts, they can get people moving, get the Marines out here or something."

Maxine rolled forward a few inches. "How many times do I have to say it, Brett? I'm not calling my parents!"

"Why the heck not?" he demanded, throwing his hands up in the air. "Your parents can probably afford to buy a small country. Why can't you get them to help us?"

"Because they don't want to talk to me!" Maxine yelled.

Brett didn't reply. He and Abby just looked at Maxine in astonishment. Her cheeks were flushed, hands balled into fists. Abby wondered for a moment if Maxine was going to attack Brett. If that happened, what she would do?

Luckily, it didn't go that way. Maxine visibly calmed down, her fists unclenching. Her shoulders slumped, and she stared down at her roller blades. "Sorry," she said simply. The word hung in the air for a long moment, surprising Abby and Brett. It was the most contrite they'd ever heard Maxine sound. In the short time they'd known her, she had never apologized for anything.

Abby cleared her throat. "Um, Max...what's going on? With your parents, I mean."

The soccer player continued to stare at her feet, not meeting their eyes. She sighed heavily, the gust of breath easily visible in the chilled air. "My parents are divorcing," she said finally, her voice barely audible. "I don't think they've really ever gotten along…as long as I've been alive, anyway. Growing up, I didn't see much of them. They were always away, managing their cosmetics empire, jet-setting all over the world."

Brett rubbed his chin. "Did you live at home growing up?"

Maxine nodded. "If you can call a giant museum a home," she said, bitterness rendering her tone icy. "I went to private schools in my hometown until now, when they saw fit to send me off to this stupid boarding school. To get me out of the way, I guess. Not that they ever really articulated to me why it was happening. One day, they told me I was leaving my old school and being shipped off here and that was that."

She was quiet for a long moment. With small movements of her legs, she rolled around in a slow circle, her hands in her pockets. When she came around to face them again, her dark eyes were focused somewhere on the horizon.

"You see…it's hard to explain. You had to be there, to know your parents were splitting up and splitting up everything else. Fighting over all their stuff. The houses, the art collection, the cars, the money. But not once did they fight over me. It's like all that other stuff is all that's important to them."

Abby's heart went out to Maxine. She was separated from her parents, certainly, and while it hurt her in different ways, she knew that ultimately it was because her parents loved her and wanted her to be safe. But to be shuttled out of the way, treated like an inconvenience; she couldn't imagine what that would be like.

She glanced at Brett, who looked like he didn't know what to do, yet was concerned nonetheless. Abby could almost see his reporter's mind thinking back on his brief time with Maxine. If he was thinking the same thing Abby was, it was that this piece of Maxine Drury went a long way to explaining why she was the way she was. All the abrasiveness, all the anger, all the indignation; it masked a girl who desperately wanted the love of her parents.

Abby wasn't used to reaching out to other people, but instinctively she knew she should do something. If someone like Maxine got this vulnerable, it was because she either trusted her new friends or simply couldn't contain her anger and sadness anymore. Perhaps a combination of both. Maxine was like a porcupine crossed with an armadillo: both prickly and hard-shelled. With a breach in her armor exposing her true inner turmoil, Maxine needed a friend.

Seeing that need, Abby stepped up to the plate. She walked up to the dark-haired girl and placed an arm around her shoulders. "Sorry, Max," she said quietly. "We had no idea."

Maxine went back to looking at the ground. "Well, of course not. I didn't tell you."

"We also didn't ask," Abby replied. "Look, you don't have to call your parents. It probably wouldn't do any more good than calling Brett's folks, anyway. No, we need another plan."

Brett nodded. "Yeah, it was a bonehead idea of mine, champ. Happens from time to time, I guess."

Maxine half-smiled. "Only from time to time?"

He favored her with a crooked grin of his own. "Don't expect it to happen again anytime soon. Anyway, let's put our heads together and plan our next move. What are our assets?"

"Our powers," Abby pointed out. "We don't necessarily have a whole lot of expertise in using them, but we do have them." She let Maxine go but remained by her side.

"And the Empowerer," Maxine said. "Reeve shoved that thing into our hands to keep it away from the Smiling Shadow. I'd say right now that's our biggest ace-in-the-hole."

"You also have me," came a familiar voice from nearby. Startled, they whirled to see Michael Alvarez hovering there, hands in his jacket pockets and obscured in shadow.

"The vanishing man is back," Brett remarked.

"Quick, tell us whatever you need to tell us before you go away again," Maxine said, rolling towards Michael a few inches. She wondered if she should try and grab him by his coat, as if her physical presence would anchor him in that spot.

But he shook his head. "Don't worry, I think everything is back under control. Whatever disruption the Smiling Shadow did to my powers has faded. Well, mostly faded anyway. I can control my teleporting again, but I'm still intangible, unfortunately."

"Oh no!" Abby exclaimed. "Do you think it'll ever get better?"

He shrugged. "I bet it will, but we can't wait for that. The Smiling Shadow is here."

"Yeah, we know," Brett said. "We saw him, big as life and twice as spooky. Flew through the campus like a banshee, laughing all the way."

Michael looked around, seeming to notice his surroundings for the first time. "Holy cow," he said, his eyes widening. "What's happened here? It's so dark…and the people…"

Maxine threw up her hands. "We were hoping you'd be able to tell us. It's like the Shadow froze the entire campus. The time capsule didn't say he could do anything like this."

"He can't," Michael said, floating over to a nearby student. He peered closely at the slack-jawed, utterly still teenager. "At least, we've never known him to have this kind of power. We need to see how far this effect extends."

"Already done," Maxine reported. "It's just the campus. The outside world is normal, and not only that, from the outside it looks like everything is fine in here."

Michael looked at them closely. "Yet you three are unaffected. Interesting. Well, the Shadow told me he'd learned some new tricks; this is obviously one of them."

"But why?" Abby asked. "What good does it do him to put the whole campus into a deep freeze?" Shivering, she zipped Brett's jacket up to her chin.

"I don't know," Michael admitted. "I've never known him to be capable of anything on this scale…unless…" He trailed off, rubbing his chin.

"What is it?" Brett asked. "Come on, Mike, don't hold out on us. You got us into this crazy mess, after all."

"Sorry, I was just thinking. The Smiling Shadow has been going around taking out old Pure Shore Club members. What I think he's been doing is taking their powers."

"Which puts them into a coma!" Abby exclaimed. "Because what gives all of us these powers are little pieces of technology…I guess you'd call that nanotechnology…that are synched up with our bodies. Remove those, and it has some kind of traumatic effect, right?"

"Right," Michel agreed. "But I think the Shadow hasn't just been taking those away to knock out the Pure Shore Club alumni."

Brett realized what Michael was getting at and whistled. "He's somehow using that technology. He's adding it to himself…making himself even more powerful!"

Michael nodded somberly. "I think that might be it, Brett. It's increased his power and given him new powers. And now he's gunning for the Empowerer."

Maxine, Abby, and Brett all looked askance at each other. How much had Michael heard before he'd spoken up just moments ago?

"Okay, let's all be honest with each other here," Michael said, holding up his hands. "We're in a serious situation and we can't mess around. The Smiling Shadow and his gang of not-so-merry men have taken over the clubhouse. Now, I know you three know something about the Empowerer. Please tell me what that is. There's too much at stake to keep secrets."

"Nice speech, coming from you," Maxine snapped. "The guy who has us peering at murals looking for clues, traipsing through forests, and spending time in a hole in the ground talking to a hologram of a geriatric alien computer."

Michael winced. "Sorry, the circumstances have been less than ideal. We haven't been able to be square with you guys. But please know that I…we…need your help. We can't beat the Smiling Shadow without you."

"We need to talk among ourselves," Abby announced, after noticing the ambivalent expressions on Brett and Maxine's faces. "Can you, um, give us a few minutes?"

The floating man looked surprised, but recovered and said, "Oh, sure, go ahead. I'll just be drifting around in the land of the statue-people." He moved away, his form soon becoming all but invisible in the darkness.

"What do you think?" Abby asked.

Maxine crossed her arms across her chest. "I think we should just give him the stupid ball and be done with it."

"Maybe so," Brett agreed. "It's really his problem now."

Abby blinked in surprise. "You guys really just want to give it up? I mean, and not help him, too?"

"Why should we?" Maxine asked. "I mean, what's in it for us?"

"Why does something have to be in it for us?" Abby demanded, surprising herself with her directness. Maxine evaded her gaze, so she continued. "Max, you were so upset earlier that your time had been wasted by all this Pure Shore Club stuff. Now you're just going to walk away?"

The soccer player snorted. "Do you think any of that matters now? You're right, I was pretty upset. But I just don't care anymore. Let Alvarez handle this. Let's get back to our own lives."

"I still want to know what happens," Brett put in. "For my story, I mean. But otherwise, Max is right. Let's just turn the oversized marble over to the ghost-man over there and be done with it."

Abby threw her arms out, gesturing at the shadow-shrouded campus. "Our own lives? Your story? Will you two listen to yourselves? Look around you! You two seem to think we can just pass the Empowerer on to Michael and call it a day. Like we can just go eat dinner together and forget about all of this craziness. Well we can't! Don't you two get it? We don't have normal lives to go back to now!"

She walked over to a nearby girl who had brown hair and wore a long gray coat. Like all the other students on the campus, she was staring off into space. Abby waved a hand in front of her eyes and got the expected lack of reaction.

"Who are you going to play soccer with now, Max? This girl here? And you, Brett. Do you think the staff of the newspaper is in any better shape? Do you think we can just show up for our classes tomorrow and the teachers will all be there, ready to give lessons?"

Brett and Maxine seemed taken aback by Abby's sudden outburst.

"But…we could leave…" Brett replied.

"And go where?" Abby asked, her voice rising in pitch. "And do what? Have you two stopped to think that, if the Smiling Shadow has become so powerful he can do this to the Jefford Academy, what happens when he gets even more power? What happens when he gets his hands on the Empowerer? I bet he wants the Empowerer so he can make himself as powerful as he wants. Then what's to stop him from doing this to the entire state? The country? Maybe even the whole world? Where will you two go then?"

Abby ran out of gas and stood before her friends, slightly out of breath, suddenly aware her hands were clenched into fists. With a slow intake and release of breath, she willed herself to calm down. Brett and Maxine were staring at her, wondering what had happened to the timid Abby they had gotten to know over the course of that eventful weekend. Abby thought of her parents, in that far-off land. She thought about what would happen if this shadow effect reached them.

"I don't know about you guys," Abby said, her voice low, "but I can't sit by and let that happen. I can't let everyone in the whole world get turned into these…zombies. If there's a way to save the world from that fate, I'm going to fight for it. With or without you."

With that, she began to stalk away, determined not to look back.

"We didn't chose to be part of this," Maxine spoke up, sounding somewhere halfway between indignant and uncertain.

Abby slowly turned to regard the other girl. "I'm learning that people seldom get choices. Did any of us get a choice in coming here?" With that, she turned and continued on her way, steering herself towards the floating Michael Alvarez, who was off in the distance, trying to make himself discreet.

He saw her approaching and drifted over to meet her. Abby couldn't believe she had just done what she did, said what she said. She wasn't sure if she wanted to lie down and cry right there or run back to her room and hide under the bed. But she knew, deep down, that she had crossed a threshold, and there was no turning back now.

"Ah," Michael said as she got within earshot. "Good, I see all three of you are on board."

Abby was confused for a moment, then turned around. Her green eyes grew wide. Maxine and Brett were just a few steps behind her.

"Well, we've got nothing better to do," Brett said, making a show of examining his nails.

Maxine's mouth was turning up in the beginnings of a smile, and her dark eyes sparkled in the darkness. "We've got to get the campus back to normal," she said.

"Can you imagine what all this dark and cold will do to enrollment?"

Abby chuckled. "Yeah, the pictures in the brochures would be horrible!"

All three of them faced Michael Alvarez. And they told him everything.

CHAPTER THIRTY-SIX
CAPTIVES OF THE SMILING SHADOW

Mr. Santillian drifted back to consciousness slowly. His first realization was that pretty much every part of his body ached, and he couldn't remember why just yet. Then he opened his eyes and the harsh gavel of his present reality slammed down on him.

Looking around, he saw that he was in the AmazeHeart chamber. The floor had been extended, making plenty of room for everyone to stand. And it was a good thing, a lot of room was needed. Along the walls, standing like grim gray sentinels at least three ranks deep, were Outriders. Mr. Santillian had no doubt they were ready to spring into action at the orders of their dark master.

The Smiling Shadow was hovering next to the AmazeHeart. Dark tendrils extended from its inky form, each one touching the AmazeHeart's glowing purple surface. Obviously he was trying to steal the Empowerer again, Mr. Santillian realized, his heart sinking. And with Reeve switched off, and no other opposition, it was going to be even easier to break into the AmazeHeart than it was five years ago.

With the eerie sight of the Smiling Shadow and his henchmen dominating his field of vision, Mr. Santillian almost missed Even Steven. Santillian blinked in surprise. The Smiling Shadow had survived, and Steven had too?

He was standing back and to the right of the Shadow, an oddly pensive expression on his face. Mr. Santillian wondered what was bothering him. Perhaps the young man was unsure about his evil alliance. He thought Steven looked very small, very out of place, in the company of his sinister colleagues.

He almost felt sorry for him, but then he reminded himself that Steven's betrayal of the team five years ago led to Stacy's death. Familiar feelings of anger and guilt returned, and Mr. Santillian strained to escape. He found himself held fast by dark manacles, doubtless produced by the Outriders. The manacles pinned his wrists and ankles to the wall, each one a freezing cold stripe across his skin. He noted his distinctive cuff links, which he could transform at a touch into his powerful multi-pistols, were missing.

Ignoring his discomfort, and finding the shadowy bonds were not to be broken by his human strength, Mr. Santillian looked for his young friends. They were arrayed to his left, each similarly bound as he was. Cruiser still wore her Crimson Cruiser helmet, but its faceplate was cracked and one side of it was dented. Mindy was bloodied and bruised, as Mr. Santillian imagined he probably was, too. Both of them seemed to be awake. He assumed Mindy and Cruiser were somehow blocked from using their superpowers.

"Ah, our illustrious guests are awake!" the Smiling Shadow remarked, without looking in their direction. "I trust you three brave heroes had a nice rest with pleasant dreams?" The Shadow chuckled, his Outriders all laughing along with him. Steven laughed too, but not as long as the others did.

He strode over to the captive Pure Shore Club members. His hands were behind his back, and he had a mocking smile plastered on his round face.

"What a reunion this is!" he said, talking loudly enough to make Mr. Santillian's already-throbbing head hurt even worse. He longed to break free of the dark manacles and knock Steven out. Not that it would work, of course, with Steven's superpower, but Mr. Santillian knew it would certainly feel good to try.

"How amazing it is, to be back in the clubhouse after all these years," Steven said, pacing back and forth in front of them. "After such a terrible defeat, to have returned as a conquering hero. Marvelous, wouldn't you say?"

"You may see yourself as a conquering hero, Steven," Cruiser said, her voice muffled by her helmet. "Delude yourself all you want. What you really are is a no-good, lousy, stinking skunk of a Benedict Arnold. I'm almost glad you're back from the dead so we can kick your sorry butt again!"

Steven gritted his teeth, his eyes narrowing. "Such bold talk from one so helpless! Let me make myself clear, chauffer-girl. Let me make myself clear to all of you. I have spent the past five years waiting, healing, convalescing. It was long, bleak, and tedious. All I had to sustain me was my hate. My hate for all of you, my hate for the club, and the sweet fantasies of the vengeance I would take upon you! Death itself was not enough to separate me from my revenge."

He stopped in front of Mr. Santillian, and coldly regarded his former teacher. "I have proven why I should have been leader and not that fool Alvarez. Mine is the superior power, mine is the superior will."

Mr. Santillian's eyes smoldered. "It takes more than power and will to lead the Pure Shore Club, Steven. There is wisdom, selflessness, and compassion, too. And several other qualities you know nothing about."

Steven's jaw tightened, and veins bulged in his neck. Mr. Santillian wondered if Steven was about to strike him. But the young traitor chose not to rise to his bait.

"Mr. Santillian, Mr. Santillian," Steven said, gazing upon him with an expression that dripped pity. "Ever the idealist. What good do your ideals do you now, old man? You're the one pinned to the wall while I roam free. The Smiling Shadow will soon crack the AmazeHeart and supreme power will belong to us. We have won through patience and cunning. We laid a trap for you, and you walked right into it like a dumb animal lunging after a lure."

Mindy spoke up. "How did you survive, Steven? The last we saw of you, you got fried in this very room."

Steven grinned. "Do not underestimate the power of Even Steven, my dear Mindy. The energy expended by that explosion was tremendous, nearly more than my power could handle. It certainly couldn't counteract it, so it did the next best thing. It removed me from the scene. And since the Smiling Shadow managed to latch onto me at the last moment, he came with me."

"It removed you?" Mindy asked. "Where did you go?"

The young man looked troubled, bad memories obviously replaying behind his eyes. "Far away. Very, very far away. I'm still not sure where exactly. But the explosion hurt both of us, very badly. I might have died if the Shadow had not spun a healing cocoon about me. I lay in that cocoon, the Shadow's energies keeping me alive while he repaired himself. I was halfway between asleep and awake, a long, gray nothing. Floating in fog. But then I emerged, as good as new, and we began to plan our revenge."

Mr. Santillian grunted. "A nice story, truly. Yet I fail to understand how a traitor can plan any kind of revenge. Really, we should be the ones planning revenge on you." His words bore such menace that Steven actually looked worried for a moment. Then his smug expression returned.

"Bold talk, from a man who got played like an accordion," he snapped. "The only reason you're our prisoners and we're in control is because of your pathetic, pitiful, predictable guilt."

"Shut up, Steven," Cruiser said. "Maybe Mr. Santillian's guilt over what happened to Stacy caused him to be blind to what was going on until it was too late. At least he can feel guilt. That's a human emotion, something you don't know anything about!"

Steven glared at her. "Talk to me like that again, woman, and I swear I—"

"You'll what?" she challenged him. "Talk me to death? Really, what can you do to someone who isn't directly fighting you?"

Mindy laughed, and Mr. Santillian smiled. Same old Cruiser, defiant to the last. And she was right. Steven stood there, seething, his fists clenching and unclenching. He knew she was right, too. Without an outside force acting against him, his superpower wasn't terribly useful. He couldn't do anything but stand there and be angry.

After a moment, Steven said, "Again, bold talk from ones so helpless. The facts remain evident. Your Pure Shore comrades across the world are in comas, the result of my partner ripping their superpowers from them and adding them to his already-considerable might. The clubhouse is breached, you are all immobilized, and soon the Smiling Shadow will break into the AmazeHeart and seize the Empowerer. With that power under his control, he shall be unstoppable!"

Steven grinned, looking quite pleased with himself.

Mr. Santillian thought it was an opportune time to point out something that had been stirring in his mind ever since he'd found out Steven was still alive. "And what is in it for you?"

The young man's grin wavered. "What do you mean, Santillian?"

"I get what the Smiling Shadow gets out of this: supreme power, and all that jazz. But what about you? What's in all of this for you, now that you've won?"

"I...You see, I..." Steven fumbled, his eyes darting around.

Lauren Saint—if that was truly her name—strode up and backhanded Mr. Santillian across the face. "Silence, you old fool! We've all heard quite enough from all of you. If you wish to stay alive, I suggest you keep quiet!"

Mr. Santillian's face stung, and he tasted blood inside his cheek. His former students were looking on with concern, and he did his best to give them a reassuring glance. But he knew, on some level, it didn't matter how much they needled Even Steven. The only Pure Shore Club member still at large was Michael Alvarez, and from what he'd been told, Michael's powers were malfunctioning. There may not be much he could do to help them.

He looked around at the dark forces occupying the clubhouse, about to lay their hands on its ultimate power, and he grimaced at the reality of awful history repeating itself. Before, he'd only failed Stacy. This time, he'd failed not only his former students, but every other Pure Shore Club member alive. He'd allowed his grief and guilt to blind him to the truth, to deafen him to the concerns raised by others.

And now it was far, far too late. He didn't know what the Smiling Shadow planned on doing with them, but he reckoned it would not be pleasant. So, this is how it ends, he mused. An utter failure as a teacher, the enemy occupying the fortress. Outwitted and outmaneuvered at every turn.

There was no one to rescue them now.

CHAPTER THIRTY-SEVEN
ALL ABOARD THE TURBO TRAIN

"There's a subway running from the campus to the clubhouse?" Abby asked in disbelief. Michael was flying as fast as he could while still allowing them to keep up. Maxine rolled along easily, Brett close at her heels, and Abby brought up the rear.

"We call it the Turbo Train! The club members need a way to go between the school and the clubhouse unnoticed," Michael Alvarez shouted over his shoulder. "What better way than a subterranean high-speed train?"

"It makes sense!" she cried, a nagging question from the back of her mind finally answered. "I'd wondered how Mr. Santillian had arrived at the clubhouse to turn off Reeve, and left again, without running into those Outriders!"

"I hadn't thought about that at all," Maxine said. "I'm sure glad we have some brains in this outfit."

Brett chuckled. "Don't sweat it, champ. Every team needs a dumb jock or two."

She veered close enough to run into him with her shoulder, and he staggered briefly off course. "We'll see who's dumb when the report cards come out, wise guy."

"Assuming any of us live to see our next report card," Abby said, looking worriedly at the frozen, slack-jawed students they were passing.

"Not something I would miss, I gotta admit," Brett replied.

Maxine snorted. "I'm with you there."

Abby didn't like report card time either. But that was because, for her, it was usually a time of agonizing over any A minus grades that might show up on it. She decided it would be wise to not tell Brett and Maxine that. They were just starting to become her friends, after all.

They arrived at a small stone house just behind the library. The stone house, Abby remembered from the Student Handbook, used to be the campus caretaker's house a long time ago. Now it served as a guest house for distinguished visitors. There were no lights on—not that there were any lights on anywhere on the campus right now, she thought—and it was reasonable to assume no one was staying there.

"If you were to closely examine the interior of this house," Michael told them, "you would find it to have a little more space on the outside than on the inside."

"Another space-warping trick?" Brett asked. "Like how that old barn disguises the entrance to the clubhouse?"

Michael nodded. "Pretty much. Reeve can do some amazing things. Now, to get to the Turbo Train…"

They followed him as he circled around the cottage and halted at a blank stone wall. Without a look back, he floated right into the wall, like it wasn't real. Or he wasn't.

"Sheesh," Brett said. "I forgot Mike was still Casper the Friendly Ghost."

"That's all well and good for him," Maxine said, staring at the wall as if the force of her gaze would topple it over, "but how are we supposed to get through?"

Abby examined the wall closely and was startled when Michael's head and shoulders reappeared. "Sorry, guys, I forgot to explain. Just walk through the wall. It should know you're Pure Shore Club members and let you come through."

Maxine was the first to try it, and Brett and Abby were astonished to see her pass through the seemingly solid barrier with no problems at all. They followed, both flinching, expecting to slam into the rocky surface and fall back onto the cold ground. But that didn't happen. They found themselves in a dark room illuminated by a single dim light above. Abby found the hidden room to be warm, a welcome change from the frigid, darkness-shrouded campus. Even with Brett's coat on, Abby's hands, nose, and ears were quite chilled. She rubbed her hands together to banish their numbness.

The next instant, Brett and Abby were floating downward.

"Whoa!" Brett exclaimed, pinwheeling his arms. When they'd entered, it had felt like there was solid ground under their feet, but really it was another anti-gravity elevator.

"It's like back at the clubhouse!" Abby cried. She tried her best not to think about the fact there was no solid ground under her feet.

"Good of them to use the same hootenanny, huh?" Brett asked. "You know, in case we'd think they were made by different people or something."

They arrived at the bottom to find Michael Alvarez and Maxine waiting for them. A tunnel stretched off into the distance, illuminated by alternating blue and red lights every few feet. The tunnel's floor was lined with a single white track. On the track, near Michael and Maxine, was what looked like a streamlined subway car. It gleamed in the tunnel lights, its surface a muted pewter color. It had doors on both sides with ramps that extended down to the ground.

"Wow!" Brett said, walking up and down the car's length. "How long has this been down here? How does it work?"

"This thing was the idea of Reeve, working with Hugh Ellwand. I'm assuming the time capsule told you who Mr. Ellwand was. As for how it works, it runs off the clubhouse's power. Try not to touch the track…it's kind of like the third rail on a subway. Lots of power coursing through there."

"What are we waiting around here for?" Maxine said, striding towards the Ellwand Express. "We've got butts to kick, people to save."

"Not so fast," Michael said, holding up his hand. He belatedly realized how ludicrous he must look, an intangible man acting as if he had control over anyone. "I'm assuming that the Outriders have never seen any of you without your costumes. Not only that, but if we're going to a superhero-type rescue, we should look the part." With a thought, he switched to his gleaming white Quantumax attire. Abby, Maxine, and Brett regarded him for a long moment, then, almost as one, they summoned their own superhero outfits.

Maxine had been wearing her golden roller blades all along, but now she had the white speed skater suit on, topped with the golden bicycle helmet. Brett was in his blue suit and cowl, his blue dot floating nearby. Abby's golden crown glinted in the tunnel's light, and she unsheathed her heart-wand. Maxine thought Abby looked a foot taller in her superhero clothes, the cape and crown making the timid girl look quite regal.

If only she could see herself like that, Maxine thought. It would do wonders for her self-esteem.

"Excellent," Michael said, surveying them gravely. "Also, if you haven't already, you must decide on code names."

"Say what?" Maxine asked.

"I see what the ghost-man is getting at," Brett said. "It wouldn't do very well for us to yell out, 'Hey, Maxine,' in the middle of the action, now, would it?"

"Like you'd really use my real name, King-of-Nicknames," Maxine said.

"Why don't you just call us champ and Blondie?"

Brett snorted. "Hey, you call me 'Ace'."

"Doofus," she shot back. "Haven't you figured out that I do that to make fun of you?"

"Um, guys," Abby spoke up. "I think Mr. Alvarez probably wants us to get going. We should decide on some real code names."

"Well, I think your name is obvious," Brett said, looking at Abby's regalia. "Queen of Hearts."

She shrugged, making her cape ripple. "I guess. I don't really know what it has to do with transforming objects, but it's the most obvious name. What about you?"

Brett smiled and held out one index finger. He willed his blue dot to land on it, and willed it to change size, growing to the size of a dinner plate. "Call me Blue Circle."

Maxine laughed. "Sounds like a gas station chain!"

"Oh, put a sock in it, champ, er, Maxine," he replied. "What brilliant name do you have dreamed up for yourself? Really-really-fast Girl? Ultimate Soccer Woman? Roller Blade Baroness?"

"Oh, I don't know," Maxine said, putting her hands on her hips. "I feel stupid even thinking about this. I don't care, just call me whatever sounds good."

"Speedster!" Abby exclaimed. "Why not Speedster? Well, um, unless you don't like it, and—"

Maxine smiled. "No, I like that. Speedster. Has a nice sound to it."

Michael Alvarez swept one hand towards the open door of the Turbo Train. "Now that that's settled, ladies and gentleman," he said, "please follow me. I fear we have already spent too much precious time."

They boarded the subway car. Rows of shiny, forward-facing black seats filled the interior of the cabin, divided by a single aisle running down the middle. Through the car's front window, they could see the tunnel extending off into the distance like the throat of a massive dragon.

The moment they were all on board, the car went into motion. They hurriedly found seats as the train sped up. And sped up some more. The tunnel walls flew by in a blur, and the train made absolutely no noise.

"Beats riding on the Boston subway," Brett quipped. "Say, Mr. Alvarez, there wouldn't be a way for a guy to wear his superhero zoot suit and one other garment from his regular clothes, would there?"

Seated in front of them, Michael turned, peering through his red visor. "Come again?" he asked, clearly confused.

"It's his hat," Maxine spoke up. "He wants to wear his hat."

"Nice guess, Speedster," Brett replied. He was seated across the aisle from Maxine and Abby. She was in the aisle seat, and she launched a swift kick at his shins, which he managed to avoid by scooting against the wall. "But yeah, that's what I meant. My hat. Is there a way to summon that back from the limbo-land of banished clothing?"

"Oh, yeah," Michael said. "About that hat…What is up with that hat? I mean, I'm all for fashion statements and all, but it's kind of unusual for a guy your age…"

"It's a long story," Abby said.

Michael shrugged. "Maybe you can tell me later." If there is a later, he thought, but didn't vocalize. "And the answer is 'no'."

"Probably just as well, Brett," Abby said. "Um, it kind of kills the point of a mask and a codename if you wear that hat as the Blue Circle."

Brett threw up his gloved hands. "I know, I know. I'd thought of that. I…just wish I could wear it. This is probably one of the biggest things I've ever done and…"

Abby leaned forward to look at Brett past Maxine, who was looking between them. "For what it's worth, Brett…I think your grandpa would be proud of you."

Brett gave her a crooked smile. "I…I hope so."

Maxine squinted at Abby. "I get the distinct impression I missed something along the way."

"I'm sure he won't mind telling you someday," Abby said.

Brett snorted. "Only if she stops trying to hit me."

They noticed the subway car was beginning to slow down.

"What, we're getting close already?" Brett asked. "Short ride."

"Fast train," Michael explained. "Yes, we're getting close. Do we need to go over the plan again? Are you all okay with what we need to do?"

All three teenagers nodded. Michael looked at their faces, seeing the nervousness of Abby, the determination of Maxine, the courage of Brett. For the first time, Michael felt doubt about what they were doing. *They mean well, but they're so young.* He swallowed.

"I'm sorry, again, for how all this has turned out," he said. "There should have been so much more time to prepare. All I can say to you three is thank you for helping us in our hour of need. That…and that you may be some of the bravest young people ever."

"Or some of the most foolish," Maxine muttered.

"Don't worry," Michael said, "our plan is sound. Abby, do you have it?"

Abby reached under her cape and produced a magenta orb. At the same time, Brett willed his blue dot to grow to the size of a serving tray. Carefully, Abby placed the orb on the blue dot. As she did so, they felt the Turbo Train lurch to a stop. She was amazed how short the trip was. It'd taken the three of them two hours to hike through the forest to the clubhouse. The Turbo Train had gotten them there in twenty minutes.

Looking out the windows, they saw no Outriders rushing to attack them.

"Guess they didn't think the subway was worth guarding, huh?" Maxine asked.

Brett snorted. "Everyone who knows about this crazy underground train is laid up in the hospital or their prisoner. Well, except for Mike, here, of course."

"And they think he's dead," Abby pointed out.

"A critical oversight on their part," Michael said. "The Smiling Shadow wants the Empowerer. What say we go give it to him?"

CHAPTER THIRTY-EIGHT
TEST OF THE NEW HEROES

The Smiling Shadow had been quiet for a long time as he concentrated on opening the AmazeHeart. Abruptly, he let loose a mighty cackle that echoed inside the chamber and chilled all who heard it.

"Success!" he cried. "I have gained access to this infernal container!"

Steven ran to its side. He was eager to watch the moment of triumph. The moment they had planned for five years. When the Smiling Shadow would seize the instrument of ultimate power and spread its dominion over the entire world.

The shadowy tendrils of the Shadow were no longer on the surface of the AmazeHeart, interfacing with its workings and trying to gain access. Now they were plunging right through the glowing surface of the giant orb, probing inside for the prize he sought.

"I have it!" He withdrew his tentacles, and right through the surface of the AmazeHeart, as if it weren't even there, or was just a construction of light, came the magenta globe known as the Empowerer.

Steven had only seen pictures of it. Even in the heyday of the Pure Shore Club, Reeve didn't show off the contents of the AmazeHeart too often. It seemed strange to him that such an innocent-looking item could be the agent that granted superpowers to people.

The Smiling Shadow held it up into the air. The Empowerer was firmly gripped in its tendrils, some of them looping around it several times like dark snakes constricting a miniature world.

"Hear me, my Outriders!" he shouted. "The key to ultimate power lies within my grasp at last! Once I internalize this device and access its unlimited power-granting potential, there will be nothing I cannot do! No foe shall oppose us, no challenge shall be too great for us! From the fallen fools of the Pure Shore Club, my power has already increased exponentially. What I have done to the Jefford Academy, blanketing it in eternal night and making its denizens my hypnotized subjects, I shall do to this entire world! I shall rule it as its everlasting emperor of night, with all of you as my barons and dukes! At last, we have triumphed!"

The Outriders let loose a cacophony of victory cries, raising their dark guns, swords, and black-gloved fists in the air. Steven cheered too, although not quite as loudly as the sinister host around him. This was what he always wanted, wasn't it? Power to rule, to dominate, to be in charge? If so, why didn't this moment feel better?

His brooding ended as the Smiling Shadow drew the Empowerer to itself. It sank into the pool of its shadowy form, a magenta gem sinking in a dark sea. This was it,

Steven thought, there would be no turning back now. All eyes in the room were riveted on the Smiling Shadow as it concentrated on the Empowerer.

Mr. Santillian couldn't bring himself to look at his former students. He had no doubt they would all soon be executed or turned into slaves of the enemy. There was nothing he could do to stop any of it. He wondered how long it would take for the Smiling Shadow to access the abilities of the Empowerer.

The Smiling Shadow was floating in the air, drifting to and fro, its dark mass undulating. Then it stopped moving. It just hung there, all motion arrested. Its ever-present grin did not waver. The Outriders glanced at one another. What was happening to their lord and master?

The answer came suddenly, and it was an answer no one expected.

The Smiling Shadow exploded with a sound like a balloon bursting.

Blobs of darkness sprayed all over the room, showering the walls and the floor and bouncing off many of the assembled Outriders. There was no sign of the Empowerer, Mr. Santillian realized, but there was a giant blue circle floating in the space the Shadow had just occupied.

Before the Outriders could react, several things happened at once.

The shackles holding Mr. Santillian, Mindy, and Cruiser prisoner turned into cotton balls. A golden streak flashed past them, and Mr. Santillian suddenly had his special cuff links in his hands.

Then Michael Alvarez soared up into the room through the floor, shining with white light, an avenging specter. Extending his hands, he blasted several of the still-confused Outriders with brilliant beams of energy.

"Let's take this clubhouse back!" he yelled.

Mr. Santillian and the others didn't know what exactly had just happened, but they didn't need to be told twice. Twin bursts of energy crackled in Mr. Santillian's hands, and his flintlock pistol-shaped cuff links transformed into his silver wonderguns. Pulling the triggers, he let the Outriders have it, both barrels. Lightning flashed across the chamber and every hit exploded an Outrider into a puff of noxious dark smoke.

The Outriders didn't remain stunned forever. They summoned their dark shields, swords, axes, spears, and guns, and charged at the newly-freed Pure Shore Club members. Mindy found an Outrider coming at her from each side, each brandishing a dark blade. Concentrating, she triggered her own superpower, causing herself to shrink. In a split second she was the size of a doll. The two Outriders didn't have a chance to react, and they plowed into one another, knocking each other out.

"Watch out, Mindy!" Cruiser cried, and she dove to the ground and scooped her miniaturized friend out of the way of the trampling feet of several Outriders.

"Thanks, Cruiser," Mindy said, sitting up in the palm of Cruiser's hands.

"I guess I'm a little rusty at this. Hey, watch out yourself!"

An Outrider was swinging an axe sideways at Cruiser. The red-clad driver ducked, and while she was moving downward, she gripped Mindy in one hand and pulled off her scarlet helmet with the other. With all her might, she used her helmet as a bludgeoning weapon, connecting with the Outrider's skull. He crumpled to the ground and didn't move.

Mindy clapped her hands. "Nice hit!"

"Not as good as this one," she replied.

Just then, the chamber's door smashed inward, throwing bits of metal everywhere. The roar of a powerful engine filled the room. With the Smiling Shadow's power-blocking manacles gone, Cruiser's mental link to her Chameleon Car had returned. From the moment she had been freed, she had willed the car into the form of a sleek, crimson motorcycle and summoned it to her. The motorcycle raced through the room, scattering the Outriders as they tried to get out of its way. A few of them tried shooting at it, but because of the close quarters ended up shooting each other more often than not.

"Well, I hate to be left out," Mindy said. "Time to show these jokers why they used to call me Heights!" She hopped out of Cruiser's hand, and grew back to her normal size, and grew some more, rapidly turning into a giant version of herself. The Outriders reeled in shock, some getting off shots at the suddenly enormous woman. She shrugged off the bolts and kicked out a massive foot, sending a dozen Outriders flying. Then she crouched down and swept one hand from side to side, batting Outriders down like toy soldiers.

Mr. Santillian took cover behind her ankles and continued to blast away at the Outriders. They'd taken out many of the black-garbed enemy, but more were flooding in the door. Cruiser drove around the room on her red motorcycle, knocking the bad guys left and right, while Michael flew around and fired off his white light beams. He was at a distinct advantage in the melee because of his intangible state. The Outrider's dark bolts and dark throwing stars just passed straight through him.

"Michael!" Mr. Santillian yelled to be heard over the ruckus. "I appreciate the rescue, but what happened?"

"You might say I brought in some reinforcements," he explained as he flew by Mr. Santillian. "Sorry, no time to explain much else!"

Mr. Santillian saw his point and decided to just keep fighting. But with so many Outriders storming into the room, they were in very real danger of being overwhelmed. Yet what could they do besides make a last stand?

•   •   •

"Holy Toledo!" Brett exclaimed. "It sounds like they're having the rhubarb to end all rhubarbs in there!" They were right where Michael Alvarez had left them, in an empty hallway near the AmazeHeart chamber.

"I wish we could help them," Abby said.

Maxine grunted. "We could if Mike hadn't made us promise to stay out of it. This is just so unfair. Abby's matter-manipulating power made the fake Empowerer. Brett's blue dot, hidden inside the fake Empowerer, discorporated that Smiling Shadow. I gave the good guys their weapons back, and Abby frees them from their bonds. We do all of that, but are we good enough to participate in the final battle? Nope!"

"I think he wanted us to stay out of this for our own safety," Abby said.

"An excellent notion that is unfortunately rendered moot," said a voice off to their left. They whirled to find Even Steven standing there, his hands on his hips, an expression of fury twisting his face like a ball of dough.

Brett gallantly stepped between Steven and the girls, but he could feel Maxine jostling him from behind.

"What do you want, Steven?" he demanded, hoping he sounded formidable but worrying he just sounded like a scared underclassman.

"Poor, poor young fools," he said, shaking his head. "Did you have any idea what you were getting yourselves into when Reeve gave you your powers and costumes?"

"Um, no," Brett admitted. "But I have to say, it's been a heck of a way to spend a weekend."

"What are you doing out here, Steven?" Maxine asked. "Shouldn't you be in there, helping your Outrider buddies?"

He chuckled, a low, nasty sound from the bottom of his throat. "The Outriders can handle things. I saw what happened to the Smiling Shadow and deduced that Michael Alvarez had some outside help. I decided to go poking around, and here I find you. Cowering like the simpering children you are."

"That does it!" Maxine cried. She sped around Brett and closed the distance between her and Steven in the blink of an eye. But before she reached him, she abruptly stopped.

"What the…?" she asked to no one in particular, looking around, clearly confused. She tried to rush Steven again, but the same thing happened. She halted just before reaching him.

Steven threw his head back and laughed.

"Remember his superpower!" Abby cried. "He always has the perfect countermeasure for any attack against him! Somehow, he's stealing your momentum every time you try to hit him!"

Maxine knew that made sense, but it didn't stop her from trying to strike Steven again. And again. And again. Each time she inched slightly closer but couldn't reach him. Eventually she rolled backwards a few inches and glared at him. He just laughed some more.

"Go on, laugh," Maxine said with a snarl. "If that's the worst you can do, then your worst is pretty pathetic!"

"Let's get out of here," Abby said. "Come on, guys." She began walking away, down the opposite way from where Steven was standing.

"Hey, Blond-er, Queenie," Brett said. "I know you're new to this whole superhero business, but I don't think you can just stroll away from a bad guy."

She turned to regard Brett. "Sure we can. What good is Steven's power unless we attack him?"

Maxine flashed Steven a look of contempt, then rolled after Abby. "She's right. In this case, the best offense is a simple cold shoulder. Something I could do very well long before I got these funky roller blades. Coming, Brett?"

Brett looked between the girls and Steven. This was totally counterintuitive for him. Back in his old neighborhood, you stood your ground and fought. Nothing was ever gained by ignoring someone who wanted to fight you, it just made them try all the harder. But in this case, he realized Abby had the right idea. Without a backward glance, he turned and followed the girls down the hallway.

Steven was at a loss for words for a few moments. His mouth moved but no sound came out. His eyes bugged and veins popped out in his neck. "What…what are you doing?" he cried when he found his voice. "Come back here, you brats! Come back here and fight! What kind of superheroes are you, anyway?"

"Smart ones!" Maxine called back. She laughed. "What a moron that guy is. Good call, Abby. Now, what say we join in on the fun happening in the other room?"

They rounded a corner and came face-to-face with the woman known as Lauren Saint. She grinned at them, baring her teeth like a she-wolf. Her eyes were a mystery behind her inscrutable sunglasses. In her hands she held a long, two-handed shadow sword.

"Going somewhere, kids?" she asked.

"Y-you're the FBI agent!" Abby exclaimed. "What are you doing here?"

"Look at that sword she's handling," Brett said. "She's no FBI agent!"

"Quite right, young ones," she said. She advanced towards them, giving her sword a few swift, menacing twirls. "That was all a ruse to get close enough to Mr. Santillian to find out if and when he turned off Reeve and left the clubhouse open for the taking. I think it's all worked out quite marvelously, don't you?"

"I can't say I agree, ma'am," Brett said. "But if you think you can intimidate us, you've got another thing coming!"

"Oh, really?" she asked. She continued to stride slowly forward, her dark blade held before her. She towered over them, looking down at them with a mixture of contempt and amusement. "And here I am, thinking I'm doing quite a fine job of intimidating you."

"That's enough!" Maxine yelled, and she zoomed at Lauren Saint before Brett or Abby could even think of stopping her. Saint moved faster than they thought possible, lashing out with the hilt of her sword and sending Maxine flying into the nearest wall with a powerful blow. Abby gasped as Maxine slid to the ground and lay there, dazed.

"You're fast, with those snazzy roller blades, girl," Saint said, looking down at Maxine's semi-conscious form. "But we Outriders are fast too. Now, who's next?"

Brett stepped between Saint and Abby. "If you want her, you're going to have to go through me!"

"Gladly," Saint said through a wild grin. Then she closed the distance between them in a split second and brought her dark blade slicing down at Brett.

He hadn't thought about the fact that his blue dot was solid when not acting as a gateway through a wall. The fact that it was solid sometimes meant he could do other things with it than make it an impromptu doorway. It had been Abby's idea to create a fake Empowerer globe as a Trojan Horse and hide the blue dot inside of it. Under the power of Brett's mind, the dot had grown from the size of a particle to massive size in a split second, effectively disrupting the Smiling Shadow and removing him from the field, at least temporarily. Now, with barely any time to react, Brett desperately utilized his blue circle as a shield.

Willing it to the size of a garbage can lid, he placed it between himself and Saint. Her slicing sword bounced off it like she'd hit the metal shield of a medieval warrior.

"Clever," she remarked, peering at the blue barrier that floated between her and her young prey. "But not clever enough!"

She struck again, and again, and again. The blue circle began to wobble, and Brett had to concentrate more and more to keep it in place. Sweat broke out underneath his cowl. The circle began to waver and wobble.

"Abby, run!" he gritted out as he concentrated. "I'll hold her off!"

Part of her wanted to take him up on the offer. Just run away, hop on the Turbo Train, and go…but that was just the thing. There was nowhere to go. And she couldn't leave her new friends. She wouldn't.

Brett was startled when Abby's heart-wand appeared next to his head, extended towards Lauren Saint. Abby concentrated on Lauren's slashing sword. With a flash of pink sparks, the sword was transformed into a sunflower.

Saint didn't realize what had happened at first and continued to hack away at the blue circle for a few more moments with the limp sunflower. If they hadn't been so scared, Brett and Abby may have laughed at the sight of Saint gradually realizing she no longer held a sword, and holding the sunflower in front of her, her eyebrows raised and her mouth hanging open.

She composed herself, suddenly no longer smiling. "Nice," she muttered. Tossing the sunflower aside, she generated another dark blade and came at them again. "You stupid children and your stupid tricks!" she shouted, punctuating each word with a blow to Brett's blue circle.

Maxine groaned and began shakily getting to her feet. Saint stopped assaulting Brett's blue circle and instead whipped her sword around until its tip was at Maxine's throat. Maxine froze in place, looking at the dark blade with wide eyes. She knew the wrong movement would mean certain death.

"Surrender, or I slay your friend," she said, her voice low. She was breathing heavily, sweating, and wisps of her hair had come loose from her hair clip and stuck out in all directions. It made her look like a sword-swinging Medusa in black clothes.

"Don't move, Maxine," Brett warned her.

Abby raised her heart-wand again. "I'll take care of her weapon again—"

"She'll just make another one," Brett snapped. He willed his blue circle to shrink to dot size, and made it drift away, off to his right. "Okay, okay, Ms. Fake-FBI lady. You get what you want. We surrender."

"Excellent," she said, her wolfish grin returning to her face. Suddenly, a score of Outriders showed up and surrounded Brett and Abby. They all held dark guns and looked grim and mean.

"Good work, Saint," came Steven's voice. He was walking down the hallway.

"Where have you been?" Saint snapped, removing her sword from Maxine's throat and allowing two Outriders to grab the girl's arms and haul her to her feet.

"Never mind that," he replied. "First things first. That was obviously not the Empowerer the Smiling Shadow ingested."

"The real thing is out there somewhere," Saint said, the truth of Steven's words dawning on her. "Perhaps hidden by the accursed Reeve, or one of these pathetic children!"

"Precisely," Steven said. He surveyed the three teenagers with cold eyes. "Tell us what you know regarding the location of the real Empowerer."

Brett gulped but didn't reply. Abby looked at the floor, unable to meet Steven's icy gaze. Maxine stared right back, her gaze as icy as Steven's. None of them said a word.

"Young fools!" Steven spat. "What do you have to gain by not giving us what we want? What loyalty can you possibly have to Mr. Santillian and the rest of those dolts?"

Maxine cleared her throat. "You really think we want to live in a world dominated by the likes of you and that living ink blot? Where these biker gang refugees patrol the streets? Think again, buddy."

Steven looked as if he might attack Maxine right then and there, but instead he willed himself to calm down, and simply nodded to Saint. Her dark sword evaporated, and she willed in its place a dark pistol. She pointed it directly at Abby's face.

"There are three of you," she said. "If I kill one, there are still two who can spill the beans. Sing for us, little songbirds, or your precious Queen of Hearts here dies."

"Leave them alone," Brett said. "If you're going to point a gun at anybody, point it at me. Wouldn't be the first time…"

"Brett," Maxine said, "has anyone ever told you you're the last of the true gentlemen?"

"Wow, champ," he said. "That's the closest I may ever get to a compliment from you. I think I'll enjoy it."

"Shut up, both of you!" Steven shouted. "Do you think this is all some stupid game? We are dead serious! Tell us what we want to know, or the girl dies!"

Abby had been quivering in fear, her green eyes riveted to the black gun barrel stuck in her face. She wanted to cry, to beg for her life. But another part of her won out. "Go ahead!" she cried, her voice cracking.

Maxine and Brett were shocked. "Abby!" they yelled in unison.

"I think I can speak for all of us," she went on, "when I say that our lives don't mean a thing compared to the whole world. The needs of the many, and all of that. So go ahead, lady, blow us all away. At least then we won't have to look at any of your ugly faces ever again!"

Steven's eyes widened at her audacity. Saint gasped, recoiling ever so slightly. The assembled Outriders grew very still and quiet.

"Those foolish words, girl," Saint said, "shall be your epitaph." She re-aimed her pistol at Abby, whose green eyes flashed with defiance. As if her glare alone could stop the black bullet to come.

"No!" Brett cried. "Don't do it! I'll tell you everything!"

"Brett, what are you—?" she began to ask, surprised at his sudden caving in. Maxine remained silent, watching everything with her dark eyes.

"You don't need to do this," Brett told her. "Look, the Empowerer was given to us by Reeve. He asked us to hide it somewhere, which we did."

"Where?" Saint and Steven asked at the same time.

"The headmaster's office, back on campus. In his private safe, behind the portrait of Aloysius Jefford III."

"A-ha!" Steven said, slamming one fist into the opposite palm. "Victory shall yet be ours! Come, Saint, let us return to the AmazeHeart chamber."

Saint and Steven strode away, with the Outriders herding Abby, Maxine, and Brett along, poking them in the backs with their dark firearms.

"You...you didn't have to do that, Brett," Abby whispered.

"I couldn't just sit there and let them kill you," he said, not looking her in the eye.

Maxine rolled her eyes. "What a couple of heroes you two are. I'm not sure if I should admire the two of you or smack you both upside the head."

"So, this is it," Abby said, dread filling her stomach. "We're toast."

"Not yet," Brett said. "We might still have the opportunity to be heroes today."

Maxine grunted. "I'm not so sure that's a good thing."

CHAPTER THIRTY-NINE
THE FEAR EFFECT

Mr. Santillian, Mindy, and Cruiser were pinned down behind the AmazeHeart. Luckily, the alien artifact was tough enough to take cover behind, and none of the hits it had taken had so much as scratched its purple surface. Dark energy bolts shot past them, blasting holes in the walls. Smoke filled the air and debris littered the floor. Mr. Santillian's marksmanship and Michael's white light beams were holding the Outriders off so far, but there were simply too many of them.

"What do you think, sir?" Cruiser asked Mr. Santillian as incoming fire raged all around them. Her motorcycle was lying near her, pitted and scarred from numerous hits. She'd thought about transforming it into something more useful, but none of its other forms were practical given the size of the room.

Mr. Santillian fired one of his wonderguns around the AmazeHeart, hoping to keep the Outriders at bay. "Well, I've been in better situations."

"This is all my fault," Michael groaned. "I didn't think there were so many of them. I thought we'd have more of a chance."

"Your fault?" Mr. Santillian said, glancing at his former student. "I'm the idiot who shut off Reeve. It's my fault we're in this position in the first place. You tried your best, Michael. That's all any of us can do."

"Any ideas?" Mindy asked. She'd shrunk to doll-size and was perched on Cruiser's shoulder. Her titanic sized form was excessively easy to hit in an enclosed space like the AmazeHeart chamber, so she'd reverted to her smaller stature to more easily take cover.

"Michael, you're intangible," Mr. Santillian pointed out. "You can ghost out of here at any time. Or just teleport yourself out. Why don't you get out of here?" He winced as a shot to the ceiling rained flakes of plaster down on them.

"And do what?" Michael asked as the plaster passed right through him and settled on the floor. "There's nowhere for me to go to, sir."

Mr. Santillian sighed and shook his head. "Apparently, my own tendency to play the martyr has spread to my students. Very well. If this is to be our last battlefield, let us go out well." He looked to Cruiser, Michael, and Mindy. "Are you ready? One last charge, over the hill, into the valley of death?"

Cruiser mounted her motorcycle. Its engine roared to life. "I'm all in."

Michael and Mindy nodded their agreement.

"All right then," Mr. Santillian said. "On three, everyone. One, two…"

Abruptly the incoming barrage stopped. Dust settled and bits of wall and ceiling clattered to the floor. Mr. Santillian stopped his countdown.

"Santillian!" yelled a voice. They all recognized the voice of Even Steven, the traitor. "Surrender now, or the Pure Shore Club's three newest members die in pain!"

Mr. Santillian glanced at Michael, his eyes wide with fear. "Michael, you didn't bring those kids into this mess, did you?"

Michael shrugged. "Who do you think freed you all, or enabled us to blow up the Smiling Shadow? I couldn't have done it without them. But I told them to stay out of the fight."

Cruiser held out hope that Steven was bluffing. "Mindy, who does Steven have hostage out there?"

"Two girls and a guy," Mindy reported, peeking around the AmazeHeart. "One girl's dressed up like a queen of hearts, the other has on white with gold roller blades on her feet. The guy is all in blue."

"Darn. That's them, all right," Cruiser said grimly. "What's our next move, teach?"

Mr. Santillian considered. They could still attempt a desperate charge. It was unlikely any of them were going to live through this, anyway. But if there was a chance…even the slightest chance…and with those three youngsters' lives at stake…

"We give up," he told them. His wonderguns disappeared and became his trademark cuff links once more.

They didn't argue. He stood up and walked out into the open, and they followed his lead. Dozens of Outriders stood before them, pistols and rifles leveled. They saw Even Steven and Lauren Saint near Brett, Abby, and Maxine. Lauren Saint held a pistol to Abby's head, while other Outriders kept the other two teenagers at gunpoint.

"We surrender," Mr. Santillian announced, his voice booming off the walls of the large room. "Let them go and we'll come quietly."

"Looks like you already are," Steven said with a smirk.

"We know where the Empowerer is," Saint put in. "The real one."

A chilling voice came from nowhere. "I am glad to hear it."

From around the room, bits of darkness were flying towards the center. Tiny, almost imperceptible blobs of shadow coalesced into a black mass. Soon the process was complete, and the Smiling Shadow hovered before them, restored to its normal state.

The Outriders bowed as one.

"Your excellency," one of them said, "it is good to see you are well."

"Your concern is appreciated, Daniken," the Shadow said. "It took me a while to pull myself back together. Now that I am, I must let our enemies know…I am not amused!"

With that, he unleashed his fear effect upon the Pure Shore Club. As one, they recoiled, abnormal, unnatural fear and panic filling their minds. Mr. Santillian fell to his knees, shaking. Mindy curled into a ball, while Cruiser gasped, doubled over the handlebars of her motorcycle.

"That's better," the Smiling Shadow said. "It is good to see your enemies overwhelmed with terror, wouldn't you say, Steven?"

"Yes…yes," Steven said, stammering a bit. As much as he wanted to see his enemies suffer, it was disorienting to see defiant, proud people reduced to quivering wrecks on the floor.

"Leave them alone!" Maxine cried. "You know where the Empowerer is now. Why do you have to hurt them?"

"Because it's fun!" the Shadow snapped. Saint, Daniken, and the other Outriders howled laughter. Steven half-heartedly chuckled.

"You say you know where the Empowerer…the real Empowerer…is?" the Shadow asked his henchmen.

"We do, your majesty," Saint replied. "The young ones hid it at the Jefford Academy. At your pleasure, we can lead you right to it."

"Please do so. Saint, you will stay here and keep an eye on our prisoners. The fear effect should keep Santillian and his lapdogs in line and the young ones should pose no threat. Leave some men here. Steven, Daniken, and the rest, with me."

The Shadow floated out of the room, leaving the air cold and musty in his wake. Daniken sneered at the teenagers and followed. Somehow, through unspoken communication, the Outriders split up. Three-quarters followed Daniken, while the others, including those holding the teenagers hostage, stayed. Steven was the last to leave, looking back at his old teammates, an odd expression on his face.

"What's the matter, Steve?" Brett asked. "Don't have the stomach for this stuff or something?"

"Shut up, boy," Steven said through gritted teeth. "You're lucky we might still have a need for you and your girlfriends as hostages, or we'd kill you all right now. But that's coming, you can count on it!"

"Sure," Maxine replied. "But it won't be you doing the executing, will it? Your superpower doesn't really lend itself to that kind of thing, does it?"

Steven's eyes lit up with fury, and they wondered if he would attack them right then and there. Instead, he turned and stalked out the door.

"That joe has some serious issues," Brett muttered.

"He has his uses," Saint replied. She turned to watch Mr. Santillian and the others flail about in irrational fear. They flopped around like dying fish, uttering incomprehensible cries and occasional shrieks. Abby shuddered, grateful that awful power hadn't been used on her, but desperate to find a way to help.

"Can't you just tie them up like you did before?" Maxine asked, nodding towards the helpless heroes. "This seems a little…cruel."

"Cruel? We're Outriders, girlie. Cruel comes with the territory! Eh, boys?"

The assembled Outriders laughed from their positions around the room.

Saint removed her weapon from Abby's temple—for which the girl was profoundly grateful—and walked over to the prone form of Mr. Santillian.

"We want them to suffer, and they are," she said. "Plus, this way, you can't free them with your magic tricks." She knelt down next to Mr. Santillian. "Ah, Santillian, you fool. So easily led, so easily drawn into the Smiling Shadow's web of deceit. I don't know what terrors haunt your brain right now, but surely none can be worse than reality!"

Abby's eyes widened as she saw Saint draw from her pocket a silver object that looked like a brooch in the shape of a cutlass. She held it up to the light, turning it around, looking at it from all angles.

"We found this little trinket in your pocket when we searched you, Santillian. I wasn't an Outrider when your last battle with the Shadow took place, but from my understanding this belonged to a late student of yours that perished. How completely tragic."

She chuckled, and the other Outriders followed suit.

"I was there," one of them spoke up. "A girl, she was. They called her 'Buccaneer'."

Abby glanced at Brett and Maxine. They all knew who they were talking about. Stacy McNiece. And unless a miracle happened, they were going to end up like her. Dead, with no one really knowing what had happened to them.

Abby's mind whirled. Maxine could conceivably get away with her super-speed, but she and Brett wouldn't be so lucky. She knew Maxine wouldn't take that chance, despite the other girl's bravado. No, if they were going to escape, it had to be another way. But what options did they have? Everything seemed hopeless. Their plan had failed. Their cause was lost.

"Buccaneer," said one of the Outriders. It was a woman, dressed all in black like any Outrider, her eyes hidden behind dark sunglasses. She was holding a dark pistol on Maxine. "Buccaneer," she said again, testing the word, enunciating each syllable carefully.

Saint got to her feet, still brandishing the silver brooch. "Yes, that was the name of the dead girl. Do you need me to spell it for you?"

"No," the Outrider replied. "No, what I need…is for you to give me my property back."

Her dark pistol abruptly vanished, and she extended the same hand towards Lauren Saint. Saint's body jerked as the brooch was snatched out of her hand by an invisible force. In a split second, the brooch sailed across the space between them and landed neatly in the palm of the other woman's hand.

"What the—?" Saint started to say.

The Outrider erupted in a flash of light. When it faded, the dark clothes, dark hair, and sunglasses were gone. She now wore gloves that went up to her elbows and tall boots folded down in a jaunty pirate style. She wore a broad sash about her waist, and a floppy hat with a long plume in it crowned her head. The brooch had transformed, too. In its place was a long, gleaming, silver cutlass, which the Outrider held by the hilt.

Saint reeled, and the other Outriders froze in shock, their mouths hanging open, eyebrows raised over their sunglasses.

"Who…?" Saint croaked.

Abby could hardly believe it herself, but she spoke up. "Outriders…meet the Buccaneer."

CHAPTER FORTY
RETURN OF THE BUCCANEER

"Kill her!" Saint yelled, pointing at the flamboyantly-dressed young woman. She had no idea what was going on, how one of their own had transformed into a Pure Shore Club Member, let alone one that was supposed to be dead.

"You can try," Stacy replied, a smile forming on her lips.

Multiple Outriders pointed their shadowy firearms at her and fired. Maxine, Brett, and Abby watched in awe as Stacy's sword flashed before her, deflecting the dark blasts into the walls or, in some cases, back at the Outriders themselves, felling several of them with their own fire.

Seeing that tactic to be ineffective, they dissolved their dark guns and brought swords, spears, axes, and maces to their hands, and descended on her, a grim tide of black-clad warriors.

"Fight if you can, kids!" Stacy cried. She went on the offensive, plowing right into the midst of the enemy, leaping and ducking, her sword flashing as she struck and parried all around her.

"You heard the lady!" Maxine roared, activating her super-roller blades and zooming across the room to clothesline an Outrider. Brett and Abby didn't need to be told twice. They had no idea what had just happened, but they sure weren't going to look a gift horse in the mouth. The Outriders who had been covering the three of them were so surprised by Stacy's sudden appearance they'd failed to pay close attention to their captives.

Brett's blue circle, the size of a serving tray, rammed one Outrider between the eyes, sending him sprawling to the floor. Abby waved her heart-wand, and with a few pink sparks, the woman who was covering her found her weapon had turned into an ice cream cone. The woman gritted her teeth and threw the cone aside. Abby waved her wand again, and the lens in the woman's sunglasses turned into grapefruit juice. She howled in pain as the liquid suddenly stung her eyes. She fell to her knees, clutching her face. Maxine took the opportunity to race back across the room and kick the Outrider solidly in the jaw. The woman went down heavily, knocked unconscious.

Abby looked at Maxine in amazement. The other girl shrugged. "Nothing I don't wish I could do in a soccer game," she explained.

They looked over to see Stacy taking on at least twenty Outriders single-handedly. They were hampered by their numbers, unable to strike without hitting each other, whereas Stacy could strike wherever she pleased.

Her silver sword flashed left and right, cutting through the Outrider's weapons like they weren't even there. She was a breathtaking sight, whirling and flipping, somersaulting and spinning, graceful and deadly. Each one of the enemy she slashed or stabbed burst into a cloud of smoke, and soon the room reeked of sulfur.

"What the heck…?" Brett asked. "Why do those guys explode like that? Did they all eat dynamite before coming to this party or what?"

"It doesn't matter," Maxine said. "We've got to help her!"

Stacy somehow heard them over the din of battle. "No! Go get the Empowerer!"

"But—" Abby began.

"No time to argue!" Stacy yelled. "I've got this situation well in hand. I've seen how fast the girl in the roller blades is. You can beat the Smiling Shadow back to the campus!"

"She's right," Maxine said. She had no idea what they would do with the Empowerer if they got it, or what they would do if they had to face the Smiling Shadow. She chose to cross that bridge when they came to it.

Abby summoned her giant playing card and hopped onto it, gathering her cape around her.

"Hop on, Brett," she said. "Max, we're a motorboat and you're the motor."

Brett clambered onto the giant card and sat behind Abby as Maxine pushed the card through the air. They zoomed out the door, leaving a golden streak of light in their wake. A trio of Outriders broke off from battling Stacy and chased after them.

•   •   •

They arrived at the Turbo Train tunnel in no time, thanks to Maxine's amazing roller blades.

"All aboard, ladies," Brett said. They ran on board, Abby shrinking her playing card back down to its normal size. Too nervous to sit down, they braced themselves by holding onto the seat backs. Abby realized they had no idea how Michael had started the train in the first place, but somehow the train knew they were all aboard. It began to move, causing them all to lurch and bump into each other. It picked up speed and the tunnel walls flew by.

"Are you guys all right?" Brett asked. "How's everybody doing?"

Abby shivered. "I guess I'm okay, if you don't count being scared out of my mind."

Maxine nodded. "I agree. It's not every day you get a sword held to your throat or a gun to your head. Well, no one said this would be easy."

"Speaking of which, that was quite a hit you took back there," Brett pointed out. "Are you all right?"

"Fine," Maxine reported. "Eager to get revenge, but I guess that'll have to wait."

"Do you guys really think that was Stacy McNiece?" Abby asked. "Back from the dead and all?"

Maxine snorted. "Just add her to the list. I mean, the Smiling Shadow and Even Steven were supposed to be dead too."

"Welcome to being a superhero," Brett joked.

•   •   •

Mr. Santillian was held in place by a thousand irrational terrors. He couldn't do anything but wallow in his own fear. He tried to form rational thoughts, to drive this horrible scourge from his mind but it was no use. He was utterly ineffective.

Then he heard a familiar voice. "Too afraid to fight a dead girl, Ms. Saint?"

That voice…His eyes, clenched shut, opened. Something about that voice cut right through his fog of fear like a laser beam. Despite the Shadow's fear effect, he was able to look around.

And he thought he must be hallucinating. There was Stacy McNiece, in her Buccaneer outfight, battling a gaggle of Outriders. She was slashing, punching, kicking, flipping, dodging, keeping the Outriders at bay. Occasionally she would score a decisive slash with her blade, and the dark warrior would literally go up in smoke. She was laughing and mocking her foes.

"St-Stacy?" he murmured, his jaw quivering. Could it be? Could it truly be? Or was this a cruel trick by the Smiling Shadow? He had to find out.

With a supreme effort, he willed the phantom fear invading his mind to recede. Slowly, he stood up. He touched each of his cuff links, and with brilliant explosions of light, they were transformed into his wonderguns.

•　　•　　•

"Uh-oh," Brett said. "Trouble. Three ugly mugs on our six."

Abby and Maxine spun to look out the rear window. Following the train were three Outriders, each on a black motorcycle. They were steering their cycles along the sides of the glowing rail, taking care not to touch it with their wheels.

All three of them hit the deck when the back window suddenly shattered.

"They're shooting at us!" Abby cried.

"Did you expect them to give us flowers?" Maxine asked. Another blast hit the train car, and debris rained down on them.

Then the shooting stopped, and they looked up.

An Outrider with a midnight blue Mohawk and jagged, brown teeth was looking down at them.

"Hello, kiddies!" he greeted them, his voice a fingers-on-chalkboard screech. "Care to come out and play?"

They scrambled to get out of his way as he launched himself into the car, landing with a THUD that shook the entire vehicle. Beyond him, the rear of the train car was a giant hole, and they could see the other two Outriders still chasing them. The Outrider who'd boarded the train had obviously chosen to send his motorcycle back to wherever they summoned their equipment from.

The Outrider cackled as his fingertips began to grow until they were three-foot long talons made of solid shadow.

"Nice nails," Maxine said. "You've gotta give me the number of your manicurist."

The Outrider didn't seem to hear her. "Slice and dice!" he cried, sweeping his hands back and forth in front of him. The talons were razor-sharp and sliced the tops off several seats. "Slice and dice!" he cried again, and he advanced on them, sweeping his terrible talons from left to right. Pieces of seat flew into the air.

"Where was this guy the last time I had to make a salad?" Brett said as they backed away.

"Slice and dice!"

"Man of few words, isn't he?" Maxine asked. They were almost backed up to the other end of the car. Soon there would be nowhere to retreat to. The Outrider kept coming, like a lawnmower merged with a human being.

"Abby," Maxine said, "now might be a good time to transform those funky claws of his into cotton candy or something."

"How about we just be rid of him, instead?" Abby asked. Before Maxine or Brett could ask her what she meant, the Outrider suddenly went flying up into the air and slammed into the ceiling. They quickly realized what had happened. Abby had, on the sly, placed her flying playing card on the train's floor and allowed the

Outrider to walk onto it. Then, with her mind, she'd taken control of the card and used it against the taloned warrior.

The man bounced off the ceiling and fell onto the card. Before he could react, the card zipped to the rear of the car and dumped him out the hole. They could hear him yelling as he hit the ground.

The other two Outriders ignored their fallen comrade and resumed their chase, pouring on more speed to catch up to the Turbo Train.

"We need to lose those clowns!" Brett said. "Come on, everyone on the card!"

"What's your plan, Ace?" Maxine asked.

"Hurry!" was his only response. They clambered on the card. It wavered a bit as Abby wasn't used to supporting three people on it, but it remained aloft.

Brett threw his blue circle against the ceiling as the Outriders resumed shooting at them. The Turbo Train began to come apart around them, shards of pewter-colored material flying.

"Through the circle, Blondie!" he shouted over the screams of incoming fire.

Abby concentrated, and they flew up through the gap the circle had created for them in the ceiling. Suddenly they were out in the tunnel, its roof hurtling by overhead, wind ripping at them. Abby's cape billowed and nearly made Maxine and Brett topple off the card.

Brett got his balance, then commanded his blue circle to leave the roof of the Turbo Train and return to him.

"Now what?" Maxine yelled over the rushing wind. "Now we have zero cover! Once those guys realize we're not inside anymore—"

"Just trust me, all right?" he demanded. "Kill our speed, Abby!"

Abby stopped keeping pace with the Turbo Train and the car swept past beneath them. The Outriders were unable to stop in time and zoomed by.

Brett closed his eyes and concentrated as hard as he could. His blue circle shot out, slashing through the air like a discus launched from a cannon. He'd never guided it this far before. It streaked over the Turbo Train, then made a ninety-degree turn directly towards the ground. There was a loud CRACK! Accompanied by a burst of light, and Abby understood what he'd done. Brett had severed the track.

The Turbo Train, with a gap in the track, flipped onto its front end with a horrendous scream of metal scraping rock. Sparks flew everywhere. The train flipped all the way over, now on its roof, all of its forward motion halted. The Outriders crashed right into it. Their black motorcycles twisted and vanished, while the men flew up and over the upended train car. They tumbled roughly across the tunnel floor and didn't move.

Suddenly the tunnel was silent. The smoke drifted their way and they coughed until Abby guided the flying card over the wreckage and continued their progress down the tunnel. Along the way Brett mentally 'found' his blue circle in the rubble. It flew, dot-sized, into the palm of his hand.

"Wasn't sure if that would work," he said, plopping down to sit on the card.

"How did you do that?" Abby asked over her shoulder. "Cutting the track, I mean."

"Just a little theory I had," he answered. "If I put some spin into the circle while it's in flight, it becomes like a buzzsaw. Sharp-edged. Amazing what innovations desperation can bring, huh?"

Maxine noticed he was breathing like he'd just run up a flight of stairs. "You okay?" Maxine asked, kneeling next to him.

"These powers take a lot of effort to use," he said. "It's like they're just another function of our body, and the more we use it, the more we push the limits, the more tired we get."

"I've noticed that, too," Abby said. She looked back at Brett. "That was…well, that was pretty incredible, Brett. Thanks."

"Yeah," Maxine said, slugging him lightly on the shoulder. "You did good, Ace. Now, Abby, touch down. Let me handle it from here. No offense, but with the Turbo Train out of commission I'm our best hope for beating the bad guys to the Empowerer."

Soon Brett and Abby were seated on the flying card with Brett's blue circle in front of them, acting as a windshield so Maxine, who was pushing them, could go as fast as she needed. The tunnel walls became a blur as they sped to the campus.

"Next stop, Smiling Shadowland," Brett quipped.

• • •

Stacy was surprised when an Outrider next to her was blasted into the wall by a bolt of blue lightning. She whirled to see Mr. Santillian, pale and trembling, on his feet and brandishing his wonderguns.

"S-Stacy?" he said, his voice little more than a whisper.

The Outriders tried to take advantage of her distraction and attacked. She cartwheeled out of the way, and turned the cartwheels into a series that took her all the way to where Mr. Santillian was standing.

"Is it really you?" he asked, his eyes alive with awe.

She squinted. "I think so. It's really hard to tell."

"How?" he asked, his mind reeling.

From the corner of his eye, he could see the Outriders closing in, Lauren Saint among them, all brandishing dark weapons. They seemed to be moving in slow motion. The unreality of this entire moment, coming face to face with Stacy, was making everything seem very strange.

"I was an Outrider," she said, as if that would solve everything. "Which has its benefits. For example…" She concentrated in the direction of the still-prone forms of Mindy, Michael, and Cruiser. Abruptly, all three seemed to be released from the Smiling Shadow's fear effect.

They sat up, startled and bewildered, especially when they saw Stacy standing there with Mr. Santillian.

"You may have returned from the grave, girl," Saint shouted, "but I'm going to send you back!"

"Not on your life," Mr. Santillian spat out. "Pure Shore Club!" he bellowed. "Maneuver Fifteen!" He lowered himself into a crouch and fired his wonderguns at the floor right in front of the charging Outriders. Instead of lightning, his guns now fired blindingly white ice-beams. The floor was frozen into a sheet of ice, and the Outriders began to slip and fall.

The Pure Shore Club wasted no time taking advantage of the Outriders distraction. Cruiser mounted her motorcycle, and its engine revved up with a mighty roar. She went from a standstill to top speed in moments, colliding with another Outrider, sending the woman flying across the room.

Mindy grew to giant size in an instant, and with one mighty kick sent two other Outriders soaring like birds. Michael Alvarez extended his hands and shot blasts of white energy that exploded two other Outriders.

Suddenly, only Lauren Saint was left. She had been in the rear of the pack of Outriders and avoided slipping on the ice. She leapt up into the air, avoiding the ice and sailing in a downward arc towards Stacy McNiece, her black sword raised and howling like a crazed banshee.

Stacy did the unexpected and threw her sword right at Saint while the Outrider was in mid-air. The force of the throw was so great it went right through her. Saint's face only had a moment to register a measure of surprise before she exploded into a burst of black smoke.

The smoke was already dissipating when Stacy summoned her sword back to her hand. She willed it back into its brooch form and pinned it to the sash around her waist. With that done, she looked up to see Mr. Santillian, Cruiser, Mindy, and Michael all staring at her.

"What?" she asked. "Never see a girl come back from the dead before?"

Mr. Santillian was the first to speak. "How?" It was no more than a whisper, filled with awe and fear.

She sighed. "The same way the Smiling Shadow and Even Steven survived, I guess. His crazy superpower got me out of the way. But for some reason, I ended up in a different place." She thought about the jumbled pieces of her past and present, her eyes becoming unfocused as she concentrated. "A place far, far away. I had no memory of who I was, or how I'd gotten there. I was homeless. I wandered. Ironically enough, the Outriders approached me about joining them."

Michael nodded. "The perfect Outrider recruit. Young, no past. No family ties. Lost in the world."

"Yeah," she said. "So they took me in. Made me one of them." She shuddered. "The Smiling Shadow…changed me. Filled me with a piece of its power like it did all the others."

"Why didn't it recognize you?" Cruiser said. "I mean, it fought against you so many times."

"It'd never seen me without my mask," Stacy said with a shrug. "And by then I'd dyed my hair, become a bit out of shape. For some reason it didn't sense that I already had superpowers."

"Maybe because you didn't have the brooch," Mindy said, pointing to the gleaming piece of jewelry on Stacy's sash.

"That could be it," Stacy said with a nod. "And Even Steven never pays much attention to the Outriders. I think he sees them as a faceless mob. He never spotted me, even though I was right there in plain sight."

"What made you suddenly regain your memories?" Mr. Santillian asked.

She touched the brooch lightly. "That Lauren Saint woman brandished this. It was the first time I'd seen it since…the last battle. I guess enough of 'me' existed, deep down, to override the Shadow's programming and bring my memories back."

"But you still have some Outrider powers," Cruiser said, sounding both hopeful and suspicious. "I mean, you were able to cancel the fear effect he put on us."

"Even now those powers are fading away," Stacy said, holding up her hands. "I can't even summon shadow-weapons. I don't feel the Shadow's presence in my mind. I guess transforming into the Buccaneer has purged all that nastiness out of me."

Cruiser smiled. "Thank goodness."

Stacy returned the smile with a patented gleaming grin. "Yeah."

"Stacy, I can't believe it's you!" Cruiser cried, and she raced over to wrap the younger woman in a huge hug. The others crowded around, trading hugs and back-slaps with their long-lost friend. Stacy seemed taken aback by all the joy but laughed and joked with her old friends like no time had passed at all.

Then she noticed Mr. Santillian had not joined the surge. He stood apart, alone, his hands stuffed into the pockets of his trench coat.

She broke away from the others and approached him. "Sir? Are you okay?"

His mouth moved but no sound came out at first. Then he said, "Stacy, I don't know an easy way to tell you this. We had a funeral for you. Your mother…your father…all your other family. Your other friends. They all think you're dead."

She frowned. "For all you knew, I was. It's okay, we'll figure it all out. The important thing is everything is set right again. Well, almost everything. While we're standing around here chatting, aren't there bad guys to stop?"

"Sounds like a job for the Pure Shore Club," Mr. Santillian said, a small smile cracking the stoic rock of his face.

"Good to see ya again, teach," she said.

Tears brimmed in his eyes. "And you, Buccaneer." And the teacher embraced his long-lost student. All the guilt embedded inside of him began to evaporate, and the great burden on his back became lighter. He had to get used to the idea of Stacy really being alive. But here she was, he thought. Real as the day is long. And if she's back, then truly, anything is possible.

"Now," he said, breaking off the hug, "what's the situation? What happened to the new kids? Are they still hostages?"

"Nope," she said. "Yours truly helped free 'em and I sent them back to the campus to head the Shadow off at the pass. I figured that girl with the Mach-5 roller blades could get them there first."

He nodded. "Good plan. But we can't let them deal with the Smiling Shadow and Even Steven on their own. What say we go give those kids some reinforcements?"

Michael Alvarez, the old team leader, smiled. "All together, then?" He held out one white-gloved hand, palm-down.

"I'm all in," Stacy said immediately. She attempted to place her hand on top of Michael's and was startled when her hand passed right through his.

"I'll explain later," he murmured sheepishly.

Stacy settled for hovering her hand above Michael's, and the others followed suit. They stood that way for a moment, in a circle of friendship, staring at each other. No one had to say anything, they all knew it.

The Pure Shore Club was back.

CHAPTER FORTY-ONE
EMPOWERER PURSUIT

Maxine, Brett, and Abby raced to the Administration Building. The campus grounds and structures flew by as Maxine navigated an obstacle course of buildings, trees, statuary, and frozen students and faculty. While she concentrated on steering them, Abby and Brett kept a lookout for any sign of the Outriders or their terrible master. So far, it seemed that they'd arrived at the campus before the enemy, but they couldn't count on that state of affairs lasting for much longer.

Maxine raced them directly towards the closed front entrance of the Administration Building. Brett threw his blue circle out just in time, and it stuck to the doors, enabling them to pass through into the lobby unharmed.

Brett and Abby hopped off the playing card, and Maxine bowed, her hands on her knees, breathing heavily.

"You okay there, champ?" Brett asked.

She stood up. "Just need to catch my breath a little," she told him. "Like we noticed earlier, using our powers a lot is pretty tiring. Come on, time's wasting, let's get to the headmaster's office!"

Just then, they heard a pounding sound. Turning, they saw dozens of students and faculty and other people, their eyes totally dark, pounding their fists on the doors of the Admin Building.

"We see you, children!" one of them cried.

"You can't keep us out forever!" yelled another.

"The Empowerer belongs to us!"

Abby gulped and backed away. "What's happened to them?"

"It's the Smiling Shadow," Brett realized. "Somehow, he's hijacked all of their brains. Turned them into zombies. Must be part of the weirdo night-spell he put on the campus!"

Maxine's eyes narrowed. "If the Smiling Shadow gets the Empowerer, I bet he'll have enough power to do this to the whole world. Take control of everybody! Which means we need to get upstairs, and fast! Come on!"

•   •   •

Steven thought it would have been faster to take the Turbo Train back to the Jefford Academy, or at the very least use the tunnel. But the Smiling Shadow's ego would not allow for it.

"The Jefford Academy is our beachhead, our prelude to the invasion of darkness that shall soon spread over the entire Earth! We should not visit the scene of our first triumph, burrowing through the ground like frightened woodland animals! No, we shall soar in like the conquering birds of prey that we are!"

Steven was held aloft by the Shadow's power, while the Outriders did their best to keep up, traveling cross-country on their dark motorcycles. If anyone happened to see them race past, their grim looks were enough to dampen any curiosity.

"I can't believe it," Steven said. "That fool Michael Alvarez, still alive, despite our best efforts. Coming in and disrupting our plans like this…"

"Patience, my friend," the dark one replied. "It is but a momentary setback. The children think they are quite clever, hiding the Empowerer on the campus. But it shall avail them naught. It is we who shall rule eternally over a planet covered in darkness and ice."

"What if they lied?" Steven asked. "What if this is just a trick, to throw us off the scent?"

"Then they shall learn what it truly means to fear the dark."

•   •   •

The headmaster's office was dark when they arrived. Switching on the light as they entered, they saw Headmaster Charlton himself, seated at his desk, slumped over it facedown.

"Is he asleep?" Abby asked.

Brett shook his head. "Don't know. Only one way to find out, I guess."

He led the way, walking across the giant office. He was about to shake the headmaster when the man suddenly sat bolt upright.

"Aaah!" Brett cried out, and he staggered backwards. Headmaster Charlton's eyes were pure black, like the possessed people downstairs. The Smiling Shadow had gotten to everyone, including the guy who ran the school!

"Hi, Headmaster," Brett said. "Um, no hard feelings about us breaking into your office, right?"

"Stupid children!" the headmaster roared. From his seated position, he leapt up to stand on his desk, crouching like a coiled spring, his fingers curled.

"Whoa," Maxine said. "Who knew the headmaster was so spry?"

"He's not normally," Abby said. "The Shadow's enhancing him. Watch out!"

With a ferocious growl, the headmaster sprang from his desk, launching himself straight at Brett. He tackled the blue-clad student to the ground, and they rolled around on the carpet, struggling to get the upper hand.

"Get the Empowerer!" Brett cried. "Don't wait for me! Remember the plan!"

Maxine and Abby raced to the large portrait of Aloysius Jefford III. Swinging the painting to the side, both girls were taken aback at the sight of the locked safe. Usually Brett's blue circle would get them inside, but he was otherwise occupied.

They heard the headmaster snarling, and Brett's voice, muffled, saying, "Headmaster Charlton, I can pay more tuition, really, I can!"

"Turn this safe door into something, Abby!" Maxine said.

Abby whipped out her heart-wand, berating herself for not thinking of this right away. With a burst of pink sparks, she turned the front of the safe into saran wrap. After that, it was a simple matter for the girls to tear into the safe and start pulling out its contents.

"Take it from here, Abby!" Maxine said. "You know what to do. I'm going to help Brett."

She rolled around the desk to find Brett had disentangled himself from the headmaster and the two of them were circling each other. The headmaster was chuckling, a wolfish grin on his face.

"I really hate to do this, Headmaster Charlton," Brett said, "but I know you're not yourself."

And he hauled off and socked the older man in the jaw. It was a solid, perfect right cross, and the headmaster went down like a ton of bricks. He didn't get back up. Brett was watching the headmaster's prone form, making certain he didn't get back up and start fighting again. Maxine looked at Brett, then the headmaster, then Brett again.

"Brett, do you realize what you've just done?"

He shook his hand, wincing. "Broke my hand?"

"You just knocked out Headmaster Charlton!" Maxine said, sounding somewhere between shocked and amazed. "I mean, you just laid him out!"

"What did you want me to do? Play poker with him? The guy was trying to tear me apart like a dog!"

"I know, it's just…Wow, how many kids get that opportunity?"

"All done!" Abby called from across the office. They ran to her side.

On the carpet in front of her she had three magenta spheres, all exactly the same size and color.

"Take your pick," she said. They each grabbed one.

Just then, the wall to the office exploded. They cried out and shielded their faces as debris battered them. Cold air suddenly whooshed in from the outdoors, and through a cloud of pulverized plaster drifted the Smiling Shadow. With him was Even Steven and several Outriders.

"Well, well, well," the Shadow said, its voice filling them with dread. "I don't know whether to be furious with you three young pups or congratulate you for your boldness. I think I'll just kill you instead."

Abby swallowed her fear and yelled, "Go, go!"

Maxine raced out the office's front door, scorching the carpet and hopping over the unconscious form of Headmaster Charlton along the way. Brett willed his blue circle onto the carpet and dropped straight through the floor. Abby pointed her heart-wand up and at the same time flew upwards on her flying playing card. Pink light flashed, and she turned the ceiling into the first thing she thought of, sugar.

White granules rained down on her, getting in her eyes, mouth, and hair. With a rush of speed, she burst through the downpour and out into the night. Luckily, she'd been on the top floor of the building. With thoughts of good luck for her friends, she vectored away from the Admin Building as quickly as possible.

"After them, fools!" Steven howled. "Get the Empowerer!"

The Outriders were frozen in place. "Which one?" one of them asked. "I counted three of them!"

"ALL OF THEM, you morons! We'll figure out which one is the real one later!"

•   •   •

Brett realized his escape route was not the most brilliant in the world. Certainly, he'd escaped the top floor, but now he was on the next level and falling towards that level's floor. At the speed of thought, he summoned his blue disc from the floor above and got it underneath himself just in time. When it touched the floor, he passed through to the next floor. He repeated the process, and actually began to enjoy it. Empty offices, desks, hallways, restrooms, all went speeding by. He was free-falling through a building! It beat bungee-jumping any day.

His elation was short-lived as he realized the ground floor was coming up. Unwilling to go splat, an idea occurred to him. When he fell into the ground floor, he willed his blue circle underneath him, but rather than allow it to land on the floor, he willed it to pull up.

It took a supreme effort of willpower, and he almost overdid it, coming close to slamming into the ground floor's ceiling. The very top of his blue cowl scraped the ceiling, but otherwise he was fine.

He floated there for a moment, catching his breath. The Empowerer was still in his grasp; he could feel its spherical form tucked between his chest and the blue circle. His eyes widened when he realized what he was doing. He was floating on his blue circle! Much like Abby could do on her flying playing card. And if he could do that…

The stairway door at the end of the hallway burst open, disgorging a horde of Outriders.

"Check you later, gents!" he called out, and he willed his blue circle to take him in the opposite direction. He was still laying down on it, and he cautiously got up into a crouch. Low-hanging light fixtures and signs had to be maneuvered around. I'd never hear the end of it if I knocked myself out against an Exit sign or a chandelier. He managed to find the front door, only to find the mob of zombie students and faculty had broken it down. Clinging to the blue circle, he raced over their heads. They reached up to bring him down, but he was too fast. He slipped out into the night.

If only you could see me now, Grandpa, he thought. I'm flying!

•　　•　　•

Maxine was out of the building in less time than it took to say it. She raced across the campus, the Empowerer tucked under her arm like a football. She realized that the golden trail she left when she roller-bladed was pretty, but in the shadows of the campus it alerted everyone to her location. Soon she had Outriders closing in from all directions on their motorcycles.

And they weren't the only obstacles. The zombie students stood in her path no matter which way she went. It seemed like at every turn, there was a human wall blocking her. She worried if she rammed them at top speed, she might hurt somebody. Sure, they were pawns of the Smiling Shadow, but they were also innocent people. They didn't ask to get put in this situation and they didn't deserve to get hurt.

The sound of a motorcycle engine came from her right rear, and she looked back to see an Outrider creeping up on her. To keep up with her, she realized, he had to be gunning his engine for all it was worth. Her eyes widened when she saw him brandishing a dark sword.

He swung his blade at her like a modern-day cavalry soldier. She ducked just in time, and ducked again as the man tried to decapitate her once more. Then the tall form of the Jefford Rocket loomed before them, its crimson surface barely visible in the gloom. At its base was the mural Michael Alvarez had painted of the Jefford Academy in olden days. Maxine recognized it, the very mural that had started off this entire crazy weekend.

At the last moment, she zoomed around the base of the rocket, skirting its edge and narrowly avoiding a bone-jarring collision. She hoped the Outrider's reflexes wouldn't be quite as good, and he would smash into the school's monument. No such luck. The Outrider drove the other way around, and came back at her, sword swinging. That would have been too easy, she thought bitterly.

Maxine grew so focused on her pursuer she neglected to pay attention to her other surroundings. Zombie students were suddenly all around her. She'd inadvertently steered herself into a crowd. Hands reached out, brushing her, trying to stop her forward motion. She found the Empowerer knocked from her grasp.

The zombie students flailed for it, each trying to get ahold of their new master's prize. It bounced from person to person, no one able to get a secure enough grip on it. Maxine doggedly followed it, her dark eyes riveted to the magenta orb, which stood out like a giant firefly in the dark campus.

Super-speed combined with soccer skills won out. She elbowed, shoved, and even slide-tackled her way through the mob, until she found herself racing on open ground once again, this time kicking the Empowerer before her like a soccer ball. Outriders were closing in from all sides again, their dark cycles roaring like angry beasts.

"You want this thing, suckers?" she cried out. "Just try and catch me!"

She became a blur, setting the grass alight, slicing through the air like a white and gold scimitar. The random zombie students tried to make a grab for the Empowerer, but all it took was fancy footwork, and the sphere stayed safely out of their grasp.

"Maxine Drury races down the field!" she cried. "No one can stop her! She's near the goal!" She looked left and right and saw Outriders flanking her. She stuck her tongue out at them and poured on more speed, hoping to leave them behind.

Then she realized she'd once again not paid close enough attention. The Outriders had been hanging back because they were boxing her in, funneling her towards…

The Administration Building. Right where she'd started. Its tall, monolithic form loomed before her, getting closer and closer with each passing millisecond. Every route around it was cut off by Outriders and zombies. She flipped the Empowerer back into her arms with the tip of her foot and raced on. There was only one thing left to do now.

Roller-blade up the side of the building! Leaving the ground, she continued on her straight course, only this time it was straight up a vertical surface! She pumped her legs furiously, holding the Empowerer close. Maxine didn't know whether she should be terrified or laugh her head off. She chose to laugh as she zoomed upwards like a rocket, the stone wall of the building a blur under her golden wheels.

Her laughter quickly turned into screaming as she ran out of wall. Her momentum carried her far up into the air, and for a moment she could see the entire campus, shrouded in shadow. She went up so high, she actually left the Smiling Shadow's dome of darkness, and saw the real sky. The sun was going down; a gorgeous autumn sunset that lit up the horizon with multiple shades of orange, red, and pink.

Time slowed. She realized that if this was to be her last sight, then so be it. It was good enough. As she reached the apex of her ascent, and gravity began its inevitable work of bringing her down to earth, an odd peace took over. Maxine found herself regretting the fact she couldn't say goodbye to her parents, or her brother.

If only I'd had more time…

A jarring impact shook her, and she found herself racing sideways instead of down. Her eyes had shut somewhere along the way. Opening them, she got a face full of billowing fabric. Pushing it aside, Maxine realized she was on Abby's flying card, lying right next to the other girl.

"Abby?"

"I thought you could use a lift," Abby joked weakly. The other girl was pale, and she was gripping the edges of her flying card with manic intensity. Her own Empowerer was wedged between her chin and the flying card itself.

"Well, I appreciate it," Maxine said, forcing herself to take some deep breaths. "Now that you've done your good deed for the day, what say you take us on the redeye Queen of Hearts express out of here?"

"I keep trying," Abby said.

"What's stopping you?"

Maxine had her question answered when awful laughter seemed to erupt from all around them. She looked up and back to see the Smiling Shadow flying right at their heels.

"Never mind," she said.

The Shadow lashed out with a dark tentacle. It hit Abby in the side like a sledgehammer. The card went off course, and the two girls struggled to hang on.

"Happy landing, ladies!" the Shadow called after them.

"Pull up, Abby!" Maxine shouted. Abby was too stunned from the Shadow's blow to comply, but she managed to soften their landing somewhat. Instead of crashing directly into the ground, the flying card leveled off, then one corner dug into the dirt and the card flipped completely over. Both girls screamed as they were flung roughly across the ground. They lost their grip on their Empowerers, the magenta spheres rolling across the grass like croquet balls.

Maxine and Abby couldn't move for several moments. Maxine recovered first. She sat up groggily, every part of her in pain. She could only imagine the bruises she'd have after that tumble. Then she was slammed back to the ground by a booted foot. Looking up, she saw the grinning, doughy face of Even Steven looking down at her.

"You led us on quite the chase, little girl," he said. "But playtime's over now."

"Ow!" came a voice to Maxine's left. She turned her head to see Brett laying there, his blue costume dirty and torn in several places.

"The lad put up a valiant struggle," the Smiling Shadow said, drifting down to settle over the grass just near their heads. "But ultimately fruitless."

An Outrider, one that Maxine recognized from their first encounter with them outside the clubhouse, stepped forward. "Shall we kill them now, my lord?"

"No, Daniken," the Shadow replied. "First things first." Three shadowy tendrils shot out from his inky mass, and each one wrapped around one of the three Empowerers. He pulled both to himself, seeming to examine them carefully, his ghostly smile never wavering.

Maxine flinched as the Shadow suddenly constricted two of the magenta orbs, crushing them into powder. "A courageous gambit, young ones," he told them, "but your decoys have been flushed out. Really, what did you three hope to accomplish?"

"Keep them…away from you!" Maxine managed to grit out.

"Well, you've certainly failed at that, have you not?" the Shadow replied. He laughed, and Steven and the Outriders joined in, creating a chorus of evil merriment.

"Why?" Abby asked. She'd regained her senses. She was propping herself up on her elbows, her golden crown askew. "Why are you doing this, anyway? I mean, what's the point?"

The Smiling Shadow seemed surprised by the question. His shadowy mass stopped undulating, though its ghostly smile remained fixed in place. The

Outriders stirred uneasily. Steven looked between Abby and his dark partner.

"Come again?" the Shadow asked, still gripping the Empowerer.

"I mean, I know what you want to do," she said. "You want to make the whole world…like this." She gestured to indicate the shadowy spaces of the Jefford Academy.

"Indeed, girl," the Shadow said. "You are quite perceptive. What I have done to your precious little school is a trial run, if you will. I shall make this world over in my image. It shall be a place of eternal night. It shall be a place of eternal cold. It shall be a place of eternal fear."

"What will you do then?"

Maxine and Brett glanced at Abby, shocked. They were both scared to death of the Smiling Shadow, they couldn't believe she was questioning it like that.

The Shadow floated in place, its inky form undulating slowly in the chilly air. "Do?"

"Yeah," Abby said. "I know what you really are. You were made on another planet and sent here to stop Reeve and everything he did to make this world a better place. Once you've accomplished that, what do you do next?"

The Outriders shifted uneasily. Abby wondered if they knew the true nature of their dark master. She doubted it. They probably thought he was a shadow come to life. A creature of the supernatural.

"Shut your mouth, girl!" Daniken snarled, striding up and knocking the crown off of Abby's head with a swipe of his hand. She flinched but didn't cry out.

The Smiling Shadow seemed to be thinking. "I don't know what I will do," it said at last. "I shall rule this world, I suppose."

"Do you have any plans?" Abby asked.

Brett saw where she was going. "Yeah, Smiley. What does a guy do when he's the boss of the whole world?"

Even Steven was still standing near Abby. She noticed him looking uneasily at the Smiling Shadow. "And you!" she addressed Steven. He jumped, startled. "What do you get out of this if the Shadow wins?"

"Vice-President, maybe?" Maxine asked. "Secretary of Cold and Dark?"

"I…I don't care!" Steven barked. "All I care is the Pure Shore Club being torn down and destroyed, once and for all!"

"Why?" Brett asked. "Just because they wouldn't make you the leader?"

Steven's eyes went wide. "How do you know that?"

"Doesn't matter," Brett replied. "It's a legitimate question."

"I deserved to be the leader!" Steven cried, his hands balling into fists. "I am the most powerful Pure Shore Club member ever!"

"Yeah," Maxine said, chuckling. "We saw how powerful you were back at the clubhouse. How did we beat you? Oh, yeah. We just ran away."

The Outriders laughed, a low rasp that rippled through the throng of evil warriors. Steven looked around, glaring. He knew the Outriders had never feared and respected him as they did the Smiling Shadow. "Shut up, all of you!" He stepped close to the Smiling Shadow. "Once you take on the power of the Empowerer, and remake the world in your image, I want to run my own Pure Shore Club!"

The Outriders stopped laughing.

"Pardon me?" the Shadow asked, its voice low and containing menace.

"You heard me," Steven said. "I want to run my very own superhero club." He gestured to Abby, Maxine, and Brett. "I want them to be my first class of students. They're young, pliable. I will be able to train them, mold them in my image!"

"I'll show you who's pliable, buster," Maxine muttered. Brett shushed her.

"Unacceptable," the Smiling Shadow said, its whispery voice taking on a new edge of menace. "Everything connected to the accursed Reeve must be destroyed. It is my mission. Nothing else."

"You owe me!" Steven shouted, pointing a thumb at his own chest. "You wouldn't be here today if not for me. You owe me your life. The least you can do is give me this one thing!"

Abby took a deep breath. She was about to go out on a long, fragile limb. "Why should he, Steven? He doesn't care about you. You're just a tool to him. A weapon. A get-out-of-jail free card in case things go badly for him, like last time. Once his mission is accomplished, do you really think he's going to keep you around?"

Steven looked at her, his mouth hanging open. He looked back at his shadowy partner. "That's not true!" He sounded like he was trying to convince himself.

"Ignore the girl, Steven!" the Shadow thundered, its smooth voice suddenly booming. "She's using a silver tongue to divide us! Now leave me alone while I access the workings of the Empowerer!"

"No!" Steven yelled. "Not until you tell me what I will do once you've taken over the world!"

"We can discuss that later, Steven!" the Shadow snapped. "Now, I must concentrate!"

Two Outriders took up positions on either side of Steven. He looked at them with contempt. "You can't stop me," he told them. He looked around at the Outriders. "None of you can!"

The Smiling Shadow let out a long sigh. "In that, you are wrong, Steven. I'm sorry it had to be this way. You saved my life, and for that I will always be grateful. But I'm afraid you are no longer an asset to my cause."

With a suddenness that startled everyone, the Shadow grew a dark tendril that snapped out and covered Steven's face with a blob of solid shadow. He began to struggle, his hands wrapped around the tentacle, but it was no use.

The Shadow was not attacking him directly, Abby realized. It was doing to him what it had done to all the other Pure Shore Club members. It was stealing his power. She looked to Maxine and Brett, who were looking on in horror, unsure what to do. She had to admit she wasn't sure what to do either. What do you do when you divide, but can't conquer?

Then she heard a sound. In the distance but growing louder and louder with each passing moment. The Outriders were looking around, confused.

"Sounds like a helicopter," Brett said.

He was right. From around the side of the Administration Building's stone bulk came a bright red helicopter. The second it came into view it switched on a dazzling spotlight mounted on its nose. Even the sunglasses-wearing Outriders had to throw their arms in front of their faces.

"What kind of helicopter is that?" Abby asked, squinting and bringing her cape up to cover her face.

"It's an Apache attack helicopter!" Brett said. "Behind the blue circle, ladies! It's about to get pretty crazy around here!"

He put his blue circle up in front of them. Cruiser watched from the cockpit of the helicopter. The moment the teens were ensconced behind their shield, she triggered her weapons.

Machine gun fire ripped through the night air. Outriders exploded in bursts of dark smoke. Grass and dirt flew into the air as bullets chewed into the ground. The only sounds Abby could hear were the cries of the Outriders and the deafening noise of the helicopter's weapons.

The blue circle quivered as it took a few hits. It was even moved backwards a few inches. Brett concentrated mightily, trying to hold it in place.

"Is that the Crimson Cruiser?" Maxine asked.

"I think so," Brett answered, straining to focus. "Who knew she could turn her car into an Apache?"

"The cavalry's here!" Abby said. "Well, the air cavalry, anyway."

Before the Outriders could get organized, the rest of the Pure Shore Club attacked.

CHAPTER FORTY-TWO
THE BATTLE OF JEFFORD ACADEMY

It had been a long time since Cruiser had used one of her Chameleon Car's war machine configurations. They tended to attract a lot of attention, so she didn't use them very often. But she had to admit, it was nice to cut loose.

The helicopter was a two-seat aircraft. From the front, Cruiser controlled the weapons and the flight operations, while Mr. Santillian sat in the back directing the attack through the communications devices the club used from time to time.

"Michael, go," Mr. Santillian ordered.

The Outriders had their attention focused on the helicopter pumping hot lead into their midst, so they were taken by surprise when Michael Alvarez flew in from the rear, standing out like a beacon in the darkness. Surrounded by a nimbus of white light, he dove upon the Outriders like an avenging angel, blasting the enemy with bolts of retina-searing energy.

"Mindy, Stacy, your turn," Mr. Santillian said. Cruiser could hear him stumble a bit at the last name.

She couldn't blame him. It was hard for all of them to accept, Stacy being alive and well after all these years. Now they had to make sure she stayed that way.

That we all stay that way, she thought as she continued to fire her weapons. Several Outriders approached from the left, tearing across the campus lawns on their motorcycles. They'd likely been patrolling the campus perimeter and were racing back to render assistance.

We'll see about that, she thought. One missile was all it took, and Outriders and cycles blew up in a fireball that threw a pillar of smoke into the air.

Meanwhile, Mindy and Stacy dropped from their perches on the sides of the helicopter and joined the battle. Cruiser halted her fire, lest she accidentally hit one of her teammates. The Outriders had found cover and were returning fire now. The helicopter's hull clanged and clanked as the marksmen zeroed on her. One shot destroyed the copter's spotlight, plunging the area into darkness.

"Take us down, Cruiser," Mr. Santillian said. "We can't let our teammates have all the fun, can we?"

"Any special requests, sir?" she asked as they made their descent.

He considered. "Desperate times call for desperate measures. If I recall, in your repertoire of vehicles is a main battle tank."

The young woman smiled under her red helmet. "Hoo-ah, sir."

•   •   •

Brett peeked around the edge of his blue shield. The helicopter had halted its barrage, and what Outriders were left were fighting back. Oddly enough, the Smiling Shadow didn't appear to be helping his minions. He seemed frozen in place, still gripping Even Steven in one shadowy tentacle and the Empowerer in another.

"What's going on?" Abby asked, she and Maxine joining Brett in looking around the blue circle.

"Holy Toledo," Brett said.

They had never seen the rest of the Pure Shore Club in action before. The Outriders were being stomped and swept aside by Mindy, who had grown to the height of a giantess. And in the midst of their foes, a modern-day swashbuckling pirate did a dance of punches, kicks, flips, and sword slashes, cutting through the Outrider ranks like a one-woman hurricane. The most remarkable thing was, she was smiling and laughing the entire time, like it was a walk in the park.

"She's a jolly pirate, all right," Abby said.

Brett grunted. "The lady's a female Errol Flynn."

"Who?" Maxine asked.

He sighed. "Never mind. Anyway, I'm sick of hiding behind my blue dot. I want to jump into that rhubarb and whip me a few Outriders. Who's with me?"

The girls were shocked when Brett didn't wait for them to respond, but stood up and ran towards the fight, taking the blue shield with him.

They looked at each other, shrugged, and followed.

·   ·   ·

The Outriders were already thinking they were facing much more than they'd bargained for; then the helicopter landed and morphed into an M-1 Abrams tank. Every Outrider from around the campus was charging into the battle, only to be met by withering cannon fire. Cruiser traversed the turret, finding groups of Johnny-come-late Outriders and launching powerful shells to their midst.

Mr. Santillian observed the goings-on from the top hatch. The three new Pure Shore Club members—Brett, Abby, and Maxine, he recalled—were charging to join the battle. His gut clenched at first, his instinct to run out there and yell at those kids to get off the battlefield. To tell them this was no place for people their age.

Then he saw Stacy, leaping into the air to kick two Outriders in the face at the same time, her merry laughter rising above the din of combat. Perhaps he'd been wrong to deny the three newcomers membership into the club. Maybe he'd been wrong to let his guilt over Stacy's supposed death drive him to shut the club down. Looking at the scene before him, he realized the world still needed heroes. And like anything else, it was best to grow heroes young. If not for those two girls and that boy, he knew they would all likely be dead by now.

Yes, them and Michael Alvarez. His eyes found Michael swooping low over the action, blasting

Outriders like a luminescent dive bomber. Maybe swooping a little too low…

An Outrider swept a quarterstaff made of solid shadow up and caught Michael in his side. The blow knocked him out of the sky and he fell roughly to the ground.

•   •   •

Of all the times for me to regain my normal solid self, Michael thought. He groaned and tried to get up, just in time to see a tall Outrider with spiky hair charging, a long, dark spear thrusting towards him. Still dazed from the blow, he couldn't react in time.

Daniken howled with laughter as he charged at the fallen superhero plucked out of the sky like a bird brought down by a hunter. The Smiling Shadow would reward him greatly for this, and the tide of the battle could yet turn in their favor.

•   •   •

Mr. Santillian knew that if Cruiser fired the tank's mighty cannon in an effort to save Michael, many of the others were likely to get hurt too. Everyone else was too busy to notice Michael's distress. Mr. Santillian knew it was up to him. He summoned a wondergun to his hand.

He couldn't fire from the top of the tank—Cruiser was turning the turret way too much to give him a stable platform—so taking care to avoid being crushed by the main gun, he leapt from the top of the tank, hit the ground rolling, and came up in a marksman's stance, both hands gripping his wondergun. He knew he would only have one shot at this. The Outrider was almost upon Michael.

Mr. Santillian aimed and fired.

Five years of disuse hadn't affected his marksmanship. The single bolt of lightning lanced out from the barrel of his pistol and streaked across the field. The Outrider known as Daniken lit up with blue fire and then exploded in a burst of smoke.

Mr. Santillian ran to his side.

"Whoa," Michael said, obviously still dazed from the blow. "Nice shot, teach."

Mr. Santillian helped him to his feet. "The least an old fool could do for one of his former students. A former student, by the way, whose advice I will never, ever ignore again."

Michael laughed. "I should hope so! Anyway, that won't be worth much if we don't live through this."

"So let's make it worth something. Come on."

"Steven…who is that?" the Smiling Shadow asked. He had drifted a distance away from the fray, spellbound by what he saw. Realizing Steven couldn't answer at the moment, he released him. Steven nearly fell, staggering but managing to stay upright.

"Who's who?" Steven asked, his face red, obviously shaken by the near-theft of his superpowers. Then he looked out across the battlefield and saw her. "Stacy…?" he said, his jaw dropping wide open.

"How? How?" the Shadow raged. "How can she be alive? She was annihilated! Utterly destroyed! Her death has haunted that fool Santillian for the past five years! How can she be here, fighting my Outriders?"

Steven thought about it for a moment, then sighed. "Probably the same way we're still here. Even Steven strikes again."

"Her being alive provides hope to Santillian," the Shadow said. "That angers me! Now I have to kill her again!"

CHAPTER FORTY-THREE
ZOMBIE ASSAULT

The fight quickly turned into a total rout. The Outriders were already reeling from the unexpected assault by the Pure Shore Club. Abby, Maxine, and Brett provided icing on the cake. Maxine was everywhere, her super-speed making her impossible to hit, punching and kicking Outriders, then gone before their comrades even knew she'd been there. Abby flew above the brawl on her flying card, her heart-wand sparkling, transforming Outrider weapons into flowers, lollipops, umbrellas, and other things not useful in a fight. Brett used his blue circle like a buzzsaw, cutting swords and guns into pieces, and managing to punch out a couple of Outriders in the meantime.

Soon it was over. Every Outrider was either knocked out or dispatched in a cloud of dark smoke. Stenches of ozone and sulfur drifted through the air, along with smoke from the multiple discharges of the tank's cannon. The ground was torn to pieces, littered with knocked out bad guys, mashed here and there with massive footprints, gouged with tank tread marks, and pitted with burning craters. Abby looked around at the scene and thought of Dante's Inferno.

Cruiser popped up from the commander's hatch of her crimson tank. "Whoo-whee!" she whooped. "That'll teach those leather-wearin' yo-yos to invade the Jefford Academy!"

Brett looked around, looking surprised to find himself still standing. "What happened to those guys? I mean, they all turn into smoke when they die—"

"It's the Smiling Shadow's power," Mr. Santillian explained. "A result of how it changes them when they become Outriders. And his power burns their bodies out after a while. If they don't die in battle, they die prematurely, anyway."

"Hate to break it to you guys, but this party isn't over yet," Stacy warned. She pointed the tip of her sword at the Smiling Shadow and Even Steven, standing a few yards away.

"What's the matter, Smiley?" Brett called out. "Too chicken to back up your flunkies out here?"

"Hey, kid," Mindy muttered, "ix-nay on the icken-chay. That's the Smiling Shadow!"

"Yeah?" Maxine said, standing with her hands on her hips and glaring at the Smiling Shadow as if her eyes alone could destroy him. "Well, he's obviously scared of us. He had to hide behind his glorified biker gang, and now he's got nothing!"

"She's right," Mr. Santillian said, impressed despite himself at the moxie of these new kids. "Shadow, your army is destroyed, your plans are foiled. I suggest you hand over the Empowerer. You can't hope to defeat all of us at once."

The Smiling Shadow let loose a peel of his unnerving, chilling laughter. "You are so certain my army is gone, Santillian? You forget you are dealing with a new, improved Smiling Shadow. I've developed powers that you haven't dreamed of."

Everyone's attention was focused on the Shadow except Abby's. She thought she heard something strange. Almost like…

She turned around. Like a hundred or so people running this way.

Before she could shout a warning, a mob of possessed Jefford Academy students, teachers, and staff members enveloped them.

"They're in the Shadow's thrall!" Michael shouted. "Try not to hurt them!"

"Tell that to them!" Brett yelled back as several boys and girls tried to tackle him to the ground. He hopped up on his blue circle and tried to raise himself into the air, but their combined weight pulled him back down.

"Brett!" Maxine cried, seeing him disappear under a pile of black-eyed bodies. She tried to zoom to his aid, but there were too many people in the way to get a running start. Ironically enough, she found herself surrounded by girls from the soccer team. "No hard feelings I got to be on the varsity team, right?" she quipped as they ganged up on her.

Abby was dragged off her flying card by three students who had a hold of her cape. They dog-piled her, one of them sitting on her wand-hand, keeping her from directing any transformation zaps. The students were clawing at her, almost like they were trying to rip her apart. Abby gritted her teeth and tried to buck them off but there were too many of them. She wanted to scream but a girl's elbow was mashing her mouth shut.

Then, they all went limp and toppled off of her. Abby sat up to find Mr. Santillian running towards her, one of his odd pistols in each hand. Several people stepped into his way, and he blasted each one of them with yellow energy that came out in waves.

"Neutralizing rays," he explained. "They stun a human's nervous system. An elegant way of stopping people without hurting them." He didn't know why he was explaining this to her. He realized he was unnerved, seeing so many familiar faces from his work at the school turned into pawns of the Smiling Shadow, their eyes turned into pools of darkness. They fought hard, worked into a frenzy by their dark master, yet they fought in utter silence, which only served to further unnerve Mr. Santillian.

Abby stayed at his side as he blasted several more students who ran at them. "Can you do that do the whole school, sir?"

He grimaced. "Probably not. We need to get out of here." He looked to Cruiser's tank. It was barely visible, covered by people who were crawling over every inch of it. Cruiser herself was at the very top, like a soldier defending a hill, kicking and swinging her red helmet around. Mr. Santillian's knew Cruiser could switch her

Chameleon Car into helicopter mode and get them all out of here, but he realized that if she switched to helicopter mode now, with innocent people all over her vehicle, the rotors would tear them to shreds.

Abby came to the same conclusions. "Can't she switch to her airplane mode?"

He glanced at her. "I'm not sure I want to know how you know about the airplane mode. And yes, she could, but there would be no way for her to take off. Not enough room. And we'd risk sucking someone into an engine…"

Abby reached out with her mind, summoning her flying card to herself. Maybe she could airlift everyone out of the melee one at a time. Unfortunately, a horde of zombie students saw the card and jumped on it, pinning it to the ground.

"So much for that idea," she said, crestfallen. Mindy had shrunk to doll-size and was riding on Stacy's shoulder. Stacy had ditched her sword and was holding her own with a series of throws and by flipping students over her shoulder. She couldn't see Michael, Maxine, or Brett.

Then, it didn't matter. It had all been a distraction. While they were occupied fighting the mob, the Smiling Shadow had moved in. Multiple tentacles lanced out and found each of them, pressing into their faces and knocking to the ground those who were still standing.

"Fools," the Shadow rasped. "You forgot one thing. I still have the power to take away your powers and leave you little more than vegetables, just as I did to all the other Pure Shore Club members. And now that I have the Empowerer, I can't see what use any of you are to me."

Even Steven realized the Shadow had forgotten about him. He watched the Shadow drain the power from his old teammates. It was what he'd always wanted, wasn't it? Wasn't it?

"You are all the last of the Pure Shore Club," the Shadow went on. "Let your chapter in the book of history close. Let the chapter of the Smiling Shadow…be opened."

Then it was over.

CHAPTER FORTY-FOUR
A NEW GENERATION OF HEROES

The zombie Jefford Academy people now stood around, their dark eyes staring at nothing. The Smiling Shadow withdrew his tentacles and didn't spare the fallen heroes another glance. He turned instead to the Empowerer, gripped tightly in another shadowy tendril.

"Now…now the world!" he exclaimed.

Steven didn't know what to do. The Smiling Shadow had no use for him, yet the Shadow could render him useless as easily as he'd done to the others.

Or had he?

Steven looked around and saw the fallen, crumpled forms of his old teammates. Mindy, Stacy, Michael, Cruiser, Mr. Santillian.

But not all of them were down and out.

The three young ones were actually standing up.

Unsteadily, hesitantly, but they were getting to their feet. Somehow, the Shadow's power-sucking whammy hadn't worked on them!

Steven's life flashed in his mind's eye. The privileged yet loveless upbringing. The cold, distant parents.

Always disapproving. Always wanting their boy to be the best at something, yet always disappointed with his mediocre grades, his mediocre performance in sports, his shy and unforceful personality. The Pure Shore Club had been his chance, his one chance, to prove he could be the best at something. He'd wanted so badly to be the team leader, to have that position of honor. Even if his parents would never know about it, he would have known, and that would have been enough.

He realized now how foolish he'd been. Reeve and Mr. Santillian hadn't granted him that honor because he wanted it for the wrong reasons. The Pure Shore Club was a company of superheroes, not a place to satisfy selfish ambition. He'd made a deal with an entity that was living darkness personified, just because he hadn't gotten what he'd wanted. Steven realized how wrong he'd been. He didn't deserve to be the leader of anything, or anyone.

Yet, he thought, they'd invited me to join, those many years ago. The AmazeHeart chose the students who would join, picking ones with noble character, with heroic potential. In Steven's case, a tragic character flaw had bloomed into something horrible over the years, but in the beginning it had been different. He'd been worthy of being a superhero.

He clenched his fists. Perhaps he was still a superhero after all.

•   •   •

Abby, Brett, and Maxine looked at each other warily. The Smiling Shadow was either ignoring them or didn't realize they were even there. It seemed totally occupied by the Empowerer. The only other people standing were the zombie students, who all seemed to be in some kind of standby mode, and Even Steven.

Abby squinted through the darkness. She could tell Steven saw them, but he wasn't alerting the Shadow. In fact, he seemed to be circling around it, drawing its attention even further in the opposite direction.

Was he distracting it on purpose? Abby looked to her friends, who both shrugged. They obviously had come to the same baffling conclusion. Maybe finding out the Shadow didn't have his best interests in mind had altered Steven's attitude. Or maybe it was something else entirely. Either way, he was giving them a chance, and they couldn't blow it.

But what could they do? They couldn't speak to each other and make a plan, otherwise the Shadow would be alerted.

Think, Abby told herself. She closed her eyes. The cold air brushed her face, rippling through her strawberry blonde hair and tossing her cape a bit. She tried to calm herself, to approach this situation like she would a school project.

Break it down, she said to herself. What are our assets? Brett's blue circle had blown it apart before, but the Shadow had pulled itself back together. And that had only worked because they'd hidden his blue circle inside a Trojan Horse of a fake Empowerer. Maxine's fast, but what can she do to the Shadow? It probably couldn't lay a hand on her, but she couldn't do much to it. It wasn't going to be beaten with physical force. How do you fight a living shadow?

A living shadow…

Abby realized that wasn't true. The Smiling Shadow, for all its dark, scary looks, wasn't a living shadow. She used not her superpowers, but her natural photographic memory, and thought back to the time they'd spent inside the time capsule, getting information about the Pure Shore Club. Holo-Reeve told them the Smiling Shadow was an alien construct. Not made of shadow. A machine. Whatever it was made out of, plastic, metal, or something else entirely, it was just a machine. Abby looked down at her heart-wand, gripped in both hands. She couldn't use her superpower to transform a shadow.

But she could transform a machine.

•　　•　　•

"So, um, no hard feelings?" Steven asked.

The Shadow's ghostly smile turned in his direction. "You're still here, Steven? I would have thought you'd have run for the hills by now."

He swallowed. "No, I've decided to stick around. I figure if you're going to, um, be in charge, better to be on your side than not."

The dark entity regarded him for a moment. "A wise decision," it finally said. "Now, I must calibrate the Empowerer to my own circuitry, making its abilities my own."

Steven frowned. "Um, how's that going? The calibrating, I mean." He didn't dare look in the teenager's direction. He hoped to everything he knew that they had some idea what to do. He certainly didn't. He didn't know how the teens were immune to the Shadow's power-draining effect, but Steven knew it was likely he personally had no such immunity.

"It will only take moments," the Smiling Shadow replied. "In our previous battle with the Pure Shore Club, all those years ago, I learned a great deal from my very brief connection with the Empowerer, before the Buccaneer cut the connection and ruined everything. I learned how it worked, which as you know, enabled me to learn the technique of taking the powers of these fools and adding their might to my own. Similarly, I learned I can make the Empowerer part of myself, generating as much power as I will ever need. Enough to take over the whole universe if need be."

"The whole universe, eh?" Steven said. He was beginning to feel sweat trickling down his temples. "That would be, er, pretty neat."

Whatever you're going to do, kids, do it fast…

"Indeed. Now shut up and let me finish my work."

Before Steven could reply, a pink flash of light dazzled him.

●　　●　　●

Maxine and Brett had been wracking their brains trying to think of what they could possibly do next when Abby had hopped on her flying card and zoomed right up to the Smiling Shadow, her wand extended. With mighty bursts of pink energy, she began…doing something to the Shadow. It reeled away from her, screaming like a banshee, dropping the Empowerer in the process. Abby was relentless, keeping pace with it no matter where it drifted, keeping up the pink bursts from her wand.

"I'm going to need your help here, guys!" she shouted.

They didn't have to be told twice. Maxine was at her side in an eyeblink.

"What do I need to do?" she asked hurriedly, looking at the Shadow nervously. So far it wasn't fighting back. Its dark form was rippling madly under Abby's onslaught.

"Keep them off of me!" she ordered, gesturing with her free hand to the throngs of zombie students and teachers all around them. The Shadow was beginning to fight back, directing his minions to attack. The zombies left their positions and were running in from every direction.

"Right!" Maxine said. She knew there was only one way to do this that was going to not only keep all the zombies at bay but also not seriously hurt any of them. She began racing in a circle around the Shadow, Abby, Steven, and Brett. Faster and faster she ran, her roller blades leaving streaks of lightning at her heels, burrowing a trench into the ground. The air began to whip up around her.

Brett looked on in awe. He realized what Maxine was doing. She was creating a tornado!

A small tornado, to be sure, and not a very destructive one, but generating enough wind to force the hordes of possessed innocents back. They kept trying to move forward, but the mighty winds blew them away. Some were even taken off their feet, sailing across the grass and asphalt.

"Go, champ, go!" he yelled, pumping his fists. "You too, Blondie! Whatever you're doing, kick that living ink blot's butt! Well, I'm not sure if it has a butt. You know what I mean!"

Then he saw what he needed to do. The Smiling Shadow was reeling from Abby's attack but was sending several counter-attacks her way. Multiple tentacles were extending around the edges of her assault, winding through the air in oblique vectors and making their way towards her.

"Look out, Abby!" he shouted. She didn't even look at him, so intent she was on her task. Her mouth was a grim line and sweat poured down her face. Brett directed his blue circle into the mix, sending it to block the path of each tentacle. Each time one tried to bridge the distance between the Shadow and Abby, the circle was there to block it.

After a few seconds the Shadow gave up on that tactic. Brett watched the tentacles withdraw. Then the Shadow let loose an all-out attack. Dark bolts of energy shot out from its form, flying in arcs, vectoring in on Abby from every direction.

"Oh, boy," Brett said. He moved the circle faster than he'd thought possible. It seemed to be everywhere at once, deflecting the deadly bolts, racing furiously from one spot to another, never lingering, never halting.

Brett felt his mind beginning to tire, and a physical tiredness began to weigh on him. Moving his blue circle at this pace was draining him rapidly. He wondered how much longer Maxine could keep up generating the tornado, too. The girl was in great shape, but every person has their limits. And she was the only thing keeping the zombies off their backs.

The blue circle zipped to and fro, now moving so quickly it looked like there was a giant igloo of blue energy all around Abby.

Brett couldn't keep up with every single blast of dark energy. There were simply too many for a human being to track. One barrage slipped past the blue circle, angling towards Abby, who was too focused on her attack to care.

Luckily, Even Steven was there.

He stepped into the path of the dark energy, his fists outstretched. From each fist came blasts of white light, countering the Shadow's assault.

"You're going to have to do better than that!" he mocked his former partner.

The Smiling Shadow did not reply. Although mostly occupied with defending itself against Abby, it managed to spare a lightning-quick black tentacle that lanced out and struck Steven in the face. His powers couldn't counter it, because it was the Shadow's power-draining tactic.

Brett looked on in horror, even as he continued to protect Abby with his blue circle. Steven was down on the ground, unmoving, his breathing shallow and skin deathly pale.

Whatever you're doing, Abby, Brett thought as sweat got in his eyes, *I hope you wrap it up in a New York minute!*

·   ·   ·

Abby realized the Shadow was somehow resisting her. Her transforming energies and its dark form were locked in battle, and it was a battle of wills. And it was a battle she wasn't sure she could win. She felt her knees quivering, and her hand gripped the wand so tightly it hurt. The Shadow's form was naturally malleable, she thought, so it made sense it could resist her power.

Or was that truly it? She realized that most of the things she had transformed so far, she had some idea of what they were. Even the Outrider's weapons were solid objects, dark energy given a physical form. Abby had a sense of their weight, their mass, their volume. The Smiling Shadow was a different story. Its form was ever in motion, undulating like a cloud, yet not a gas. Not a liquid, either. It was some kind of solid object.

She wasn't looking at it the right way. Her normal vision told her it was a shadow. But what if she had other vision? What if she could perceive an object as it truly was?

Then it happened. Reality took on a new appearance as she began to see microscopically. The dark void of the Smiling Shadow was gone. In its place, she saw that it was in reality made up of millions…trillions…of dark objects. It was a gestalt entity, a swarm of microscopic machines. They were in constant motion, buzzing around like bees. And they looked like insects, Abby saw. A swarm of black, electronic insects, all working together, an awful machine made for sinister ends.

It was time for the machine to be shut down.

She dropped to one knee. Her arm shook, and she gripped it with her other hand, keeping her wand steady. With a supreme effort of will, she focused on the swarm, on each and every robotic bug in it, and unleashed an explosion of pink light.

Right before it happened, Brett noted through his haze of weariness and total concentration, the Smiling Shadow seemed to realize it was beaten. Its ever-present ghostly white smile curled downward into an expression of dismay. The Smiling Shadow wasn't smiling anymore.

Then came an explosion of pink energy, and the Smiling Shadow was gone. Many other things happened at that same moment. The dark dome concealing the campus vanished, revealing a star-filled, night sky. The zombie students all groaned and collapsed where they stood, crumpling like marionettes with their strings cut. Maxine halted her mad circuit and fell, exhausted, plowing chin-first into the ground, passing out. Brett stopped his manipulation of the blue circle. Instantly his tiredness overtook him, and he fell backwards.

Abby was thrown back by the explosion. She lost control of her card, and it slammed to the earth. She found herself on the ground, her wand lost. Her fingers searched for it, found it, but it was burning hot, hurting her even through her glove. She let it go, yet lacked the energy to even say 'Ow!'

She was looking straight up. She wanted to get up, to see how Brett and Maxine and all the others were. She wanted to see if they'd truly won.

But she was just too tired.

Unconsciousness began to overtake her. Her eyelids fluttered as she gazed up at the night sky. The real night, she realized, not the icy evil dome of night created by the Smiling Shadow. The stars and their constellations twinkled at her, as if hailing her victory with a celestial salute. And all around her, she realized, were small brown leaves falling to the ground. She'd done it. She'd turned all those tiny pieces of the Smiling Shadow into something harmless. It was over.

Abby smiled a small smile as her vision blurred. She allowed her eyes to close, and she didn't wake up for a long time.

CHAPTER FORTY-FIVE
A NEW MORNING

When she awoke, Abby didn't quite know where she was. She'd been dreaming of her old home in Charleston. Her old school, her old friends, not far enough removed to truly be her old anything.

Looking around, she saw her dorm room, and the bizarre events of the previous few days rushed back. She sat up abruptly, her blanket falling from her. She was wearing her Winnie-the-Pooh t-shirt and pajama shorts. A pink twinkle of light notified her she still wore her heart-ring.

Abby realized she was not alone. Maxine was sitting next to her bed, slumped down in the dorm room's standard-issue desk chair, her head titled to one side and drooling on herself. She had on jeans, sneakers, and a Jefford Academy Girls Soccer hoodie.

"Um…Max?" she asked. Her throat felt raw, like she hadn't used it in days.

Maxine awoke with a start, her dark eyes wide. "Who's there?" she blurted out. Then she locked gazes with Abby. "Abby!" she cried. "You're awake!"

Abby tried to get up, but every part of her protested, pain running all through her. She slumped back onto the bed. "I'm awake," she groaned, "but my body sure isn't happy about it." She looked at Maxine. "How did I get here? How long have I been here?"

Maxine handed her a glass of water. "You sound horrible. Drink something."

Abby accepted the glass gratefully and began to drain it. "Oh, I'm really, really hungry, too!"

Maxine shrugged. "Makes sense. You've been out for three days."

Abby almost choked on a swallow of water. "Three days?" she spluttered. "Why?"

The dark-haired girl frowned. "You do remember what happened, right? You know, destroying the Smiling Shadow, and all that jazz?"

Abby grimaced at the memory. She doubted she'd ever forget it. She'd taken herself past all limits she thought she had. "Yeah, I remember. I guess I passed out after that." She sat up slowly and brought her knees up to her chin. "You guys, and the others, you weren't out as long as me, I take it?"

Maxine shook her head. "We were messed up, but not as much as you. Reeve and Mr. Santillian say you pushed your superpowers further than anyone your age has ever done before. They say you're lucky you didn't die."

Abby shuddered and put the glass of water aside. "That's a cheerful thought." Then she jumped, flattening her legs. "Wait, the others…Brett, Mr. Santillian…Cruiser! And…wait, did you say…Reeve?"

Maxine laughed. "A lot's happened while you've been in here snoring away. You in a mood to stretch your legs?"

•   •   •

Abby felt like she was in a dreamworld. She got dressed and went outside with Maxine to find a normal morning at the Jefford Academy waiting for her. It was mid-morning and a brilliant autumn sun drenched the campus in its golden light. Students walked to and fro, carrying books, backpacks, and sports equipment. A crew of groundskeepers were tending a large flower bed outside the girl's dorm. Abby heard birds chirping in a nearby tree.

She looked around. The last time she'd seen all of the people, they'd been possessed by the Smiling Shadow and trying to kill her.

"Hey," Maxine said, "careful. Your head's turning so much you might give yourself whiplash."

Abby turned to regard her. "Um, you have to understand, I was just getting used to my classmates all being a bunch of zombies. Heck, the last time I saw this campus it looked like a warzone!"

"Keep your voice down," Maxine said. People were giving them curious glances. "Come on, let's walk." She pulled Abby by her arm for a few steps. After a while, Abby shook Maxine off and walked on her own.

"So, what happened?" she asked, her green eyes darting all around.

"I'm no science whiz," Maxine said, "so forgive me if my explanation sounds a little goofy. Basically, when you beat the Shadow—turned it into a bunch of leaves, I might add—all the students and teachers were released from its control. They were free, but the strain of getting loose from the evil inkblot's influence knocked them all out."

"I see," Abby said. "What you had, I guess, was a whole bunch of unconscious people, if you count Mr. Santillian and the others. By the way, are all of them okay? Gosh, Maxine, you're driving me nuts, here!"

The taller girl threw up her hands. "Hey, relax. They're all fine, don't worry about them. I'm just trying not to pile too much on you at once. It's a little overwhelming."

Abby sighed. "Sorry, this has just been the zaniest week of my life."

Maxine snorted. "Tell me about it! I was right there with you for most of it, remember?" They continued walking, a meandering stroll towards the middle of the campus. "Anyway," she continued, "while all the zombiefied kids and teachers blacked out, the opposite effect happened to Mr. Santillian and the others. The Shadow's defeat somehow snapped their powers back into them. That's what the Shadow had done to them, by the way, drained their powers."

"The same as it did to all the other alumni," Abby realized, "putting them all in the hospital." A sudden thought occurred to her. "But wait!" She stopped, jabbing a finger towards Maxine. "The Smiling Shadow took us down along with them. Yet they stayed down. We were still awake. We still had our powers! How?"

Maxine gave her a lopsided smile. "We're special, what can I say? Apparently, when the Shadow tried to access the Empowerer in their last encounter, the Shadow learned how to take powers away from Pure Shore Club members, but Reeve learned some stuff too. He learned that the existing members had this blind spot that could be exploited. I guess there was nothing he could do about the old-timers, but he made changes so any new recruits wouldn't be vulnerable in that same way. Hence us shrugging off the bad guy's battery-draining power while the others were out like lights."

Abby bit her lower lip. "Wow, so Reeve really planned ahead. Good thing, too."

Maxine knew what Abby meant. She looked around at the sunny day, the people walking to and fro. None of it would be there if not for Reeve's foresight, and Even Steven becoming a turncoat for the second time.

It was as if Abby had read her mind. "But what about Steven Endicott? Did he get his powers back too? What have they done about him?"

"They let him go," Maxine said simply.

"What?" Abby cried, loudly enough that some passersby shot them startled glances. "Sorry," she muttered, her cheeks turning red. "You're telling me that…that villain…is out there running around free?

After how he betrayed the club? After he turned on his friends and helped the Smiling Shadow?"

Maxine squinted at her friend. "I thought I was the one who was supposed to get indignant around here."

"I have a very strong sense of justice, I guess," Abby said with a shrug.

"Gee, I hadn't noticed. Well, from what I hear, Mr. Santillian and Reeve said he could go free but on the condition Reeve removes his powers. Reeve apparently has a way to do that that doesn't put people in comas. They figured he would be pretty harmless then, and they knew we wouldn't have won without him." She went on to explain that the surviving Outriders, with the Smiling Shadow destroyed, had lost their powers too, and had also been let go.

"Can Steven be trusted to keep the club a secret, though?" Abby said. She envisioned him on some talk show, busting the hidden superhero club wide open to the world.

"They seem to think so," Maxine said with a shrug. "The guy's pretty messed up. In fact, his life sounds a little bit like mine, the more they told me about him. He has the super-successful, not very lovey-dovey parents. Anger, resentment, the whole package."

Then Maxine was quiet, walking on and staring straight ahead, her mind evidently on something far away.

"You couldn't turn out like him, if that's what you're worried about," Abby told her.

Maxine glanced at her in surprise. "How did...? Never mind. I'm getting used to your scary smartness." She smiled, but only for a moment. "I am worried about it. I can tell myself now that I won't end up like that, but I can't predict the future."

"No one can, Max," Abby said. "Well, um, unless that's the superpower of some Pure Shore Club member I haven't met."

They arrived at the center of campus, a green lawn soaked in sunshine. Kids were throwing Frisbees and footballs, others were sitting on the grass in groups or alone, reading books and talking. Just another normal school day. Abby found herself grateful that such a 'normal' sight was there to be seen. The Jefford Rocket stretched up into the sky, casting a long shadow across the ground. Abby looked at the shadow and thought of the foe they had vanquished. Despite the warm sunshine, she shivered.

"I assume all of these people don't remember what happened to them, then?"

"Reeve has some pretty amazing powers," Maxine said, stuffing her hands into her pockets and gazing up at the rocket. "There's a reason they were so desperate to have him switched off before they invaded the clubhouse. The guy apparently can edit people's memories. It's helped the club stay a secret all these years."

"Gosh, I'm glad he's on our side!" The thought of such a thing being possible made Abby slightly queasy.

"He did all of that…for all of these people…in three days?"

"Like I said, he's pretty amazing. No one was going to remember what happened to them while they were under the Shadow's control anyway, so he filled in the gaps for them. He also fixed the damage to the campus so no one would freak out when they came to." Looking around, Maxine couldn't believe a huge super-battle had been fought here. Everything looked exactly as it had before. It all seemed like a dream now, like it had never happened.

But it had happened. Her dark eyes swept the sparkling grass and found the Senior Rock. Near there and under the ground was the time capsule. At the base of the rocket was a mural with a hidden clue to an off-campus superhero clubhouse. Out of sight was the brick guest house, entry point to the Turbo Train. And, of course, normal-looking people walking around with superpowers. So much hidden, some of it just out of sight, some of it in plain view. It made Maxine and Abby wonder what else was hidden just under the surface of everyday life.

"What becomes of us now?" Abby asked, her green eyes focused on the sky. "Does Mr. Santillian want to keep the club closed down? Do we lose our superpowers?" She rubbed her heart-ring subconsciously. She was still getting used to the feeling of it on her hand.

Maxine grinned. "I was getting to all of that. I think seeing Stacy McNiece alive and well, and the fact the

Pure Shore Club was the only thing that stood between the world and forever night, has made old Mr. Santillian more amenable to the idea of bringing the club back."

"So it's happening?" Abby asked, unable to keep the excitement out of her voice.

"Sure is. This year will be the first year an active chapter of the club will be in operation in five years. He talked about it with the headmaster and everything."

"That's great!" Abby exclaimed, doing a little jump. She immediately regretted it as her legs started to hurt twice as much. "So…are you and Brett joining up too?"

"Of course we are," Maxine said. She noticed Abby's face break out into a giant grin. Maxine understood why. She had friends on the soccer team, and Brett had the school newspaper. Abby didn't seem like she was involved in anything else.

The more she thought about it, she realized that a superhero club was a perfect fit for Abby. While she herself was good at soccer, and Brett was probably born a journalist, Abby was a true hero. Maxine had seen the other girl, despite her fear and insecurity, rise to the occasion time and time again. And when it came down to the final fight, it had been Abby who had stepped in and made the plan that saved the day. Maxine admired Abby's courage, and wondered if she could ever be so noble, so brave.

She looked sidelong at Abby as the other girl continued to survey the peaceful, idyllic campus before them. Despite Abby's kind words, Maxine still worried that the seeds lay within her to grow into a vengeance-fueled villain like Even Steven. But maybe being friends with Abby and Brett could change that. After all, they were unlike any friends she had ever had before. Maybe she could learn from Steven's mistakes. Maybe she could deal with the mess that was her home life and move on.

But she vocalized none of this. Instead, she said, "Well, it looks like you got your adventure, Abby."

Abby smiled and folded her arms across her chest. They stood together in silence for several moments, taking in the wonderful normalcy they had fought for. She thought of a line from *The Scarlet Pimpernel*.

Silence and joy, for those who had endured so much suffering…

Then, thinking of books made her think of something else.

"Maxine!" Abby cried out abruptly.

"What? What?" Maxine demanded, her head swiveling left to right. Abby sounded so alarmed, she expected to see the Smiling Shadow returned from the dead and hurtling towards them with a cohort of Outriders backing him up.

"How long did you say I was asleep?" she asked.

Maxine looked at her, noticing the other girl was pale, wide-eyed, and biting the nails of both of her hands at the same time. "Um, three days," Maxine told her. "Why?"

"I've missed three days of classes!" Abby cried. "My GPA must be ruined!"

CHAPTER FORTY-SIX
FAREWELL

"Stacy, are you sure you want to go to your parents?" Mr. Santillian asked.

She and the other members had stayed at his house since the final battle with the Smiling Shadow. They were all sore and feeling strange after having their powers ripped out of them and then returned, but Reeve told them that sensation would go away as the alien technology inside them recalibrated itself to their bodies and minds. So mostly they had slept and contemplated the future.

Stacy walked out to the front porch, a duffel bag she'd borrowed from him slung over one shoulder. He followed her, carrying her suitcase. Stacy had returned to them with nothing but her black leather Outrider clothes and her Buccaneer outfit, prompting an emergency shopping spree to build up her wardrobe. She had done it because it was necessary, but it served to remind her in very stark terms that she'd missed five years of her life. She wondered if her parents would have any of her belongings still.

"I'm sure," she told him, putting the duffel bag down. "I can't not go to see them, or my brothers and sisters."

Mr. Santillian nodded. "I understand. We can only hope the reunion is a good one."

"Yeah," she agreed. The fact was, she really had no idea how they would react. How do you deal with your daughter, thought dead for half a decade, suddenly turning up on their doorstep one day? Talk about the ultimate shock.

"You don't have to stick to the cover story, you know," Mr. Santillian said, leaning back against one of the porch posts and putting his hands in the pockets of his jeans.

Stacy looked at him in surprise. "What? And blow the Pure Shore Club's cover? Don't let Michael or Reeve hear you say that!" She laughed, and he chuckled along with her.

"I'm serious," he said. "Some things are more important than the Pure Shore Club. If you think it will make things easier…"

"I don't think anything will make this easier," she told him. "Besides, I still believe in the club. As you know, the Smiling Shadow isn't the only threat out there, known or unknown. We operate best when people don't know we're here."

"That's true," he admitted. "I just thought I'd give you the option, if you needed it."

"Thank you, sir," she said, smiling. "But I'm going to stick with our fairy tale of me wandering the back roads of America with no memory. It actually isn't that far from the truth."

Mr. Santillian studied her, this girl he had once known, now turned into a young woman in the blink of an eye. Stacy was the only person who had been an Outrider and a Pure Shore Club member. She hadn't talked much about her experiences with the Outriders, working for the Smiling Shadow, and he could only imagine what it had been like. He didn't press her on the subject; she would talk about it when she was ready.

The Chameleon Car came into view at the end of Mr. Santillian's street. Cruiser pulled into the driveway and waved from inside the car. He waved back. He was looking forward to having Jolene as his teaching assistant again. He'd pulled a few strings with Headmaster Charlton—who was for some reason nursing a very sore jaw—and got her hired back.

The headmaster was blissfully unaware of the full story, but he knew that the alumni were getting better, the FBI was gone, and things were getting back to normal at the school, all things he believed Mr. Santillian to be responsible for. It had been no problem to get a few favors from the man, such as overlooking a few days missed homework for Abby, Brett, and Maxine, and agreeing to reinstate the Pure Shore Club as an official club. That last decision had been made when the headmaster had personally met Stacy McNiece, alive and well, negating the taint that had stuck to the club for the past five years.

Mr. Santillian helped load Stacy's bags into the trunk and then they hugged, an embrace of beloved teacher and long-lost student.

"Thank you, sir," she told him. "For everything."

He struggled to find words. It was overwhelming to have her back after all this time. He still wondered if it was all a dream, or if she would disappear like a mirage. "You don't have to call me 'sir'," he told her. "You're not a kid anymore."

She let loose her patented daredevil laugh. "That depends on who you talk to. I'll be in touch, sir."

He smiled and shook his head as Stacy got inside the Chameleon Car and it zoomed down the street. Mr. Santillian stood in the driveway, watching the car until it disappeared around the corner. Going back inside, he was startled to find Michael Alvarez and Reeve in his living room, sitting in his twin armchairs, watching TV.

"Oh, Blake, good," Reeve said. "You're just in time. A rather fun movie is coming on. Have you ever seen *Sky High*?"

Mr. Santillian laughed. "So, this is what being reconciled means. You two characters teleporting into my house and making yourselves at home whenever the mood strikes you."

"Hey, you have to take the bad with the good," Michael joked. "Is everything set for Friday?"

Mr. Santillian shrugged. "As ready as we'll ever be." Friday was the official start-up day for the new Pure Shore Club. The three of them, plus Cruiser and Mindy, would be there, along with some older members coming in for the event. Many of the alumni were excited at the prospect of their old organization returning. Of course, part of the festivities would be an initiation ceremony for Abby, Brett, and Maxine.

"We're here to let you know the Alvarson girl has woken up," Reeve proclaimed.

Mr. Santillian was elated. He couldn't have lived with another young life on his conscience. "How is she doing?"

Reeve shrugged. "Fantastically well, I would say. They make them tough these days, I think."

Michael grunted, stroking his chin and not watching the television. "Yes, the only reason any of us are here right now is because of those three. With no training, without even knowing exactly what the Pure Shore Club even really was for much of it, they saved the day."

"The world," Reeve put in. "Truly, what other trio of teenagers can say that?"

"As long as it doesn't go to their heads," Mr. Santillian said. He thought about how he'd thrown them out of his office, declaring the Pure Shore Club would never start again. If anything, the past several days had served as much-needed deliverers of humility for him. He'd been wrong about so many things. Including the young man and the alien computer who were at that moment in his living room.

"Oh, I doubt it will," Reeve said. "The AmazeHeart generally picks the good ones, eh, Michael?"

"Some better than others," the young man replied. Mr. Santillian knew Michael was thinking of Steven

Endicott. Michael had disagreed with the decision to let Steven go, and Mr. Santillian couldn't blame him. He sincerely hoped Steven would find his way in the world, and that another Smiling Shadow didn't prey upon his worst tendencies and set him on an evil course once again.

Mr. Santillian folded his arms across his chest, and he could feel the familiar cuff links at his wrists. Those weapons could not help him with what he was about to do. "Listen," he said, in such a serious tone that Michael muted the TV, "I have some…things to say to you two. We've been so busy getting everything squared away the past few days that—"

Reeve interrupted him. "If you're going to apologize, Blake, save your breath. Everything turned out well. Indeed, I think you switching me off was one of the better things to ever happen to me!"

Mr. Santillian had to admit Reeve had a point. Most of the computers he knew of had to be turned off and rebooted every so often. It turned out that Reeve had never been rebooted, and thus had missed out on many updates and diagnostics. Now the living computer was back and better than ever, apparently more powerful and in better condition, his battle damage totally repaired.

Even his holographic avatar had changed. Instead of an image of an elderly, wild-haired professor in tweed sport coat, he was a younger, taller, slender bespectacled professor with sandy brown hair in a tweed sport coat. Reeve jokingly referred to the image as 'Reeve 2.0'.

"Still, I was very wrong to do what I did," Mr. Santillian continued. "I should have trusted both of you, and I didn't. I am guilty—"

"Of nothing," Michael interrupted him. "Only of caring to an insane degree. Normally that's not a bad thing, when you don't have a shadowy enemy manipulating you. Let's not dwell on these things, sir. It's all water under the bridge."

"Michael, you don't have to call me s—" he began, then he chuckled. "Never mind."

CHAPTER FORTY-SEVEN
STORYTELLING

Brett realized that if he stared at his laptop screen much longer, he'd probably start seeing through it. For the past several weeks, he'd resumed going to class—a surreal experience, after everything that had happened to him—and doing assignments for the school paper. He'd taken time to visit Abby a few times, and all three of them had been out to the clubhouse, getting acquainted with Mr. Santillian and the new, rebooted and improved Reeve. They weren't learning how to be superheroes quite yet. Mr. Santillian said that would start after the initiation ceremony.

That meant Brett had time to think about writing his exposé on the Pure Shore Club, compiled from his notes and personal observations. This is what he wanted, the story of a lifetime, the big one that would propel him to reporting stardom.

But was it really what he wanted now? He was alone in his room, the light of the laptop screen and his desk lamp the only illumination other than the soft orange glow of the October sunset outside. Maxine and Abby had no idea he was still thinking about writing this article. Or at least, they hadn't asked him about it. Brett figured they'd forgotten about it by now.

Or they assumed he'd given it up.

And should he give it up? He reflected on the past few weeks. He'd learned things about the world that had turned his perception of reality on its side. Aliens from other planets were real. People with superpowers were real. Underground clubhouses and turbo trains. Sentient shadows made of tiny nano-machines. It was like he'd been living a life inside a house with all the blinds down and all the curtains drawn. All at once, the blinds and curtains had been opened and now he saw the universe for what it really was. Didn't the rest of the world deserve to know the same extraordinary things he did?

His notes were on his phone and all he had to do was start typing.

But three things were keeping him from doing it.

For one, even though he'd lived it, it all sounded crazy. His editor would either think he'd lost his mind or made it all up. He had no witnesses, not bothering to interview Michael, Cruiser, Mr. Santillian, Abby, or Maxine because he knew they wouldn't go on the record. No proof, no story.

Second, he mused as he sat back in his desk chair, the Pure Shore Club did a lot of good. Who else could have stopped the Smiling Shadow and the Outriders? Who else could have depowered Even Steven? And though they hadn't heard specifics, Brett guessed the Pure Shore Club had secretly stopped other similar threats throughout the years. What if his story made them less effective? Wasn't it better for them to operate anonymously?

Third, it would mess up the lives of some people he'd really grown to like. If anyone believed him—and that was a very big if—the scrutiny of the whole world would be trained on Abby, Maxine, Mr. Santillian, and the rest of the club. The government would doubtless want to have Reeve to themselves to study. Not to mention all the living Pure Shore Club members who enjoyed anonymity now.

He recalled how his grandpa talked about his old buddies from the military. Brett figured his friendship with Maxine and Abby was a lot like that. They'd gone through danger together and were really the only ones who knew what it was like. Those shared experiences bound people together like no other. He'd only known them a few weeks, but Brett had not only bonded with them, he'd grown to respect them. Even Maxine, who still drove him crazy sometimes. They didn't deserve to have their lives upended because of him and his ambition.

Besides, he reminded himself as he snapped his laptop shut, *no one would believe me anyway.* Something else would have to be the subject that would make his journalistic reputation. For now, he had to get ready for the initiation ceremony that night, and then it was time for superhero school.

What would Grandpa think of all this? he wondered.

THE END

ABOUT THE AUTHOR

Jason is an Army brat who grew up moving seven times to military bases from Germany to Fort Knox, Kentucky. At each new base, Jason would star all the kids in his classes as characters in his own stories and comic strips, creating bonds between kids from all over the country. Jason's Magic Pen Adventure book series have been accepted to numerous festivals, and his second book, *Super Problems*, was a Maxy Awards finalist. When he's not writing, Jason is into 1980s pop culture, follows the Cleveland Guardians, and has a goal to visit all the MLB baseball stadiums. Jason lives with his wife in Cleveland, Ohio. *The Pure Shore Club* is his fourth novel.

JASON R LADY
MONSTER
PROBLEMS

NOTE FROM JASON R. LADY

Word-of-mouth is crucial for any author to succeed. If you enjoyed The Pure Shore Club, please leave a review online—anywhere you are able. Even if it's just a sentence or two. It would make all the difference and would be very much appreciated.

Thanks!
Jason R. Lady

We hope you enjoyed reading this title from:

www.blackrosewriting.com

Subscribe to our mailing list – *The Rosevine* – and receive
FREE books, daily deals, and stay current with news about
upcoming releases and our hottest authors.
Scan the QR code below to sign up.

Already a subscriber? Please accept a sincere thank you for
being a fan of Black Rose Writing authors.

View other Black Rose Writing titles at
www.blackrosewriting.com/books and use promo
code
PRINT to receive a **20% discount** when purchasing.